HER GRIP
ON THE PISTOL.

"I'm going to have to break you of this habit you have. Guns aren't for playing." His arm banded like iron around her lower back, forcing her tightly against him. He didn't try to disarm her. He should have. The man was a missionary, no matter who put him there.

Men like Simon Wells didn't allow people to pull guns on them.

Instead, contrary to every expectation, his free hand slid up her back, mapping her spine. As his fingers dug into her hair, cupping the back of her head, her smile faded. "Let me go."

"Will you shoot me?"

"Count on it, Agent Wells."

"Oh, well. Even a dying man gets his last request."

The kiss stripped away every thought of denial, of protest. He didn't tease her or gently engage. He claimed. He took. His lips covered hers, scorched where they touched her. Sent tingling shivers from her lips to her spine to her fingertips.

To her molten, swirling insides, suddenly too hot.

Too wild . . .

By Karina Cooper

KARINA COOPER

SACRIFICE the WICKED

A DARK MISSION NOVEL

AVON

An Imprint of HarperCollinsPublishers

AVON BOOKS
An Imprint of HarperCollins*Publishers*
10 East 53rd Street
New York, New York 10022–5299

Copyright © 2012 by Karina Cooper
ISBN 978–0–06–212769–3
www.avonromance.com

First Avon Books mass market printing: October 2012

Avon Trademark Reg. U.S. Pat. Off. and in Other Countries, Marca Registrada, Hecho en U.S.A.
HarperCollins® is a registered trademark of HarperCollins Publishers.

Printed in the U.S.A.

10 9 8 7 6 5 4 3 2 1

For Kyle. You put up with me day after day, but the strength of your tolerance shines most when I begin an IM session with "Okay, say you're a witch hunter and the woman you totally dig has just kneed you in the balls . . ." Thank you for wearing with such grace and charm the many hats I force on you.

CHAPTER ONE

A metal edge pressed against the back of his skull.

Missionary Simon Wells froze even before the *click* told him a pistol had just been unnecessarily cocked.

"You have more guts than I gave you credit for," came a low, feminine voice, husky from sleep and so goddamned sexy that it stroked all the way from his ear to his dick.

Parker Adams inspired that visceral response just by breathing; had since the moment he'd strode into the Mission director's office early last summer. That she was his boss didn't seem to matter to the rest of his body.

He raised his hands, the docket he'd found in her desk drawer obvious in one. *Operation Wayward Rose*. The classified stamp on it looked black in the faint seam of blue-white light rimming the curtained windows.

"Good morning," he said easily. As if he didn't know what she meant, as if she didn't have the business end of a pistol locked against his skull. "Is now a bad time for a social call?"

He heard her teeth grinding; reflexive, he figured, especially around him. "Give me that file," she demanded through them.

A corner of his mouth twitched.

So did his erection.

"I can't do that."

The increased pressure at his head warned him before she moved. He pulled the folder out of her reach, spinning away from her gun at the same time.

He didn't touch her. Didn't have to. As an administrative missionary, she wasn't trained to fight. Not like he was.

Not that *he* exactly ended at *missionary*.

She drew up short before she collided with his chest, put distance between them so fast he couldn't help but grin.

He made her nervous.

Good. Because right now, in the dark and the quiet, with her sleep-tousled hair and her midnight blue eyes dangerously bright, she made him think about things she didn't want him thinking about.

Lots of things he *shouldn't* have been thinking about, anyway.

Witch hunters didn't like witches.

Of course, with her gun trained steadily at his chest, Simon bet this particular missionary wouldn't like him anyway.

It was a struggle not to grin.

"You break into my home," she said, her voice arctic. Her eyes snapped in frigid warning: *Don't even breathe.* "You steal my property—"

"The Church's property."

Her jaw tightened. "Give me that file," she repeated, every word a knife. It didn't fit the sex-kitten look, a look an entire world away from the mask she cultivated at work.

He wasn't prepared for the Parker he found here.

Her hair gleamed like a blood red ruby in the dark, and while the cool copper color had always caught his eye, now it begged for his touch. Falling in disheveled waves past her shoulders, it framed her high cheekbones and dark blue eyes.

As if that wasn't bad enough for his peace of mind, she wore silk pajamas. Thin, flowing pants, a button-down shirt. The pale blue material cupped her body like a lover—shit, like *he* wanted to—and outlined every curve of her body like it'd been poured on. Her round, full breasts, the line of her hip. The sweet, teasing contours of her thighs.

The night made her look softer. Much younger than a Church director had any right to be, infinitely vulnerable.

So much more fuckable.

Lust tightened his chest. Curled in his already too-damned-aware cock. Vicious, demanding. Hungry.

His fingers tightened on the file. "Sorry, *Director* Adams." He drew out her title deliberately. "I'm going to have to confiscate this."

Anger—real fury—lit her eyes to twin diamonds. The gun leveled between them. For all her lack of hand-to-hand training, the Church made sure all its witch hunters knew how to shoot. He didn't doubt she could nail him square in the chest at this range.

His side twinged in vividly remembered pain.

Maybe it said something about him that the last woman to put a bullet in him had been a redhead, too. Although the through-and-through wound had healed over the past two months, the idea of a matching set made his skin itch in nervous anticipation.

Given Parker'd been the one to bandage him up, he wondered if she'd really pull the trigger on him now.

Probably. She was one determined woman.

Which explained why he was in her—up until recently *extremely secure*—condo in the dead of night, rifling through her office. Simon had known of the director's interest in the events locked inside this folder. He'd suspected she'd kept the classified information despite the order to destroy it.

He didn't know until today what she'd been doing with it. The stupid—clever, relentless, dedicated—woman.

The docket in his hands held secrets she had no business sticking her nose into—secrets that others would kill for.

Were *actually* killing for.

Simon should know. He had a list in his comm and the blood on his hands to prove it.

He didn't want to add hers to the mix.

Parker's jaw shifted. Firmed. "You have two options, Agent Wells. One, you put down that file and we'll talk about this." Her eyes, softer without her careful makeup and framed with red-tipped lashes, narrowed. "Like civilized people."

Simon raised an eyebrow, tucking the folder behind his back. "And two?"

"Two," she told him icily, "I shoot you, end your grating habit of disobeying my every order, and expose you for the witch you really are."

Like he'd thought. Clever. "You wouldn't."

"Try me," she replied, her gaze dead-straight.

But he didn't have to. Another time, another man, and maybe he'd have bought it. Simon knew better. "You're a good woman, Director. You can't even bring yourself to arrest someone without hard evidence, so you sure as hell won't shoot me down. That's inhumane."

A bell jingled from the kitchen, shrouded in blackness through the second entry. Simon didn't look away. He'd already met her cat— a white bundle of inquisitive fluff.

One more reason she wouldn't shoot him. Anyone who owned a cat that ridiculous couldn't pull the trigger on an unarmed man.

God damn, she was adorable.

The gun shook, ever so slightly. "Inhumane is what's in that file." And too fucking curious for her own good. "Put it down, Mr. Wells. Now."

Simon grimaced. "Fine. Let's take option one." Slowly, his eyes on hers, he set the folder on the desk behind him.

She didn't drop her guard. He didn't expect her to. Instead, she cupped one hand under the other, a two-armed stance that only brought attention to the roundness of her breasts beneath thin silk. And the divot her nipples pushed into the fabric.

Maybe *adorable* wasn't the word. How about smoking hot? Drop-dead sexy.

Hands-off erotic, like every *screw the boss* fantasy every man had ever entertained.

"Good. Now, let's talk."

Bad idea. Every beat of his heart pumped a surge of raw need through his system.

He needed out. He needed to get this folder away from her grasping hands. She needed to leave him alone.

Or else he was going to show her what *need* really was.

He'd already spent too fucking much time entertaining his own fantasies. How she'd respond to his touch; to the feel of his fingers against her softest skin, what she'd sound like when she climaxed against him.

His back teeth locked as blood surged to his rapidly hardening erection.

Bad timing. Bad choice.

On everybody's part.

"How about I leave now and we can talk tomorrow?" A thin chance.

One she ignored. "The Salem Project. GeneCorp. Human testing, Mr. Wells." She watched him like a hawk, clever gears obviously engaged under all that red hair. "How deep does Sector Three go?"

"What makes you think I know?"

Her gaze dropped to his left shoulder. Flicked up again, cold as any frozen hell he could imagine. She was good, signaling scorn without having to open her mouth.

He liked them spiky.

He didn't rub his shoulder, the spot where a black ink bar code marked the flesh beneath his Mission tattoo. That block of thin lines marked him as obviously as any neon sign—for those who knew what to look for.

Lab subject. Witch.

Dead man walking.

"Fine," he allowed. He leaned back against the desk, perched on the edge. "What makes you think I'll tell you?"

"Because I have the gun." As if she knew how little that seemed to count for her, her unpainted mouth quirked—a thin smile angled toward self-deprecation in the shadowed office. His gut kicked. "And if you don't, I'll keep sniffing out the answers without you, Mr. Wells. Whatever it takes."

Her eyes flared, smile fading as he pushed off the desk, took a step forward. "Going to warn you once, Mission Director."

The gun jerked in her hand. Then rose in silent warning as she took one barefoot step back.

Goddamn, her toenails were red. Bloody lust red.

"This is *way* over your pay grade," he told her. "This goes so far, no one's going to think twice about dropping your body into the burning chambers without so much as a trial. Leave Sector Three alone."

Her chin rose. She stepped back once more, butt of the gun cupped in once-more steady hands. "I've had meeting after meeting with Director Lauderdale," she said evenly. "With the bishop, even with clerical offices the Mission has never had a reason to deal with. All because of Operation Wayward Rose. So why don't you tell me what that op was *really* about?"

"Juliet Carpenter is a witch. That's what."

"Bull." Her mouth twisted. "Up until seven

weeks ago, she wasn't even a footnote in the Mission database."

"Obviously, you're wrong."

Again, that fine edge tensed in her jaw. He tested her patience. He knew he did; loved that he did. It was one of Simon's secret pleasures. "Where is she?" she asked evenly.

"I don't know." Truth. He'd barely made it out of the lab facility alive; there was no way for him to know where Juliet and her rescuers had vanished to.

"But you didn't arrest her."

This was old ground. His debriefing had already covered all this. He didn't care that his smile flashed a hell of a lot more tooth than amusement required. "I was bleeding to death at the time."

The gun vibrated, a nearly imperceptible tremor as the weight dragged at her arms. She wouldn't be able to hold it forever. He could just wait it out. Wait her out. Know that if he did, she'd hate him all the more.

He recognized how much the Mission director valued her control. Of herself, of others. Of her surroundings.

Simon wasn't the type to fall in line.

And she knew it. "You're a witch," she said quietly, voicing the accusation that had hovered between them all these weeks. All the meetings, the briefings, the fucking eye contact in the halls on the rare occasions he found himself topside.

He went still. "Yes."

Her eyes locked on his; infinitely deep, bottomless pools of something unreadable. That icy mask of hers served her so well in boardrooms and briefings, but his fingers twitched now. Standing in the darkness of her office, hair tumbled, ice blue silk luminescent around her, Simon almost groaned at the fierce surge of denial—of want—forcing itself through his skin.

He wanted to mess her up. Dirty her pale skin, grab her long hair and watch color suffuse her cheeks. Strip the ice from her, inch by silken inch.

"Who else is like you? How deep does the infiltration go?" she asked him, and he thrust his brain into gear. Forced himself away from a precipice he didn't completely understand.

She *fascinated* him.

"You know I can't tell you."

"Can't?"

"Won't," he acknowledged, setting his jaw. *Can't.* She was in enough shit with the director of the Church's secretive research and development sector. Lauderdale had reach.

Worse, he had the bishop's ear.

"Not even if I take you in?" Her voice remained low. Taut. The unspoken threat easily implied.

Taking him in, taking a *witch* like him in, meant interrogation.

She didn't have every secret—if she did, this would be an entirely different conversation—but Simon heard the tensile steel in her voice and wondered how far he could push.

How fast he could run.

He shook his head. "You won't be able to," he said, not unkindly. It wasn't her fault. Months of clandestine preparation, weeks and weeks of politicking had all but stripped the control over the Mission she supervised.

Parker just didn't know it yet.

She jerked her face aside, forcing the sleep-tangled curtain of her hair back from her face as if in emphasis of the frustration he clearly read in her tone. Her expression. He bit back an unwelcome surge of sympathy. "All I want is answers, Mr. Wells. I'll do anything I have to."

Shit. She had no sense of self-preservation.

"You play a dangerous game." He took another step forward—threw up his hands as her arms stiffened, gun barrel aimed at his head. "I'm not going to sit back and let you kill yourself."

Her eyes flashed. "Nobody *lets* me—"

Clatter. A white mop darted out from under the desk, bell tinkling merrily with every scrabbled footstep. Her gaze flicked down to the cat, one foot moving aside as if she were used to the animal's antics.

Exactly what he needed.

Simon lunged, faster than she was ready for. Exploded into calculated aggression, so sudden she had no time to do anything but strangle on her own sound of surprise as he closed one hand over the gun slide, wrenched it back, thumb on the catch.

He crowded her, all in the same fluid motion, until her back slammed against the door frame and Simon was keenly aware of her breasts against his chest. Of her thighs cradled by his, the soft silk of her pajamas under his hand. The warmth of her skin under that.

She smelled warm and sweet, like a woman just out of bed. Traces of her perfume clung to his senses; the very same perfume he'd ordered her once to wear again.

Of course he noticed that she did. Probably in some misguided attempt to assure herself he had no control over her, but she wore it all the same.

Sexy.

He dropped the detached slide to the carpet.

"How dare—"

Her words caught on a hard gasp as he locked the fingers of one hand around the smooth, slender column of her throat. Her eyes snapped wide, chin jerked high, as if that would allow her to keep breathing.

He didn't squeeze. Knew how easy it would be, but that wasn't his goal.

Not here. Not now.

Not, if he got his way, ever.

But he needed her to back off, or else he wouldn't get the choice.

"Stop," he said, nearly a growl. She shuddered in the crook of his arm.

Beneath his thumb, her pulse hammered, hard and fast.

"Forget about Juliet Carpenter." Every syllable fell in low, even tones. Unbreakable. "Forget about GeneCorp, me, Sector Three, everything you read in that file."

Her eyes widened, fathomless and shadowed. "I can't."

"You need to. This has been going on long before you, and it'll keep going after you're dead," he told her. Maybe it would help. God, he hoped it did.

Because if the conspiracy unfolding under her feet didn't get her, he would. He couldn't avoid it, avoid her, any more than he could avoid breathing.

The hard ridge of his cock nestled firmly against her abdomen.

As the awareness of it slid into her gaze, he felt it in the way her back arched. The faintest tilt. A curve. Subtle as hell.

He turned her on.

Jesus, he could have gone the rest of his short life without knowing that.

His voice softened. "Do you understand me, Parker?"

She swallowed hard, her throat moving under his palm. But she didn't answer.

He leaned in, until there was no space for her to breathe. Until he could feel her blood quickening through her veins, echoed in the slam of her pulse beneath his grasp. Her nipples hardened beneath her thin silk shirt, impossible not to feel through the insufficient barrier of the tank top under his synth-leather jacket. Erotic as hell.

From ice to inferno in nothing flat.

The useless gun hit the floor at his feet. A bell jangled, padded footsteps springing away into the dark.

"Get off me," she whispered.

But her eyes went soft and smoky. Dazed.

Simon should have stepped back.

He couldn't. "Christ," he whispered, and to seal the impression—to get a taste of the woman he couldn't shake—he closed the gap. Covered her mouth with his, claimed her soft, warm, trembling lips in a kiss that had nothing to do with anything but the need he'd tortured himself with for two long, eternal months.

Mission Director Parker Adams froze.

This man worked for her. Sort of. He worked for Sector Three, which was so classified even she didn't know what they really did. He wasn't her friend.

He sure as hell wasn't her lover.

He was a *witch*, and she was better than this.

But there was nothing cold about the ragged edge of lust exploding under her skin. Slow, saturating heat gathered between her legs, swirled low in her belly as his lips covered hers.

Somehow, Agent Simon Wells, spy for Sector Three and irritating thorn in her heel, was kissing her.

No, not kissing her. *Devouring* her.

Two months of forced civility, eight bloody weeks of tension, finally snapped between them.

His mouth was firm, aggressive. Undeniable. She gasped as his fingers slid away from her throat, up over her jaw. He dug his thumb against the corner of her mouth to coax it open, and nerves tingled to life. Her skin, her senses, her lips.

That part of her brain that had nothing to do with common sense and everything with wild, primal abandon.

His tongue slid between her lips, tasted her, and sensory fireworks flared behind her eyes. She shuddered. Her hands fisted by her sides; she closed her eyes because she couldn't stand to look at the handsome angles of his face while he played her body like a fine-tuned instrument.

And she couldn't pull away. Didn't want to.

A whole other problem she wasn't equipped to handle. Not now.

Not when her world had turned into a cage of politics and lies around her.

His teeth nipped at her bottom lip. Hard enough to force a shattered moan from her throat. Every torturous nerve turned to liquid flame, and just with a kiss. With the feel of his broad, leanly muscled chest against hers. His leg slid between her own, and God help her, her silk pants were so thin that she might as well have not been wearing anything at all.

He'd trapped her. Not just between hard doorjamb and harder man, but by the sensations sweeping through her body.

Lust. She recognized that one easily. It'd been a long time, but she knew the chemical taste of it as the secret parts of her body went soft and liquid with need.

Fear. Fear of his touch? Fear of her own response?

Fear of him.

That one spiked as his fingers tightened on her chin. Holding her still, forcing her still.

No.

His tongue twined with hers, demanding, wet. His hips tightened against her own, locked her down, pinned her until all she could think about was the hard length of him trapped behind his jeans. So very, very close.

No!

Parker grabbed his sides. Felt the faintest uneven ridge under her thumb where a bullet wound had healed into a ridged, puckered scar. She'd been the first one to tend him—clean entry, messy exit, on the front and back of his left side. Courtesy of a mission she didn't authorize. It had bled too much, but she'd done it.

Blood. The very thought pitched bile into her chest. Gave her enough to work with, to separate herself from the unyielding assault on her senses.

It was enough. Wrenching her mouth away, Parker jammed a thumb into the tender scar.

Simon swore, jerked back so fast it left her off-balance, staggering into the opposite side of the doorjamb. She grabbed onto it, jerked her hair out of her face to glare at the missionary as he covered the front of his side with one hand.

Pain etched dark edges into his features. His eyes glittered. By day, she knew they were a mixed green and brown. Hazel eyes; sometimes one, sometimes the other. Sometimes gold.

"Damn," Simon said, sucking in air with a painful hiss. But his white teeth flashed in a thin smile. "I'll remember that next time."

Nerves, anger, pitched in her belly.

Parker forced her knees to lock, her shoulders to straighten. Unflappable Mission Director. That's what she had to be.

That's what she *was*.

"There won't ever be a *next time*," she said, proud when her voice remained even. As self-possessed as he was. "Get out, Mr. Wells. We'll discuss this in the morning."

When his smile slanted into an arrogant, self-satisfactory curve, she bit out, "At the *office*."

The fact she even had to clarify galled.

He turned, presented her with his broad back, and picked up the folder again. The triptych sigil on its cover gleamed. Operation Wayward Rose.

She wasn't going to stop him this time. The damage was done. Nothing he did could keep her silent. Unless he killed her.

He could try.

"Oh, and *Director* Adams?" He paused in the office door frame. The night painted his features in shadow, turning the hollows under his cheekbones and the beautifully angled line of his jaw into something sinister. "Believe it or not, I'm on your side."

She raised her chin, forcing her gaze to remain on the back of his head. Not on the powerful line of his back, leaner than some of her more built missionaries, but no less muscled for it. She'd seen him in various stages of undress—hard to avoid it in the training facilities and in such close quarters. She'd seen most of her missionaries.

But *his* body put her tongue in knots.

"I don't believe you," she told him, cool as the air she pulled into her lungs. "You're a spy for the witches, for Lauderdale."

"But I'm on your side," he repeated.

Was he insane as well as a heretic? She muffled a laugh before it slipped from her lips, knowing it would only come out razor sharp. "Come talk to me when you're ready to share what you know. Until then, Mr. Wells, count yourself lucky I'm content to let you stay."

"You can't—"

"Trust me," she cut in, drawing herself up to her not insubstantial height. Her chin rose, but her gaze pinned him where he watched her from the door. His eyes narrowed, a dark slant of . . .

surprise? "This is my Mission. There is *nothing* I won't do to keep my people safe from you."

Simon raked long fingers through his short, coffee brown hair, turning away. "You have no idea what you're promising." But then his head turned, throwing his angled jaw into sharp relief. "And I can't be there all the time. Stay out of this, Director. At least for your own good." It wasn't a reply. He didn't give replies.

It was an order. As arrogant as it always was with him, dismissive of her intent. Of her authority.

Locking her teeth together, Parker said nothing as he left her office. Held onto the door frame with cramping fingers until she heard the final click of her front door. It beat her first choice, which was to find the nearest portable object and pitch it at his smug head.

Her temper sizzled, a fraction of a degree cooler than the physical lust still riding her. As tempting as it would have been to give in to either, Parker didn't dare.

She didn't sleep with missionaries, and she sure as hell didn't flirt with witches. Simon was both.

Only by the narrowest margin.

That traitor. He hadn't come *in* through her front door.

She'd have to figure out how he'd breached her security. Shore it up if she expected to play a game she wasn't sure she'd built herself up enough to handle.

Politics were bad enough, but this . . . chemical warfare of need and confusion only added to the months-long political shitstorm Nadia Parrish had forced on her with Operation Wayward Rose.

Parker was tired.

Her lips throbbed. They felt damp, swollen. Her skin prickled, but it wasn't fear. Or *all* fear.

She couldn't deny it. A part of her, the simple woman, wanted Simon Wells.

No, not precisely. She wanted his strength. His fearlessness. His control.

And the Mission director she'd become couldn't afford any of that.

A warm bundle of fur leaned in against her ankles, as if in apology. Parker bent to gather Mr. Sanderson into her arms. His heavy weight settled into her chest, collar jingling, and the happy rumble of his purr rattled through her ribs. Stranger gone, problems over.

Not for her.

She wanted answers.

The Church had them. Somewhere. As the director of the witch-hunting Mission, she should have been in on everything the research and development branch of the Church was planning. Had planned. Whatever Sector Three was doing, it affected her Mission.

Aside from a classification hierarchy, the two directors were equal. The blasted Church law demanded it. Order of hierarchy put the bishop of the Holy Order of St. Dominic above all things, the directors of Sector Three and Sector Five—the Mission—next, and the civic body of government last. *Period.*

But two months ago, Nadia Parrish had knocked down Parker's typically apolitical door with demands Parker didn't have the clout to deny. Simon, supposedly a missionary but trained under Sector Three's meddling eye, had been a problem ever since.

Along with Sector Three's interference, names like GeneCorp and the Salem Project had cropped up.

Words like *human testing*.

Having Operation Wayward Rose end in bloodshed and disaster, end with more questions than when it began, grated Parker's sense of responsibility.

And her pride.

But she hadn't been able to learn much before the order had come down from the Church brass—destroy the data, classify everything. Hide whatever dirty fingerprints the operation had exposed.

Parker surveyed her dark office. The drawer she'd put the folder in was still slightly ajar, but other than that, Simon made for a neat thief.

One goal, in and out. And a kiss.

Why? Why had he kissed her?

She bent, let the cat jump lightly to the floor, and tried not to think about the reminder her body wouldn't let go. She was a grown woman. She knew what the damp ache between her legs meant.

Lust wasn't nearly a good enough reason to ignore Simon's loyalties.

Her Mission. *Her* people. She'd had to sign death certificates for enough of her missionaries to feel responsible for every last one.

But she wasn't sure what to do about it. Yet.

Nothing in his thirty years of life had prepared him for Parker Adams.

Simon's heart pounded in his chest, a rhythmic *thump, thump* of anxiety, of surprise and adrenaline, and a ragged, visceral need. It had taken everything he'd had to leave that apartment—to leave her, tousled and off-balance and—"Fuck," he rasped as he leaned against the elevator wall.

He shouldn't have kissed her.

He couldn't *not*. What the hell was it about the woman?

Forcing himself to slow his breathing, his fist clenched on the railing as another surge of adrenaline lanced through his chest. Found an echo in his head.

He'd gone in expecting a fight. Expecting to go toe to toe with her in the only way he'd stand a chance—as the kind of man even the ice bitch of the Mission couldn't bend to her will.

More fool him. What was it about her that left his palms sweating, his heart pounding?

The doors hissed open.

The lobby lights slanted through his skull like a straight razor to the eyeballs. "*Fuck*," he repeated, gritting the word out as his senses cracked without warning. Shapes, living bodies, individuals. They piled up in his head—thirty floors of people, stacked up like the pieces in a jumbled puzzle.

Not now.

As pain fractured through the back of his skull, Simon staggered out through the lobby doors, grabbed a fistful of brick. The ground shifted out from under him. The folder slipped from his fingers. Pale in the stark fluorescent lights surrounding the complex, it fluttered as if in slow motion. He squinted at it.

It blurred.

Degeneration. That's what the scientists called it. What Kayleigh called it. A sign of the end.

In about eight seconds, his sight would go. With

it, the sensory radar that constantly pinged the back of his head, where his witchy ability lived.

Where the worst of the headache screamed.

Shit. Not the time. Not the place, either.

The street beyond the carefully manicured strip of fake grass dipped and swayed, rolling inward on itself as he struggled to think through the screws drilling through his skull.

Time was running out. In a very terminal sense.

"Hey, man."

The voice sheared through his overwhelmed brain. Slammed into his senses like a thunderclap.

Masculine. Grating. Simon jerked, surprised when his back straightened and he fell against the side of the building. He didn't realize he'd bent over.

Squinting, he couldn't see more than the vaguest impressions of a shoulder, a muted face. Black on black.

He clenched his teeth. "Operation number," he managed.

"Oh, man." A hand grabbed his shoulder, steadied him. "You look like hell. Just lean right there, okay?"

The brick wall dug into his back. Simon braced his hands against it, felt the gritty surface but couldn't see it. "Who are you?" he demanded. His voice locked down on a taut edge of pain.

Of anger.

This *sucked*.

"Don't strain yourself." The man patted him on the shoulder and let him go. Simon jerked his head around, searching vainly through black streaks for the owner of the cheerful voice.

Paper scraped along cement.

When it spoke again, it seemed farther. Or his ears were tunneling from vertigo. "Thanks for this. You saved me a lot of work."

As if Simon weren't buckling in pain.

"Fuck you," he growled.

"Aw, and here I thought we were friends. Oh, well. Take care of yourself." The sound didn't come at Simon from in front, or beside him. It slammed into him like a wall. All-encompassing. Overpowering.

Sensory overload.

"Get back—" He choked. Coughed as blood filled the back of his throat. His tongue prickled, like he'd licked an exposed wire, harsh and metallic.

As his knees buckled, as his back grated against rough brick, Simon coughed into his cupped hands and realized they cooled, tingling and wet, in the dark.

He didn't know if the thief was gone. Couldn't see, couldn't open his senses.

Couldn't do anything but hemorrhage from the nose and wait for the worst to pass.

CHAPTER TWO

She was late.

At half past nine, Parker strode out of the mirrored elevator and into the interior offices of the Mission. The din of over two dozen voices conferring lowered as every eye shifted to her.

Damn it, she was *never* late.

She resisted the urge to pat down hair that didn't need patting. The reflective elevator walls told her that she looked exactly like she always did—confident, polished, and untouchable. She'd bound her copper hair in its customary smooth coil, her makeup was perfectly applied. Not too heavy, a few subtle passes to highlight her features.

Under her tan trench coat, her navy blue pantsuit covered her neatly from neck to ankle, tailored to her body, accompanied by a cream-colored blouse too high-necked to be inviting. Although overall damp from the summer shower pattering the walkways outside, she didn't look anything like the disheveled woman Simon had accosted.

Exactly the point. She wasn't that woman, and she'd be damned if anyone else saw her that way.

Parker strode past the first three rows of desks, aware that the missionaries watched her go out of the corners of eyes not completely focused on computer screens and field notes. Even the dialogue around her quieted.

She didn't like speculation. Speculation led to questions, at a time and place no one could afford them. If she'd learned anything in her years in the Mission, she'd learned first that trust wasn't just essential—it could save a missionary's life. These missionaries needed to obey her every word. To have no reason to doubt her.

Nothing Parker did—or wanted to do—would be allowed to jeopardize that. Already in the hole due to her predecessor's betrayal last year, she had to tread extremely carefully. Over a year of dedicated service had made dents in the agents' collective armor, but she wondered if she'd ever stop struggling against the tide.

Probably not. And she couldn't blame them. Peterson had served over a decade as director. To have him exposed as a witch had been a terrible blow for the men and women who'd followed him. And to have had her appointed by the bishop didn't help. At twenty-eight, she was young for a director. That counted for a lot of the doubt.

Head held high, she crossed the fake wood floor. Her heels clicked with every step, authoritative enough to announce her approach and loud enough to give her agents warning.

It was a small favor but one she didn't mind giving them. Parker remembered what it was like to be a cubicle jockey. Her missionaries worked hard. She didn't mind straddling the hard-ass line now and again.

The cubicle area served as the information hub of the Mission. Most of the missionaries here were information analysts, technical specialists, and a few street-level operatives catching up on paperwork. Topside didn't see as many active witches as the streets below the security line, though it wasn't entirely unheard of.

The décor, at Parker's insistence, was tasteful. Expensive because it had to be, and as harmonizing as the decorator could safely make it without losing its working edge. The floors were kept clean by routine maintenance, and even the faux wooden cubicle panels gleamed.

Agents came here to work, but that didn't mean they couldn't be comfortable. Missionaries led hard lives. Harder for the active operatives. Among the offices, jail cells, and training facilities in the Mission side of the Holy Order's quadplex, there were suites of recovery rooms, isolation rooms, and a whole floor of suites specifically for those agents on the brink of mental breaks. Parker did her best to make sure her agents found some solace between operations.

"Agent Trapp." Her voice snapped across the open floor.

A sudden, muted flurry of determined industriousness followed.

Henry Trapp, a slight, dark-skinned man with a propensity toward outlandish ties, half stood from his station at her left. "Ma'am!"

It was time to get to work. Late or not. "Is there an update on last night's surveillance?"

"The report is compiled and in your in-box," he said smartly. "Patterns suggest that activity is climbing. We're up thirty-seven percent over last year."

General surveillance, the kind the Mission kept up to study patterns over the long term, was the lifeblood of the Mission's success. Fully half of her analysts were assigned to day-to-day maintenance, and Trapp had been nominated the de facto spokesperson for the month.

Parker didn't begrudge them the efforts to minimize contact with her as a whole. She just made sure to keep track of who drew the short straw.

"Climbing?" She stopped, facing him directly over the head of another analyst who didn't seem to be paying attention. A glance at her screen showed four columns of figures. Statistics.

Last year around this time, the Coven of the Unbinding—a semiorganized cell of witches with ties throughout every major city in the Church's fold—had only just been decimated by the collective efforts of the Mission. It had put a massive dent in witch activity figures for the next few months. A successful raid.

Well, successful with the aid of rogue elements the Mission had never found.

Maybe an internal coup from the coven's own ranks, maybe external sources. All the investigative team had been left with were a lot of charred bodies and a dead operative.

And one traitor director turned into so much melted flesh.

Maybe it didn't say much that activity was up this far. The Coven of the Unbinding—or at least the city's witches—had plenty of time to rebuild.

"The mid-lows have reported no less than two separate sightings in a six-hour window," Trapp explained. He adjusted his tie—today's offering was electric orange stripes on a field of sunshine yellow. "Both known heretics. Although teams attempted to take down both, the witches and the individuals they'd met with were gone by the time they mustered."

Parker frowned. "They're not mustering fast enough. Send out a notice to keep two teams and three analysts per district on round-the-clock standby."

"Yes, ma'am."

"Director?"

She turned, followed the raised hand three cubicles away. "Agent Neely. What do you need?"

If Peter Neely could have chosen any other field of work, he'd have served admirably as some kind of waiter or catering staff. He was plain, not unattractive, with brown eyes and thick black hair he kept fashionably styled. His build was average, his height was average. He didn't stand out. He didn't have to.

It made him an excellent candidate for those operations requiring close-quarters surveillance.

He spun around in his chair, adjusting his thin black tie with one hand. A nervous habit she'd long since learned to ignore. "Eckhart from the mid-lows got back to us. He sent the files you requested," he said, as matter-of-factly as Parker could have wished.

Straight to business always made her day.

She shrugged out of her damp trench coat. "And?"

"I went through all the operations for the past year," he continued, gesturing with his pen. Parker's gaze flicked to it. Neely lowered the offending utensil. "Topside and below the sec-lines. I highlighted all the markers that *might* link Operation Ghostwatch to other cases, but it's looking pretty slim."

"We know he's been working with various members of society, heretics and otherwise. We need to find our leads where we can."

"Yes, ma'am. But without knowing how he operates, it's all guesswork on my part. I've sent the files up to the profilers for verification," he added.

"Make sure they get in touch with Mr. Stone. He'll have the best tools to get you what you need."

"Yes, ma'am."

"Has Agent Silo reported in?"

"Early this morning." Neely tapped his computer screen. "There's a list of new reports in your in-box. Over half are marked as urgent."

"I'll handle them immediately." She folded her tan coat over her arm, glancing toward the dubious safety of her office. Slatted blinds in the same off-white color covered the glass window.

She never closed her blinds.

Her eyes narrowed. "Who is in my office, Mr. Neely?"

"Not sure, ma'am." Neely's gaze flicked to the side. Just enough. "I'll get to work on these links."

"Do." Damn it. Parker turned, but she only made it five steps before another voice rose in her direction.

"Director Adams?" A petite woman with pixie-short light brown hair waved a bangle-ridden hand from across the room. The sound jingled and clattered through the operations floor.

Without hesitation, Parker detoured. "Agent Foster. News on Red Balloon?"

"No, ma'am." The girl—woman, Parker corrected silently—beckoned her to come around the chest-high cubicle divider. Elizabeth Foster's records put her in her mid-twenties, even if her freckled cheeks and wide blue eyes gave her the appearance of a teenager. "I'm looking at Operation Domino."

Damn. "Tell me it's good news, Ms. Foster."

"Sorry, it's bad."

Parker leaned over her shoulder, bracing one hand on the cubicle lip for balance. She was acutely aware of every ear on them.

Sign enough that *bad* didn't begin to cover it.

The images on Foster's screen . . . screamed. Vivid red. Mottled pink and gray. Streaked brown.

Blood and brain and bone.

Parker steeled herself, forced her eyes to glide from one photo to the next. There wasn't anything left to identify the operative with. Not without scraping it all together and dropping it into a man-shaped bucket.

"Who am I looking at, Ms. Foster?" she asked coolly.

"Jesus," came a whisper from somewhere beyond Foster's desk.

Ice bitch. She didn't have a choice. If she let herself think about the face, the personality, the mind behind all that smeared gristle and paste, she'd be as useful as a two-legged chair. The men—*her* missionaries—deserved a foundation stronger than that. She'd learned long ago to compartmentalize her emotions from the job.

All good missionaries—all successful ones—did.

"David Carver." Foster's voice wasn't quite as steady. "Rookie, ma'am. Came in on the last recruitment drive."

She searched her brain. On cue, an image of the rookie surfaced—pale skin, dark blond hair cut close to his scalp. Green eyes?

No, blue.

Her frown tightened. "Where was he on the training regimen?"

"Level three," Foster said quietly. "He was training under Eckhart's crew."

"He flew through level two," another voice offered, and Parker glanced across the divider to meet Neely's serious gaze. "Bright kid. Real talent. Scouted him from the selection myself."

A hush fell over the office. Parker straightened, her hand coming down on Elizabeth's thin shoulder. Brief. There and gone. "Neely, Foster, put a rush on the samples from the scene. Where was he found?"

They exchanged a glance Parker didn't miss.

"His home, ma'am," Foster said when Parker's eyes narrowed. "The bastard got him in his home."

Parker nodded. "That makes five." She turned, pitched her voice to carry. One by one, the agents she knew had been watching her met her eyes. "Five of our agents have been murdered, missionaries. Five of your friends and teammates. Do I need to make any clearer the importance of Operation Domino?"

"No, ma'am," came at her in a rippled chorus. A few headshakes.

A lot of hard-eyed stares.

Parker met each set of eyes in cool appraisal. "Those men and women below the sec-line are counting on us. Let's not let them down."

"Yes, ma'am!"

"You have your tasks. Everyone get back to work." The sudden flurry of activity that followed jangled. "Make sure all the evidence is given highest priority," Parker added to Foster. "I want the labs on this immediately."

"Ma'am," Foster replied, already lowering her attention back to her computer screen.

Parker strode to her office. Every step earned eyes pinned to her back.

Anger? Probably. Confusion, she was sure. Fear among the non-street teams.

Carver made the fifth dead operative in the past two weeks. The nature of each varied. Carver, so much meat. Hannah Long, another rookie, had been nothing but ash. The other three had been shot, one in the back and two execution-style in the forehead.

The only connection seemed to be their occupation.

Someone was hunting witch hunters. Many someones, given the differing MOs. And those someones, she thought, her mouth set into a grim line, were very good at it. Operation Domino had just blown the rest of her priorities out of the water.

But she couldn't ignore Ghostwatch, either.

The former was an obvious problem. The perpetrator behind Domino's string of murders needed to be found. But the latter was an ongoing issue. Initially, Ghostwatch began as a shadow in her lead technical analyst's radar, then morphed into a monster of a problem within weeks. A hacker was infiltrating previously secure systems across the city and causing her lead tech specialist unending amounts of trouble.

Jonas Stone was a fine missionary, the best tech the Mission had. Possibly anywhere. He could go into any database, learn anything, filter out data from the most complex systems. Parker didn't understand it all; she'd tried for a while, but that language belonged to a whole other, much more foreign world.

What she did know was that when Jonas talked about the Ghostwatch hacker as if the second coming of Christ was on its way, there was a major issue.

Ghostwatch and Domino weren't the only dockets on the Mission's collective desk, either. The city's witches weren't being kind enough to wait their turn. The lower-level teams had their own problems, and according to the reports flooding her in-box, they were all contending with a spike of witch-related activity.

To say nothing of her murdered missionaries. If they didn't get a lead on this soon, she was going to lose more men. She couldn't afford that.

She pushed open her office door, schooling her features into a mask of cool appraisal as she found it unsurprisingly occupied. A blond head lifted from a digital readout; artfully tousled waves slid off shoulders clad in a stunning red designer blazer. Cheerleader perfect.

As Parker hung her trench coat on the hook in-set by her door, her back teeth ground.

Dr. Kayleigh Lauderdale. Just Parker's luck.

If Parker was the ice bitch of the Mission, then the daughter of Sector Three's director was her classified equivalent. With her wavy blond hair, innocuous gray-blue eyes, and expensive suit, she gave the same air of *hands off* that Parker polished to perfection.

Only her shoes, Parker noticed as the woman rose to her feet, were flats. Contrasted black against her red suit.

"Good morning," the woman said in cheerful greeting. She didn't offer a hand.

Parker didn't care. "Dr. Lauderdale." She shut the door behind her with an emphatic, quiet *click*. "I was unaware you had an appointment."

If Parker's frosty greeting scored any hits, she couldn't tell. There had to be something in the Sector Three water coolers. Every employee she'd ever had the bad luck to deal with had matched Parker attitude for attitude.

The fact that the director of Sector Three was this girl's father wouldn't help Parker's case.

"I'm sorry." Kayleigh sat as Parker sank into her own chair. "I'm given to understand you're always prompt, Miss Adams."

"Director Adams," Parker corrected coolly. She didn't address her punctuality—or lack thereof. "We're very busy, Doctor, excuse me while I get to the point. What does Sector Three want with the Mission this time?"

Score. Parker watched the woman's smile fade. "You are referring to Nadia Parrish?"

Mrs. Parrish was only the tip of the iceberg. Parker had so many questions. About Mrs. Parrish, the folder Simon stole, the order that demanded the Mission seal their own operation and destroy the data.

There was a lot Parker referred to.

When she only studied Kayleigh, steepling her fingers on the polished surface of her light wood desk, the scientist sighed. "I understand that relations between Sectors Three and Five have been strained, Director. It's my hope to change that."

No real answer. "You can start with explaining what you want." Parker's voice didn't soften. Didn't warm.

She didn't want this Lauderdale—any Lauderdale—in her office. Not even in her Mission. Parker had to deal with the fact that the sector's Magdalene Asylum headquarters occupied the quad across from the Mission. If she looked out of her office windows, Sector Three's side of the quadplex towered even above Mission levels.

The first ten served as hospital wings, topside's premier facility. The next seven as rehabilitation centers. The rest was classified. What was worse was that all the labs the Mission had access to fell under his purview.

And that bothered her.

Laurence Lauderdale kept a tight rein on his division. As tight as Parker kept on her own, only he had the temerity to walk all over hers.

She'd happily return the favor. On those rare occasions when the notoriously secretive sector came out to play, anyway.

"Right to the point, aren't you?" Kayleigh murmured. Her mouth twisted, rueful. "I can't blame you. Director, you know from previous debriefings that Mrs. Parrish is no longer with us."

"I wonder, are you referencing the spiritual sense or professionally speaking?"

The remorseful line to Kayleigh's mouth deepened. "I understand that she was an obstacle, but I've spent the past two months going over her projects. It's my hope that we can work together on future matters."

That wasn't an answer, either. Although Parker didn't need one. Through Simon's post-op report, she already knew Mrs. Parrish had met an unfortunate end in the lower streets. According to official channels, however, the woman had simply retired.

Well, according to the top-secret official channels that Parker had access to. As far as most were aware, the woman had never existed. Much like Sector Three.

Translated? None of her business, and Parker didn't have a choice.

Her eyes shifted to the wide glass window separating her office from the information hub beyond it, but the vertical blinds remained closed.

She liked to keep an eye on her operatives. That this woman had closed the blinds regardless told Parker everything she needed to know about the nature of this relationship.

"Cut to the chase," Parker ordered evenly, flicking away the doctor's worthless olive branch with a gesture. "What do you want? What does Sector Three want?"

The doctor's eyes cooled. Ice and diamonds. Like

father, like daughter. Only her father was eighty if he was a day. Parker placed his daughter at somewhere just under thirty. Close to her own age.

"Very well, Director Adams." Kayleigh sat back in her chair, crossing long legs in classic *fuck you*. "I understand you're working on an operation you've called Domino."

Parker resisted the urge to rub at her forehead. It thumped in muted echo of her heartbeat; a twitch of temper she wrestled into place. "So you've been keeping tabs on our lab requests."

"Of course."

"Why?"

The woman rested an elbow on the chair arm, one hand splayed over the reader in her lap. "Because the Mission's interests are Sector Three's interests, believe it or not."

"Oh, I believe it," Parker replied, acid in the dry words. "What's your point?"

"We'd like to arrange a joint task force."

Over Parker's dead body. "All evidence points to witchcraft. This places jurisdiction squarely with the Mission." And she'd had enough of Sector Three's spy witches to last her a lifetime.

The question was, did Kayleigh know? She had to.

"It sounds like you can use the help," the woman pointed out.

Not from her. Not when it came with strings, like Simon so obviously did. Parker shrugged. "Sector Three won't take over this investigation, Dr. Lauderdale. It's useless to ask."

Kayleigh tilted her head, eyes wide and earnest. "*This* investigation, Director?"

Parker's gaze narrowed. "You must think I'm stupid."

"Not stupid." Lauderdale straightened, leaning forward, broadcasting a sincerity Parker didn't believe. "Cautious, yes. And that's understandable."

She'd just bet it was.

Politics. Mrs. Parrish had failed in her demands, Simon failed in his retrieval, so they sent the sweet-faced cheerleader to make friends.

Not today.

"We have it well—"

"An exchange, Director." Kayleigh raised her hand as she cut Parker's denial off. "We're willing to offer something for the information."

An eyebrow climbed. How serious was she?

One way to find out.

Parker met her gaze, mouth curving into a faint smile. "I want Operation Wayward Rose declassified."

The doctor hesitated.

"And in exchange for having access to my missionaries, you will tell me why two of your men were stamped with a bar code. I'll even give you Agent Wells to lead your task force." But she wouldn't admit that she knew what the bar code meant. Not yet.

Not until she figured exactly how far this political corruption went.

But Parker didn't have to be psychic to know Sector Three would never meet her demands. Dr. Lauderdale's face shuttered, her eyes sliding up to the ceiling for a brief second. It was enough.

"I didn't think so." Parker stood, bracing the tips of her fingers against her desk, and looked down at the terrier on Director Laurence Lauderdale's leash. "You can compile your own team if Sector Three thinks it necessary." Parker's tone frosted. "But let me be clear. If your people interfere with mine in any way, we will arrest them. Conspiracy against the Church is a dangerous accusation to contend with." *True or otherwise.*

Kayleigh didn't stand. As the friendliness cooled from her gaze, as chilly resolve settled under her skin like a mask, Parker didn't look away.

Her stare, direct and uncompromising, had been known to put even her toughest missionaries in a cold sweat.

The Lauderdale girl held up well.

But in the end, her gaze dropped to Parker's desk. Flicked up again immediately as she rose, but Parker counted it a win. "Director—" Kayleigh paused. And then, quietly, "Parker. I'm only here to help."

"You can help by compiling a report on exactly what Sector Three is doing with my missionaries."

"They aren't your missionaries."

Another finger of icy resentment snapped into place.

No. Not all of them were, were they? Parker's weight lifted off her hands. She rose to her full height, taller than her unwanted guest, especially in her black spiked heels. Her shoulders tensed under her suit jacket, but Parker's voice didn't raise. Didn't ease above frigid calm. "You want to help?" She stabbed her index finger against the surface of her desk. "Get your people out of my sector."

When Kayleigh only studied her, Parker smiled in thin, red-lipped humor. She circled her gleaming wood desk, her heels clicking loudly as she strode to the door. "As I thought. Run back to your father and inform him that we're Mission, Dr. Lauderdale. We look out for our own."

"Parker—"

Parker yanked open the door. "That's *Director,*" she cut in with arctic dismissal. Her voice lashed through the suddenly much more open space.

Every head on the floor turned.

"We *will* remain in charge of Domino, and we *will* catch the perpetrator. Your only job is to get your spies out of my teams. I trust that's clear enough." She watched as Kayleigh picked up her reader. Noted the set to the woman's shoulders beneath her red blazer. She was angry.

Probably a little humiliated.

Good. Maybe it'd give her something to chew on. What was a little political suicide between rivals? Parker swallowed the tense ball of anxiety in her throat, meeting the woman's gaze.

"Very well, Director Adams." The doctor hesitated outside the door. Turning, her full mouth tilted at a hard angle, she added, "I sincerely hope you don't come to regret this."

"A threat, Doctor?"

"No." Kayleigh smiled. "In the interim, records show you're behind on your medical ex—"

Parker couldn't help herself. With a flick of her wrist, the door swung shut. Slammed firmly into place, right in Kayleigh Lauderdale's surprised face.

It wasn't enough. As anger streaked through her veins, sizzling hot, Parker stalked back to her desk. Sat in her custom-fitted chair.

The nerve.

She breathed in through her nose. Out, hard and angry, through her mouth.

For that *brat* to pretend like her own predecessor hadn't put Parker's teams in jeopardy? Risked Parker's missionaries like they weren't anything but pawns in some greater political game?

Her temper simmered.

For the woman to make her little offer as if Sector Three weren't sitting on some of the deepest, darkest secrets of the whole Church?

Oxygen was key. Cool air. Long, slow breaths.

This wouldn't stand. It couldn't. Parker didn't have all the information. All she knew was that Sector Three forced Wayward Rose on her, on the Mission; forced Simon Wells on Parker. All in the name of what looked like a nasty cover-up.

Her fists clenched on the smooth desk surface.

Her agents worked hard. Lived dangerous lives. Every day, they hit the streets looking for signs of witchcraft, ready at a moment's notice to take them down. Blood, bullets, fear, and pain. Her people understood the risks.

Took on those risks to keep the city safe.

Nobody would be allowed to drag them into danger. Nobody but her. Parker cleared every operation. Sector Three wouldn't be allowed to change that.

Not as long as she sat at this desk.

Only now the truth was staring her in the face. Parker keyed in her password to the computer without looking at the screen. The password was twenty-two digits long, comprised of mixed-case letters, special characters, and numbers. All of her passwords, when a thumb lock wasn't available, were different. And just as complex.

Parker memorized everything.

Within moments, a list of missionaries filled the screen.

How many of them were still hers? How many of them could be trusted?

That hard knot of tension bubbled into something sickly. Something heavy as lead and cold. All of her life, she'd dedicated herself to the cause. To the men and women who made the streets safe. Whether she'd been an information analyst or the Mission director, that dedication hadn't changed.

But had they changed around her?

Unbelievable. The amount of damage done since Peterson's betrayal would never be undone. Even if Parker could get to the bottom of Sector Three's machinations, what would it prove?

Bracing her elbows on the desk, Parker covered her face with both hands and allowed herself a brief moment of rest. But even as the darkness pressed in on her eyelids, her mind flicked through information, siphoned through the facts as she knew them.

The Holy Order of St. Dominic ruled over all of New Seattle. Ruled, in fact, over much of the country—or what remained of the stable cities scattered across it. With power in the minimalistic federal government, it surprised no one that the Church maintained an active interest in the day-to-day affairs of the city the Order had rebuilt from the Old Sea-Trench up.

The end result was a system of checks and balances that was listing too far to one side these days. The civic body took care of day-to-day business, the clerical stuff every city needed to run. The Holy Order's Cathedral occupied one wing of the quad, providing holy communion for most of top-side every Mass. It also served as the bishop's seat of power.

Bishop Applegate oversaw everything, from the secular to the ecclesiastical.

Between them sat Sectors Three and Five. Research and Development and the Mission, respectively. For all intents and purposes, Sector Three's clearance outstripped the Mission's—Parker's—but according to Church regulations, both directors remained on equal footing.

Until now.

Her first few petitions to the bishop had gone unanswered. Now, she wasn't sure Applegate had even seen them. During her last debriefing, she'd spoken to a room full of advisors.

And to Laurence Lauderdale, director of Sector Three.

Parker had tried the usual channels. Now, with her missionaries' lives on the line, she needed alternatives.

Straightening, she unhooked her comm, flipped it open with a thumb, and keyed in Jonas Stone's comm frequency by rote. Attaching the speaker to the shell of her ear, she waited.

The line clicked over. "Uh . . . Great timing, Director."

Parker had stopped being surprised by the clarity of her lead tech analyst's warm tenor. A few years and a set of living parents, and he could have become a fine singer for the culture feeds.

Instead, he had to deal with her. "Operation Domino," she said by way of greeting. She'd ease into the subject. "Talk to me."

"Oh." The word was a sigh on the speaker, beset by a faint line of crackling static. "This sucks, ma'am," he continued, as serious as she'd ever heard him. "We've got samples from the scene, hope to find something there. Every scene has come back negative."

"Of what?"

"Anything helpful," he replied dryly. "No fingerprints, no DNA aside from the dead hunter's."

"What does Mr. Eckhart say?"

The clatter of keys—as much a part of every call she'd ever had with him as his voice—halted for a moment. "Basically, ma'am? We've got no leads, no evidence, and nothing but speculation. It's as bad as Ghostwatch."

"Timely lead in," Parker said, frowning. "Where are we there?"

"About the same." But irritation colored his voice. "Whoever this hacker is, they're damn good."

Parker shook her head as she rose. "All our leads are frozen. This is not efficient, Mr. Stone."

"I know, I know." A keyboard ruckus undercut his frustration. "Every time I put a tracer on this guy's electronic footsteps, it leads to a dead end. It's like he's got something warning him every time I get close to his turf."

"A program?"

"If so, he'd have to infect the entire city grid with markers. It'd be one fuck almighty of a program," Jonas replied, then added quickly, "Er, sorry, ma'am."

Language was the least of her concerns. "Impossible?"

"Impossible to hide," he corrected. "It's possible to make."

"But actually *impossible* to hide?"

He hummed a thoughtful note. "Okay, really difficult. Even for me. To hide something like that, it'd be an extremely sophisticated piece of programming. It'd have to not just attach itself to city systems but disguise itself while it did it."

"Explain."

"Okay, say I'm a virus piggybacking on another system," he said patiently. "The system is designed to sweep for anything out of the ordinary, like unapproved data or stagnant bits of code. So, I'd basically be sending out two parcels of data—a stream of encrypted communication, and a stream of junk data disguised as valid information to fool any seekers. The encrypted data would ride under that. Follow?"

Parker let out a deep breath, perching on the edge of her desk. "So possible."

"Possible, and I'll start looking for that," he allowed, "but improbable."

She stared at the covered window, eyes narrowed. "I had a thought, Mr. Stone."

"Yeah?"

"Someone is hunting missionaries," she said evenly. "Someone is learning not only who they are but where they live, where they like to operate, where they *are*."

"Are you thinking the ghost is behind it?"

"The thought had occurred to me." But no, that's not where she was going. "Follow me here. Ms. Long was murdered in the restroom of a lower street club. Although she was on duty at the time,

Mr. Carver was not. He was murdered in his own home. Someone with intimate knowledge of the Mission has to be—"

The frequency rattled, dissolving into static as Jonas's sudden fit of coughing overwhelmed the mic.

Parker's eyebrow raised, her glance shifting to the comm unit on the desk. "Mr. Stone?"

"Sorry!" He cleared his throat. Tried again when it rattled. "Sorry, I inhaled my energy booster. Man, that burns."

She rubbed at the bridge of her nose with one finger, grasping for what calm she could wrap around a sudden surge of impatience. "If you're finished."

"Sorry," he said again, a little rougher around the edges, but accompanied once more by clicking keys. "Ma'am, do you think Simon is *murdering* our people?"

Did she?

She looked down at her desk, stared through the clean surface. She didn't want to believe it. Didn't want to think that the man who'd tested the last dregs of her patience with a kiss that still sent flickers of aftershocks through her could be so . . .

So evil.

"Ma'am?"

But why else would he be here? Just spying didn't seem enough.

"He's the only link we have to the data from Wayward Rose," she said crisply. "With Nelson dead, we have no way of knowing who else may be working for Lauderdale."

Jonas sucked in a breath, the air hissing between his teeth. "You're talking full-scale conspiracy."

"At this point in time, I'm willing to track down any leads. No matter how—" *Terrifying. Infuriating.* "—disheartening."

"Aw, man." She could hear the worry as thick as paste on the line; a worry she echoed. "All right. Where should I look?"

Parker frowned, pushing the heel of her hand against the needling threat of a headache centered behind her forehead. Where should Jonas look? Simon was the only stamped agent she knew of.

She needed an inspection. But all inspections were done by qualified medical personnel, and she couldn't just order her missionaries to strip for her. Well, she could, as she'd done when Simon and his partner had first been placed with her, but that had been to inspect the seal specifically.

And she'd skirted a few regulations in doing so.

All medical personnel came from the labs, which meant Sector Three influence there, too.

Damn it. And that was even supposing all of Sector Three's spies wore the bar code.

She needed Simon's help.

Wouldn't get it.

"Start with everyone Simon's age, give or take a year or two," Parker said, calculating quickly. "Disqualify anyone assigned before—" She hesitated.

"I'd start with sixteen months," Jonas cut in quietly.

Her mind made the connection immediately. "Peterson's exposure?"

"I don't know," Jonas said, "but if I wanted to slip a mickey into a drink, I'd wait for a little confusion to serve as distraction, right?"

"Good point." And that would mean Sector Three had launched its campaign almost immediately upon her appointment. It was, she had to admit, what she would have done. If she were a backbiting political snake. "Do that."

The sign on the line echoed the one she wanted to give. "Okay, I'll start running background checks on any agents acquired in the last sixteen months. I'll bring up medical records, too. This'll take a bit."

"I want you to go over the murdered agents with a fine-toothed comb, too," she ordered. "We weren't looking at them very closely. See if there's a link between them."

"Aside from a tendency to hunt down witches?"

A flicker of a smile tugged at her lips. "Aside from that."

"I'm on it."

"Good." That was one thing covered. "Be in—"

"There's something else."

She raised an eyebrow as she studied the unit on the desk, raising a finger to the bridge of her nose. "What is it?"

Jonas cleared his throat. "Are you, um, somewhere safe?"

The other eyebrow joined the first. "Safe?"

"I mean private," he amended quickly. His voice, normally fairly casual even when talking to her, now strained. "Somewhere, you know, without ears."

"Yes," she said slowly, glance flicking around her empty office. Bookshelves, coatrack, chairs. Lamps. "What's going on?"

He took a deep, audible breath. "While we're on the subject, I have some information about that . . . thing. With the bar-code tattoos and stuff."

Her chest tightened with anticipation. "Gene-Corp."

"Yeah." He drew the word out slowly, and for the first time, Parker realized he'd stopped typing. As if he needed to focus intently on what he said.

Or what she said.

She worked to keep her eagerness out of her voice. "Well? What about it?"

"So, you know that I . . . know people," Jonas hedged. "I mean, you sort of have to, in this line, right?"

"Get to the point, Mr. Stone."

"Yes, ma'am." She could practically hear the wince in the acknowledgement. "I have a lead in to something that sounds big, and it's from a source that really needs to not, uh . . . have questions aimed at him. If you know what I mean."

Following that took effort. "He . . . is willing to give us information in exchange for a certain amount of immunity?"

"Yes," Jonas said in relief. "That."

"About GeneCorp?" About the witches GeneCorp was cultivating. The human subjects churned out in lists longer than her arm. Anticipation gripped her.

"Er . . . yes."

Parker slid off the edge of her desk, straightening from her perch, and carefully tucked stray tendrils of her hair back into place. "So meet with him."

"Um . . ." He sighed. "Ma'am, he wants to meet with *you*."

Her eyebrows knitted. Her? Unheard of. "This sounds like a trap, Mr. Stone."

"I promise you, it's not," he said hurriedly. "Really. It's just that it's really complicated."

She studied the surface of her desk, neat to the point of obsession, and traced two fingers along the ledge in absent thought. Complicated.

Wasn't it always?

"I won't ask you what you know," she finally said, her lips turning up into a humorless smile as Jonas's sigh of relief filtered through the speaker. "Yet."

"Right."

"But I need to know how credible this is."

He didn't even hesitate. "Absolutely, one hundred percent credible, ma'am. Whatever he's got, it's going to be worth it."

And if whatever it was could help her in her Mission, then it would be exactly that.

She nodded, once. "When and where?"

CHAPTER THREE

Kayleigh strode down the hall, her head buried in her digital reader. Like Simon knew it would be.

He didn't bother with greetings. "Where's the docket?"

She jerked in surprise. "Simon! What are you doing?" Her question ended on a surprised note as he grabbed her arm, pulled her out of sight around the corner. She stumbled, but she didn't fold.

She was too much her mother's daughter to fold.

Simon let her go as she pulled at his grip, her pretty blue-gray eyes narrowed in anger. Color rode her cheeks. "You have no right—"

"Shut up," he said over her, cornering her into the alcove wall.

The shock in her eyes made the act worth it.

The Magdalene Asylum had damn good security. Practically unbreakable. Compared to the other three sides of the Holy Order quadplex, the place was a veritable fortress.

Fortunately for him, his security clearance allowed for a certain amount of free reign in the building. Not as much free reign as she got, but being the Sector Three director's daughter had its perks.

It was only a matter of time before she'd come back to her office. So he'd waited.

With some really bad vending machine coffee to keep him company. After the morning he'd had, it'd do.

"No one knew about that folder but me," he said, ignoring her wide-eyed surprise. He kept his voice low, but the intensity of his anger didn't need volume to translate. "I broke every reg in the book, but I got it and got out, no mess. Only to lose it to some jackass shadowing me. How did you learn about it, Kayleigh?"

Although she had no room to sidle in, less room beyond Simon where the alcove ended abruptly into the instant coffee machine, she didn't give in. He let her shake off his grip from her arm.

Her mouth thinned, practically white with anger. "Don't you *ever* jump me like this again," she hissed. "Ever. I don't know where your goddamned folder is! *My* operative never got inside."

Simon frowned at her. "What the hell do you mean?"

"Exactly that." When she pushed at his chest, he stepped back, giving her the space she needed to peel herself off the wall and straighten her red suit jacket. "Are you telling me someone took that file from you?"

"Motherfucker." As an answer, it said enough.

Kayleigh bent to pick up her dropped digital reader, light brown eyebrows furrowed. "That's not what I wanted to hear."

"That's all I've got," Simon growled. He turned, glared at the coffee machine. It had no answers for him. "How did you learn about it?"

"You aren't the only eyes and ears in the Mission." She sighed behind him. "I assume you'll track that folder down?"

"Yeah." He glanced over his shoulder. "Speaking of, what were you doing in Adams's office?"

Kayleigh dropped her gaze to the reader braced on her forearm. Her fingers moved quickly, keying in a sequence for something he couldn't see. "That's classified."

"Oh, for God's sake." Simon raked a hand through his short hair. He didn't have to check the halls to know they were still alone. People—impressions—pinged across the back of his mind, all tucked in offices along the corridor or in the floors above and beyond.

When he wasn't catastrophically bleeding through the nose, his ability worked just fine.

"Simon—"

"Look," he said, cutting her off. "I've got a job to do. Give me the tools so I can. Who else is reporting to you?"

She didn't bat an eyelash. "Try again."

His back teeth ground. "Fine. What did you and Director Adams talk about?"

She stared at him. Weighed it. He watched the struggle in her face, forced himself not to smile in victory as it gave way. With a small shake of her head, she said, "Operation Domino."

Of course. "You're afraid the Mission might get too close."

"Exactly so. The evidence they're sending our labs is liberally laced with Salem markers, but they're ours. For obvious reasons. We can't risk them learning any more of the truth than what Carpenter's case revealed."

Jesus Christ. Kayleigh Lauderdale had no conception of the truth. Simon shook his head. "They won't." Not without some help, anyway. He turned back to the hall, his jaw set. "If that's all, I need—"

"Why haven't you checked in, Simon?"

He hesitated.

"Your last report was two weeks ago." The reader chirped in her hands. "And last you reported, you were, let's see, 'back to one hundred percent.' That's it."

A dozen different excuses all filtered through his mind, even as a shape detached itself from the others in his sensory awareness. A body on the move.

A smile tugged on the corner of his mouth. "It's true."

"You're not in the Mission for your health," she snapped, lowering the reader to her side. "The only reason I know you're doing your job is because of the Domino reports. Simon, you have to keep me apprised."

No. No, he didn't. He shrugged. "You need lab rats killed." His teeth flashed, a smile he knew wasn't kind. She flinched. "I kill lab rats."

Her knuckles whitened over the reader. "We'll see how smug you are when—" As his smile widened, as he folded his arms over his chest, she bit off the angry words he knew she couldn't possibly mean and amended them to, "At least check in with me now. No pain or headaches?"

No one deserved death by degeneration.

"None." He told the lie without so much as a twinge of conscience. She made it so easy.

"Nausea? Vertigo?"

"Nope."

She hummed the tone that doctors everywhere cultivated. The one that hid her thoughts beneath a mask of intellectual study. "What about your abilities? Are they starting to fluctuate?"

His smile hardened. "Like Carver?"

He didn't have to look at her to know she winced. "David was a unique case. He wasn't showing any signs of degeneration, molecular or otherwise."

Or maybe the witch just didn't want to report it. Didn't want to end up lying on some slab while they cataloged every step of the process.

Yeah. Simon knew the feeling.

"Domino's going to be a problem for us if this keeps up," she continued quietly. "They can't possibly think witches are taking out their soldiers."

"That's exactly what they think," Simon countered dryly, turning back. And they weren't exactly wrong. He counted as a witch. So did the other few cleaners in Director Lauderdale's camp. "Give me time."

"Time isn't on your side. You need to report in for weekly examinations," Kayleigh said. "The others are already starting to degenerate. You'll need to be somewhere safe when it happens to you."

"I'll cope."

"Simon, every chance I have to study this thing is a greater chance for me to break it," she pressed. "Don't you want to help the others?"

No. He really didn't. Simon raised an eyebrow, studying her with barely leashed scorn. "You sound like your father."

Color flooded her cheeks. "My father is right to be concerned."

"Your father is the reason you're in corpses up to your pretty smile," he replied evenly. "Let's not get ahead of ourselves."

"Screw you."

His tone lightened as he once more gave her his back. "I'll check in when I'm done."

"Simon—"

"Someone's coming," he told her, shooting her a grin over his shoulder. An easy, no-worries kind of smile. With teeth. "Better not get caught in a corner with a missionary, Doctor. What would Daddy say?"

Setting her jaw, Kayleigh pushed past him, clutching the digital reader to her chest as if it'd provide a shield between her and his mockery.

"You're an ass," she muttered.

"You said it yourself, Kayleigh. Enough time, and I'll be out of your hair." Venom coated his tongue as he added, "Unless I explode. Like Carver."

"Damn it, Simon." She stopped, didn't turn around. He studied the back of her head, her wavy blond hair that wasn't anything like her mother's. But the obstinate set of her shoulders, well, he recognized that one.

Reminded him of her mother. And of himself.

But Kayleigh was one hundred percent natural.

He wondered what she'd say if he ever sent her the DNA data he'd destroyed. What she'd do.

Confront her father, maybe. It wouldn't get her anywhere.

"I didn't *choose* this, you know." The corridor sucked out her words, sent them bouncing along the plain, unassuming hall.

He was too tired for this shit. "That makes both of us. Guess your family should have thought of you before they started making me."

Her indrawn breath wasn't as silent as she probably hoped. But when she spoke again, she'd leashed whatever emotion she entertained into a thin, even line. "Just do your job, Simon. And check in on time."

Simon didn't say anything. Whistling softly, a breezy little tune, he slid his hands into his jeans pockets and sauntered back toward the elevators.

He was two floors down when his comm vibrated against his hip.

Simon unhooked the device from his belt. As he dropped his gaze to the small case, pain licked across his temple—*eighty people in the fifteenth floor of the Magdalene, mice in a maze*—and lanced through his forehead.

Did he get headaches? Oh, yeah.

But that was the way a Salem Project witch went out. With a goddamned bang.

Rubbing at his forehead, Simon flicked open his comm.

The list was growing. Fully a quarter of the names were marked as completed, some he'd done himself, but it didn't end.

More names he knew. More faces he recognized.

More bodies he'd have to hide.

Splat.

Simon blinked. The comm screen blurred red.

Splat, splat.

God damn it, not again. Lifting his hand to his nose, he swore thickly as a metallic tang filled the back of his throat. Blood splattered his hand.

Tilting his head back sent waves of pain through his skull.

Two headaches in twenty-four hours? That couldn't be a good sign.

Parker strode into her office. The door was already swinging shut behind her when the rest of her attention caught up. "For the love of Christ, Mr. Wells!"

Simon didn't get up. Sprawled in her office chair like some kind of decadent god on a throne, his long legs stretched across the gap between chair and desk, ankles crossed on the polished surface. Hazel eyes narrowed, he studied her over the raised hem of his blood-soaked T-shirt.

It bared the lean muscles carved into his abs, revealed one flat nipple.

Nausea warred with heat.

Won.

Parker clenched her teeth. "Why aren't you at the infirmary?" More importantly, why did he keep showing up to *bleed* in *her* office?

His teeth flashed in a grin, as lazy as she'd ever seen him despite the blood saturating the fabric of his T-shirt. He lowered the hem. "Stopped bleeding. You said you wanted to talk. Is now a bad time, *Director* Adams?"

The way he stressed her title made her teeth ache.

The way he seemed to think he could bleed all over her things was worse.

She reached for the doorknob, mouth tight with the effort not to throw up the bile clinging to the back of her throat. She was an executive missionary, not a fighter. She didn't do blood.

Hadn't ever.

As they went, it was a hell of a phobia.

"I can leave, of course," Simon added, his tone wickedly knowing. Mocking. He straightened, dropping his feet to the floor. It only served to pull him upright, to send every muscle in his torso flexing. Moving.

Like a well-oiled machine.

He had a body most women drooled over. Parker was trying very hard not to be one.

Lust and nausea, these things shouldn't cohabitate.

Parker glanced at the doorknob, an inch from her outstretched fingers. Her skin crawled.

And tingled.

Oh, God, this was bad.

"You owe me an explanation, Mr. Wells," she said quietly, appalled at herself for even forcing herself to endure that much. She turned, drawing her professional demeanor around her like a shroud. Cool, collected. "I'm eager to hear what you have to say."

"Yeah. I'll just bet." Simon stood, a powerful surge of his lean body, and stripped his T-shirt off.

Parker tried not to swallow her own tongue. "What are you doing?"

He pitched the bloody shirt into the small trash can behind him, every move flexing the muscles stacked under his swarthy skin. The man was shirtless in her office. Shirtless, and no sign of any fresh wounds. The puckered scar decorating the front of his left side shone healthy and pink, starkly pale against his tanned skin tone.

She frowned. "What happened to you?"

"Nosebleed." He rubbed at his nose, which showed no trace of any lingering blood. "Sucker punch in the training room. It happens."

She swallowed as his gaze settled on her.

Less than four hours ago, she'd met that gaze wearing nothing but thin silk pajamas and the cloak of darkness. Now, in her suit and severely pinned hair, dismay filled her as her body responded in the same, pulse-knocking way.

"You often wear your street clothes in the training room?" she asked pointedly. Part of her knew he lied. The rest of her remained torn between visceral memory and the reality. Which was that he broke into her home. Bled on her desk.

Disobeyed every order.

His smile flashed.

Parker's shoulders straightened as she strode across her office. "Get out from behind my desk."

He stepped into her path.

She stopped just shy of running into him, jerking her gaze to his, mouth set in a cold line. Enough games. Enough flex of social muscle, physical muscle.

Enough with the sudden awareness of his body heat, of the warmth emanating from his bare chest. Flashing in his eyes.

"You're walking a thin line." She ignored his

quirked smile. "Make no mistake, Wells, you're here on my tolerance. Regardless of who put you here," she added as he raised one condescending eyebrow, "all of my agents answer to *me*. That includes you."

He raised a hand, fingers reaching for the side of her face.

She seized his thick wrist in a tight grip, held it away from her. "Don't," she said tightly. "Don't touch me. Don't test me, or I'm going to screw the consequences and move heaven and earth to see you thrown in the cells."

"I have no doubt you could." A beat. "Parker."

The way he said her name sent a ripple of heat through her insides. Her chest, her belly.

Between her legs.

Her grip tightened. The tendons and muscle beneath her fingers flexed; so much corded strength.

He raised his other hand. Slowly, making no effort to disengage from her grasp, giving her every opportunity to dodge him, the tips of his fingers touched her cheek.

Callused. Roughened. Gentler than she expected. They burned a path down the line of her face. Across her jaw.

"Relax," he said. Ordered, more like. His tone didn't leave room to compromise. "I'm not your enemy."

"You're a witch," she scoffed, but she couldn't pull away. Couldn't look away from the heat in his gaze. "Don't patronize me, Mr. Wells."

"Yeah, I'm a witch." The rough edges of his fingers grazed her lower lip. "So why haven't you thrown me out yet?"

Because she wasn't positive she had the clout. Because she wasn't sure that the rest of her Mission was prepared for the political storm that would follow.

Her eyes narrowed as his fingertips traced the line of her throat. "You lie to me, Mr. Wells. You make a habit of it. I don't like liars. I don't like *witches*." He skimmed under her jaw, as if he were seeing her through his touch. Memorizing the feel of her skin.

His other hand remained locked in hers, rock steady. Completely at ease.

His smile pulled one side of his sculpted mouth higher. Sexy. And too damned smug.

When he reversed the position of her hand and his, it twisted so fast Parker couldn't react. Suddenly, her wrist flexed in his fingers, shackled in an unbreakable grip, and his other hand circled her throat.

Not like he had last night. Not in anger, or in a bid to hold her still. This was slow, deliberate. A symbol, she thought wildly, a point. But what? Why?

Her heart pounded. Why did the feel of his palm over her pulse send her body into meltdown?

"Only I noticed," he said, lowering his face so that his breath wafted hot against her temple, "this thing that happens when I'm near you." He inhaled deeply, which slid his chest against hers. Warm and hard and male. And *bare*.

She shuddered, caught in his spell.

Trapped by his assault.

"You're wearing that perfume again. Do you know what that does to me?" His words should have made her snort in mockery of his arrogance.

But she couldn't force it out of her too-dry throat. Instead, she gasped.

"When you're turned on"—his mouth lowered to her ear, lips brushing her sensitive skin—"your scent changes. Subtle. Real subtle."

It should have turned her *off.* It should have sent her into convulsions of laughter. It should have . . . Oh, God, it should have made her cringe.

Instead, as if he touched a flame to her body, need swamped her. Wild. Sexy.

She wasn't any of those.

But he made her want to try.

Parker closed her eyes as his tongue darted out against the overly sensitive shell of her ear; a flick, a taste. She nearly jolted out of her skin.

As he leaned back, his chuckle filled her senses as deeply as the scent of him; musky and faintly tangy. Woodsy and man and lust.

He let her wrist go with a deliberate slide of his callused fingers against the inner skin of her arm.

Parker swayed as he pulled away.

Her fists clenched. Enough was goddamned enough!

"Sit your butt in that chair," she said, every word tamped down to an arctic chill, "and stop playing games."

This time, to her vast relief, he obeyed. Mostly. "No games," he replied. "Just facts." As he sat, the leather chair cushion creaked. Absurd counterpoint to his all-too-nonchalant drawl.

"Then give me some more facts," she retorted. "Real ones. Which of my missionaries are working for you?"

"Me?" He grinned. "You give me too much credit."

Her fingers twitched. Nearly curled into a fist

before she forced them still by her side. "How many of my agents are mine?"

"I don't know."

"Then what does Sector Three want with the Mission?"

There. Simon's expression shifted, an almost imperceptible change. Except to her. Parker didn't sit. She braced her hands on her desk, met his eyes directly.

Deliberately.

"Why is Kayleigh Lauderdale trying to seize control of Operation Domino?" she pressed.

He raised his fingers to his lower lip, a gesture she was sure he intended to look casual. She didn't buy it.

"Why is Juliet Carpenter so important to—"

"Are you looking for a funeral, *Director*?" The question came slowly. Lazily. It didn't match the calculated scrutiny of his gaze.

"What?" Parker frowned. "I'm looking for answers. Answers to questions that are putting *my* people in jeopardy. And if you don't give them, Agent Wells, I'm holding you for obstruction."

"Good luck with that."

There. Another so-casual reminder of his independence flung in her face. Her patience cracked. "I can't nail you for witchcraft as long as the labs are held by that cheerleader," she said flatly, "but I damn well can hold you for insubordination. The cells are on my wing."

His mouth quirked. "I can think of better things to do with a woman bent over a desk like that."

She straightened so fast that her thighs slammed into the wooden lip. Heat flooded her cheeks. Temper spiked a wrecking ball through whatever control she had left. "Are you asking me to lock you up?"

"And if I was?" His eyes glinted.

Parker stared at him. "I can't, can I?" But it wasn't defeat fueling her as she pointed at him. "You're protected."

"For now."

"Fine." Only one answer to that. "Leave your gun and get out."

He rose with the same ease with which he did everything else. "Are you firing me, Director?" His smile knowing, he rubbed one hand down his bare chest.

Insufferable, infuriating . . . *spy*. She gritted her teeth. "You're on the payroll, but I don't have to schedule you for anything. You're suspended. Run back to your Sector Three masters and inform them you won't be spying for them anymore. I've had it."

"You sure you want to do that?"

Now? Oh, yeah. "Bring them on, Mr. Wells." She may not have much choice in regards to the slow infiltration of her own people; she may not be able to handle Sector Three directly, but she'd draw the line somewhere.

Somehow.

His smile twitched higher, a deeper curve echoed in his eyes. "You impress me." His eyes glinted. "Director."

Parker's fingers twitched. So close. So close to a concussion, and he didn't even know it. Forcing herself to remain still, to glare icily at his back as he sauntered for the door, she said nothing.

Until she realized her gaze pinned to the middle of his broad, defined back. His very *bare* back.

The man was going to walk out of her office half naked. Bare-chested, smiling like a lunatic.

For God's sake, was he trying to ruin her? Every

agent on that floor would see him leave her office like that. There'd be rumors, speculation.

Another damned hole to climb out of.

She gritted her teeth so hard that the noise filled her ears. "Try not to go through the main areas."

"Sorry." He tossed her off a salute that couldn't have spelled *too bad* more clearly if he'd said it aloud. "Only one way to leave. See you." That pause, that grating halt before he dug in with a final drawled "*Director.*"

As the door clicked shut behind him, Parker seized the first thing that came to hand and pitched it.

Pens clattered against the door, rained to the ground. The container glanced off the panel, leaving a dent and bending the thin metal.

It bounced back across the floor.

Silence descended. Silence, and the ragged edge of shame as she realized she'd let the bastard do it again. As the blood hummed in her ears, Parker stared at the mess.

This wouldn't do. Not as a Mission director, not as Parker Adams.

She took a deep breath. Reached for her comm.

Jonas answered within seconds. "Ready to go, Director?"

She shook her head. "Almost. I want a trace on Simon Wells's comm at all times."

Silence filled the line for a long moment. Then, slowly, "Ma'am? You what?"

"Crack his comm frequency, Mr. Stone." Parker sank back into her chair, fingers tapping on the desk as she glared at the door.

And the memory of the bare, muscled chest that had filled it.

"I want to know who he talks to, for how long,

about what. I want every message transcribed, am I clear?"

Jonas cleared his throat. "Sure, Director. I'll, uh. I'll get right on that. If you hang on, I can tell you where he is now."

A muscle in her temple throbbed. "I know where he is right now, Mr. Stone." In the middle of her operations floor, drawing too damned much speculation. "Just keep me posted on anything he does out of the ordinary."

"Right, then."

"Good. I'm headed out to meet your informant now. I'll be in touch."

"I'll have your list compiled when you get back."

She disconnected, set the comm on the desk, and stared at it while she mulled her orders in her mind.

Impetuous? Yes. She couldn't argue that.

But he was hiding more than she could allow. Suspending him, removing him from the Mission offices would either put a hole in his espionage plans or free him to do whatever else Sector Three might want him to do. If the former, score one for Mission Director Adams.

If the latter, then Jonas would be able to track him. And she could gain more information than she currently had.

One way or another, she'd draw his secrets out.

Until then, she had an informant to meet.

CHAPTER FOUR

She'd suspended him. Demanded his gun and kicked him to the curb.

Surprising as hell. And too much fun to worry about the consequences of it. He didn't even bother reporting the sentence to Kayleigh; what did it matter? She'd made it clear she had other eyes and ears in the Mission.

Eyes and ears he'd have to ferret out, eventually.

Simon knew he should be less obnoxious, but watching Parker turn into a twitching mass of nerves with every calculated touch made him feel human in ways nothing else could.

Which was as much a problem as anything else.

Feeling human was the last thing he needed to do.

The drive along the New Seattle byway gave him plenty of opportunity to consider his options. Suspension wouldn't fly for long. Sector Three wouldn't allow it, and Parker was going to hate that.

He couldn't blame her. Nadia Parrish's ill-conceived plans had shoved too much of Sector Three onto her turf.

And Director Lauderdale wasn't giving up the ground he'd already gained. Not without a fight.

The conspiracy—because it was exactly that— would only get worse with time. If it hadn't already. Two months of closed-door meetings had shifted the balance of power subtly in the wrong direction. Kayleigh didn't know half of it, but she'd learn what he only suspected.

He didn't envy her when she did.

Simon leaned against the sodden brick wall outside the lower-street diner, one foot planted on the rough surface. High above, too far to get more than funneled echoes, thunder boomed and clashed.

The storm rolled in only an hour or so ago. If summer patterns held, it'd stay for another few hours and dissipate into a fogged mist. Which would settle into the depths of the city, infiltrate the streets, and turn them into humid pits.

While the upper echelons cooled off with whatever breeze ghosted along at those heights, these poor bastards trapped below the sec-lines would swelter in a heat made of damp and rot.

It didn't get *hot* in New Seattle. Not really. Some days were warmer than others during the summer months, but the sun didn't reach far enough to heat the streets. It just got sticky and wet. Skin-clinging, sweat-gathering, pore-saturating wet. Exactly the kind of weather that turned a man lethargic and slow.

Simon scraped his forearm across his forehead,

grimacing as it came away damp with sweat. The rain didn't fall in straight sheets. It hit the upper streets first, pooled and gathered in gutters designed to siphon the puddles away. It slid down buildings like the one he leaned on, fell like streams from gouts overhead.

Whole different worlds. Of course, he couldn't judge. He'd spent most of his life down here, and even he had to admit he preferred the open spaces topside.

Too bad the walls surrounding the whole city still made it feel like the largest mousetrap in the world.

Simon checked his watch. It'd been exactly twenty minutes since the last missionary had left the diner. Seth Miles, recognizable everywhere by his usual fedora, didn't see him around the corner. Simon made sure of that. The kid was a fine missionary. One of the good ones.

Exactly the kind of guy who'd try and interfere with Simon's objective.

Not that he could blame Miles for it. Missionaries were sworn to go after witches, not other missionaries.

Of course, like Simon, Jonathan Fisher wasn't just a missionary. He'd recognized the name on the list this time. Part of Simon's own generation. His own rapidly disappearing generation.

He blew out a breath, scraping his sweat-damp hair back from his forehead.

Now or never.

He ignored the front entry, following the alley back around the building. The neighboring structures sat close enough to give the alley a three-foot span, cramped together so tightly that he had to turn sideways as wall-mounted pipes narrowed his passage. He stepped over piles of refuse, the forgotten remains of rotting garbage and discarded crates. Algae and black moss clung to everything, climbed up the base of the building to spread slimy green fingers through pitted and corroded brick. The smell permeated everything—decomposition blended with the festering miasma of old cooking oil and worse.

The diner, as far as Simon could recall, hadn't always been a place that served food. Or what passed for food for those prices. The building had remained untouched for years, probably hosted more than just squatters in its time. It had picked up a great deal more of New Seattle's charm than was strictly *charming,* but it had somehow turned into one of those places where people went to eat, waste time, and have a pint of bathtub beer.

The alley opened into a wider square. The smell seared through his nose, pungent fingers of decaying moss and burning oil. Black clung to the edges of the diner façade, spread out from the kitchen door as if it had long ago caught on fire and nobody had bothered to scrape the soot off.

Simon approached the entrance, shoving his hands into his pockets. Jonathan wasn't exactly a friend, but they knew each other well enough. And they sure as hell both knew the score. If Simon asked, the man would follow him. Just out into this alley, which was all the privacy Simon needed to—

Somebody was coming.

His senses picked it up seconds before the door

flew open, slammed back into a discarded pile of bottle-filled crates, sending glass ricocheting into the wall. A man staggered through, tripped over the jagged lip where building merged with asphalt. Hacking, choking, his arms flailed as his legs gave out from under him.

Cursing, Simon looped an arm around Jonathan Fisher's stocky chest. Blood speckled the air, red-tinged foam spattered Simon's arm as he braced the man's body weight against his own.

The smell of iron undercut the choking stench of oil and refuse, and a seismic roll of magic power jammed into the narrow alley around them.

"Son of a bitch," Jonathan gasped. He clung to Simon's arms, flecks of foam spraying.

Not good.

Simon's magical gift wasn't among the combat-ready. Useful as a rule, it nevertheless couldn't compare to the more practical applications of fire calling, lightning-wielding, even the telekinetic abilities that had ripped Carver apart.

Jonathan's was like Simon's. A kind of bio-magical control over his own body. Internal; useful without being obvious. The kind of thing a good missionary could use to keep himself at the top of his game.

Until it broke down.

"Hey, buddy," Simon offered quietly.

"Simon." Jonathan didn't straighten. As his body trembled in Simon's arms, tremors rippling under his skin, he coughed. Choked on the effort and expectorated a sticky, crimson mass to the broken pavement at their feet.

Simon's grip tightened. "Losing it, huh?"

The missionary didn't have to say anything. It

was obvious. Whatever degeneration affected the Salem subjects, it hit fast and it hit hard.

A goddamned bang.

"Yeah, you and everyone else," he said grimly. "I got you, Fisher. Don't struggle." Simon braced his shoulder under Jonathan's, leveraged him to the pavement and away from the kitchen exit. Carefully, he wiped the rim of pink foam from the witch's lips with his sleeve.

No one followed him. The bundle of sensory nodes in his awareness remained gathered in the diner proper, only a couple remaining in what he assumed was the kitchen. He'd know if someone detached from the group.

It'd give him time to see to a man who'd never been his friend but who shared a part of Simon's past. And his future.

Jonathan deserved better than to go like this.

The man gasped for air as it rattled through his lungs, his eyes wide and staring. Not quite sightless. Aware enough that as Simon bent over him, Jonathan reached up and grabbed his shoulder in a grip that bit.

Simon couldn't be sure, but as waves of power pressed outward, rippling from the dying man's skin, he guessed the overkill was wearing down his body. Eating at it to fuel its own power surge.

Shutting him down.

"Damn," Simon muttered. "Fisher, you look like hell."

"Feel it," he croaked. But his mouth twisted, a caricature of a smile. "No . . ." He coughed, hard enough to force bloody saliva from his throat. "No coincidence, right? You. Here."

"No coincidence."

Jonathan's laugh died in a choking spasm.

Grimacing, Simon covered the man's hand on his shoulder and waited for the worst to pass.

"Knew about Hannah. Peter and . . . rest. Too late for them. You . . . you, too?" Jonathan demanded, trying to raise his head.

Simon met the man's eyes, brown and shimmering in a bottomless well of pain and, somewhere in there, recognition. He saw himself in Fisher's eyes.

A laughable concept, if it weren't too close to the truth.

"Me, too," Simon agreed. "Carver bit it last night."

"Too soon." Even on the verge of implosion, the man didn't give up.

Simon could have liked him. If . . . well, if everything had been different. "Yeah. Hannah and Carver didn't last nearly as long. We hold the dubious distinction of lasting the longest."

Fisher grunted, scorn and—not that Simon could blame him—anger.

Simon covered his hand with his own. "You're on the list, buddy. You want me to leave you alone?"

He wouldn't, but what did it cost him to let Fisher have a say in his own end? One way or another, he'd die. Either at Simon's hand or at the end of a long, bloody breakdown.

Simon had only made it down here in time for this by pure luck. How many other Salem witches were suffering like this? Like Carver?

Simon couldn't be everywhere.

The man didn't disappoint him. Letting his head

fall back to the spongelike growth infesting the uneven asphalt, Fisher took a deep, rattling breath.

"Nah," he managed hoarsely. Lightly, even. "End it clean, while you . . . while you can. Took forever to get . . . rid of Miles. Good kid."

"Seems like it."

He frowned. "Simon, this won't end . . . You just—" Phlegm caught in his throat. Gargled.

"Easy—"

"Be careful," Jonathan gasped out. He closed his eyes, fingers twisting in Simon's wet shirt. Stretched the already abused fabric. "They all know . . . the missionaries, they . . . the new ones. They're not like—Agh!" Power shuddered against Simon's skin.

Fluctuated, just like the remaining dregs of Fisher's life.

Simon stared down at him, at the ruined shell of what had once been a man just like him. Jonathan's flesh mottled, moving as if fingers tried to work themselves out. Worms of motions, writhing. Twisting.

His mouth gaped as he choked, teeth bloody.

"I know," Simon said quietly, answer to the unspoken threat. He smiled ruefully. "Everything's going to be okay. I won't be that far behind you."

"Wells—"

Simon caught his free hand, held it as the man struggled.

"Listen to me," he gasped, pulling on his shirt. "It's . . . it's different. Changed. No one's working alone." He spoke quickly, every word forced through mucus and blood. "Watch . . . your back, man. Something's not . . . It's all sideways."

Simon unholstered his gun, the one he didn't

bother leaving behind when Parker suspended him. Jonathan's eyes flared, and Simon's gut twisted in shared horror and sympathy as he realized the whites were stained pink. A film of blood.

Degeneration wasn't nearly strong enough a description for this hell.

"I'll be careful," he promised and pressed the muzzle to the missionary's forehead. "Ready?"

"*Do it.*"

His heart slowed. Evened. "Go with God."

Red tears leaked from the corner of Jonathan's eyes, even as he croaked a bitter laugh.

God had nothing to do with this.

As the gunshot cracked like thunder in the small alley, ricocheted from wall to wall and filled the near silence with echoes, Jonathan Fisher's laughter stopped. Blood and gray matter splattered the pavement. He jerked once, a full-body shudder, and Simon flinched as the man's power erupted on a wave of red and pink; like a sonic boom.

Harmless, if uncomfortable. It blew through him, formless as the wind, and faded before Simon could do more than brace himself. It left the filthy alley, left the world for all Simon knew. Left him, bloody and raw with emotions he couldn't stop to give voice to, bent over the corpse of a man whose end would mirror his own.

He closed his eyes, holstered his weapon without needing to look, and took a deep, blood-saturated breath of rotten air and humid temperatures.

All the Salem witches knew what was coming. They all carried the same memories, the same so-called childhood. The cells, the needles, the drugs. None of it had ever brought them anything but a short life and a single opportunity to make it worthwhile.

Killers and spies for Sector Three might have been enough for some. It wasn't for Fisher.

And it wasn't for Simon.

Matilda Lauderdale had wanted something else for him. Something she'd refused to say, even when he'd stood over her dying body, demanding answers.

Now more than ever, he had to find out what. Before it was too late for him, too.

With steady fingers, Simon unclipped his comm, flicked open the screen. A few keystrokes put a check by Fisher's name.

Done.

By habit, he scrolled through the list one more time, double-checking every entry. As it came to the end, he stilled.

The list had expanded by one.

P. Adams.

"Motherfucker."

The whole game had changed.

Testament Park wasn't the only park in all of New Seattle. It remained the only one cultivated by the city, however—marked by a large, memorial fountain commemorating the rebirth of a city torn apart by Armageddon, placed squarely at the front gate so all the passing cars could marvel.

Or, as the case typically was, ignore it. Even Parker had stopped seeing the swatch of green as she passed it every day for work.

Only one kind of plant really did well in the

mostly cloudy environment. Tough evergreens, scrublike bushes, anything that thrived in lots of rain and no real sun. The civic sector—the governing offices that took up the third side of the Holy Order quadplex—had decided that tithes should be set aside for the park.

As if anyone cared anymore about greenery and nature.

Parker sat on the edge of the fountain, one hand buried in her trench coat, the other holding an umbrella open over her head. The rain cooled the air, gave it enough of a mild bite that she didn't relish getting a soaking.

Pedestrians passed on the other side of the fountain, a long line of black umbrellas and the occasional colorful designer pattern. Cars glided by, wheels forging through the collected rainwater as the built-in gutters worked to direct the flow away from the streets.

On the park's side, the paths remained empty.

As far as Parker knew, only the occasional jogger or strolling couple wandered through the meandering trails. It wasn't big enough for a full run, and there were better places—gyms and cultivated tracks—where exercise could be more comfortable.

She tended to stick with the Mission facilities herself. How long had it been since she'd last wandered through the evergreens?

Years, at least.

Her clearest memory involved an eager set of hands and the risk of getting caught.

A faint smile touched her mouth as she shook her head. That was a long time ago. A somewhat less difficult time, though the orphans collected in the Mission boardinghouse always knew where they'd eventually end up. The Church cultivated everything—parks, people.

Conspiracy.

She shifted on the cold, hard ledge, transferring her umbrella to the other hand. Her gun was in reach, but she couldn't leave it out for anyone to see. It'd take some doing to get it if she needed it.

She hoped Jonas was right.

She couldn't risk extra backup on this one. Not if what the analyst said was true. Anything, any clues, as to GeneCorp's nature and interests would help her.

Help the Mission.

She resisted the urge to check her watch.

"Miss Adams."

Her head whipped around so fast that the umbrella tilted. A man caught the edge, sent water leaping out from the waterproof material in a miniature version of the fountain.

He wore a long coat, virtually identical to hers but for the black color, belted over what looked like dark jeans. Not exactly suit-and-tie wear. His lean build and wet curls didn't offer anything to make him stand out, though his angular features were handsome enough.

Not as striking as Simon.

And she really didn't need to be making *that* comparison.

His smile reached his warm brown eyes. "Pleasure to meet you face-to-face," he said lightly. He let go of her umbrella. "May I sit?"

Her eyes narrowed as the memory clicked into place. "Phi—"

"There's no need for that," he said hastily, folding to the ledge beside her with elegant ease. "Let's just keep this as informal as possible."

"So you say," she said slowly, shifting to keep distance between them. Not that she expected Phinneas Clarke to do anything but charm her to death.

The man had a reputation. A little less than a year ago, he'd run the city's premier resort and spa for the wealthiest and most elite. Coming from a prominent family himself, the spa had done very well among the wealthy set.

Until a rogue missionary had infiltrated it, culminating in its destruction—and the defection of one of her top agents.

Phin Clarke's mother had died in the ensuing fallout. Parker had tried to keep tabs on them, to get to the bottom of the events that had ended in so many questions, but a few months later, the Clarkes had vanished completely.

That made them guilty as hell in her book, but she'd never had anything to go on.

Until now.

He studied her, a kind of half smile shaping his mouth. "I suspect you have a lot of questions."

"You have no idea," she said evenly. "Let's start with where you've been."

"Safe." He leaned forward, lacing his fingers, elbows braced on his knees. If the rain dripping through his sodden hair bothered him, he didn't show it. "I have a lot of contacts, and I'm only telling you this because I think you're going to need my help more than you know."

"I'm listening," she said.

"You've probably figured out by now that there's a pretty big shake-up in the Holy Order."

"I'm learning that."

"After everything that happened at Timeless," he said, studying the wet, dripping park laid out in front of them, "we waited out your investigation, pretty sure you'd never find anything to pin on us. After all," he added, a glint in his dark eyes as they slid to her, "he was *your* missionary."

Not quite. Joe Carson was a rogue element from another city, a transfer with an agenda all his own. But she let it slide. "It was the witchcraft that bothered us," she replied, every word mild as spring rain.

His eyes crinkled warmly. "The people who revealed themselves weren't our witches, either. What was left of the Coven of the Unbinding took an interest in Timeless."

"So you say."

"It doesn't matter now." He clasped his hands loosely, elbows braced on his knees. "Not long after Joe Carter, a handful of covert operatives came after us."

Parker narrowed her eyes in sudden anger. "I ordered no such thing."

"We know," he replied, shrugging his rain-soaked shoulders. "We figured that out. But we also figured out that until the power play balanced, we weren't safe. So, now we are. Or," he amended ruefully, "were, until Juliet Carpenter ended up on one of your lists."

Fine, but that told her virtually nothing except that this had been going on for too long. Covert operatives? They weren't hers, which meant either her missionaries were acting without her orders, or Sector Three had involved themselves. She'd long suspected the latter.

She hated that she suspected her own people.

"So why am I here?"

"Because I have something you'll want to look at," Clarke said. He reached into his coat pocket, hesitated when Parker stiffened. "Relax. It's not a gun. I'm just getting out a package."

"Why you?" she demanded. "Why do you have this?" Whatever it was.

Clarke's smile revealed dimples at the corners of his mouth. "Can I say that you're not alone? Is that cheesy?"

It might be, but hearing it managed to worry her and soften the knot of anxiety in her gut at the same time. "Who else is working with you?"

"Can't say." Thin plastic crinkled. He drew out a wrapped container, a zippered bag no bigger than his palm and too opaque to see through. Balancing it on one hand, he offered it to her, his gaze steady. "And we're not *exactly* on your side. But you need this."

"What is it?"

"An answer," he said cryptically. As her fingers closed over the mysterious bag, his other hand covered them. Pinned her hand between his and held her. "Be careful. If I've learned anything this past year, it's that the people you're playing against don't play by the rules."

Parker bit her lip, her grip tight on the umbrella handle as she stared at the man she should have been arresting. "How do you know what's going on?"

"We're very well informed." Again, his smile, and a somewhat sheepish duck of his head. "*Surprisingly* well informed, even. But we're . . . sort of stuck. Giving you this might move things along."

"To what end?" she demanded.

"You know what?" He gave her hand a squeeze. "We really don't know. But you've got the scientists and labs. And now you have something that could change the outcome of this fight. Maybe you'll figure it out. If you need me," he added, blinking away the rainwater, "talk to Jonas. It's not easy to get up here, but I'll do anything I can."

Confusion made her slow. Shaking her head, she extricated her hand—and the bag. "Tell me what this is, and maybe I can do more for you."

"It's a piece of the puzzle. It's . . ." He hesitated, obviously working through an answer. "It's something Sector Three will want. Wants now, actually. I'd give you more, but the time you'll spend figuring that out is going to give us time to move. You understand our caution." His teeth flashed—a smile charming enough to melt the pants from most girls, she was sure. Parker wasn't most girls, but even she could admit Phin Clarke had a way about him.

Maybe it came from having two mothers. Maybe it was raw genetic luck.

But she was Mission Director Parker Adams. She couldn't be charmed.

"I see," she replied coolly. And she did. He had to know that she'd have him tracked the instant she could.

"Just keep it out of their hands," he added, sobering. "We're taking a big risk here. If they get that, it all goes to hell. Okay?"

"I understand." Only that part she didn't. Not completely.

Clarke nodded, pushed a hand through his wet

hair, and got to his feet. Shaking off his soaked coat, he sighed deeply. "Well, lovely meeting you. Be careful, Miss—"

"It's Director."

He paused, looking down at her with a trace of one dimple at the corner of his mouth. "For now," he said cryptically and tipped an imaginary hat.

It was such an old-fashioned, out-of-place gesture that Parker's eyebrows flew up as a grudging whisper of appreciation flickered.

She throttled it back behind an icy mask. "This doesn't clear you, Mr. Clarke."

He winced faintly. "Somehow, I don't think anything short of an act of God would do it. Good-bye, Director. Good luck."

Turning his collar up, Clarke strode deeper into the park. She watched him, her jaw shifting as she fought years of training—of duty.

She should have arrested him.

Instead, his black coat and dark hair quickly faded, swallowed up by the shadows clinging beneath the rain-soaked trees.

Her fingers tightened on the soft plastic case. Glancing down, she studied the oblong container. What would it hold?

Was it a trick?

It didn't *feel* like one.

Parker glanced left to right. Seeing no one else, she plucked at the zipper, pulled it open, and cautiously spread the flaps apart.

A single syringe nestled in the bottom, filled with a murky liquid that didn't slosh so much as ooze when she tilted the case for a better look.

Drugs? Something else?

This day was just getting stranger and stranger.

Her comm vibrated. Jumping, Parker grabbed the unit from its pocket clip and checked the frequency number. Jonas. Not surprising. She flipped up the screen but held it to her ear instead of bothering with the earpiece. "You have impeccable timing, Mr. Stone."

"Yeah," he said slowly. He didn't bother to deny the accusation she didn't have to say. "You have a million questions—so do I, trust me, Director. But I'm afraid that I'm not calling about that."

"What is it, then?" She righted her umbrella as it threatened to slide off her shoulder, pocketed the case with its mysterious contents.

"There's been another murder. Within the hour."

Parker rose. "Who?"

"Agent Jonathan Fisher." His voice strained. "He was one of my team."

Her mouth tightened. "Is a crew on site?"

"Two."

"Make sure Mr. Eckhart sends me the report."

"Yes, ma'am."

Parker closed the comm, already striding away from the fountain. Mystery or not, the city's witches weren't doing her any favors. She had work to do.

CHAPTER FIVE

She was short on answers. Short on leverage.

Long on questions.

Rubbing at her eyes, Parker hung her wet coat on the hook by her front door and set her purse down on the table beneath it. She stretched until the joints in her hips and shoulders popped in muted relief.

The day hadn't ended well.

Jonathan Fisher had been found like so much garbage, his head a morass of barely recognizable flesh and tissue. The bullet they'd pulled out of the ground had matched half the Mission-assigned armory. Most of her field agents carried a .45. So did any criminal looking to make a sizeable hole.

Signing off on the data made something in Parker's soul twitch. More evidence, more proof, sent to the Sector Three labs. What else could she do?

With every murdered missionary, her questions grew—and the data they sent the labs continued to fail them.

Was Dr. Lauderdale withholding information?

A laughable question. Of course she was. But Parker needed to know if her labs were compromised so badly that Sector Three would keep all data from Domino's scenes out of Mission hands.

How would she find out? A heart-to-heart with one of the lab techs, maybe. If Sector Three stayed true to form, the grunts wouldn't know anything about the politics at work. Parker could play on loyalty. Hell, for this, she'd fight dirty and go right for the career throat.

Parker made her way to the bedroom, stripped out of her work clothes, and stepped into a pair of jeans and a white blouse. Mr. Sanderson yawned blearily at her from the nest he'd made on her bed, displaying prominently pointed fangs.

"Hey, baby," she murmured.

Her hand hovered over the gun she'd stripped off with her work clothes. Would she need it?

She grimaced. Of course she would. She was expecting company, wasn't she?

Feeling spiky, more on edge than she ever wanted to in her own home, Parker grabbed the gun, checked the safety, and tucked it into her waistband.

Every new murder cost her more than just manpower. Six of her agents were dead, and she had no reason to think it'd slow down now. The strain of the day weighed on her—too much time spent directing missionaries who were losing heart.

And gaining an aggressive edge.

As she returned to the living room, shadowed by the sleepy cat, she flicked on a lamp, rifled through her purse until the case filled her fingers. She stepped over Mr. Sanderson, entered her office, knelt, and inputted a digital sequence into the safe, where she kept what few valuables she considered worth storing. A few nice pieces of jewelry, her backup gun, some documents.

And now, one mystery syringe.

The door swung closed at a touch, the tumblers smoothly clicking into place.

Within minutes, she made herself a cup of strong coffee, fell into her armchair, and stared into the hot, black brew.

She almost laughed. Somehow, she'd gone from a neat, orderly existence to playing hostess for a secret so big—or so Phin Clarke suggested—that it would . . . what did he say?

She rubbed at her eyes with one hand as her gaze unfocused in brief, too-stressed exhaustion.

Oh, right. *Change the outcome of this fight.*

To what end?

How could a little syringe do it? What was it? A drug? What kind?

And how could she find out? Dr. Lauderdale all but admitted to keeping tabs on everything coming in and out of the Mission labs. Parker could coerce some information relating to Mission cases from a lab lackey, but she'd be pushing it if she tried to sneak in an extra test.

Her grip tightened on the bridge of her nose.

She had one option, then. Private sector.

Tomorrow, she'd deliver the material directly to a corporate laboratory. Somewhere run by someone she could keep a close rein on. Maybe Toller Industries. They'd done some work for the Church before.

No, that wouldn't work. Anyone that big would have Church ties. Maybe a smaller company. One desperate for a little monetary edge. If she had to, she'd dip into her own funds to facilitate the matter. Easy as pie. So why, she wondered as she briefly touched the gun in the back of her waistband, didn't she feel better?

Fatigue, sure. And stress. She was angry.

She felt hunted.

And she needed a break. Parker lifted one foot as Mr. Sanderson prowled out from under the chair, and allowed herself to melt bonelessly into the cushions. She set her mug on the small stand beside the chair. Rain slammed against the window, accompaniment to the thoughts spinning around and around in her head.

What did she know?

Precious little as fact.

Sector Three had decided to infiltrate—possibly even take over—Sector Five. The Mission already struggled under a new director. Parker wasn't so arrogant that she thought everything was coming up roses, no matter how hard she'd worked for the past year and a half. The agents who'd worked under David Peterson had had a massive chunk blown out of their trust quotient. Those who'd come out of training since his betrayal were suspect.

That didn't leave Parker with a lot of steadfast players.

Jonas. She could count on him to support her, but at what cost? He knew about the Salem Project—about Simon Wells and Juliet Carpenter—but he also kept company Parker couldn't approve of. Phinneas Clarke was wanted for questioning. So, for that matter, was the company *he* kept, wherever it was he hid.

But what were her options? At this point, neither the devil she knew nor the angel she didn't looked like sure bets.

Simon Wells? Talk about a devil. No matter how hard she tried, she couldn't grasp his angle. He was a product of this human testing lab, she got that much. A marked witch. The exact thing she and her people should have been hunting down, sentencing for his crimes.

But he was protected by the very Church she swore to uphold. Protected, and allowed the run of the Mission Parker had prided herself on directing smoothly. Why?

Amy Silo. If Jonas was the technical god of the Mission, then Agent Silo doubled as his research equivalent. She'd earned her place in the Holy Order's massive library, the undisputed queen of the research stacks. She kept a sharp watch on everything going in and out of her library, and not even Lauderdale himself had the clout to have her removed. A missionary, yes, but even the bishop had to answer to his favored librarian when it came to the Order's treasured books.

Nothing would turn her from the cause. And the cause had never been the Mission.

The librarian's cause was knowledge. Knowledge didn't play politics.

Exhaustion turned Parker's body to useless fluff. She usually spent long days at the office, but this trumped most. The lunch she'd picked up on her way back from the meeting with Clarke hadn't lasted past eight, and at somewhere just before midnight, her stomach now felt as if it'd latched onto her spine. Desperate for nutrients.

She was too damned tired to cook.

Parker let out a long, slow breath, staring past the circle of light shedding golden illumination over her chair. Her spacious condo remained dark, one part from the evening hour and mostly from the storm clouds. She turned off every light as she left the room it belonged to. Outside of the lamplight, the living room and kitchen beyond it glinted with the occasional flash of lightning, shadows dancing wildly.

She didn't like wasting electricity. Not that it mattered in New Seattle. The heights of the metropolis were among the most well-maintained on the electrical grid. Even should the summer storm raging outside cause the power to short, generators redirected all currents back to the top.

It was one of many perks of living high above the rest of the city.

"Damn," she breathed, smoothing one hand over her copper hair.

Thunder rattled the windows, echoing a flash of lightning that turned the fluorescent light rimming the drapes into purple-white luminescence. At her feet, Mr. Sanderson jumped. Collar bell jingling, he skidded out of the living room so fast that his claws caught at the carpet.

Parker hid her smile.

"It's just thunder," she called. "Scaredy-cat."

"Not," corrected a low, masculine voice just behind the armchair, "*just* thunder."

Parker's heart surged into her throat. The man

was a damned ghost; how the hell did he *do* that?

The hard edge of a pistol muzzle pressed into her skull. "No sudden moves," he warned.

The action mirrored her own only hours before. He wouldn't *dare*.

Of course he would. "Mr. Wells, you have ten seconds." To her relief, her voice didn't shake even a little. Ice cold, it lashed as deeply as the thunder rolling across the sky.

The point of pain under his gun lifted. "Ten seconds is too long," he said, but unlike every conversation she'd ever had with the man, there wasn't anything *easy* about his tone now. "It's time to go."

"You must be joking."

"Not even a little." He circled her chair, stepping into the pool of lamplight like some kind of golden god rising from the dark. Dramatic. Oddly erotic. Was it the light? The shadows sinking into the carved angles of his face?

The new, unstained T-shirt clinging to every muscled line of his torso?

Parker shifted. Met his gaze, raised an eyebrow. "I'd rather sit and talk."

Holstering his gun in one smooth motion displayed the muscles in his upper arms and shoulders, outlined by his nylon shoulder rig. His khaki-colored T-shirt clung to the lean definition of his chest, beads of water dripping from his hair. She watched a droplet slide across his temple, trace the sculpted line of his angled jaw as he stared at her.

Challenge.

"Sorry, sweetheart. We can't do that."

Something had changed. Between his suspension and this confrontation, something felt different. Even when he gave every appearance of seriousness, his eyes usually laughed at her. Now, she saw nothing but impatience in their glittering depths.

Did he know about her meeting with Phin Clarke?

Would it matter if he did? The gun's grip nestled into her palm, hidden at the small of her back.

"Trust me," he said quietly.

What did it say about her that she wanted to? *Idiot.*

Because she wanted him off-guard—because she wanted to touch—she slid her left hand into his. He pulled her to her feet with the same easy surge of power he gave everything else. Pulled too hard, folded her too neatly into his embrace, one arm banded across her back.

It pinned her to him. Tucked her against his longer form as if she were made to fit in the hollows of his body.

Parker's breath caught.

His exhaled on a hissed curse as the unyielding muzzle of the pistol in her right hand slotted into the groove of his sternum. His eyes narrowed, thick dark lashes shielding whatever gears ground in his head.

She didn't know. Couldn't read him. All she knew was that every breath only highlighted how much space there *wasn't* between them. Clarified how much the smell of him filled her senses. It sparked a chain reaction from head to chest to that knocking ache between her legs, no matter how much he made her angry.

The man was a menace.

For a long moment, only thunder split the silence.

Parker allowed herself a small smile. "I never make the same mistake twice, Mr. Wells."

"So I see." His answering smile revealed the edge of his even white teeth. It crinkled the edges of his eyes, forcing a knotted weft of appreciation through the determination she clung to.

Her grip tightened on the pistol.

"I'm going to have to break you of this habit you have." A silken promise. "Guns aren't for playing." His arm banded like iron around her lower back. Forced her so tightly against him that she knew he had to feel the knot of a bruise forming around her gun. He didn't try to disarm her. He should have. The man was a missionary, no matter who'd put him there.

Men like Simon Wells didn't allow people to pull guns on them.

Instead, contrary to every expectation, his free hand slid up her back. Mapped her spine, traced over the seal of St. Andrew nestled between her shoulder blades.

As his fingers dug into her hair, cupping the back of her head, her smile faded. "Let me go."

"Will you shoot me?"

"Count on it, Agent Wells."

"Oh, well." The tone should have warned her. "Even a dying man gets his last request," he murmured.

She stiffened. "Don't you—*Mmph*!"

Simon's kiss wasn't the same. This wasn't a simple meeting of lips and breath and skin. Something had changed.

Something infected his laid-back façade.

This kiss stripped away every thought of denial,

of protest. He didn't tease her or gently engage. He claimed. He took. His lips covered hers, scorched where they touched her. Sent tingling shivers from her lips to her spine to her fingertips.

To her molten, swirling insides, suddenly too hot. Too wild.

The end-of-shift shadow at his jaw scraped her sensitive skin as he tilted her head, changed the angle to deepen the kiss, set fire to her blood and made her forget about the gun in her hand. The syringe in her safe.

The secrets, the lies.

Somehow, he always managed this. Managed to get in under her skin. Beneath her guard. Closer than she ever wanted him.

Her hand flattened against his chest, just by the gun he ignored. Muscles flexed, leaped under her touch.

Everything in her wanted to feel skin, not damp fabric. *His* skin, his heartbeat trapped beneath his flesh. Her fingers found the hem of his shirt. Slid under.

Something ragged and unrefined guttered in his throat as she found smooth, ridged muscle; something that raised every hair on the back of Parker's neck and curled like a rough hand between her legs.

Like steel given flesh. Like . . . like shaped aggression, strength made human.

Everything about him turned caution to arousal. Fear to need. She wanted him. She couldn't deny it, not when her body thrilled with every flick of his tongue against hers. Her eyes had drifted shut; she didn't know how. She didn't command it.

Her body wasn't hers.

Simon invaded her space, her thoughts. Her peace. Claimed what he wanted, left her starved and wild in his wake.

Parker didn't *like* men like him.

She'd never *met* a man like him.

Pulling her mouth away left her gasping, her lips damp from his kiss, tingling. He let her; she had no reason to think otherwise. As her eyes fluttered open, as she clung to his chest and tried to force her body to suck in the air his kiss had stolen, Simon stared down at her.

His gaze bored into hers, smoldering with the same inferno licking at every measure of restraint she possessed. Knowing. All too aware of the way her heart pounded in her chest.

"I'm going to give you one chance," she whispered. One chance was all she had it in her to give. "Talk to me, Simon. Tell me what I need to know." Holy God, was that her voice? So husky and inviting.

His fingers tightened around the back of her head. As if the very sound of her voice did to him what he did to her.

Not that it'd help. "Sorry." For the first time since Simon Wells had walked into her office days ago, sincerity filled his quiet tone. "You really have to come with me."

Parker's kiss-swollen mouth quirked even as she firmed her grip on the gun. "Then we're at an impasse, Mr. Wells."

"You have no idea what saying my name like that does to me, do you?"

She blinked. "What?"

Simon's smile uncurled slowly.

No. Not this again. This time, this was her scene. She moved quickly, gave no warning; calculated it with the same precision she did everything else. As the gun dug into his sternum, as his hand tightened at her back, she pressed the fingers of her free hand together and jabbed them—hard—into the hollow of his throat.

His curse strangled, an unintelligible grunt.

She followed up with a barefoot stomp on his instep, spun out of his suddenly loosened grip as he grabbed for the back of the armchair with one hand, and ran like hell.

Parker wasn't an idiot. He had height, reach, and weight on her, not to mention whatever powers that Salem gene bestowed on him. She sprinted for the hall leading to her bedroom—and the escape route out the window. She'd formulate a plan later, but for now . . .

For now, she had him on breaking and entering, assault and battery. If he pushed her, she'd add a self-defense plea to the mix and shoot him. Let the Church try and cover *that* up.

While they tried, she'd have him in interrogation.

A growl hard on her heels warned her it wouldn't be easy. She didn't think it would. As a hand closed on the back of her neck, Parker stopped abruptly—too fast, no warning—and slammed her elbow into his gut.

He took the hit. Took it as if her elbow was made of feathers and foam. Stepped into it, into her, slamming her sideways into the hallway wall. Shelves in her living room clattered. His free hand curled into her blouse front, shoved her hard against the wallpaper.

The back of her skull bounced off his palm.

His eyes gleamed, mere inches from her face. His features, already angled, were drawn taut, skin flushed. Mouth set.

She'd surprised him.

Good.

She shifted; he let go of her head to grab the wrist with the gun, pinning it to the wall above her head. "Stop it," he ordered.

Like she would. "Breaking and entering, Mr. Wells," she panted, too aware of his greater strength over hers. Of his leg shoved hard between hers, his hip pinning her tightly.

His rain-saturated clothing slowly soaked through her blouse. Warm and suddenly too intimate for the setting.

"The least of your concerns," he growled back, jerking the damp strands from his forehead with a hard shake. Raw impatience. "Listen to me, you *need* to get out of here."

"I'm not leaving my home on your say-so."

His teeth flashed in a hard smile. "You're a smart woman. You know I wouldn't risk my neck if it weren't important."

She knew no such thing. Far as Parker could tell, Simon Wells was a certifiable lunatic.

But still, she hesitated.

"You're important enough to kill," he said quietly, slowly relaxing his grip in her collar. His fingers grazed her throat. Her collarbones. Smoothed over the sensitive curve where her shoulder met her neck. "Which makes you important enough to keep alive. Come with me, Parker."

"Director," she corrected coolly, even as her

skin heated from the rasp of his callused fingertips. From the damp heat of his body against hers.

"Fine, if it'll get you out of here."

She shook her head. "I don't trust you."

Again, that edged smile. A flicker of approval. But before he could say anything, it vanished as his gaze snapped to the living room beyond the hall. His features settled into hard, dangerous lines. "Shit."

"What?"

"Quiet."

The intensity of the order drilled through her outrage.

Her pulse kicked hard.

His mouth thinned. Anger, she read that much. Concern? "Listen to me," he whispered. "There are three men circling this complex."

"What?" Her voice slid up an octave.

"You know how you aren't a field agent?" He turned, slid his hand against the back of her now clammy blouse and snagged her wrist with the other hand. Almost as if they were dancing. Only she couldn't pull away. "I am, and I'm talking to you *as* an agent. Move your ass, Director."

Was he telling the truth? Aside from the continual rumble of summer thunder and pattering rain, she couldn't hear anything but her own heartbeat. And his.

The holster carrying his gun—illegally worn, now that she'd suspended him—bumped her elbow as he leveraged her past her office. "Clearly, the strain is getting to you," she said evenly.

He didn't rise to the bait. "You have no idea. Is there a fire escape out your window?"

"Yes, but—"

"Good." His footsteps didn't so much as rasp on

the colorful runner protecting the hall's hardwood flooring. Hers dragged.

Parker dug her heels in. His grip on her wrist twisted; she winced. "This is absurd. You need help. Whatever GeneCorp did to you, Simon—"

His face shuttered. The light flickered behind them. "Time's up."

With a low, wheezing drone, the electricity guttered to dead silence.

Thick black night corralled them in utter darkness.

This was his fault.

Simon followed Parker's gaze as she whirled in the dark hallway, her face a bone-white shadow of surprise in what little lightning residue crept through the dark hall.

He couldn't give her time to adapt. Not this time. Her name on his list proved even the Mission director was fair game. And he wasn't the only cleanup agent on the roster.

There weren't that many operatives out there yet, but taking on three by himself wasn't his idea of a good time. They'd already hit the power grid in the block; not even streetlights remained visible.

"Wait!" she whispered. She took a step back toward the lamplight—and the bull's-eye target it'd make of her.

He caught her by the shoulders, fingers tight in her blouse. "Leave the cat," he said tightly. "They're not after him."

"It's not—"

"Now!" he snapped. As his senses unfolded, as the individual bodies pinged on his witch-born radar, he dragged her back further down the hall.

Parker's mouth flattened into a hard white line. She caught up with his urgency—and to her credit, she caught on fast. Saying nothing, she pushed past him, a red-capped shadow.

Although only an administrative missionary, she had serious spirit. He liked that about her.

He liked a lot of things about her. Her copper red hair, always so tightly wound. Her midnight blue eyes, the way she thrust out her jaw when things didn't fall into place. Her red lipstick, sultry as hell and one more plate in her polished armor.

The sweet curve of her ass in the jeans he hadn't thought she owned.

Amid the wild rush of adrenaline, the thought slammed home in a surge of heat.

Focus, damn it.

She crossed the room, her stride long. Her feet bare. Lightning flashed outside, streamed through the flirty sheer curtains he'd never have expected from the uptight director. It painted her bedroom in fluorescent purple and blue, sank it back into darkness made all the worse for the memory of it.

Simon knuckled at his eyes. "Move it," he ordered quietly, shutting the door as softly as he could. She'd put a lock on it.

Paranoid?

In this case, just paranoid enough.

He slid the metal catch into place, hurried across the room as she forked right.

She ignored him, flinging open her closet and kneeling to rifle through God only knew what. Simon growled a curse.

The look she shot him might have been censure. He wouldn't doubt it. But spots of color rode her cheeks, and fear shimmered in the depths of her usually so steady gaze.

Maybe there was hope for her yet.

He twitched the curtains aside. Rain splattered the window, hammered the metal fire escape clinging to the building wall. Contrary to his earlier assertion, nothing moved outside, though a muffled series of thuds faded beneath a wild clap of bone-rattling thunder.

"Let's go, Director."

"I need shoes," she half snarled, waving sneakers in one hand and her Beretta in the other. Simon flung aside the curtain and unlatched the window. It opened easily.

Rain splattered the brick windowsill, blew a fragrant blend of wet cement and acid through the room. He braced one hand against the glass over his head, leaned out far enough to study the dark path through the fire escape.

It was a long way down.

"Ready," she breathed behind him. Simon turned. Offered a hand by rote and raised a surprised eyebrow when a wild fork of lightning turned the room bright as daylight.

Somehow, she'd managed to pack a bag. It hung over her shoulder, a simple canvas rig. Her bare feet now sported laced sneakers, and a black neoprene jacket covered her blouse, hiding the curves he'd had too much time to admire.

"Always prepared, huh, Director?"

If looks could obliterate, he'd be a pile of ash on the carpet. Thunder swallowed her response, but Simon bet on a talk on their immediate future.

Then again, he'd bet on a whole lot more than

talking, but not if he didn't get her out of this net right fucking now.

Biting back a hard little smile, he gestured gallantly to the open window. "After you." The door creaked as something—someone—tested the lock. Simon's humor vanished. "Now," he added, wrapping his hands around her waist and all but spilling her onto the slippery metal platform.

The metal groaned beneath her sudden weight. Telling enough to anyone listening. And Salem Project operatives weren't stupid.

Under the cover of the storm's rage, the door exploded open behind him, lock tearing from the doorjamb. Splinters rained into the room.

A man in black plasteel body armor followed.

"Move!" Simon yelled, but he didn't have time to draw his gun. The operative came at him so fast, Simon couldn't even gauge any details about him. Black-clad, face covered, build lean and lethal. Gun ready. That was enough.

He lurched to the side, grabbed the man's gun hand, and yanked him into the room, hard enough to hear his shoulder pop. The operative stumbled, grunting, but twisted sideways. Simon cursed as the motion snapped tension through his side, pulling at his wounds.

Who was he? One of his own generation?

A newer breeding pool?

Three operatives. *Nobody's working alone.* Fisher's warning repeated itself in his brain as Simon caught the fist flung at him, rotated his grip, and rammed the agent face-first into the window frame under his own momentum. The whole wall shuddered.

The operative righted himself but staggered. Simon danced away from the boot lashed back in lethal intensity. It grazed his shin. Too close.

As Simon wrenched his gun free, his opponent turned, hands splayed. Giving up?

Simon hesitated.

No. It didn't matter. Setting his jaw, he pulled the trigger, twice in quick succession. He didn't even stop to check as the man dropped mid-lunge, skidded face-first on the carpet.

Known or not, the operative made his choices.

And Simon had just sealed his own.

He half dove out of the window, adrenaline pounding in his veins. Another impression in his awareness suddenly changed direction; as if Simon were the center of a compass, he felt it—saw it— alter course. And fast.

Nothing broke stealth like gunfire.

Rain sluiced down the fire escape, making the rails treacherous. He caught sight of Parker's soaked form two platforms below him, scaling the escape as if she did it every day. She'd hit the ground first; he still had two floors to go.

Humor skated through apprehension.

Faded as a shadow detached from the corner of the building beneath her.

"Parker!" he roared.

She looked up, pale features furrowed with intense concentration.

Only to curse in mingled surprise and anger as the operative grabbed the bag across her shoulders and plucked her, kicking and fighting, from the ladder. Her feet flashed, reflectors on her sneakers throwing back glints of silver. One collided with the operative's knee.

The man staggered but held tight.

Simon holstered his gun, snapped it in place. Didn't stop to consider the alternative. Seizing the railing in both hands, he vaulted over the edge and hit free fall. His stomach launched into his chest. Vertigo slammed through his head, wrenching his senses lopsided, even as his feet scraped against the operative's shoulders. Slid down his armored back.

Silver glinted in a flash of lightning; a metal edge colored blue, and fire seared up his side as Simon hit the ground, took the operative down with him and felt the impact all the way to his bones. He cursed savagely as pain wrecked every nerve from heels to hips. But the operative hit the ground tangled with him, sending Parker sprawling in the opposite direction. The knife flashed as it buried itself in shadow.

He didn't have time to hurt.

The operative recovered first, slammed an elbow into Simon's sternum as he tried to get to his feet. Gasping, Simon caught his arm, wrenched it; rolled with it until he felt as much as heard the joint in the man's elbow give with an audible *pop*. The operative screamed.

The tattoo emblazoned into Simon's shoulder scorched white-hot as the air around him froze.

Son of a bitch!

Sucking in below-freezing air that burned all the way to his lungs, Simon rolled away from the witch. The rain-slick walkway between the condominium buildings dug into his side, his face, his back.

Ice crystallized around him. Bitter cold.

He didn't have the ability to ward this much magic off.

Lightning seared the sky, threw wild shadows across the small alley. Red glinted like molten metal in his peripheral.

His skin felt as if it would peel away from the seal of St. Andrew's warning burn.

"Simon, get down!"

He collapsed. As icy shards of witchcraft shattered the brick above him, gunshots split the storm-ridden silence.

His? No, his fingers throbbed, too frozen to have pulled his gun loose. Pain fought for dominance between his tattoo and the knife wound in his side. Simon gasped for breath. "Parker?"

Warm hands grabbed at his. Pulled hard. "Agent Wells, get on your feet!"

It took effort. A hell of a lot more effort than it should have. The pain merged somewhere over his entire right side. A tear he couldn't take the time to poke at, a fall he probably should have thought twice about before he rolled onto his knee.

Oh, yeah. He was a real goddamned hero.

He forced his eyes open, bared his teeth as he grabbed a handful of cold brick. "Dead?" he managed.

"Down, at least." Concern shaped her beautiful face as she slung his arm over her shoulder. Concern, and more than a trace of impatience. "He launched ice like a missile, which means we need to go. Now. Can you walk?"

With inhuman effort and her support, he struggled to his feet. Agony shredded through his side.

"Car," he gritted out from between tightly clenched teeth. "Corner. Just need to get there."

A slim arm slipped around his back.

Grateful for her supportive shoulder, he let her take the lead. Let her guide him as he turned his focus inward and combed the immediate area for anyone else on the move.

People lived in the condos around her; they registered easily. Living things, pinpointed with almost exact accuracy. It was a hell of an ability. Made getting caught by surprise pretty hard.

But every time he forced it, he risked an episode. Degeneration.

Rain pounded them, soaked through his clothes. He couldn't tell what was precipitation and what part bled through his shirt.

He'd find out. Sweet Parker Adams would have to patch him up again.

She'd just love that.

"Tan sedan?" she demanded.

"That's the one."

"Keys?"

He could have forced his hand into his pocket, but right now, straining any part of his body seemed like a bad idea. He leaned on her, just a little bit more. "Pocket," he said.

She muttered something he didn't hear, and without warning, she shrugged him against the hood of the car. It pressed into his back, supported him even as she flattened a hand against his chest to keep him standing. He couldn't help but grin—a painful flash of teeth—as he felt her other hand slide into his wet denim pocket.

It nudged at flesh too focused on the ragged line of fire along his side to respond appropriately, but he was man enough to appreciate the gesture anyway.

"Get that smile off your face, Mr. Wells." Her tone slid into arctic so easily.

But he knew the truth; she hit inferno just as fast.

When his blood wasn't trying to escape the confines of his shredded skin, he'd prove it. Again. As much as he wanted.

Until then, he had to make do. As her fingers groped for the small set of keys, he caught her face between his palms.

She stilled.

Simon stared at her. This moment, right now, with the rain sliding over her skin, her mouth wet and red and raised toward his, he could pretend everything was going to be okay.

Nice fantasy.

The keys jangled free of his clinging pocket.

She was a rare woman. Maybe that explained the attraction he had no right to claim. The bone-deep need he'd felt for her since that first day in her lower street office.

Parker's gaze dropped to his side. Lightning filled the street, painted every hollow and pale curve of her face as she gasped. "Simon."

He followed her gaze. Blood saturated through his sodden T-shirt. Spread like a gory flower along his side.

"Oh, yeah," he murmured, and realized he didn't mind leaning against the car quite so much. Fuck, he hurt. "Maybe you ought to drive."

"Yeah." Her voice shook. "Maybe."

CHAPTER SIX

Parker slammed the car into drive and did everything she could to keep her gaze focused on the empty street. The rain poured in sheets of gray, rattling the metal roof and pinging off the hood like liquid bullets.

She could drive in the rain. No problem there.

What she couldn't handle was the bloody T-shirt and the man beside her. What she couldn't stop thinking about was the man in black missionary armor collapsing into a twitching tangle of limbs as the bullets she fired tore through him.

She knew as well as anyone else the weaknesses of that armor. It was her job.

But she'd never killed a man before.

Now what?

That part came easily to her hastily compartmentalizing mind. The operative they'd fought off was a witch. Like Simon. One of Sector Three's? He was too outfitted not to be; that was *her* armor. Her people's designated uniform. Either Lauderdale was requisitioning her uniform, or his people had already supplanted her own.

Just like Simon had tried to tell her.

Damn it.

Right now, she focused on getting them the hell out of the area.

Her fingers tight on the wheel, she flattened the gas pedal without warning. The engine revved loudly, and Simon hit the passenger side door with a muffled grunt of mingled pain and alarm.

Don't look.

She didn't have to. The flash of red in the reflected glow of the car's dashboard told her more than she ever wanted to know. Her stomach twisted up so tight, it corkscrewed all the way into her throat in a splash of bile.

Setting her jaw, she guided the four-door sedan—in better shape than she expected, given its age—along the dark street. It took less than a minute to break out of the ring of darkness.

Parker unclenched her jaw before it locked. "Start talking, Mr. Wells."

He took a slow, deep breath, audible even over the car's still-warming motor. "Parker?"

Her temples throbbed. "What?"

"Thank you."

That just about stuck her tongue to the roof of her mouth. She shot him a quick, suspicious glance, sparing her attention from the road for a fragment of a second.

He stared down at his shirt, the hem pulled out

as if to ease the pressure from his side. But his mouth turned downward. A thin, tight line. "You saved my life." His gaze raised to her. Flickered. "Thank you."

She looked away. For a long moment, all Parker could do was drive. The silence filled the space between them, so thick she could imagine reaching out and seizing a handful. Twisting it up into knots; shaping it into the words she wasn't sure how to say.

What *could* she say?

The truth.

"You're welcome," she said quietly. "I'd do the same for any of my people."

"I'm not your people." But his voice didn't lash; didn't even harden. Truth given right back to her, easily spoken.

Her shoulders stiffened. "Which brings me to my questions. That was witchcraft activating my seal." And she'd forgotten how badly it hurt when it flared. The skin between her shoulder blades still itched. "One of your peers?"

A flicker of a smile, dry as dust. "Yes."

"Why are you fighting them?"

"Because they want to kill you," he replied, voice strained and muffled beneath the hem of his raised T-shirt. Motion beside her drew her gaze as easily as if he'd flashed a neon sign; she couldn't stop herself. Her gaze flicked to her right.

Her head spun.

So much blood. Bright red, spreading like a gory flood. Soaking into his shirt, painting his skin.

His eyes glittered. Narrowed. "Parker? Parker!" He lunged, cursing, and seized the wheel as the vehicle drifted onto the curb. The car rocked, righted under his control.

Parker sucked in a hard breath, smelled the coppery fragrance of his blood and hastily jammed a finger onto the window control. "Stay over there," she said sharply, just as he ordered, Keep your eyes on the road!"

She slammed the back of her hand against his wrist, forcing him to let go of the wheel.

"Agent, I just shot a man." Every word blasted out of her on an icy promise she wasn't sure she had it in her to fulfill, but she was close. Damned close. "You need to start talking, or I will pull this car over and take my chances with whatever witches are left."

Blood. Bullets in the dark, a body she'd dropped with a well-timed shot from a gun she'd never had to fire off the range. And in her safe neighborhood, too. Things like this didn't happen in topside New Seattle. Sec-comps routinely patrolled the streets, streetlamps lit the residency districts to near daylight. Curfews in the residential districts kept the loiterers away.

Of course, Parker didn't know how many of these security measures had counted on witches posing as clandestine operatives.

And she sure as hell didn't understand Simon's role in it.

"I'm sorry." His voice gentled, even if the hard line to his mouth didn't. "If I could go back and change it, I would."

It meant nothing. "Did you know they were coming?" The cold night air whipped through her half-open window. Shivering as it slid through her damp clothes and hair, Parker gritted her teeth. The alternative meant closing her only avenue to fresh, bloodless air.

Simon muttered something rough and annoyed as he stripped his T-shirt off. Followed it up with a rueful, "Another goddamned shirt."

Because he needed *another* reason to go without one.

Nausea warred with a sudden burst of unwelcome heat.

"Mr. Wells—"

"I'm supposed to kill you," he cut in, balling up the wet fabric and pressing it against his side. At the best, it hid the bloody tear just over his ribs.

At the worst, it revealed more of his swarthy, beautifully defined skin than she wanted to cope with.

Her internal struggle between throwing up and wanting to lick the surface of his abs would have been worth laughing over if she weren't soaked to the skin, driven from her home, and spiraling into a nasty spike of temper.

She took a deep breath, hands hard on the wheel, and forced herself to meet his eyes over the bundled cloth. "Okay," she said, ever so gently. "And you're not going to."

"No." He smiled, even through lines of pain bracketing his mouth. "I like you just the way you are."

A finger of temper jostled loose. "I appreciate that. Explain to me why I just shot a witch wearing missionary armor."

"That's a better question." But the humor drained from his voice as he shifted, leaning back into the passenger seat. His long legs didn't quite fit, forcing his knees into the dashboard. "I assume you actually read the Wayward Rose report."

"Obviously."

"What do you know about GeneCorp?"

"Not enough." Her gaze dropped to the dashboard clock. Nearly after midnight. That explained the general lack of traffic. The residences closest to the pinnacle of New Seattle lived among the safest districts, but they operated under strict rules.

Among the common appearance and maintenance demands, the civic body of the Church demanded a midnight curfew, barring emergency personnel.

And those whose authority went beyond. Like a missionary.

Still, getting stopped by the NSRF wouldn't help anything. She needed to get to safer ground. The club districts, or a late-night restaurant. Something.

He waited for her to signal, to ease into a turn, before he asked, "Exactly what?"

"I have a lengthy list of numbers, no names, and a good portion of them marked as failed." She took a turn that crossed two lanes, grateful for the quiet streets. "Which I take to mean *dead*."

"A good guess."

Guess, nothing. Jonas had been rather thorough. "I know it's a Sector Three operation, but only because Mrs. Parrish brought *you* on board the same time she foisted Wayward Rose on me." And because Jonas Stone had to go digging into the Church's closed-off mainframe to get the data she did have. "I saw the bar codes. Found the link to something called GeneCorp. Followed it to the lab site in the industrial sector where Parrish was killed."

"Clever girl."

"*Don't* patronize me."

She didn't need to look to know his gaze pinned on her, scrutiny wrapped in indolent humor. "My mistake."

She swallowed her anger. "I know it's some kind of witch lab experiment," she continued evenly. "And that its roots go all the way back to the old city. Over fifty years."

"Is that all?"

She shot him a narrow glance. Jerked her attention back to the road as the streetlamps they passed bathed his skin in crimson smears and unforgiving light. It was *just blood*. Everybody had it.

She didn't mind her blood. His wasn't all that different.

Red and wet. Harmless.

Liar.

Damn it.

She cleared her throat. The gummy texture in the back of it didn't ease. "According to the information I acquired—"

"We'll talk about how, later."

She ignored that. "According to that information," she repeated over him, "the project has been moved, shut down, and restarted a handful of times. Far as I know, the Mission wasn't involved until Mrs. Parrish assigned you and Nelson to my unit and wanted us to do her legwork on Wayward Rose. I don't know how Juliet Carpenter is related to any of it."

"You're thorough." He closed his eyes, head resting back against the car's side panel. "You know everything I know."

"I don't think so." Her tone cooled. "How is Lauderdale involved?"

"He started it."

And with that single phrase, pieces fell into place. A headache threatened behind her forehead; stress balled into an angry little knot as she said quietly, "And he's still running it, isn't he?"

"Yes."

"You're from this experiment."

"Me and a whole army." Wearily, he raised his bloody hand to his face, caught himself and lowered it again. "GeneCorp, an entity separate from Sector Three, runs the project, but GeneCorp is run by Laurence Lauderdale, ergo . . ."

Ergo, Lauderdale had his fingers in a lot of pies. She wondered if the Church knew.

"And?" she pressed when silence followed.

"And, nothing. You have all the answers."

"Bull hockey."

His snort of laughter only spiked a rising octave to her anger. He lifted the makeshift compress, checked his wound.

The hair on Parker's neck raised as she forced herself not to look. Not to see the blood smeared on his side, soaked into his hands and bandages and— "Pull over," Simon demanded.

She shook her head. Hard. "I'm fine."

"Parker, *pull over.*"

She did. But only because she was fairly sure that if she didn't, he'd make her.

And if he touched her with a single bloody digit, she was going to vomit. Her guts twisted just thinking about it.

He dropped the bloody T-shirt to the floor at his feet.

As the car drifted to a stop beside a brightly lit line of condominiums—metal and glass, unlike her quainter metal and brick complex—Simon unlatched the door and stepped into the rain.

Parker clung to the wheel and tried to breathe deeply.

Maybe he knew she needed a moment. Maybe he let her take it. She didn't know. All she knew was that she had to get it together before she lost her cool completely.

The rain slammed into the car, pounded the roof and windshield until all she heard was the force of the weather. Thunder, pellets of water.

It drowned out her heartbeat.

Slowly, her grip on the steering wheel relaxed.

The driver side door wrenched open. Grabbing her arm, Simon yanked her out of the seat. Supported her weight when her feet tangled together, and tucked her, none too gently, between the car's unyielding metal frame and the half-naked, strangely warm resistance of his body.

Rain sluiced down his face, pounded into his bare skin.

Parker blinked at the sting of it in her eyes. Her mouth opened, but whatever words she'd intended vanished on a breathy sound of surprise, of raw shock, as Simon seized her jaw between thumb and fingers.

"Stop fighting me," he said, every word a low, aggressive order. "Just stop."

His thumb dug into the corner of her mouth, forcing her lips to part on a gasp. Her eyes widened. "Those men were under orders to kill you, do you understand that? Do you know what I just threw away to haul your stubborn ass out of there?"

Cold rain slid down her cheeks. Pooled into the collar of her jacket, sent fingers of ice down her spine.

So at odds with the heat of awareness low in her belly. Of her heart's frightened hammer and the wild fluttering in her gut.

So conflicted.

But the rain washed away the blood. Ruined the only excuse she had to avoid looking at him. He gave her no choice, fingers hard at her jaw, forcing her face to lift to his. Pinning her in place. "Make this easy on me, Parker."

Her hand splayed on his chest—warm skin, hard muscle. Something about him pulled at her. Why? Because her hormones said so?

She couldn't lose control of this. Couldn't let him bully her. She was a director. The boss. The ice bitch of the Mission.

But as his eyes blazed into hers, wild and angry, Parker wondered what he'd taste like. What he'd feel like, wet skin to wet skin, moving over her. Into her. Taking her, dominating her. Right here in the rain.

He could. She knew he could.

And she couldn't let that happen.

"I'm grateful," she told him. The rain slid over her lips, cool and tangy. She watched his eyes trace her mouth. Darken. "I think that makes us even. Get off of me, Mr. Wells." Before raw lust and temper overwhelmed whatever good sense she had left.

The woman needed a lesson. A thorough one.

Logic assured Simon that he didn't have time to do it now. Still, he couldn't help himself. His left hand cupped her skull just over the sodden knot she kept her hair in. Tendrils clung to her cheeks, forced loose by the rain. It helped soften her appearance.

But her eyes, blue and bottomless, hardened. Iced over, as if it'd help her.

It wouldn't. Simon knew her tricks.

His thumb stroked the corner of her mouth, smearing the surprisingly durable red lipstick she'd chosen. "Simon," he corrected. Rain splattered across his shoulders, down his back. It dampened the heat emanating from his skin, but not by much.

Was he running a fever? Just his luck.

The inevitable just crept closer and closer.

But not yet. Not before he got Director Parker Adams out of the mess he'd helped create. Whether she liked it or not.

She shoved at his chest. "This is ridicu—"

"Simon," he said over her, and she gasped as his thumb once more dug at the corner of her mouth.

This time, he didn't stop with *making a point*. The tip of his thumb slipped between her lips, slick with rain. Her skin, pale in the unforgiving fluorescent lights, flushed with sudden embarrassment. Heat filled her eyes.

She couldn't hide that.

He wanted her to submit. To his protection, to his touch. To *him*.

Not something they trained him for at the lab.

Her tongue darted against the pad of his thumb, as if it could push him out.

As if she couldn't help but taste it.

Her fingers at his chest tightened, nails digging in so suddenly that he inhaled on a harsh sound of lust as it tightened low in his balls.

Focus. "I'm a witch," he said, voice rougher than he meant. "I'm part of the Salem Project. I'm the only thing standing between you and a shit storm none of you saw coming. You're going to have to trust me." And—because why the hell not?—he went for broke. "At this point in the game, I *need* you to trust me, Parker."

Her teeth nipped at him; on purpose? He couldn't tell. Her eyes locked on his, hazy. Banked with something so focused, smoldering, he couldn't be positive she heard him.

She would. His fingers clenched in her hair. Tight enough to secure the silken knot in his hand; hard enough to force her back into a steep curve, thrust her breasts against his chest.

"You call me Simon," he said into her wide eyes. "I'll call you Parker. Because we're going to be stuck together for a while." Longer than she probably hoped.

Too long for his peace of mind.

Too late for that.

"Do you hear me?"

Her lashes, brown at the base and tipped with red, flickered. Down to his hand; his thumb aching, caught between her teeth. Her gaze rose.

The lust he read there—raw, scorching, wild—reached into his blood and boiled it over.

Her mouth closed fully around his finger.

His thoughts fled on a ragged growl. "And we don't have time for that, either."

But damn if he didn't let those sexy red lips pull on his finger.

The feeling tightened in his dick, squeezed as if her lips wrapped around him there instead of his thumb. Erotic as hell.

So not the right time. He slipped his thumb free, his smile flashing as her teeth scraped along the callused edge. "Jesus, you're dangerous."

He leaned back. Far enough that he couldn't feel her body against his bare chest. That he could breathe without smelling the rain-drenched fragrance of her.

And her perfume, sweet and refreshing. The smell haunted him.

The director had a streak of something wild in her. Simon would explore that. He couldn't *not*.

But he'd have to do it later. When his side wasn't throbbing and the threat of Salem operatives didn't ride his ass.

"Get in the car," he ordered, and let her go.

As her gaze cleared, mouth twisting and one hand raised to her lips, Simon folded into the driver's seat and slammed the door shut.

His heart hammered. A steady thrum of arousal. And of excitement. Bad timing for it, but then, there wouldn't be any time for anything if either of them got killed now.

It was time to come clean. At least as much as she needed to know to be comfortable.

Hell, maybe she'd have more to add than what he knew.

Maybe it was time to trust someone else.

Then again, maybe he just wanted in her pants.

The passenger door jerked open. Color high in

her cheeks, Parker climbed into the seat, droplets scattering with every sharp gesture, and slammed the door shut again.

Thunder crashed. Perfect counterpoint to the twisting in his gut.

Simon guided the car back onto the street. "You know that the Salem Project has been around since before the quake."

"Yes," she said, once more the ice queen. Like that night in her home, it didn't fit the rain-drenched, fierce-eyed creature shivering beside him. "But the trail for that project ended well after the quake. I assumed the records didn't survive."

He reached out, turned on the heater, and flicked the vents wide.

Because he didn't have it in him to risk another wrestling match with his own need, Simon didn't deflect her with humor. Not this time. "That, and because the Salem Project started as something else." His tone flattened, eyes flicking from rear-view mirror to the road at regular intervals.

The rain didn't make spotting a tail easy.

"At the time, knowledge was worth more than results," he continued when she said nothing. "Dr. Laurence Lauderdale and his wife, Matilda, pioneered a new track into an ongoing project, but they both worked for GeneCorp."

"They didn't own it?"

"Not then. After the quakes, they rebuilt the company. Or, more precisely, the Church rebuilt the company."

"What *is* it?" she asked, but not impatiently. She'd put her director face on.

The one that said she was listening not as a person on the wrong end of a bad decision but as a tactical advisor. A decision maker.

He'd have to rid her of that notion real quick.

"I get that it's rolling out witches on some kind of"—she gestured—"factory belt, but why? Is it a supersoldier project? A genetic study on witches? What's their goal?"

Even he didn't know that. It'd changed, somewhere along the way. Changed enough that Mattie had fled.

He flicked her a quelling frown. "My story. Simmer down."

Her eyes narrowed. "Of course, Ag—" She caught herself. "Simon."

His name on her lips shouldn't have lanced a bolt of lust to his cock. It did.

Because she'd listened.

God, that was sexy.

"I don't know how it started, or what the intent was, but it graduated to gene therapy shortly after the Salem genome was discovered."

"Why? To . . . cure it?"

He shrugged. "Maybe. The Lauderdales focused on retro-engineering the genome first. For study. They were only in the fledgling stages when the quakes hit."

Parker glanced down to the floor. Blanched, and pulled her sneakered feet up.

Simon hid a smile. "Sorry about my shirt."

"It's fine." It wasn't, but he'd give her points for bravado.

"After the quakes, the witch hunts started." Simon glanced in his side mirror. Frowned when a single light winked out of view.

"The witches created the imbalance," Parker replied. Like a good little Church mouthpiece.

"I've never met a witch who could cause an earthquake."

"Enough blood makes a powerful focus for—"

Simon's back teeth came together so hard that they audibly clicked. "Take off the Mission face paint for one second, Parker, and listen to me. Witches *do not* have that power. Period. It'd take an entire city of blood to cause something like that—" She opened her mouth. "*Not* that there's any proof it's even possible. There were no city-wide sacrifices before the disasters started."

Her mouth closed, red eyebrows knotting. She sat back in her seat, back angled into the corner. To keep an eye on him. Put distance between them.

And rightfully so.

He forged ahead anyway. Might as well rip the stitches out all at once. "Think about it. In the handful of years before the quakes, there were other cities hit by other things. Superstorms, earthquakes, tsunamis, tornadoes, floods. Don't you think if there were any articles, any recordings, *anything* about witches conducting mass sacrifices, the Church would have shown it by now? As pure propaganda, if nothing else."

Her eyes narrowed again, but it wasn't in anger. Score one point for logic.

Negative five hundred for indoctrination.

Simon rolled his shoulders. It didn't ease the tension. "I realize it goes against everything you believe in, but you're going to have to face this. I'm part of a legacy that spans over five decades. I know what I'm talking about."

She said nothing.

"Somewhere along the time line, they successfully retro-engineered the sequence." He frowned again at the mirrors. The single light doggedly followed. In and out of view. Too far to get any details.

"But why wasn't anyone told?"

"Because witches are bad, remember?" He didn't bother mitigating the scorn out of his answer. "At that time, the populace was just antsy enough to pull a torch-and-pitchfork routine on anyone caught playing with witches. Even if those witches were innocent of anything."

"I guess so. But why would Bishop Applegate want soldiers genetically modified with the Salem genome?" she demanded. "It goes against every doctrine he's ever preached. They're making *witches*."

Simon's smile lacked humor. "He doesn't. The program isn't for him. I doubt he even knows."

Her gaze dropped to his torso, though he knew she couldn't see his seal—or the incriminating bar code—from where she sat. "How old are you? Where were you born?" Her frown twisted. "Are you from outside the city?"

"I'm thirty. And I wasn't born, Parker, I was vat-grown. Cultivated in a test tube and incubated by a machine, right here in New Seattle."

Every word seemed to shape her expression. Narrowed it, refined it. Hardened it. Her mouth flattened into a thin, white line.

He might as well go for broke.

"The Salem Project isn't for the Church." He

glanced at her. "It makes witches out of genetic material with the greatest odds of survival. Hatches them, raises them, and turns them into soldiers. The problem is in the longevity."

"What do you mean?"

His smile twisted. "There's something in the DNA that's . . . broken or fractured or not complete. I don't know, I'm not a scientist." He glanced at her, then again at the mirror. "That's what has the Lauderdales so wrapped up."

She shook her head. "I don't understand."

"It's easy. Director Lauderdale made himself an army, but his wife made sure he couldn't use it."

"His wife." Parker smoothed her hands over her hair, but it wouldn't help. Gone was the sleek coil. Tendrils hung around her cheeks in a sexy frame he couldn't help but notice. She looked good ruffled. He wanted to ruffle her some more. "You mean Mattie," she said, so suddenly that he couldn't help his smile.

"Yeah. I called her Mattie."

"But she died. Matilda Lauderdale passed away years ago." Her voice now slanted what was common fact up into a question. "You had to be, what, six years old?"

Approval had him nodding, but not in agreement. "That's a lie Lauderdale gave his suddenly motherless kid. Mattie died two months ago." He reached up, adjusted the rearview mirror. "And she didn't abandon us completely. Hang onto your bucket, sweetcheeks."

"What?" She gripped the seat belt over her chest. "Why?"

Simon shifted his grip on the wheel. "We may have a tail."

CHAPTER SEVEN

Kayleigh knocked on the door as a courtesy.

"In," came the raspy reply.

She stepped inside the spacious office, her shoes sinking into plush carpet. The lights blazed, circles of gold and lighter yellow. It painted the office in homey tones, touched on the dark wood furniture and gave it a warm sheen.

Given the amount of time Laurence Lauderdale spent in this office, it might as well feel like home.

"Dad," she began reproachfully, only to cover her mouth with her digital reader as the tall, frail man behind the desk raised a gnarled hand.

"No, we'll need more than that if it's going to make a dent," he said, beckoning her in further. But he wasn't talking to her. His desk-mounted comm lights glowed blue, and he tilted his head to the side as he always did when a comm mic was clipped to his large ear.

Kayleigh muffled a sigh. The man never rested. How he'd managed to live well into his eighties was a secret she hoped was genetic. Well, in that *normal cause* kind of way.

As a geneticist for Sector Three, Kayleigh spent a lot of time considering the many mutations that comprised a human being. Hair colors, skin colors, eye colors. Shape, texture.

She'd never been that interested in life span.

At least until now.

Her stomach burned as she held the reader to her chest. The stress of her current project sat there like a ball of acid, and it wouldn't get better while she waited for her dad to finish his call.

She didn't sit in one of the red leather chairs arrayed in front of his desk. Giving him what privacy the large office could afford, she strolled to the wall-to-wall bookshelf, pretended to peruse titles she'd long since devoured.

"Double- and triple-check your numbers," Laurence said into his earpiece. His voice, once so strong and kind, now quaked with age. "Keep a close eye on everything, but I don't want to sacrifice too much manpower. I'll need your team prepped."

Pulling a worn, creased text from the shelf, she idly flipped through its dog-eared pages. But her glance flicked sideways.

In her memory, Laurence was still a tall, lean man with strong arms and a wide smile. Never *young,* he'd always been a man of distinguished demeanor. Kind. Gentlemanly.

But her eyes told her a different story.

Now he stooped with age, his joints gnarled and often stiff. Physically, he appeared frail. A thin skeleton with mottled spots showing through his short, cobweb-thin white hair. His ears were large, loose skin hanging, and his teeth had been reduced to dentures, but she loved him anyway.

The smart ones didn't let his appearance fool them, either. Her dad ran a tight ship. One look into his faded blue eyes, similar to Kayleigh's own, and it became clear why he remained director of Sector Three.

The man was brilliant. Truly a pioneer.

Her role model. A lot of the scientists' role model, really. She hated to disappoint him.

She slid the book back into the bookshelf.

"Good," Laurence said, flicking through something—probably data of some kind—on his reader. "Stay close and keep your comm on. Take care, now." He plucked the mic from his ear with shaking fingers, but his lined, weary features brightened. "Kayleigh."

"Hi, Dad." She crossed the office, bent to kiss his gaunt cheek. His cologne—the same light blend of subtle aftershave and soapy-scented cream he'd used for years—filled her nose.

Every year, every month, seemed to hit her harder. He just kept getting older. Thinner. *Less*, somehow.

He didn't argue as she plucked the mic from his awkward grip. "Dad, how many times have I told you to get the new earpiece?"

"I don't need a new earpiece," he argued good-naturedly. "The old one works just as good as it ever did."

She slotted the bit into his desk comm. "Except it's too small for you to handle well. I'll order you one tomorrow, okay?"

He sat back, eyes twinkling. "What brings you to my office, Kayleigh? Shouldn't you be home and sound asleep?"

"That's *my* question." She rounded his desk, fingers trailing on the satiny finish, and folded into a chair. Out of habit, her legs crossed at the knee. "It's after midnight, and you know the doctor said you needed to get away from the office more."

"Heh." He waved her censure away. "Barry spends his days on a golf mat in his office. What does he know?"

"He knows your blood pressure," she pointed out serenely.

Laurence's thin mouth twitched. He leaned forward, resting his bony elbows on his desk, and raised a bristling white eyebrow at her. "Did you come to lecture me, Dr. Lauderdale, or is this an official visit?"

"Official visits ended hours ago," she replied with a long-suffering sigh. Her chest squeezed, as it always did when he looked at her with that mix of devilish humor and stern expectation. And her insides rolled over.

She looked down at her digital pad. "But you're right, as usual."

"As I suspected."

Swiping her thumb across the print-lock, Kayleigh pulled up her report. A quick scan refreshed everything she needed to share. She'd start with the good news. Good-ish. "I have the Salem data from generations fifty-two through fifty-five."

"All right." He nodded. "Go ahead, at your own pace."

A smile tugged at her lips. He'd been telling her to move at her own pace for years. "Okay. First, we've lost one hundred percent of fifty-two and -three." Not a flicker on his creased expression greeted her unsurprising revelation.

This was an ongoing problem. And one she'd have to address before she left. Her stomach burned at the thought.

"We lost seventy percent before you authorized euthanasia for the rest," she continued, "but as was mentioned, degeneration was guaranteed. Patterns from fifty-four are following precedent." Kayleigh scrolled through a lengthy list. "We've lost sixty percent of that generation. Same as before. Their abilities are overclocking too fast for their bodies to handle."

"What about the field agents?" the director asked, eyebrows beetling.

"We managed to get to three when they didn't report in," she said, frowning. "They were euthanized before the damage could manifest itself beyond explanation. But we've missed the catastrophic phase for four of them. They degenerated too fast, and the Mission is reacting according to expectations. They're keeping the docket open." It didn't help that some of the euthanization orders weren't being handled as cleanly as they could.

Kayleigh didn't think it right that the bodies were left out where anyone could find them. They deserved cremation, at least. After study.

They held answers, but her father's team was adamant that missionaries not simply disappear.

They needed to be found dead. Needed to give the Mission director's people closure, keep them away from the truth.

Kayleigh suspected it was far too late for that. She needed those bodies.

"Damn," her father sighed.

She didn't begrudge him the word. It wasn't exactly the best news of the night. Putting Salem Project operatives in with the Mission, even as a field test, had been too extreme for her taste. One of Nadia Parrish's many mistakes, a mistake Kayleigh was desperately trying to rectify.

Only her father constantly overruled her concerns.

Kayleigh recognized the validity of the project. The Salem genome was too understudied, especially for the level of power locked into such a tiny allele. Witches could heal, they could bestow gifts, blessings. Somehow, they had powers science could only reach for.

Unlocking a healing witch's genetic makeup could mean synthesizing the sequence to curing disease. But she wasn't so sure that was her father's plan. And she didn't know how to ask.

She'd grown up saturated in the concept of gene therapy, in genetics and biology on a macro level. She'd gone to school, top in her class, had taken every step she could to make her father proud. To honor her mother's memory.

But the extent of the Salem Project awed her. And worried her. Field-stressing the subjects had a certain logic to it, but in the Mission?

She didn't like it.

"What about the rest of fifty-four?" her father asked.

"There are still some operatives in the field," she added as a handful of photos scrolled across her reader. "Including Simon Wells."

"Wells." Laurence's face pulled into a dark frown. "Has he reported in?"

Kayleigh straightened. "Recently. He's still functioning, despite his wounds. He claims one hundred percent, but I'd put him at about eighty. The trauma he suffered during Mrs. Parrish's antics might have been enough to trigger degeneration."

"Any signs?"

"Not that are physically apparent. He's less than inclined to work with us," she added pointedly.

Her father's frown stitched deep lines into his mouth. "How was he? Did you examine him?"

"No," she admitted, bracing herself for the dismay, the disappointment, she saw in her father's scowl. "He seems to be holding up remarkably well for his generation. He was mostly trying to make sure I didn't ruin his Mission credentials, given the consequences of Operation Wayward Rose."

"That woman." One gnarled hand slammed on the desk. "She will be the death of me."

"I hope not."

His thick eyebrows knitted into a solid furrow. "What is she doing? Is she still blocking us?"

"Every chance she gets." Kayleigh sighed. "Dad, Director Adams hasn't done anything to impede our progress. Not really. Mrs. Parrish stuck her in the middle of a Sector Three problem because she got lazy. It's not Director Adams's fault. She's just protecting her people, like you do for us."

He sat back, eyes flashing. "We'll just see about that."

Kayleigh grimaced. Her dad's temper flares weren't good for his heart. "Settle down, Dad. I don't want the doctor yelling at me at your next physical."

"Hmph. What about generation fifty-five?"

She switched gears easily. "On a more positive note, we've only lost seven percent of fifty-five as of today's reports. That's better than the sixteen percent we've usually tracked by now."

Her father raised his eyebrows, craggy lines settling into his forehead. "The difference?"

"A particular pattern of sequencers in the—"

Laurence suddenly grinned, raising his twisted hand again to cut her off. "Just make sure it's all in your report, or we'll be here all night."

"Right." They could spend hours on the subject, and every minute crept on past midnight. "It's already in, and I'll forward it to you right away."

"Good girl."

And now was as good a time as any for the real reason she'd come. As a knot in her stomach bubbled and frothed, her humor faded. "Now for the rest."

"Hm?" His eyes sharpened on her face, studied the arms she wrapped around the reader. "What's wrong, Kayleigh?"

Bracing her chin on the upper edge, she stared glumly at his folded hands, riddled with age spots. "The truth is . . . Dad, I don't think I can crack the Eve sequence."

"Nonsense."

She sighed. "I'm serious. I'm dancing as fast as I can, but all I'm seeing is more and more subjects dropping off my lists. My simulators are all projecting catastrophic losses." Her mouth twisted. "I've worked through seven generations in the system. First I lose them all by the time they hit fourteen, then I manage to isolate a sequence that keeps them going until thirty-five, but I can't push it past that. Whatever Mom saw in the DNA, it's beyond me."

"You're doing the best you can."

No. All she was doing was delaying the inevitable. Her simulations were proof enough—her father's project was a failure.

But how could she say so? "I know they're all lab subjects, but . . ." *They're human, too.* Sympathy for the subjects wouldn't earn her any points.

She had to be logical. Reasonable. Objective.

Laurence rose, not as gracefully as he once could and with a great deal more creaking in the joints. He circled the desk, his smile kind. Sympathetic. He knew the stakes as well as she did. "I understand," he told her, and cupped her shoulders in his thin hands. Bending, he met her gaze, held it. "That's why you have to keep working, sweetheart. Without you, without your brilliant mind, these subjects will keep dying."

"But if you stop the project—"

His eyebrows furrowed. "We can't do that," he cut in sharply. His grip tightened on her shoulders. "Kayleigh, your mother and I, we spent our lives on this. My Mattie died before she could finish the single most important thing of her career. Sweetheart, you need to complete her formula. You're the only one who can."

Her stomach hurt. It always did when she started considering the casualties. When she started considering the ethics.

Not a word her dad took lightly.

She looked down at her reader, arms tensing around its hard frame. "I'll keep working on it," she said quietly. "I just . . ." She just what? Didn't want to be in charge?

Didn't want to know the numbers?

Wasn't her mother?

She couldn't do that. He'd put her in charge, his right-hand woman. She couldn't let him down.

He took her hands. His skin was cool, paper dry, but his grip was firm as he enfolded her fingers between his. "You're every bit as brilliant as your mother," he assured her gently. "Maybe even more so. You'll crack the Eve sequence. And when you do, all our work will be worth it. A new dawn. I promise you."

Maybe. Kayleigh rose, shifting her reader to the crook of her arm, and squeezed his hands in return. "Okay, I'll keep working. Now, please, Dad, go home. You're already out past curfew, you know how the gate guard gets."

He let her go. "So are you, young lady."

True. She smiled at him as he turned, bracing one hand on the desk to walk around it and regain his seat. "Since you're probably not going to leave anytime soon, is there anything I can get you?"

He tapped the desk with his index finger. "Compile all of Simon Wells's data and send it separately. I want all of his charts. Go back to his genetic compilation."

She raised an eyebrow, unconscious mimicry of his. "Okay. I'll do that."

"Good girl. Now go home. Make sure I get that report. And, young lady?"

She paused.

"You get lots of rest."

Kayleigh nodded, tucking back a lock of her shoulder-length blond hair. Pictures of her parents assured her she took after her dad more than her mom. She sported his eyes, his hair color when he was younger.

But Matilda Lauderdale's determination lived on in Kayleigh, or so her dad often said. She had a habit of staying too long, working too late, on any project that captured her mind. Picking it apart, looking for the patterns.

"I will," she assured him and bent over the desk to drop a kiss on top of his head. "I feel fine." Which was true. Tired, a little frazzled sometimes, which led to the occasional headache and eye strain. A little heartsick on the bad days.

She was pretty sure she had an ulcer.

But otherwise fine.

"Sweet dreams, little girl."

"Night, Dad." Because lecturing *him* about the same thing wouldn't get her anywhere, Kayleigh departed his office. The door clicked shut behind her, and before she'd even made it out of the ante-room, she heard his voice again.

"Change of plans."

Another call. Another late night. Who was he meeting with now?

That was her dad, the director.

She made a mental note to find him that specially designed mic before too long.

CHAPTER EIGHT

Parker clung to the back of the passenger seat because the handle over the window had long since broken off. Given Simon's driving now, she could imagine how. "Where are you going?" she demanded.

The streets whipped by in a rhythmic pattern of streetlamps and traffic lights. They'd made it out of the residential zone, but he wasn't slowing. Deftly, Simon spun the steering wheel, taking a corner so hard the car shuddered. The tires shrieked wildly, rubber peeling against the smooth topside streets. "Somewhere to wait the night out," he told her over the din.

She twisted, stared through the back windshield. With the curfew zone cleared, more cars filled the streets, more lights in blue- and white-tinged pairs. "Who's following us?"

"Could be any number of people," he replied, as nonchalant as ever. "Could be nothing."

She shot him a look he didn't bother turning his head to see. "More of those witches?"

"Possibly." The lights they sped under pooled through the car, painting his body in mouth-watering edges of muscle and shadow. The man needed to put a shirt on.

Preferably one not covered in blood.

Parker turned, slamming her back into the seat, and glared out the side window. But she clung to the seat belt strapped over her chest. "If Sector Three sent them after me, this needs to be brought up to the Church," she pointed out. "It's illegal for them to pull an operation on another sector—"

"You don't get it, do you?" He still didn't look at her, and though she knew he had to focus on the road, the lapse grated.

She bit off her curt reply and angled for something cooler. "Explain it to me."

Simon's smile flashed. "Yes, ma'am," he drawled, in that patronizing way he had that *also* grated.

Everything about this conspired to shred her patience.

"Let me put it in plain terms." He spun the wheel, taking another corner so fast that it slammed her against the restraining belt. She gasped.

His hand flattened against her chest. Strong. Supportive.

Right between her breasts.

Parker's teeth clicked together. She grabbed his wrist, threw his hand away from her as if it reeked of something foul.

Another grin. Indolent as hell. "Anything happening now is so covert the bishop won't know it's going on. There's going to be an internal shift in the Holy Order's upper echelon. Bet on it."

"How do you know?"

"Put it together. I'm not the first witch in the Mission, right?" She flinched at his so-effortless use of the word. A *witch*. God help them all. "Peterson was only the first caught. You can count on at least half of your missionaries bought out or turned. The director is thorough. Nadia Parrish was a beast, but she knew the game better than Kayleigh Lauderdale ever will."

"Meaning I should just let this happen?" she demanded.

"No," he replied patiently. "It means that it's already too late. The whole house of cards is coming down, and *you're* on top."

Parker shook her head. "I don't buy it. There has to be something I can do."

"Don't bother. Everything's linked up. The Coven of the Unbinding, Sector Three, the Mission." Now he looked at her, smile gone. Eyes dark and filled with . . . *sympathy*?

No, it had to be wishful thinking. She didn't need sympathy. Couldn't.

"How do you think David Peterson got to be Mission director?" he pressed. "You can't skate by the tests every missionary goes through, you know that. The labs in the Magdalene Asylum do all the Mission's tests. Someone knew he was a witch."

The realization put a cold ball of fear in her stomach. And an angry swatch of stubborn impatience. "There's always something to be done," she said quietly. "Get me to the lower street offices, and I'll prove it."

His jaw hardened.

"We still have a chance," she told him. "Jonas is trustworthy, and he can get word out to—"

"Jesus fucking Christ." The car spun wildly as he wrenched the wheel, sending Parker into the door. She clung to it as the car rocked. The sedan's engine revved as the tires found traction. Brightly lit signs whizzed by, neon and lights.

As the car stopped suddenly, forcing Parker to brace her hands on the dash in nervous surprise, his hand dropped to her seat belt latch. It snapped open. She registered his intent too late.

Before she could argue, fight him off, anything, he caught a fistful of her jacket and hauled her bodily over the gearshift. Her knee slammed into the door, elbow hitting the window so hard it sent shock waves through her fingers.

But her body settled over his like a warm blanket, knees sliding to either side of his hips. Parker's breath caught—anger and something much less simple. Much more insidious.

She tried to brace her hands against his chest, leverage herself as far back as the steering wheel would let her, but he captured them in one easy grip. Trapped her hands between his body and his hand.

Right over the snug place where her legs framed his waist.

Too much heat. Not enough air.

His left hand caught her chin, forced her to stare down at his upturned face. Something angry and wild and *focused* turned his eyes to diamond facets in the neon glow of the club signs.

"This isn't a game," he said, every word a soft promise of velvet menace. "This isn't a popularity contest."

Parker's mouth dried with fear.

"I don't have time to walk you through the steps," he said tightly. "The only thing Lauderdale wants more than you out of his hair is the genetic sequence that'll unlock his army. Everything's all blown to hell, and I'm not letting you get caught in the blast, Parker."

Parker stared into his eyes, her pulse thick and fast in her throat. Too loud. "Why?"

His index finger traced her lower lip. Killed with just a touch whatever words she might have scraped together.

Damn him.

Damn her own response to him.

His finger slid from her lip. "Because you're the one good thing the Mission has going for it."

Such brutal honesty. But it was a line. It had to be. Parker turned her face away. "Let me go, Simon."

"Say please."

She stiffened. But the act only ground her against his body. Sent shock waves through her own. She sucked in a jittery breath.

"Too late," he murmured, his fingers sliding around the nape of her neck.

"But the tail—"

"Lost him four blocks ago." His voice thrummed through his chest. Seemed to lick a path across every nerve she possessed. Slowly, inexorably, he pulled her head closer. Tugged her toward him, undeniable.

The man knew how to play the game, she'd give him that.

Parker grabbed the denim ridge under her hands; felt his erection underneath his jeans, firm against her knuckles. His eyes flared, smoldered with awareness. With warning.

A warning she needed. And a warning she wanted to ignore.

But the heat uncurling between her legs told her she tread on dangerous territory. She rocked, once.

Simon's grip tightened on the back of her neck. With a low, muttered "Fuck," he pulled her close enough to seal the space between them. His lips found hers, unerring in the neon-speckled shadows. Just as firm and confident and *real* as she could want.

She leaned into his kiss, let her body soften. Tried to put a lid on it as her blood surged in wild answer to the rasp of his tongue flicking over her lower lip. It teased her. Tasted her.

"Simon," she whispered.

She needed him to let go of her hands. Before the rest of her body forgot everything but the warmth of his skin against hers, the taste of his mouth.

Sex with him would be so good. She could all but sense it, feel his leashed control as if it were a current running under his skin. He'd drive her wild. Take her in hand, mold her to fit him until she lost everything.

And he was a witch. A killer. Even if he came from some godforsaken experiment, it didn't change what he was.

He was everything she was sworn to protect the city from.

But he was also the only person who'd told her anything about any of it.

Her eyes drifted closed, catapulting her into a realm of sensory overload as his fingers slid up into her hair. Pins finally gave, loosened by rain and his own insistence. The heavy mass uncoiled, tumbled down her back. As his mouth feasted on hers, as his lips coaxed hers apart and his tongue flicked against her own, he tunneled his hand into her hair and seized a fistful.

She gasped against his mouth, eyes flaring wide.

His other hand slid into her jacket, curved around her waist. Held her firmly against him, nestling her against the hard length of him beneath his jeans. So good.

So dangerous.

He tugged at her scalp, sent a shaft of raw lust straight to her core. Something wicked in her loved it. He was strong, demanding. The warmth of his palm at her waist, her ribs, pulled a breathy sound from her throat.

His fingers slowly curved over her breast.

She flattened her hands against his bare chest.

"Playing with fire," he chided softly, his firm mouth quirking up into a knowing smirk. His eyes, heavy-lidded but still so sharp, darkened.

The heat of his palm saturated through her blouse. She could feel her nipples hardening, groaned with it as his fingers unerringly found the nub hidden beneath the beige fabric. Circled it. Teasing.

Fire filled her veins. Need rose, overwhelming logic and anger and fear. He tugged at her hair, pointedly. Firmly.

She sucked in a shaking breath as her body clenched, suddenly flooded with her own rampant craving.

How? How did he know exactly how to make her wild?

"You make my life difficult," he whispered, angling her head to send his breath over her ear.

She shuddered. "You started this."

"Oh, make no mistake. When you come to me, *Director*, it will be because you want it."

"Oh, God." Parker closed her eyes, every word a razor across her nerves. Her embarrassment.

Her *want*.

As if aware, as if sensing it, his voice roughened. "It won't be in a car, it won't be rushed or hurried. I'll draw out every second until you're begging for me. Whenever you're ready." Slowly, deliberately, his teeth closed on her earlobe, jolting a current of need through every part of her. "I'll make you scream."

She was so ready *now*.

And that was the problem.

How simple would it be for him to take her right now? In the front seat of his sedan, her back tight against the steering wheel, her body cradling his. Letting him in. Riding him.

From ice to fire. It was that easy.

It was that dangerous.

Simon's hands closed on her waist, forcing a gasp from her lips as his fingers left her breast. Spots of color rode high on her cheeks, probably courtesy of the same genes all that red hair came from. It tumbled just past her shoulders, thick and straight; all but glowing beneath the neon lights.

Redheads. So much trouble.

"But first, we should get out of view," he said into her ear. She shuddered.

And then she stiffened.

Simon didn't bother hiding his laughter as he flexed his arms, lifting Parker off his lap and depositing her back into her seat. A few feet away, standing in the circle of light beneath a street corner lamp, a small group of club-rats cheered.

The advice they offered wasn't as muffled as she probably wanted.

The color in her cheeks spread to her forehead, her neck. "You're despicable." Her voice shook.

Simon raised a slow, thoughtful eyebrow. "You don't sound embarrassed." He eased the car into drive once more and navigated through the parking lot. "Relax. Given the painted-on getup they sported, I doubt yours was the only show tonight." He glanced at her, but she didn't give him her face, staring out through her window. Her hands clenched in her lap.

Simon relented, letting silence fill the car as he concentrated on navigating through the club district.

The topside club sectors were similar to the ones in the lower streets only in that there seemed to be a prolific love affair with neon. The words spelled out in the wealthy upper stratum of the city were much more classy than the typical *Girls! Girls! Girls!* found below, and the interiors of the clubs tended toward dancing and dining rather than poles and naked flesh.

But the amount of people filling the sidewalks, waiting in line, grinding in wide voyeur-friendly windows of some of the establishments were as familiar to him as breathing.

A man could lose himself in this kind of crowd. Which was exactly the point.

He glanced at his unwilling guest. Met her scrutiny with raised eyebrows. "Yes?" he prompted.

"You're a witch." The word went sour in her voice. He couldn't blame her. "Yes."

"You were made in a lab."

"I'm a genetic smoothie, created from a missionary and a witch." A specific witch, but she wouldn't know the difference. Heresy was heresy. When her fine red eyebrows winged upward, he shrugged. "Most of them are. There's something about the way missionaries are cultivated that promotes higher survivability in the gene therapy process." Assuming one ignored the fact that they all died sooner rather than later.

He didn't want to get into that now. It was enough that she was asking questions, that she wasn't trying to get back to the quad and get herself killed.

"How?" she demanded. "How do they get material from a missionary? What material?"

"Yearly physicals. Skin, hair, and yes, even bodily fluids. They harvest the genetic material when we go in to the clinic."

Her eyes narrowed to blue fire. "The hell they do."

He shrugged again. "It's the truth. That's half the reason the Mission pulls from specific orphanages, you know. You're all trained from the moment you show up, developed along very specific lines. It does something, helps the process along somehow."

Parker fell silent, her glance sliding to the windshield. The rain had tapered off, but summer in New Seattle promised it'd be back. It always did.

He rather liked the summers. Not that he'd be around much longer to regret missing them.

Damn. What a dismal train of thought.

Within minutes, the neon haze marking the club district pulsed in the rearview mirror.

He'd take her down to the lower levels. That was his prime stomping ground. There were a few safe houses there he knew of, a handful of people he could strong-arm into hiding them for a short time. Hiding her, anyway.

"Who were your . . ." She hesitated. "Your parents?"

"Donors." This time, when she flinched, an answering pang of guilt kicked in his chest. "We don't have parents, Parker. Not like normal people do. We have genetic samples from two donors."

"That's awful."

He shrugged. "That's the way it is. Missionaries don't have parents, either."

"No, but we had—" She paused.

"A real birth?" His mouth twisted into a hard smile. "You sure?"

But to his surprise, she didn't rise to his bait, admitting softly, "No. I guess not." She clasped her hands between her knees, stared down at them for a moment. Then, oddly endearing, her gaze flicked sideways. Studied him in sidelong inquiry. "So who were your donors?"

Now it was his turn to hesitate.

What would it cost him? Not much. And in return, he'd tell her something to earn her trust.

But she'd have more questions. He'd be disappointed if she didn't.

He sighed. "I'm patterned off of Matilda Lauderdale."

Her eyes widened. "The director's wife?"

"The same."

"Does he know?"

The question earned a snort. He couldn't help it. "I don't know. Mattie did a lot of things I didn't know about. Or understand." Like drink poison rather than tell him what he needed to know.

Like make him to begin with.

Parker's fingers touched his forearm. Firm, warm. It sent sparks of awareness through his nervous system and soothed something he didn't have a name for deep inside.

Why?

"You sound like you knew her well," she said, and he didn't kid himself. It was a prompt. A fine example of what made her a damned good leader.

To his astonishment, he found himself answering. "Not as well as I wanted, but enough to know that she lived even after everyone said she'd died. Mattie was . . ." How would he phrase it?

"A smart woman," she offered.

"Incredibly. And manipulative as hell."

"You almost sound like you miss her." She removed her hand, and the spot on his arm tingled as if already missing her heat. Simon's grip tightened on the wheel. "I liked her. She was a real bitch sometimes, but I liked her. Inconvenient as hell that she's dead." And if it came out rougher than he'd meant, she'd cope.

He didn't look at her, didn't want to read whatever it was on her face. No right choice here. Guilt, sympathy, disgust—he deserved just about anything she had for him. And more.

Because it was his fault Mattie died.

"What about the witch half?"

It took him a moment to follow her train of thought. "No," he said slowly. "You've got it wrong. Mattie *was* the witch half."

"The hell she was."

He didn't begrudge her the shocked revelation. "I don't know who filled in the missionary sequences, I just assumed it was whatever characteristics she handpicked to suit her own."

Parker rubbed at her eyes. "Did Lauderdale know that, too?"

"He knew of her gift. Something about the ability to see things as they are. But he didn't know about me." Simon didn't know if that still held true, but he'd taken care of the paper trail.

"What about Kayleigh?"

A whole other barrel of very slippery fish. "Didn't inherit the genome, far as I know. She's never displayed anything useful." Simon shrugged, squinting through the windshield. "Killer mind. Has Mattie's intelligence, which might just kill her."

"Doesn't that make her your sister?"

"Only in the same way that dogs share a genetic makeup."

"Ouch."

Simon didn't bother explaining. Kayleigh was a good kid, but beyond his reach. Or his help. One damsel at a time, and Parker was a bloody stubborn damsel to field.

"You're a double agent." When he only tilted his head, Parker laughed. It wasn't all amusement, but the husky note stroked across his skin like the softest touch; warm rain and sunshine. All the things he couldn't have. "You're an honest-to-God double agent. How do you keep it straight?"

He didn't. He just played the cards he was dealt and focused on the only thing that mattered now.

The sudden chime of an incoming comm transmission startled them both. As Simon glanced at the vibrating unit on his hip, Parker jumped, turning in her seat to paw through her bag. "Maybe it's—" She flipped her screen open, shedding pale blue incandescence over her face. Her features hardened. "Damn."

"What is it?"

"It's an all-hands transmission." Her voice went arctic; he knew better. Without waiting for her to continue, he reached down and plucked the comm unit from his belt. Flicking it open, he skimmed the contents quickly.

"Fuck." The word wasn't strong enough. "They're calling all team leads to the Mission headquarters. Even the mid-lows. Eckhart'll be on his way."

Her mouth curved into a smile that had nothing to do with humor. "It's under my authorization. Needless to say, that's false."

Simon curled his fingers around the wheel and spun it hard enough to pull a U-turn in the street. Horns blared as he peeled out from traffic, lights skimmed through the windows.

Parker swayed, her fingers clamped so tightly around the unit that they whitened. Her eyes banked in hollow concern, stark with something else he couldn't read.

He could guess.

"We can't go to the lower streets," he said, forcing himself to focus on the road. The problem at hand. Forcing his voice into even tones. "They'll have the checkpoints manned and they'll search every car, you can count on it."

She said nothing, staring at the now-dark comm unit.

"We need to get you somewhere safe."

She shook her head. "All of my team leads are gathering at the Mission. I can't leave them to face Lauderdale alone."

He ignored that. "Do you have another safe house? A friend? Anything?"

She only kept shaking her head. Denial, anger. Wordless fear. He could read her like a book. What she was feeling.

What she was planning.

Hell, no. Reaching beside him, Simon covered her clenched fingers and the comm with one hand. "Think, Parker. If they're pulling the leads in under your authorization, they've got a plan. And they're going to keep a sharp eye out for you. We have to do this the hard way."

She frowned at his hand. "Why?"

"Easy seems to be—"

"No," she said, her quiet voice husky. "Why are you so intent on helping me? The truth, Simon." When she turned her head to level those stricken blue eyes on him, Simon felt something give. Something treacherous.

Something more than just a desire to dominate

her senses and leave her begging for him. For the first time since meeting the unflappable Mission director, it was Simon's heart that lurched. A dangerous move.

A stupid one. And unfair.

He let go of her hand. "I have my reasons" was all the answer he could give, knowing it wasn't any kind of answer at all.

CHAPTER NINE

There were perks that came with working for her father. Among the obvious—a salary that made sure she'd never want for anything ever again—were the ones that didn't brighten Kayleigh's day so much as make it easier to handle.

The computer system wired into Lab Seventeen fell into the latter category.

The thing was a beast, as far as corporate systems went. All she needed to know was what to look for. The computer handled the rest.

Unfortunately, the data it spewed out at her now wasn't helping.

Kayleigh braced her elbows on the workstation, fingers laced under her chin as she skimmed the data unfolding down the screen on the left. The monitor on the right highlighted all the search terms she'd used and compared them through the data streaming in.

It was all very complicated.

Kayleigh had learned to selectively focus.

"Simon Wells," she muttered. One of a handful of surviving members of his generation. Although, if the statistics held up, not for long.

The thought weighed on her.

Hell, they all did. All the doomed souls churned out by GeneCorp, year after year.

All in the name of progress.

She straightened, leaning back in her chair until it tilted precariously on its ball-joint swivel. She let her head fall back, eyes closed, and took a deep, cleansing breath.

Men like Simon were the reason she needed to figure her mother's legacy out.

"Search complete," said a pleasant computerized voice. "All data regarding subject Simon Wells, collected."

"Finally."

"Warning," it added.

Kayleigh frowned. "Warning? What warning?"

"Data corruption in sectors two hundred through two hundred and eighty-nine."

She straightened, feet hitting the floor, and grabbed the edge of the desk as the chair wobbled. "What? In English, computer."

"I'm sorry—"

She cut off the mechanized error message, tapping in the command that would translate the sectors to something she'd understand.

"Searching."

Stomach churning, discomfort and anxiety fueling the insomnia she'd been dealing with for almost two weeks, Kayleigh watched the search pattern flicker across the right monitor.

Red bars slid into focus.

"Sectors two hundred to—" She stared. Scrolled up a few pages, double-checked the computer's patterns and scrolled down again. "Impossible."

Only, not so much.

"Search backups," she said, clearer and slower than she probably needed to. The computer had a tendency to misunderstand, especially when she spoke to it in the middle of a thought.

God save her from clumsy voice-recognition software.

"Searching," the pleasant voice assured her.

That would take a whi—

"All backups show missing data," the voice continued, too fast to be a mistake.

Kayleigh surged to her feet, her white lab coat swirling at her knees. Bracing both hands on the worktable, she bent over the screen as if getting closer would make it less confusing. "That can't be right. Search again."

"Searching." She waited. "All backups show missing data."

Damn it. One hand flattened against her stomach. The other curved over her forehead as a headache flared behind her eyes.

Stress. Of course stress.

Now what?

"Find access point of missing data," she said tightly.

The system hummed.

Kayleigh paced in front of the workstation,

checking its progress over three minutes that felt like an eternity.

Finally, the system beeped. "Data manually deleted from location. Access hub forty-seven-fifteen, system eight."

"Where?" That made no sense to her. What kind of gibberish was that?

"Data manually deleted from location. Access hub—"

"Argh." She smacked the screen, because the alternative was digging a fist into the burning hole in her stomach. "Show me on a map."

A third screen flickered on, showing a portion of the city. A red marker gleamed, pulsed in place.

Kayleigh stared at it. Rubbed her eyes and sank back into the chair. Slowly, she reached for her comm.

And paused.

It was late. Too late to bother her dad with this. Besides, she didn't even know what it meant. There were any number of reasons why Simon Wells's birth charts had been altered from GeneCorp's old facility in the industrial district.

Maybe the incident with Nadia Parrish had caused a malfunction. Maybe Nadia herself had done it.

Kayleigh drew her feet up into the chair, closed her eyes, and tried to breathe away her headache.

Nothing felt right about this. Nothing.

CHAPTER TEN

Upper streets or lower, business was business. While clubs, strip bars, gambling dens, and worse operated all night in the lower streets, the all-hours café Parker found herself sitting in looked cleaner and more brightly lit than any lower street dive. The open floor plan provided an excellent view, liberally decorated with carefully watered plants and lots of polished chrome.

But it was an all-hours place with all-hours people. There'd be some measure of safety in public.

She slid into a booth, every muscle practically sighing as she sank into the comfortable cushions. It wasn't her soft, warm bed at home, but she'd take it over car seats and bullets any day. Tucking her bag into the corner, she studied the café critically.

The table, inset with colored tiles, couldn't have been more perfectly positioned if Simon had requisitioned his own floor plan. She had a complete view of the whole place.

The floor dipped in by one step in the center, and tables arrayed along the tiled indentation remained mostly empty but for a man hunched over a laptop at a single seat and two couples sharing a table across the way. Laughter from the latter bit sharply through the café, earning a faint smile from Parker.

She'd never been the type to hit the clubs and go out for food after. Or in between. Or whatever they were doing this late.

Early, she supposed, for a couple of kids with nothing better to do than dance the night away.

Her gaze settled on the man briefly, picking out all the cues. Suit jacket discarded over the back of his chair, crisp shirt rumpled from wear, open collar, loose tie. Headphones covered his ears, masking any sound the rest of the world made as he typed efficiently on his small keyboard. The smooth *click, click, clack* of each keystroke countered the music.

Booths lined the walls, each outfitted with navy blue cushions and the same kind of mosaic table. More of these were occupied by groups and couples, as if people didn't like the idea of being trapped in the center of attention.

She knew the feeling.

A pretty woman with chin-length blond hair strode from table to table, digital notepad in hand and her dark blue apron pristine. A brunette employee leaned against the back counter, watching a widescreen video feed as she nursed a cup of something that steamed. No sound leaked through the speakers, but subtitles filled the bottom half of the screen.

Entertainment and gossip feeds. The classic staples of any late-night hangout.

The kitchen beyond her seemed quiet, but Parker suspected there'd be at least two employees to handle food orders and cleanup. Probably the likeliest exit if she had to make a fast one.

Given the order still filling her comm screen, Parker didn't doubt she'd have to if the operatives found her again.

A coup. That was what this felt like. Politics more treacherous than anything she'd had to deal with before. This made Nadia Parrish look like an annoying gnat in comparison.

Her team leads—the men and women who led her street units, who trusted her—were amassing. Brought to the Mission under her name.

What would happen to them? What would Sector Three do?

How many of them were still loyal to her?

Parker had grown up in the Mission orphanage, had gone through the same training, the same schooling, as every other missionary in her order. She'd worked her fingers to the bone for them.

She cared. About her job, about her missionaries. About the cause.

She'd worked so hard to earn their trust, had even started making headway in the lower units.

Until this.

Now it ate at her. Was Simon right? Did her people all sign on with Lauderdale? Eckhart, Neely, Silo? Elizabeth Foster, with her bangles and brilliant eye for patterns and facts?

Parker dropped her face into her hands, digging at her eyes as a headache threatened to develop.

What the hell was the Church doing? Sitting on its collective thumb? How could it be so blind to—

"You need something, honey?"

Parker straightened, planting her elbows on the table and summoning a smile from somewhere that didn't feel hunted and exhausted and angry. "Coffee," she said, managing not to sound as worn as she felt. "Just black."

The pretty blond waitress studied her with concern. "We can do just about anything you need. You sure a good stiff drink won't tide you better?"

Probably. But she didn't dare. "I'm sure. Just send over a carafe and I'll plow my way through it."

Over the girl's shoulder, Simon exited the men's bathroom. His long-sleeved thermal, pulled out of the back of his car, covered the bandages he'd wound around his torn side.

They'd have to get his injuries looked at. The man had to be in a lot of pain.

It didn't show. In his faded denim, rain-mussed hair, and that shirt, with its sleeves shoved up over wiry forearms, he looked . . .

Damn it, he looked delicious.

Parker ignored the little twitch, that subtle signal that demanded she be aware of his every move. One part paranoia. Two parts attraction.

Every bit stupid.

"All right," the waitress said. "I'll bring you some napkins, too." She strode away, leaving Parker with a clear view of Simon's back as he sauntered toward the businessman with the large headphones.

Now what?

Tapping the man on the shoulder earned Simon a harried, annoyed scowl. The man pulled one speaker off his ear, then the other as Simon said something. Parker couldn't hear what either of them said, only picked out the pleasant tenor of Simon's voice as he gestured toward her.

Toward her? What was he doing?

Parker frowned. It deepened as the man met her gaze, dark eyebrows winging upward, then looked back up at Simon's rueful smile.

To Parker's surprise, the businessman fished out a sleek, flat comm from his jacket pocket and handed it to Simon. The metal case flashed silver, mirror smooth and probably more expensive than the units she outfitted the Mission with. And a hell of a lot more fragile.

Simon flipped open the case, typing something quickly.

The man glanced again at her, shook his head, and hunched back over his computer.

Parker's eyes narrowed. Had Simon just used her as some kind of excuse? A ruse?

Who was he contacting?

His Sector Three superiors? Was he reporting on her? Telling them where they were?

No. He'd made it clear that he'd given up everything to help her.

But for God's sake, why?

She linked her fingers tightly against the table, glaring at her whitening knuckles. She had some choices to make, didn't she? Where to go. What to do.

Who to trust.

Well, that one she had down. Easy answer: trust no one.

Not as easy to commit to.

The waitress returned, aluminum carafe clattering loudly as she set it down in the middle of the table. "Brought you two mugs," she said with a smile. "For your man there."

"He's not my man," Parker snapped. That it came out like a complaint only set her back teeth grinding.

"Yeah?" The waitress glanced over her shoulder as she set two plain ceramic mugs beside the carafe. "That's a shame." Before Parker could respond, the blond fished a bundle of napkins out of her apron and placed them in front of Parker. Her eyebrows, framing brown eyes much kinder than Parker would have expected, rose and lowered meaningfully. "Fix your lipstick, honey."

Her lipstick?

Red. Her *lipstick*. Of course she'd left it on. And then she'd gone running in the rain. And Simon had slid his finger in her mouth. And kissed her.

And she'd let him.

"Damn," she hissed, seizing the carafe. The brushed finish blurred her reflection, but she didn't need detail from the improvised mirror to see how little of her lipstick remained on her lips.

Heat climbed her cheeks as the waitress murmured, "Mm-hm," and walked away. Parker grabbed a napkin, scrubbed at her mouth until every last trace of red was replaced by pink, abused skin.

Simon returned as she splashed hot, black coffee into her mug. "Make that two," he said lightly, sliding into the seat across from her as if everything was all right with the world.

As if he wasn't a witch.

She wasn't a missionary.

Letting her head fall to the table would only share more of her mental state than she wanted Simon to know. Instead, she pushed her full mug toward him and filled the second. "What was that all about?" she asked.

Focus on work. She could do that.

"I needed a comm." He brought the mug to his lips, his eyes dark under the bright lights of the café. He sipped gingerly, made a face, and added as he lowered the too-hot cup, "One that isn't tracked by the Church."

Her own gaze narrowed, she set the carafe aside. "Why?"

"Because we need help."

"I need help, you mean." Parker couldn't stop the bitter words.

He cradled his mug in both hands, elbows planted on the table. Mimicry of her own stance. Exhaustion warring with nerve-prickling vigilance.

Was he all right?

Parker didn't know how to ask. Not when the memory of his mouth on hers still colored her every thought. She had to get over this.

He was only toying with her anyway.

"Take some time, regroup. I ordered us some food." As reassurance went, Simon's directive didn't go far.

But she frowned in surprise as her stomach rolled and gurgled in sudden hunger. When was the last time she'd eaten?

Hours ago. A late lunch.

"None of this makes sense," she said tightly.

"Sure it does."

"No." She jerked her chin up, leaning forward so that every icy word could plunge between his pretty, inscrutable eyes. "Why did they put you in my Mission? Why didn't you die with Nelson and Parrish? Who the hell shot you down in that lab?"

Those eyes banked. Stonewalled. "That's what you're hooked up on?"

She barely kept a snort of laughter between her teeth. There wasn't anything funny about it anyway. "Oh, no, that's only the start. What are they planning to do my agents? Are they still my agents? Why did you choose *now* to turn your back on Sector Three? What exactly are you planning?"

He let her talk, his own weight braced forward. The fingers of one hand loosely encircled the rim of his mug, and as she spoke, his index finger tapped it. Once. Twice.

Patient, wasn't he?

She flattened one hand on the table, leaned over it. Dropped her voice to a low, taut whisper. "You know what I think?"

"You're going to tell me." Amusement colored his laconic tone. His mouth.

Her palm ground against the mosaic tiles. The café vanished around her. As heat swept through her cheeks, burned at her ears, the back of her neck—sheared through her thin veneer of calm—Parker forgot about the blond waitress. The harried businessman. The couples.

Her focus narrowed to Simon Wells. Easy smile, infuriating implacability.

Witch.

"I think you're keeping tabs on me because I'm useful."

Simon's smile faded.

Hers stretched, thin with anger. "I think you killed Nelson and you probably killed Parrish. I think you're having a grand old time up here, jerking me around because it pleases you to jerk *them* around."

"Parker."

She pushed her mug aside, ignoring the ring of brown liquid the fragrant coffee left behind. Leaning in until the edge of the table dug into her ribs, Parker met his eyes and half snarled, "I think you enjoy pulling the rug out from anyone it pleases you to fuck with."

His lashes flickered at the word Parker didn't let come out of her mouth often. She was too angry to care.

"And I think you really enjoy playing me," she added derisively. "You're a wi—" She caught herself before the word escaped. "A *criminal*. You probably "

She forgot how fast he moved. Suddenly, his hand wrapped around the back of her head—that unshakable way he had of reminding her how much more aggressive, how much stronger, he was than her. Fingers tight at her skull, he pulled her half across the table and held her still as his eyes burned into hers.

Angry. She'd made him *angry*.

Good. He could join her club. The ice bitch had *long* since fled the building.

"Be very careful," he said softly. But every hair on the back of her neck rose as the words fell, deceptively calm. "I understand you're confused. You didn't expect any of this."

She tried to straighten, to put distance between them. His grip tightened.

"But my *understanding* only goes so far. You're wrong," he added. His breath smelled like the coffee they both drank. His scent, faintly acidic from the rain and faintly musky, filled her nose as she took a sharp breath.

He didn't let her interject so much as a syllable.

"I didn't kill either of them," he continued with the same soft calm so at odds with his grip. The fingers at his mug were white with it. "Other witches did—witches Nadia tried to capture for Sector Three."

Witches? Like . . . "Juliet."

"Among others," he said evenly. "I didn't set anyone on you. You might recall, *Director,* that I tried to get that goddamned folder out of your hands."

The skin over his cheekbones stretched taut with anger, drawing his features in harsh lines that sent more than just a thrill of apprehension through her.

Why? Why, damn it, did his caveman tactics send her body into overdrive?

Except she could figure that much out on her own.

She didn't dare look away. "You've been screwing with me since day one."

His smile touched the corners of his eyes, crinkling them. Warming them. And yet, somehow, he only seemed all the more dangerous. "You misunderstand," he told her. "I don't want to fuck with you, Parker. I want to *fuck you.*"

The heat in her cheeks climbed as a firestorm

ignited low in her belly. Shock warred with her instinctual, visceral response to the crudity.

"There's a difference." Simon let go of his mug, traced her burning cheek to tuck her hair behind her ear. "A small, but important, distinction."

Words jumbled in her throat. Not that it mattered, because Simon tugged at his grip, forced her that much closer, until his lips hovered scant millimeters from hers.

She stared at him, into his eyes, mesmerized by his . . . Oh, God, what was it? By his words? His smell, his, what, freaking pheromones? His simple assertion that he wanted her?

His *easy* declaration of how things were?

Everything he did was easy. She'd been accusing him of it since day one. But she wasn't.

She couldn't be.

His lips brushed hers as he whispered, "The rest is pure speculation."

Someone cleared their throat over Parker's fog-filled head. She blinked, feeling suddenly as if she'd surfaced from deep water, and sucked in an abrupt, gasping breath.

Simon let her go before she yanked her own hair out of his grip. "Great," he said, grinning at the blond waitress. "We're starving."

Parker shook her hair back, a defiant move that wouldn't take away the feel of his hand on her head. At the nape of her neck.

The knowledge that she'd wanted him to close that distance, to kiss her the same way he'd kissed her in her condo, in the car. Outside in the rain.

Too much kissing.

As the waitress set the platter down—chicken

and greenhouse vegetables and an array of cheeses probably garnered from concentrate—Parker didn't dare look up.

I want to fuck you.

As pickup lines went, she'd heard worse.

Simon ate in silence, content to let his reluctant date mull over his last volley. He ate quickly, one eye on Parker and the other on the café.

He didn't trust anything at this point.

The rest of him hovered like a mental net. The people in the café registered easily, and three more in the kitchen moved about like flies in a jar. People in the streets passed by, people in cars.

He knew exactly how many of them stepped inside from the rain-slick streets. And how many didn't.

His message should have already made it to Jonas's system. He'd memorized that damn number just in case.

He knew Parker trusted him. The tech seemed all right, and he knew Jonas was hard on the heels of Ghostwatch. He knew the ghost had taken notice of the tech in kind.

He knew where they all intersected, even if they didn't know themselves.

These things all factored in.

But if Jonas didn't show up within the next few hours, Simon would have to move to a new plan. One that involved dumping the director somewhere safe while he pulled every string he had—all of a handful, at this point—to end this.

The chances of success there settled somewhere around *unlikely*.

Everything banked on Jonas. And the tech agent's adherence to the instructions Simon had left him.

Simon didn't like that, either, but his options were slim. He hadn't expected them to come after Parker themselves, not this early. The fact the Salem team had done so told him that Director Lauderdale wasn't in the mood to be patient. Parker was in the way.

Something had shifted. Something had been decided when he wasn't looking, and without any inside intel, Simon was operating blind out here. Not comfortable.

Not safe.

Then again, safe had been blown out the window the second Parker stuck her spiked heel into the mess.

Everything had moved past the point of subtlety.

He refilled his coffee mug, pouring the last of the carafe into the white ceramic. Outside, people milled in knots, small groups out long past residential curfew and happier for it. It made keeping track of any potential threats harder.

Moving fast was something Simon did best. But he didn't like Parker's extra baggage.

She wouldn't like his.

That sort of made them even, didn't it?

"There's something you should know," she said abruptly.

He hid his smile as he wiped his hands on his napkin. "There's a lot of things I should know. Let's start with what's on your mind." He held out a hand. "And give me your comm."

To her credit, she didn't ask why. Slipping the

device from her pocket, she handed it over. "Yesterday I met with an informant."

He flipped up her comm screen, powered down the device, and set it aside. "And?"

"He showed me something I think is important."

He didn't follow. "This has what to do with what, Parker?"

She looked down at her plate and the few bits of chicken she hadn't managed to finish. The girl had a healthy appetite—he appreciated that in a woman.

Her lashes lifted, revealing the eyes he'd started dreaming about months ago. Brilliantly blue, dark like the depths of the night sky just after sunset.

And shadowed.

He deserved that much, anyway. "You'll have to start somewhere," he said gently.

He watched it play through her features— uncertainty, mistrust. Resignation.

Exhaustion.

"It was something to do with GeneCorp," she finally said. "A syringe. He told me that it would lead me to a lot of answers."

He stabbed at her plate with his fork, spearing the chicken neatly. "Who was the informant?"

She looked away. Then back, her gaze once more steady. "Phinneas Clarke."

His fork scraped against her plate. She jumped, wincing as the metal clattered to the ceramic surface. Back rigid, Simon braced a hand on the table. "Phin Clarke. Wanted Phin Clarke?"

The man Sector Three had sent operatives after—a shady fucker named Clay. Simon had never liked the witch. Cocky as hell, young but powerful.

Far as the word got around, Clay had been

killed. Probably by the same people—Matilda's people—that had taken Operation Wayward Rose apart. Then Clarke had vanished.

So had his mother.

With—Simon would stake his very short life on it—those same people Matilda had protected.

As Parker nodded, he swore savagely under his breath.

That was it. That was the key.

Motherfucker.

"Where is it?" he demanded.

She leaned back, fingers braced delicately at the edge of the table. "What is it?" she replied just as evenly.

Anger raked a bloody hole through him. Swallowing back the surge, he reached again for his coffee mug.

Swore when a bolt of pain lanced through the back of his head. The cup slipped from his spasming hand. The ceramic clattered loudly, drawing every eye.

Simon fought to keep his head up, but Parker's keen gaze settled on him with narrow-eyed appraisal. Pain etched a bass beat through his skull. Pain he knew he failed in keeping off his face.

"What happened?" Her glance flicked to his side. "Your wound?"

He shook his head, didn't bother explaining.

He'd pushed himself. Pushed his abilities, although it seemed like every opportunity he took to use them pushed it into overdrive. Damn it.

Four seconds . . . three . . . two . . .

There. The world stood up in one giant radar field and stomped all over his brain.

Simon's elbow hit the table.

"Simon?"

His forehead cradled in his palm, he squeezed his eyes shut and managed, "Headache." It was the best he could do.

The word didn't even begin to describe how it felt. As if every last body in a miles-wide radius had just all crammed into one room. Hammered on one nerve.

It was too late to shut it down.

"Simon, what's in the syringe?"

His future, if he was right.

If those witches had anything—fuck, if they had a syringe from Mattie, from GeneCorp . . . He'd thought it too late, a done deal. He'd hinged all his decisions on the knowledge of his impending destruction.

But what if he was wrong?

Even as pain ravaged his head, hope uncurled. An insidious flame.

"I don't know," he said tightly. Not quite a lie. Not entirely the truth. He suspected. "It could be anything. What did Clarke say?"

He knew she read every sign on his face, in his stiff muscles. Pain, determination. Maybe that explained her small nod; her acquiescence to his question. Maybe not. He couldn't tell as his head threatened to crack under the pressure. "He said that it held the key to the whole fight. That Sector Three wanted it."

Jesus Christ. He leaned over the table, gripping the edge until his knuckles cracked. "That thing holds the answer to—" *Life.* His life. Simon grimaced. "To everything. I need it, Parker."

She met his gaze. Flinched at the pain Simon knew she read there. "What will you do with it?"

Cure myself.

He closed his eyes as the back of his head squeezed. A vise of pressure.

As Simon knuckled at his eyes, two shapes arrowed in from the front corners of the café's building. They cut through traffic lines, bypassed collections of people.

Shapes with purpose.

Operatives? At only two, Simon would have left someone in the back. Both coming in from the front was sloppy.

The line between visual and sense distorted, until his eyeballs ached with it and Parker's face blurred into a hazy gleam. White skin. Ocean blue eyes.

"Simon?"

He shook his head. Hard. Ignoring the terrible ache in his chest—wild hope, crushing disappointment—he muttered, "Let's go."

"But—"

The café door swung open.

Simon slid out of the booth, grabbed Parker by the arm, and bodily hauled her out behind him. "Stay close."

"There they are," a man's voice said.

Eyes flicked toward them. Too many.

Parker peered around him, all that red hair a bloody gleam in his pulsating vision.

Two men wearing street clothes quickly navigated the tables. Headed right for them.

Simon pushed Parker ahead of him. "Kitchen. Go, now."

The waitress, a fresh carafe in one hand, approached with a nervous, uncertain frown. "Do you guys want your check—*hey*!"

Simon grabbed her, pulled the carafe from her grip with a smooth motion, and spun her around. Pulling her back against his chest, he used her as cover as he studied the threat.

Two men, and a lot of horrified patrons. He didn't care. One of the men, a tall older man with a sandy blond goatee, threw up his hands. "Just hear us out!" he called.

Not on his life.

The second man, athletically built and young-looking, with dark brown hair and eyes, cut a diagonal path. Right toward the kitchen exit. And Parker.

"Sorry," Simon said in the waitress's ear. With a firm hand at her back, he shoved her at the first man, flung the carafe at the second so hard that coffee sprayed from the spout in a steaming arc.

The blond man tripped over the waitress, hit the floor in a tangle of limbs and curses. The other rolled across the floor, sliding off the lip and into a chair hard enough that it rocked against the table. Coffee pooled in a growing puddle of brown.

Simon pulled his Mission-standard Colt from his waistband, fired it once into the ceiling. The shot thundered in the surprised silence. Echoed.

Like he knew they would, the patrons screamed on cue, threw themselves to the ground, at each other. Toward the door. Just like panicked sheep, cutting between him and the struggling men. Screaming, crying, shouting.

Chaos accomplished.

Simon sprinted after Parker. Without a backward glance, he pushed into the kitchen.

His head pulsed, pounded with the effort to keep his vision focused in his eyes, and not the radar flinging information at him left and right. The cooks had fled; smart move.

Simon sprinted between two low metal counters, past the grill hissing as oil overheated on its surface. He grabbed the edge of a boiling pot, tipped it too fast to sear more than the ends of his fingers. As scalding oil and water coated the floor behind him, he shoved open the exit illuminated beneath a glowing green sign. The door rebounded off the wall. The empty alley sucked at the sound, reflected it back in a series of echoes that hammered into his skull.

Where the fuck was Parker?

But even as he thought it, even as he stepped out into the rain-cool night, his radar shifted. Spiked hard through the back of his head and nearly sent him to his knees with the effort.

Sirens wailed in the distance. He didn't have time to linger. "Parker!"

The alley ate the echoes, twisting them into the growing cacophony of people who'd all missed a show and wanted a look now. His senses shut down. As if a switch had turned off his abilities. Just . . . nothing. A headache that wouldn't quit and nothing.

Useless.

Parker was a smart woman. She wouldn't go out into the crowd without knowing if there were more tangos in there. Which meant she had to go out to the parallel street, adjoined by the other side of the alley.

He'd have to bet her life on it.

He lurched into a sprint before the thought finished forming. His feet splashed in puddles, but there weren't any piles of refuse or discarded shipping crates to navigate. No lumps of homeless squatters, no mold and moss. As alleys went, this was one of the cleanest he'd ever been in.

Topside took its appearance seriously.

With every footstep, a dull ache echoed in his heart—worry, fear. Where the hell was she?

As he approached the alley mouth, a hand grabbed the back of his shirt. Without even breaking pace, he turned into the grip, crowded his assailant against the wall, and twisted the arm impeding his progress. By instinct, by a habit as familiar as breathing, his other fist drew back for a punch he only barely caught in time.

Copper flame, a corona of red in his blurry vision. Pale skin, warm curves pressed against him.

Fuck! His punch shifted into an open-palmed brace beside Parker's head, all in the space of a breath.

He growled something that might have been a word. His brain just wouldn't translate, hooked on the image of Parker's blood, her beautiful face bruised and battered under his own handling.

"It's okay! It's—"

Seizing the collar of her jacket, he pulled her up to her tiptoes. "Never sneak up on me," he managed, and covered her mouth in a kiss that seared more than just her taste on his brain.

He needed a handle on this. On *her*.

And as she stiffened in his arms, as one hand braced against his chest and her mouth went pliant under his, Simon knew he'd get it. Hell, he'd get more than just a handle.

When he raised his head, her eyes shimmered, nearly black and too wide in the bright-as-day streetlights. "Next time," she said shakily, "I'll warn you."

He let go of her wrist as if she'd burned him, but he couldn't force himself to straighten. Not yet.

He just needed a minute.

Flattened between him and the brushed steel wall, she took a slow breath, her hands tight against the cool surface. She didn't move, didn't look away, as if convinced he'd snap if she did.

She felt good. Right there, with her body tucked into his and the rest of the world blocked out around them, with her taste still on his lips and her heartbeat echoing his, she felt right. Simon closed his eyes.

No time for this.

Sirens filled the street behind them, crowded the café. The New Seattle police would get statements, block some of the streets, try to levy some kind of net to catch them, but the cops weren't much better than glorified security.

He'd worry more when the New Seattle Riot Force came to play.

"We need a way out."

"There's a car right over there."

He opened his eyes as she ducked under his arm. Humor, vicious under the ragged edge of adrenaline, filled him. "Why, Director, are you suggesting we steal a car?" The one she indicated waited at the edge of a club parking lot. High gloss, sweet curves. His tone dried to a razor's edge as he followed her gaze. "Or just *that* car?"

"I'm not *suggesting* anything," she said, flashing him a look over her shoulder that he had no trouble translating as *go to hell.* "Follow or stay here for the police."

Gauging the flow of vehicles along the two-lane street, she darted between them, leaving Simon to catch up or eat her dust.

He peeled himself off the wall, groaning.

He'd kill for a shower.

He'd commit double homicide if Parker joined him in it.

Simple man. Nothing simple about his tastes.

Parker drove, savoring some small pleasure behind the wheel of the gleaming sports car. She ignored Simon's halfhearted protests, mulled what she'd learned in the diner over and over in silence.

So the syringe was important. The way the clues were stacking up, she couldn't help but think it held some kind of genetic material. Something to fill the gap in the broken DNA sequence Simon was talking about.

Or maybe it was Matilda Lauderdale's DNA?

Even as she thought it, she discounted it. If they wanted that, they could use Kayleigh. Parker remembered enough about matrilineal lines to know it'd be similar. Unless . . .

If Kayleigh really didn't have the Salem genome, then they'd want an active genome—but why?

No, the first theory made much more sense. And would explain why Clarke warned her to keep it out of Sector Three hands.

"Damn," she muttered. As she navigated the vehicle through the sporadic traffic at the rim of the night scene, she risked a glance at the man filling the low bucket seat beside her.

He didn't look so good.

His skin stretched tautly over his cheeks and forehead, furrowed, lines drawn at his mouth and eyes as if he were in pain. She didn't doubt it. The amount of blood he'd lost after his stunt at her condo was bad enough.

Something was off about this. Something that went way beyond simple blood loss and exhaustion.

"How's your head?" She pitched her voice softly. As gently as she could, given the indents her nails were leaving in the steering wheel cover.

"Fine." But he stared moodily out the window.

"And your side?"

"Fine."

She couldn't help it. Her lips twitched as she fought back her smile, exhausted though it was. "Are you bent out of shape because I'm driving the limited edition phallic symbol?"

Now Simon looked at her. But she wasn't sure it made anything better. A gleam of something dangerous flickered in his eyes. "Forty-second and North Rainier."

She raised an eyebrow. "What is that?"

"Drive, Director Adams." The seat, smooth leather, creaked faintly as Simon leaned back into its cushion. "Where did you learn to hack into a vehicle sec-system?"

"I *am* a missionary, you know." Parker tucked her hair behind her ear with one hand, her gaze focused on the road, the few cars around them, and the street signs they passed at a decent clip.

Forty-second and North Rainier? That was somewhere near Testament Park.

"I didn't think you ever hit the street."

"I don't. I didn't," she added, guiding the sleek luxury car through traffic with ease. The power steering rolled smooth as silk in her hands. A real classy car. Status symbol, all the way. "I was an analyst before I got promoted. I spent a lot of time looking at useless facts and picking out the parts that mattered."

Simon closed his eyes, his head leaning back against the plush seat rest. "Yeah?"

Was it the lights glossing through the windows, or did he look pale? A sheen of sweat clung to his forehead. The skin around his mouth edged yellow.

Parker's brow furrowed. "Simon—"

"They teach analysts how to hot-wire sportsters now?" He drawled the taunt without opening his eyes. Right over her concern.

She blew out a silent, frustrated breath. "Bored orphans trapped in a topside boarding school taught me how to hot-wire a sportster," she replied, her tone cool because concern would only open up questions she wasn't ready to deal with yet.

Questions like *why did she care?*

No, that wasn't fair. Of course she cared. She thought of herself as a good person. The real question shaped up to be *how much* did she care?

"Among those many facts I've gathered over the years, I learned this particular model has a specific default in the outside security panel," she continued when he said nothing. "It was limited edition when it came out, so only the real money got one.

There's maybe five in the city today. People who throw money at limited edition designer vehicles don't really care about things like security defects if it never leaves the garage."

Simon shifted, one arm folded over his ribs. His mouth pulled to one side. "You'd think whoever owned this baby would take better care of her."

Shifting up into gear, Parker shrugged. "My guess is that some rich guy's son borrowed the car to impress girls. Lucky for us, that means we'll have at least six hours before it's reported stolen."

"You don't sound impressed."

"I don't care about cars," she said, checking the road over her shoulder as she flicked the left signal on. It clicked softly. "Of all the things to sink your money into, I don't see the allure." She glanced at him. Jerked upright as his head lolled back on his neck. "What—"

"Just drive," he said thickly. "Safe house, fifteenth floor. View." His chuckle guttered somewhere in his throat, as if he struggled to talk through water. "Nice view."

Reaching across the cramped interior, she pressed the back of her hand against his forehead. It all but sizzled. "You have a fever. Damn it, Agent Wells, you should have said something!"

"Drive," he said again. He raised his hand, captured hers. Palm to palm. Gently, he pulled it away from his burning skin. Held on to it when she would have set it back on the wheel.

His fingers wrapped with hers. Entangled, as if he had some right to it. To her.

His palm felt clammy, damp. Too hot. Gritting

her teeth, her heart pitched in her throat, Parker depressed the gas.

But she didn't extricate her hand.

Whatever kind of safe house Forty-second and North Rainier was, she hoped painkillers came with it. And bandages, and food, and something for him to drink. Something for *her* to drink wouldn't go amiss, either. Nor would the lucky coincidence of a doctor.

Parker didn't feel that lucky.

"What are your symptoms?" she demanded. When he didn't answer, she squeezed his hand. "If you don't want me to turn this car around and take you to a clinic, you better start talking to me."

"Don't like needles."

"I don't care," she said evenly.

His lips, that beautiful sculpted line she found so fascinating, twisted wryly. "You would, wouldn't you?" He still didn't open his eyes.

That worried her.

"Bet your life on it," she told him. Outside, the line of steel and glass buildings ended abruptly. Lights scattered throughout Testament Park outlined silhouettes of earthy green and brown, cold gray cement.

"Am," he replied, the single syllable quiet. Determined. Slowly, he raised her hand to his mouth. Pressed the back of it to his lips.

The sensations that single, ridiculous gesture caused in her belly should have shamed her. Jaw tight, Parker snatched her hand away, grabbed the steering wheel in a death grip and refused to look at him. "I'm serious, Simon."

"Too serious," he countered, but the slow way

he drawled the words reminded her too much of that day in the lower street office. His blood on the desk, his skin ashen.

A bullet wound, for God's sake, and he'd refused the clinic then, too.

There's something in the DNA that's . . . broken.

The memory clicked at the same time the street sign for North Rainier lit up in front of her.

And he was part of that. The sequence, the fractured thing.

She shook her head, navigated the turn easily. Bordered by the rain-damp street, streetlamps reflecting white-blue glares off the wet pavement, a high-rise apartment complex towered overhead. Lights glittered from inside, sparkled on balconies and shimmered in the constant wash of rain from the black sky overhead.

This was the kind of place the terminally rich came to visit. Parker couldn't afford it, not even on the Mission director's salary.

She bit her lip as she guided the stolen car into the parking garage. "Simon."

"Mm." It wasn't a word so much as a breath of sound.

"Is that syringe the key to your broken DNA?"

Silence filled the empty space behind her question. She held her breath; she didn't know why.

Let it out when he sighed, more a grumble than a breath. "It's possible."

"What would you do if you had it?"

"Use it."

"How?" she demanded.

"I don't know."

For a long moment, silence seeped into the car,

filled the space between them until she was sure she could taste its weighty solidity just by breathing in.

She reached for words, but nothing came. Nothing fell into her mouth, her head; what the hell could she say to combat the stark honesty in that reply?

His eyes opened. A gleam of hazel. "Are you going to tell me where it is?"

Trust no one.

The silence went on too long. His jaw shifted. "Fine," he finally said. "Doesn't change anything." He grabbed the door latch.

He made it halfway out before his shoulders rounded. He staggered, fell against the neighboring car, and clung to the dark red hood.

Parker scrambled out through his side, grazing her knee against the gearshift. She barely noticed. "Okay, hang on. Just put your arm over my shoulder."

"Fifteenth—"

"Fifteenth floor, I know." She grabbed Simon's arm as he half turned. The ridged lines carved into his face, bracketing his eyes and mouth, didn't bode well. His cheeks all but glowed under a sheen of sweat. The arm she pulled around her neck felt damp, even through his thermal.

The man was on fire.

He leaned against her as she wrapped her arm around his waist. He was solid under her grip, narrow enough that she could grab a fistful of the waistband at his side for balance. "Walk with me," she urged softly. "Come on, Agent Wells."

His head reared back, eyes glittering. Feverbright. "Simon."

She tried to pull him away from the car's edge.

His weight settled back on his heels. Angled jaw set into stark relief, he splayed one burning hand at her jaw and said doggedly, "Simon."

Parker winced. Jesus help her, how high was his temperature? "Okay, Simon. Lean on me, I won't break."

"I know." He stared down at her, his body curved over hers. His eyes heavy and too shiny. But his smile flashed. That sexy line that screamed arrogance. "Believe me, I know. Not worried about you right now."

But he didn't give her all his weight. As Parker walked him across the lot, managed to get him to the elevator and inside, she was keenly aware that he held the bulk of his own weight away from her shoulders.

A man thing? A missionary thing?

It didn't matter. Parker was used to being underestimated.

"Thumb," Simon said and leaned over her, reached across the elevator to lay the pad of his thumb on the scanner. The doors closed, leaving her trapped. Cornered against the gleaming wood panel.

"Greetings, Mr. Johnson," a computerized voice said. "Departing for your suite."

"Johnson?"

"Yup." Simon didn't move. Didn't draw away even once the elevator smoothly transitioned into motion.

Instead, slowly, as if giving her every opportunity to push him away, his head lowered. Parker didn't dare look up; not if it meant she would endure another one of his soul-shattering kisses. Not if it meant looking into his eyes, seeing the heat and the promise and knowledge there.

But he didn't take her face in his hands. Didn't force her to look at him. Instead, as the elevator shifted subtly, he dropped his hot cheek to the top of her head. Let it rest there, his lips by her temple.

His hands spanned the railing on either side of her. A cage of muscle and male and heat.

Her heart thumped erratically. Parker closed her eyes, blocked out the visual of his body so close to hers, but forced them open again as she realized it only made her all the more aware of his broad chest angled against her. Of his heartbeat slamming against her shoulder.

Of his breath against her temple.

The floor alert dinged, shattering the fragile peace. The doors opened into the vestibule of an apartment that could fit hers and then some.

His shoulders straightened. His jaw, shadowed by dark stubble and still too pale where it didn't burn red, set.

He pushed away from the wall—from her—and strode out of the open elevator doors on his own feet.

Parker winced as he stumbled, slamming a hand against the wall for balance. A large painting rattled dangerously.

Hurrying after him, she touched his arm. "Let me help you."

"I can walk," he replied curtly.

"Simon—"

"I'm not dead yet," he snarled, but he didn't

slow. Didn't look at her. Crossing through what Parker could only call the parlor, he clung to the back of an armchair as he passed it, braced himself against a small hip-high wall and vanished into the interior of the safe house.

Parker let him go.

CHAPTER ELEVEN

He was an idiot.

Simon perched on the edge of the bed in the master bedroom he'd never seen, heedless of the expensive bedclothes under him. The safe house was one of three he'd managed to install topside, but even this place wouldn't stay safe for long. Not once they really started looking. He needed a plan.

And instead, he hid.

He clutched his thermal shirt in both hands, the waffle weave rough in his palms, and stared sightlessly at the damp, sweat-stained fabric. Maybe it was the pounding in his head, settled now to a dull throb in the back of his skull. That headache. That same symptom promising a messy, bloody end, and soon.

Maybe it was the vertigo that pulled the world

out from under him as he'd tried to focus on not throwing up.

Or it was Parker herself. All that fire-red hair tangled around her face. The concern in her mysterious blue eyes.

The way her mouth pressed together when she actively kept herself from saying what she wanted to say.

No. No, he was just an idiot.

Because Simon was pretty fucking sure that love wasn't a part of this equation. He killed people, absolutely. Murdered the witches well on the way to degeneration, watched the woman who'd made him die in his arms. But he wasn't cruel. Not enough to put her—to put himself—through that kind of hell.

That talk of a syringe didn't matter.

They didn't have a lab, and they didn't have the damn thing to test. It could have been a tube filled with water, for all she knew. Nothing changed for him.

The only thing that meant was that he now had a compelling motive for Sector Three's action against her.

If they even suspected she'd seen anything from Matilda, Sector Three wouldn't hesitate to pull the trigger. The Church didn't like loose ends, and she was a tangled one.

"Still sulking, Mr. Wells?"

Simon stiffened, pain streaking through the raw flesh at his side. It was too late to pretend he hadn't just been sitting there. Staring at nothing. The way she leaned against the doorjamb, her arms folded under her breasts, a roll of bandages held loosely in one hand, told him she'd been there long enough to get the picture.

He didn't bother to try. "You need to get some rest," he said curtly. This time, when he rose to his feet, the floor stayed nice and firm beneath him.

A corner of her mouth angled downward. "*You* need a keeper," she said, as if he hadn't just dismissed her.

Anger curled in his chest. And more. "Go away, *Director*."

He knew how much the way he said her title annoyed her. Had since the day she'd corrected his blatantly disrespectful use of *Miss* in her name. Tweaking her temper usually amused him.

Right now, he wasn't after amusement. He felt savage. Like an injured animal.

Like a rutting beast.

Biological clock? Awareness of his own death weighing on him? Maybe.

Or maybe Parker Adams had buried herself so far under his skin that he didn't know how to get her out.

His radar had shut down. Simon was blind in the one way he knew to keep her safe, and the message his eyes conveyed to his brain wasn't helping.

Because as she strode across the large room—her bare feet sinking into the pale gray plush carpet, her newly braided hair pulled back sharply from her set features—all Simon saw was a woman he desperately wanted to fuck.

He wasn't any better than that.

He *couldn't be* any better than that.

"I came to help you with your wound," she said, her tone glacially even. "And to check on your temperature. You were burning up twenty minutes ago."

He still was. Only not in the way she meant. At least, not that he could tell anymore. "I don't need your help. Not now, not ever."

There. Something about the glint of temper in her beautiful eyes sent a jet of need straight to his dick. Any blood he had left pooled in his jeans.

Hers went right to her cheeks. Ice bitch, nothing. Parker didn't throw the bandage roll at him, but he could read the desire in every taut line of her body as she brandished it. "You need somebody's. And maybe I need your help."

"Yeah, you do."

She had the grace to flush, but her gaze pinned his. Her chin lifted. "At least I can admit it."

"I don't—"

"You've spent our entire relationship behaving as if I'm stupid, Simon." Her words sliced through his temper. His pride. "I don't know how you think I made it to Mission director, but I promise you it's not because I break. Take your damned shirt off and let me bandage your knife wound, you idiot."

He blinked. Fought back a smile.

Touching. And because it hit a low, warm note somewhere in his heart, he quashed it. "You can't help me," he growled.

She flattened a hand on his shoulder, pushed hard enough that his knees buckled. "Want to bet?"

He sat before his balance gave out. Touch him? Touch his wound?

He studied the obstinate angle of her chin. "You can't be serious."

"Try me."

Parker Adams didn't like blood. He'd figured that out already—her skin turned green when she saw the stuff. Her forehead and hands went clammy. Classic signs. How she managed to function in a society that demanded blood on a daily basis intrigued him.

One more fact he found captivating about the strangely compelling director.

The day she'd tended to his wounds, he'd known. And the fact she offered now only ratcheted up the tension, the clash of needs and wants and questions scrabbling for dominance inside him.

He wanted her. He didn't want her to want *him*.

Didn't want to keep her. Didn't want to leave her.

What the fuck was wrong with him?

"Fine," he said evenly, conceding a battle he already realized he'd lost. "You can help me with that."

Just her and his blood.

An object lesson involving her own limitations.

Simon dropped his hands to the thick bandages wrapped around his stomach and sides. Finding the edge, he jerked it loose, ignored the stretching, shifting burn as every move pulled his torn flesh.

Her gaze dropped to the unraveling cloth.

Widened as it revealed the first blotches of brown. It'd get redder as the layers peeled away. Bloodier. Messier.

The color in her cheeks faded, but she took a deep breath.

Go away. Why did she have to be so stubborn?

She didn't leave him. Didn't faint, didn't even take a step back. Despite everything he knew, everything he'd hoped—even as her lips flattened into a white line and that bloom of sweat appeared on her forehead—she stepped closer. Reached out.

His breath locked in his chest as she caught his hands in hers, stilling his rapid, wrenching efforts with only a touch. A gentle grip, so at odds with the cold sweat gathered in her palms.

She met his gaze. Her own all but screamed her revulsion.

And her resolve.

"Let me," she said, her husky voice strained.

Simon couldn't bring himself to make this worse. Couldn't bring himself to admit that he wanted her hands on him, no matter how he got it.

He let her take the bandage end. Held his arms away from his sides and watched her face as she unwound yards of stained bandages. Every layer revealed another swath of blood. Another vibrant stain where he'd left the old bandages in place to soak into the new.

Silence settled into the bedroom. Broken only by the rustle of fabric, by the hammering pulse in his ears and his determinedly aroused erection.

By her breath, a little too fast.

And by her sympathy as the no-longer-white material peeled away. "Oh, Simon," she whispered. Did she know what she did to him as she curved one hand over his ribs? Did she feel the way his heart thudded within the cage of his chest?

He stared down at the crown of her head, the lamplight picking out glints of gold in her copper hair, and he wanted to tear that fucking rubber band from the end of her braid. To sink his fingers into that cool mass of silk and flame and bury himself in everything that she was.

Her taste, her texture. The sound she'd make when he filled her.

The way she'd gasp his name.

He flinched as Parker gingerly grasped the corner of a blood-soaked square. "Just pull it," he said, gritting his teeth.

"Are you sure?"

"It's kinder."

"Oh, Jesus." Bracing her hand against his shoulder, she peeled the crusted pad from his side. Pins and fire radiated through his hip. Up into his ribs.

Simon hissed out a curse, stiffening. His hands fisted behind his back.

"I'm so sorry," she whispered. She dropped the bloody square like it burned.

But even as her throat worked, as he heard her swallow hard enough to hurt, she flattened both hands on either side of his shoulder, just over his seal and the bar code beneath it. Steadying him. Reassurance?

He didn't need her support. *Yeah, he did.* "Don't move. I'm going to get some water to clean this up."

She flitted away like a creature made of fire and light—too fast for him to stop. Too bright for Simon to do anything but stare, bemused at her contrariness. At her stubborn refusal to give in to her own phobia and make *something* in this whole thing go right for him.

It was that same core of tenacity that had her angling to get back to the Mission. Right the wrongs being done to her crew, no matter his certainty that she'd already lost them all.

Did she even consider the dangers to herself?

He breathed through the pain, his mind cataloging it, storing it away where it wouldn't impede his ability to function. He'd always been good at that.

Good at compartmentalizing all the things that weighed on his shoulders—the labs, the witches he killed. And Mattie, whose last act still haunted him.

Now Parker. What was it about her? Why did he feel so . . . so fucking *at peace* around her?

Why did he let her tend him?

Because it pleased her?

Because it pleased *him*.

Motherfucker.

She returned quickly, carrying a bowl of water and towels from somewhere in the apartment. Tendrils of hair around her ears clung damply to her cheeks, as if she'd splashed water on her face, but her eyes remained steady, her hands sure as she dipped a cloth into the water. "Bear with me," she said, professional briskness so out of place in this bedroom. "This might hurt."

Not any worse than anything else Simon had handled lately.

He forced himself to be still. To lock every muscle down, clamp down on every urge to touch her as she dragged the soft towel over his skin.

"The edges are too ragged," Parker said, copper eyebrows knitting as she cleaned the blood away. Her voice, unlike her hands, wasn't steady. "You'll need stitches."

"Hell, no."

"It'll scar."

Simon gritted his teeth. Scars didn't bother him. Not nearly as much as the feel of her soft hands on him.

The wound had stopped seeping, anyway.

She dropped the soiled cloth, picked up another,

and renewed her efforts until the second cloth turned pink. The cold cloth skimmed over his side, around his back, wiping away the blood smear.

Sending shock waves of ice and fire through his body.

"Your bullet wound looks like it healed okay," she said. As the cold cloth skimmed over his lower back, as she braced one hand between his shoulder blades, Simon's fingers curled into fists. "Was that from Parrish?"

He jerked. Her hand fell from his back as he rose from the edge of the bed, stepped away from her. All but ran. "It was just a witch," he said flatly.

Another towel hit the floor. "Simon."

"Leave it alone, Parker." He didn't dare turn.

Couldn't stop himself as she laughed, a husky sound that stroked a velvet line over his senses. "Every time you tell me to leave it alone," she said, amusement warring with the strained remnants of fear in her voice, "it always comes back to bite me."

He frowned at her, all too aware of the cool air against his damp skin. Of his shirt discarded on the floor by pink- and red-stained towels.

Of her stare. Forthright. Challenging.

"This one won't." And because he wanted her on the defensive, he smiled. A curve, a flash of teeth that had nothing to do with humor, and he knew it. "It's a last-ditch effort from a dead woman."

Parker's amusement drained, as clear as if he'd pulled a plug. "I'm sorry."

"I'm not."

Her mouth twisted. "You really aren't, are you?"

Just one more lie he'd fed her.

He was sorry as fuck.

Sorry that Mattie hadn't lived to see her plans—whatever they'd been—come to fruition. Sorry that she'd never see what became of her machinations.

Sorry as hell he'd been the one to find her, to watch her die from the poison she'd drunk so he wouldn't have to go back to Lauderdale and get caught in a lie.

Simon looked up at the ceiling. The elegantly wrought light fixture flickered faintly, a subtle glimmer.

No answers there. Only the insistent pressure locked up in his gut. The faint headache he couldn't shake and the awareness of her. In the same room.

In reach. It'd be so goddamned easy.

When his gaze met hers, he didn't even try to hide the animal need riding him. He stripped away the thin veneer of propriety, let her see exactly how much torture it was to stand here and let her touch him.

To let her think she had *any* say at all in what he did.

"Go away, Director," he warned softly.

Parker took a step back. Her red toenails gleamed in the golden lamplight; just one more shaft of heat spiraling in his gut. Lust red. Blood red.

Her cheeks flushed. "I'm not some kid—"

"Stop." Her mouth closed under his low, forceful command. "Don't . . . do that. None of that. Don't come in here and be brave for me, don't try to sympathize."

She licked her lips, and his eyes dropped to the motion.

His dick hardened to near pain.

"Don't even be in here," he finished roughly.

"Turn around and leave right now, Director, or I will make good on every threat I've ever made you."

"Parker."

His eyebrows climbed. Slow. Incredulous.

Her palms slid along her thighs, wiping the damp traces of her sweat, his watered-down blood, against her jeans. Nervous and restless. "It's Parker."

His eyes narrowed. "You don't know what you're doing."

"You're doing it again," she replied, squaring her shoulders. "You can't even trust me to know what I *want* to do." Her tongue darted out again, as if she couldn't help it. As if she didn't know what that pink swipe across her lower lip did to him.

His laugh twisted to something near pain in his chest. Came out half a growl. "You don't want to waste your time with me."

She couldn't hide her trembling as she raised both hands to the first button of her blouse. "Try me."

His mouth dried as the first button slid free. Bared an inch of skin, the line of her collarbone. And every . . . nerve . . . *detonated*.

Simon closed the gap between them, all but pounced on her before she could do more than take another step back. The backs of her knees slammed into the bed frame, sent her sprawling over the mattress. He followed her down. Crowded her, trapped her between his splayed hands on either side of her head. His knees framed her legs.

She stared up at him, her eyes bottomless and wild. Her lips parted.

Simon ignored the ache in his head, his side. Ignored the exhaustion hammering at him. Every cell in his body shuddered with the intensity of his need.

"One chance," he said, voice lashed to a taut, strained effort. It was all he could manage. "Order me to go. Tell me you don't want me here, right now. Treat me like your missionary. *Director.*" But it wasn't a taunt this time. He wielded her title like a shield; like a lifeline leading her back to safety.

All she had to do was take it.

Parker stared at him. Met his eyes and didn't flinch.

She should have.

"It hasn't worked before," she said huskily.

Holy God. "Only because I'm an asshole," he said roughly. He'd make it work. He'd have to; this couldn't happen. Not like this. Not with him. He wanted to— Christ almighty, he wanted to. That was the problem.

"Simon." Raising one trembling hand, the very tips of two fingers stroked over his bottom lip. "You told me I'd scream."

He groaned, shifting his weight to capture that hand. Deliberately, he yanked it away from him, pinned her wrist to the mattress. "You brought this on yourself," he whispered, and seized her mouth in a kiss that tasted of anger as much as it felt like finding home.

This was it. No turning back.

As Simon's lips covered hers, brushed across them and set every nerve ending she possessed on fire, Parker raised her only free hand and threaded her fingers through his short hair. As he so often did to her, she cradled his head, held him while her mouth strained to meet his passion, match his intensity.

He kissed like a man drowning. Starved for air, for the touch of someone—anyone.

Parker shuddered beneath his onslaught, nowhere near gentle but determined, sweetly savage, only barely restrained by the thinnest control.

Her body arched as heat swept from her forehead to heels. With just a kiss, he started something in her that Parker didn't know how to describe. Like heat lightning and laughter all at once; like the most insidious drug swirling through her stomach, between her legs.

And all this with just a *kiss*.

As his mouth slid to her cheek, lowered to her jaw, she sucked in a shaking breath, throwing her head back to give him easier access to the sensitive skin of her throat. He moved over her, sliding a knee between hers, his powerful shoulders flexing as he lowered his mouth to her neck. Every stroke of his lips, every flick from his teasing, tasting tongue dragged another portion of her self-control to hell.

No. It wasn't about his future. Their future. Maybe they didn't have one; Parker didn't dare assume this was anything but sex between two adults, physical and wild. Giving in to the want and the temptation.

There was too much at stake to be anything else.

The stucco ceiling offered her no answers, only a formless glow of lamplight that painted his face in harsh lines of gold and shadow. It dipped into the hollows beneath his cheekbones as his lips traced her skin to the top of her blouse. His tongue flicked out, a brief caress that pulled at her swirling insides, before his teeth closed over her flesh. A nip. Just hard enough to curl her toes.

Parker gasped, her back arching, hips raising in shameless delight and meeting only the powerful muscles of his thigh between her legs. Grinding herself against it shot fireworks through her body, too hot, too fast. Not nearly enough. She groaned on a shuddering exhale, laughed when Simon's chuckle ghosted over her sensitized skin.

Shifting his weight to his knees, deliberately pushing his thigh into the juncture of hers, he pulled her fingers away from his head and turned them palm up. His eyes gleamed, wicked green and gold as his gaze met hers. Held it.

When he pressed a kiss into the palm of her hand, something in Parker's chest tightened. It stole her breath, her voice.

His tongue flicked out. So soft compared to the solid muscle of his thigh, tight against her body. Insistent pressure where she wanted it most. He transferred her hand to the same easy shackle that held her right wrist captive and pinned her flat against the bed.

Thrilling. His strength, his needs fueled hers. His fingers at her wrists, callused, forceful enough to leave marks, warned her that he wasn't playing. Not this time.

Was he ever?

She hoped not. Arousal so sweet, molten hot, stole every inhibition she had left.

She wanted him to take her. Take her, God,

like . . . like some kind of prize or possession. Use her, make her scream. Just like he'd promised.

Was that wrong?

Did she care?

"Earth to Parker," Simon said, his voice husky with arousal mirrored starkly in his angled features. Firm and apparent behind his zipper. His smile flashed, rueful. Edged. "You along for this ride?"

Parker opened her mouth and swallowed her words as he hooked his finger at the collar of her blouse. Too easily, he flicked a button open with thumb and forefinger.

"Because I think I know what you like." His words fell over like silk, feathered delight and embarrassment through her. "But you need to be clear with me, sweetheart. I don't want to hurt you." Another button popped open, and another. "Okay?"

She nodded, once. "So . . . so far, so good," she whispered.

CHAPTER TWELVE

Again, he smiled. Mind-alteringly sexy. Slowly, as if savoring every inch of her skin each button revealed, he worked his way down her shirt.

Parker bit her lip as the last button slid free.

Would he see her as she saw herself? Attractive enough in clothes, nothing special outside of them, Parker wasn't a woman who took to admiring herself in mirrors.

But the look in Simon's eyes—awe and appreciation and raw, visceral lust—told her she didn't have to bother. As he pulled away one flap of her shirt, baring the lacy edge of her beige bra, his smile crept into his eyes. Crinkled them.

His fingers settled over her ribs. "Your skin is so smooth." Slowly, he traced her ribs, a feather-light touch. Parker squeezed her eyes shut, all too aware of the fluttering way her stomach jumped beneath his so-slow exploration. "You smell like what I always imagined the desert would smell like."

She huffed out a laughing groan as the second half of her shirt fell aside. "It's my perfume." She flexed her arms, pulled at his grasp, but it only tightened around her wrists. More erotic than imprisonment had any right to be.

"I know. That perfume I told you to wear again." She jerked, gasping as his mouth settled just over her navel. A kiss, slow. Deliberate. "That was the day I decided to get you here."

Heat climbed her cheeks, not all of it simple passion. "I just— It's my perfume, I always—"

Simon nipped at the soft flesh just over her hip. She cried out, half in pain that didn't really hurt, half in shock. All desire. "Don't lie to me, Parker," he said roughly against her skin.

"I'm not," she gasped.

"Yes, you are." With no more warning than that, he shifted his grip on her hands and yanked her upright. He didn't let her go to do it, forcing her arms straight, baring her bra to him. Parker's eyes flew open.

And then she wished she'd kept them closed.

He was too much. Too much man, too much aggression. Frightening and awe-inspiring and sensual.

He stared down at her, his jaw rigid with something she couldn't read—control or anger or determination. All of the above. His knee dipped the mattress by her hip, his other still planted between her legs. The position put her so close to his bare skin that she could feel the heat radiating off him.

Fever?

Of a sort. The same kind that infected her. Stripped away her barriers and left her needy, desperate for more.

For Simon.

Raising her chin, she met his glittering stare head-on. "Prove it," she told him. It trembled.

His nostrils flared, as if he were an animal. Starving, hunting. Fresh on her trail.

Without grace, without patience, Simon stripped her of her shirt, transferring her wrists to each hand to get the white material off. Her bra followed, unclasped expertly. And all at once, she knelt half naked in front of a man who was supposed to be her subordinate.

She was his boss.

The ice bitch of the Mission.

Not anymore. Those rules had been thrown out the instant they'd fled from her home. The instant that all-call had gone out.

Now she was just Parker Adams.

Needy, vulnerable. Aroused.

His gaze slid over her like a physical caress. Traveled over the line of her shoulders, her collarbone. Her chest rose and fell too fast to hide, and she was sure he saw her pulse hammering at the base of her throat.

He didn't touch her but for the fingers at her wrists. Just looked at her. Lazily. Slowly. Taking his sweet time. As his gaze lowered to her breasts, full and tight, Parker's cheeks flooded with heat as her nipples obviously beaded beneath his scrutiny.

His slow, sexy smile ripped the bottom out of her stomach.

"I dreamed about this." His voice filled her

senses, dark and dangerous. "You're going to come for me, Parker."

Her throat dried. Parker held his gaze, squirmed as he only stared at her. Waiting.

One dark eyebrow rose, supercilious as hell.

He knew. Damn him, he *knew* what she wanted. What he did to her. But only waited.

She looked away. "I—"

"Yes?"

Parker licked her lips. It didn't help. "I don't . . ."

"Look at me, Parker." Gentle. Coaxing. But no less an order.

She did.

Simon's eyes narrowed. Slowly, he reached behind her, found her braid and pulled it over her bare shoulder. The ends tickled the top of her breast, tickled and stroked and added another layer to the complex sensations already twisting her up inside.

His fingers brushed the same spot, and Parker shuddered. He pulled the band off, stroked those fingers through her hair until the braid unwound and most of the cool mass slid down her back.

"You don't have a choice," he said, even as he wound a lock of her copper hair around his index finger. Lust pounded through her body, wicked and wanton. "This is about what I want. Isn't that right, Director?"

She flinched. But he wasn't wrong.

The hair tightened around his finger, pulling harder and harder until she had no choice but to lean forward. Where her arms were beginning to shake, his seemed rock solid over her head. A taut line of muscle and strength, patience incarnate.

"Say it," he whispered, his eyes bottomless.

"I—" Parker took a long, slow breath. Felt it flood her chest, her belly.

Felt it burn away into nothing as he tugged on her trapped hair.

"Please," she managed, her eyes wide. Her heart pounding so hard, it overwhelmed fear. Shame. All those things she'd spent so long avoiding. "Please touch me. Take me, Simon, make me come." Her back curved, unabashedly thrusting her breasts to him. Needy, an offering she desperately wanted him to accept. "Come with me."

Every breathy word caused his eyes to darken. The smile left them. Left his mouth, drained from his features until Parker could only shiver as he studied her from a place she didn't recognize. Something not cold; God, he was too vivid, too intense to be cold. Not detached, not judging by the lust shaping every hardened muscle of his beautiful body.

Something . . . strong. Something immovable.

"You're mine," he said softly.

Oh, God. That sounded . . . so permanent. So . . . So *dangerous*. She wanted it.

Parker nodded. He pulled on her hair, hard enough to force a small sound from her throat. "Say it, Parker."

"I'm yours," she gasped. "Damn you, make me yours."

His eyes banked hard. The fingers around her wrist tightened near to pain. Letting go of her hair, he curled his hand around her throat and crushed his mouth to hers.

As if he knew. Knew how the dominant edge in him stroked something feminine and sultry and soft in her. As if he could sense how much his aggression turned her on.

Parker moaned as his tongue slid between her lips, found hers and stroked it, tasted her. Let her taste him. Finally, letting go of her wrists, he dragged his hand up her ribs. Filled his hand with her breast, stroking. Molding, shaping. It freed her to touch him in turn. His muscles were hard and defined under her searching hands, leaping to her touch as if she were a live wire laid against his skin.

He made a rough sound in his chest as her fingers stroked over one flat nipple, returned the favor in kind as his found her left nipple and pinched it tautly between thumb and forefinger. She cried out, throwing her head back and wrenching her mouth away under a flood of wild demand. Him, inside her.

Now.

He tugged her arms back, slid a hand behind her back and lowered her to the bed, springs squeaking faintly underneath him as he shifted over her.

"Grab the headboard," he commanded.

Parker's hands stilled, half outstretched. "But I—"

He twisted her nipple, hard enough to draw the breath from her lungs. Just this side of pain, so delicious that her shoulders flattened, back arching. "The headboard, Parker."

Shaking with need, she raised her arms above her head, fingers interlacing around a metal rung of the sturdy headboard. It left her exposed, open to his study.

"If you move your hands," he warned, stretching out beside her like some kind of pagan god at a feast, "there will be trouble. Am I clear?"

The man stole her breath. Her logic, her rational thought. With his jeans riding low on his hips and his chest bare to her hungry gaze, he looked every bit as decadent, as sinful, as everything the Church warned against.

She could have gone her whole life without feeling *this*. Him. His hands on her, his rough aggression surrounding her.

She nodded. "Clear."

"Good." Simon bent, very slowly, and drew her right nipple into his mouth. Parker groaned with the pull of it, with the exquisite torture of his damp, hot mouth encircling her breast. Tongue flicking across the tight bud, he bit down gently. Just enough.

Her groan shuddered to a gasp for air.

Was this the right thing to do?

God help her, it didn't matter now.

His fingers found the clasp of her jeans, and with the same easy effort, Simon unsnapped the front. The zipper hissed.

He drew back, teeth tight at her nipple, pulling it. Sending streaks of lightning from breast to belly and lower. She could feel the hot, sticky fluid between her legs, wetter than she'd ever been for any man. She wasn't a stranger to sex, but whatever Simon was doing to her transcended just sex.

He played her. Played her body like a well-oiled instrument. As he shifted his mouth to her other breast, Parker gritted her teeth, fingers clamped on the metal rung until she was sure the edges would score permanent lines into her skin.

But as his teeth closed on her skin, his fingers slid beneath her jeans. Found her warm and swollen, slick with need. The sound he made only pushed Parker higher, stripped her of inhibition and fear as her legs fell open.

"God, you're wet," he breathed against her skin, damp from his mouth. "Is this for me, sweetheart?" His fingers brushed against her, slipped between the folds of overly sensitized flesh until she was all but writhing against him. Desperate to be free of her jeans, to feel him fully inside her. When he stroked against her clit, Parker jerked, sobbing out a word that she'd meant to be encouragement but didn't make it past a raw sound of need.

Simon's laugh, his breath, ghosted across her breast.

His fingers eased out of her jeans. He pulled away, leaving her keenly aware of the loss of his body heat, but only groaned, "Oh, God, *yes,*" as he peeled the material from her hips. Slid them down her legs.

Parker clung to the headboard, her eyes squeezed shut. She could only imagine what she looked like. Her hair tangled around her shoulder, her pale skin pink with exertion and embarrassment and arousal.

"Don't move your hands," Simon warned. The denim cleared her feet, rustled as her jeans hit the floor. "No matter what."

"Got it," she whispered.

The bed dipped, squeaked as his weight settled on the mattress. Parker didn't dare open her eyes.

"You're unbelievable." She jerked as his lips brushed the sensitive skin just above her knee. "Sexy." They moved over her thigh, tracing a line higher and higher. "Strangely obedient," he added in lazy amusement.

She shook her head.

Bracing both of his hands beside her hips caused her weight to shift. Parker opened her eyes, frowning in concentration.

Only to gasp as he met her gaze. Like a god, she'd thought before. Indolent and confident and carved from perfection. His swarthy skin gleamed in the lamplight, muscles in his shoulders and arms bunching as he slowly lowered himself to her.

He didn't look away.

"Trust me," he said. Ordered. Another demand. She trembled, fingers aching around the headboard. "Why?"

As his elbows locked around her thighs, one hand flattening over her belly, Simon smiled. "Because you need someone to trust, Parker Adams."

She shook her head, her hair sliding over her cheek as she swallowed hard.

"And you need someone to take care of you."

"I can't—"

"At least for as long as I'm here." He blew against her flesh; a tease. "And you need to hold on tight," he added, just before he buried his mouth into the soft flesh between her legs.

"Oh, *God,*" she managed. It was all she knew to say as his tongue dragged over her clitoris, stroked around the tiny nub of tangled nerves. His lips pulled at it, tugged, left her gasping and twisting as he pulled away to slide his tongue deeper. Only a taunt, a torment compared to what he *could* fill her with.

But it was enough to raise her hips from the bed.

To force him to push against her stomach, hold her still as he feasted at her wet flesh. He licked her so thoroughly, so deeply that her breath came in pants, gasps, pleading.

Simon shifted, and as Parker writhed beneath his mouth, he eased two fingers into her body.

"There's no shame in wanting to be taken care of," Simon said, his voice rougher than it'd been moments before.

Parker shook her head, over and over, but she couldn't look away. Not from his eyes, smoldering. Not from his mouth, damp from her own body's arousal.

He'd tasted her. He approved of her.

Her hips jerked, bucking even without her order as his fingers stroked through the ring of nerves already pushed to breaking from his tongue. They dragged over a particular spot, curved into her inner flesh.

"You're a strong woman, Parker." His mouth curved up. "You're strong enough to fight even when you don't have a chance in hell of winning. Giving up control doesn't make you less." In and out. His fingers played her as skillfully as his tongue had, twisted inside her. "Give me everything you have, sweetheart. I want it. Every last secret." He lowered his lips once more to the tight bud of her clit.

Her mind shattered an instant before her body followed.

Parker's denial never made it through her scream.

Un-fucking-believable.

She humbled him. Rocked him down to his

shredded soul. The caliber of her response, the sweet way she gave in to his demands and let herself go stripped Simon of any words he might have said to reaffirm distance between them.

She was everything he'd fantasized. More.

As her body clenched around his fingers, twitched in aftershocks of her orgasm, Parker panted for air. Her eyes squeezed shut, a trick he was learning she employed to keep from engaging him.

It was cute.

The lovely bloom flushing her chest and cheeks fascinated him. She climaxed unapologetically, as completely as he could have hoped.

But it wasn't the way her muscles remained clamped on his fingers that knocked any last good intentions he had out of the running.

Her hands remained wrapped around the metal rungs, tight on the headboard. Exactly as he'd commanded.

Slipping his fingers out of her sent her body into a shuddering gasp.

"Jesus, you're beautiful," he said huskily. He couldn't help it. Parker Adams knew how to dress herself for maximum impact, but naked, makeup worn away, stripped of every piece of armor she carefully cultivated, her beauty outshined anything else he'd seen in his life.

Her hair spread out around her, vivid against the dark burgundy comforter. He liked redheads as a rule, but she was something else entirely.

Something he didn't dare explore.

You're mine.

What the fuck had possessed him to demand that?

Parker's feet flexed, toes pointing in a stretch he watched shape every soft line of her body. His blood hammered, erection pulsing painfully behind his restraining zipper.

"Simon?"

"I'm here," he said. Although God knew why. She was dangerous.

This was dangerous.

Her mouth curved as her red-tipped lashes lifted. Her eyes, still hazy, met his. Challenge. "You are missing a minor yet crucial step," she pointed out, her voice smoky. And so similar to his own taunting drawl that he couldn't help his grin.

"Minor, huh?"

"I did add crucial," she replied serenely. One foot slid over her other shin, an absent caress that shouldn't have been as sexy as it was. But she didn't let go of the headboard.

And that was enough.

She might not realize what it was about him that elicited her gasps and moans and panting for more, but he knew.

For now, he could pretend it was enough.

"Are you ordering me to fuck you, Parker?" His crudeness widened her eyes, but not in shock. She'd spent too much time around missionaries to worry about language.

Instead, embarrassment filled her features. She glanced away. Then back. "Is it an order if I say please?"

"Begging has its charms." Simon unsnapped his jeans, his gut twisting with it as he watched her gaze fall to his hands. To the vee of skin he exposed as he pulled his zipper down. He didn't deal with boxers or briefs; his cock sprung free of the confining denim, thick and so sensitive that he gritted his teeth.

The unadulterated wanting in her face, in the way she licked at her lips as if he were a five-star meal, thrilled him.

"Just keep looking at me that way," he said roughly. He shed his jeans. "Like you're going to eat me alive."

"Any chance I get," she whispered. Her legs opened, one knee upraised. It bared her to him, let him admire the tuft of reddish-brown hair between her legs. The slick pink flesh beneath.

His blood pounded through his dick.

That was his. *She* was his.

At least for tonight.

"Please," she repeated breathlessly. "Simon—"

"Easy, sweetheart." He climbed over her, his erection heavy between his legs. His need elevated into desperation. Her legs opened on either side of his, her hips tilting up in obvious demand.

"No," she said, her lips curving into a smile miles beyond wicked. Her elbows bent, but she didn't let go. "Not easy. Anything but easy."

As his cock nudged her soft flesh, Simon's breath caught on something between a groan and a chuckle. "Insatiable."

"Not done screaming," she managed, her hips lifting, arching, doing everything in her limited power to force him inside her body. As she coated him in her own body's juices, Simon felt the last, lingering confines of restraint slip away.

He didn't have a condom. He didn't need one. He wasn't so much of a slut that he didn't take care, and he knew without having to ask that she did the same. Pregnancy wasn't an option; all the normal missionaries were given birth control shots at every physical. He didn't have the same physicals, but she did.

Grasping her hips in both hands, Simon stilled her body. Met her gaze, held it. "Look at me," he commanded harshly.

She bit her lip. A whimper escaped as his fingers tightened.

But she didn't look away.

And as he slid into her wet, welcoming flesh, as she took him in, inch by gleaming inch, Simon lost himself. In her body, so fucking tight and wet and welcoming. In her eyes, deeply blue, wicked and fogged by desire. In her hitched breath, her broken pants as he slid out of her, and back in. Slowly. Forcefully. Nothing easy about it.

She cried out, body twisting.

Simon caught her leg as it curled over his hip, heel digging into his back. He stroked inside her, every push, every thrust ratcheting his climax higher, faster, harder.

She moaned, timed with every pump of his hips. So beautiful. Color swept her face, her body clenched around him, massaged his cock and shoved every last thought from his head.

There was just her. Just him, inside her. Her voice surrounding him, her body, her cries of ecstasy drawing him in. Erotic as hell.

"More," she sobbed. Her back arched, and Simon let go of her hips to brace his hands on either side of her shoulders. "Simon, there, oh, God—"

His name and God's in one breath. He chuckled, the sound hoarse as he buried his lips against her shoulder. Her skin tasted faintly salty, smooth as silk under his mouth as he licked a trail along her collarbone. As his hips pumped against hers, as she raised her own to grind with every thrust, his teeth sank into the muscle between her shoulder and neck.

She didn't want easy.

He didn't want to disappoint a lady. *This* lady.

As sweat gathered across his shoulders, as heat coiled tighter and tighter in his gut, his balls, Parker writhed and panted and moaned his name. Until her internal muscles clamped down around him, dragged at his sensitive cock and wrested all control from him.

His lips found hers; fused as she cried out, a scream every bit as intense as the one he'd already coaxed out of her. As his body began to shudder, as spasms of his climax rippled out from his tightened balls and Parker's fingernails sank into his back, Simon groaned in echoed release.

The fucking world flipped over.

Parker Adams, the woman who'd haunted his every waking fantasy, shuddered underneath him, her eyes blissfully closed, her lashes spiky against her sweat-damp cheeks. As his cock twitched and leaped and shattered every preconceived notion of objectivity he'd built around him—around *them*— Simon's arms gave out.

His body covered hers, pinned her, and he dropped his face to the bedclothes by her shoulder. He had to breathe. He had to remember how.

He had to disengage—his body from hers, his mind from the dangerous path it traveled—and he had to do it *now*.

But he didn't.

This was a problem.

CHAPTER THIRTEEN

Jonas Stone wasn't completely honest with the world.

No missionary was—that way spelled a messy end—but he didn't like that the world wasn't always honest with him, either. It was a complaint he'd long since learned to handle, his way. In the flickering light of the tech van he'd made his own, he watched the city through half a dozen feeds mounted against one wall.

"The police department has gone on record stating such figures are overblown, but that the public should continue to be vigilant. However, there is no statement from either the New Seattle Riot Force or the Mission—"

The shelves built into the van were custom designed by him, allowing just enough room for his chair to slide on tracks between them. Computers, screens, a veritable cornucopia of technology traveled with him wherever he went.

This was home. More than the apartment he claimed on his paperwork, more than the offices where Alan Eckhart kept track of the lower level street teams, this van had everything he needed and more.

Including a small fridge and a crate of energy boosters for the overnighters.

He'd had a lot of overnighters lately. Not all courtesy of the Mission, either.

Damn, he was skating along a thin line.

"—say they never would have suspected Walters to be a witch. Missionaries were on the scene shortly after his attack on the family—"

Jonas rubbed one thigh absently, thumb dragging across aching muscle. His chair, also custom, cradled his weight evenly, but no amount of padding could take the pain from his body forever. His right leg hurt more tonight, probably from the physical therapy he'd insisted on pushing.

At least he could walk, albeit with crutches. It was a far cry from his prior confinement to his chair.

"Witnesses say two men burst into the Avenue Café moments before the attack on an employee."

Jonas's attention dialed in to that one. Reaching over, he tapped two keys on the interface he'd built himself. Compiled of three keyboards and an array of wires, it controlled every last aspect of his tech van.

On command, the other feeds muted. Figures passed through the glass in silence.

A pretty brunette looked solemnly out through the monitor. Behind her, people milled outside the very same café Simon Wells's message had directed him to. "Although no one was seriously hurt, all three men have vanished into the chaos that followed. The police encourage everyone to keep calm and be aware for any suspicious activity."

Of course. Not that it'd help. New Seattle was rife with suspicious activity, not the least of which came from the Church itself.

He adjusted his glasses, reaching for the comm he'd slotted into its dock. The message had been wiped, but he'd already traced the source. Winston Wilkes, one of many employees at the New Seattle bank. Topsider. Clean record, workaholic, divorced once, no kids.

Nothing suspicious there. Except for the fact it came with Simon's name attached. And a set of instructions he'd already investigated.

Jonas knew what the pretty reporter didn't.

Hacking into the sec-comps didn't take any effort anymore. Jonas had so many back doors into the city's network that he could spy just about anywhere outside of the Holy Order quad. Most of the time, it came in handy for Mission operations.

Sometimes, he did it on his own.

Sad to think that despite all of that, the hacker he'd spent too many hours chasing down still managed to give him a run for his money and then some.

The data he'd accrued tonight puzzled him immensely. Why had Simon Wells been at that café? Why had the director been with him when she was supposed to have been meeting with the team leads topside? He'd watched them exit in the chaos, tracked them in their stolen car to the condos overlooking Testament Park.

He'd had to dance a finger-jig on his keyboards to do it, but he'd managed. And he'd remotely turned off the silent alarm the director's clumsy vehicle-sec hacking had triggered.

But he couldn't even say why.

Jonas had a bad feeling about all of this. And only half of it came from the bone-deep pain he lived with on a daily basis.

Fifteen years was a long time to rebuild himself. The fact he'd managed to do it after a coven nearly blew him up with his tech van was pretty much a miracle—even he thought so. He'd seen a lot of missions, a lot of screwups, and a lot of bad choices in his time.

But he liked to think that he'd been given a second chance. He recognized the good people he worked with. The director, for all her aloofness, was that type. Scads better than David Peterson ever was.

Something about her reminded him of one of the few people he counted as a friend. Although Naomi would hate to be compared to the woman she called *little Miss Parker* in that way of hers.

He tilted the comm screen, studying its carefully clean surface. The message from Simon was puzzling by itself. He knew for a fact the man was involved with the GeneCorp issue. He'd traced a few leads at the director's request—and shared what he'd learned with a couple of friends on the wrong end of Church law. Silas Smith and his team had been working on the same problem, different angle.

He figured better two interests than one.

He hadn't counted on Simon cropping up as a third. By his calculations, the man fell on the wrong side of Mission loyalties. Simon's request to meet him and the director at that café had come with alternatives. The protocols given in the same message told him to send everything he knew about the director's interests to a particular frequency.

Tracing the frequency led to a miles-long list of dummy buoys. Ones he didn't have time to investigate. Another player?

This news feed suggested there had been an altercation at the same place Jonas had been instructed to visit. Surveillance footage put the director there.

And yet, the all-call from the director's frequency had requested all the leads at her headquarters. Eckhart had gone up already.

What was he supposed to do now?

Because from where he was sitting—and he didn't think it immodest to claim he sat at the center of the wave, he could virtually tap into anything—it looked like he had cards nobody else knew existed.

Jonas blew out a breath, shoving his glasses up on his head and leaning back in his seat.

Was this it? Was this his moment?

Nerves ate at his stomach, gripped his chest with viselike intensity. He'd grown up in this Mission. Had sworn the oaths, done his duty. Through hellfire and worse, he'd overcome it. He was the best analyst out there; he knew it. The king of the wave.

Was it all for nothing?

Or was this just his chance to walk—*ha!*—where good men had walked before? To take that step, the same line missionaries before him had taken. Silas Smith, Naomi West. Missionaries he'd looked up to.

Still did.

Was he talking crazy?

"I'm talking crazy," he affirmed to the bank of monitors. And even as he said it, his long, thin fingers darted over the keyboard. He tapped in a string of code, hesitated.

Last chance. He could stop now. He could pull up stakes in his moral code, pull his big boy pants up and do his job. He could work his technological magic on the dockets the Mission gave him and keep his nose clean.

He could forget about Silas and Naomi. About the Salem Project, and the hole in his gut. The same void that had been steadily eating at him for over a year.

Slowly, pulling his glasses back to his nose, he studied the command he'd never thought he'd find himself inputting.

The cleanest resignation he'd ever tendered.

The only resignation he'd ever tendered.

What would Silas do?

Leaving the command line in place, he flipped open his comm. Plugged the mic into his ear and dialed.

The line synched within seconds. "Tell me you have good news."

His lips twitched at the order. "I never lie to a lady. Especially one that can kick my ass."

Naomi West snorted, one of her many less-than-ladylike traits. "What's up then?"

"A mystery." He slid his glasses off again, rubbing at the bridge of his nose. Quickly, he filled her in—leaving out the bits about the extra frequency.

There were some things he'd long since figured out how to filter. If Naomi suspected another threat, she'd stop at nothing to end it.

That's what made her a damn good missionary. But she had other problems now.

Jonas could handle this mystery player.

She was silent for a moment after he stopped speaking. And then, baldly, "What the fuck, Jonas?"

"Yeah, that's kind of what I thought, too," he admitted. "Nai, what did Phin give the director?"

A beat. Just enough for him to sense the lie before it came. "I don't know."

Jonas frowned. But he didn't pursue it. "Well, all right," he said lightly and slid his glasses back into place. The command line blinked at him. "That's all I got. Sounds like someone pulled a coup."

"Damn. I'll tell the team." Her tone hardened. "Don't do anything stupid, Jonas. I'm going to send—"

"Don't. I'm fine down here." He glanced at the silent feeds. His eyes narrowed, back straightening as the figure of a man detached himself from the alley next to the mid-low Mission offices.

Company?

"What about little Miss Parker? Any word?"

"Nothing since the last comm wave," he said quickly. "Nai, I gotta go."

"Wait, let me—"

Jonas winced. "Trust me, babe. When have I ever let you down?"

Maybe the worst lie he'd told. His guts gnawed themselves apart. A bad feeling, right?

A terminal one.

As he cut the line, jammed his thumb against the

security pad and let the device scrape itself clean, Jonas watched the man raise a fist outside the van.

Wham, wham, wham! Even though he'd been expecting it, the impact jerked him half out of his chair. Pain shot up his twisted legs, and Jonas grabbed the edge of the desk as he swallowed back a clenched groan. The van doors opened behind him.

"Jonas? You in here?"

Neely. "Christ," Jonas gasped, falling back to the chair. He swiveled, rubbing his right thigh with both hands as he glowered at the missionary. Neely's familiar face was a hell of a relief. Not the shadowy killer he'd half expected looming out of the dark. "Don't scare me, man!"

The man leaned in, hands braced on the van floor, wincing. "Sorry. I figured you'd have seen me coming."

He had. He just hadn't realized it was one of his own. "Been working overtime on these new dockets," he admitted. Mostly true. "Is it just me, or are we seeing a serious climb in activity?"

"Don't even get me started," Neely replied, his mouth twisting in chagrin. He jerked a thumb back over his shoulder. "You able to take a ride?"

"Huh?" Jonas rubbed at his face. Fatigue always managed to catch up in those times between projects.

"Ride," Neely repeated with amusement. "You. Me. Now."

"Why?"

"The director wants you topside."

Jonas stilled. Slowly, lowering his hand, he squinted at the man he'd known for almost a year.

A lie. Neely lied. Why?

"Jonas? You okay?"

Jonas shook his head, grimacing. "Approaching the point of no return, you know?" He turned around. "Let me power down. You want to unhook my crutches?"

"Got it." Metal clanked behind him as Jonas stared at the screen. The blinking cursor.

What would Silas do?

The right thing.

He tapped the enter key. Data streamed. One by one, the monitors in the van turned black. As the overhead lights winked out, Jonas took a deep, calming breath.

This was it. No going back.

He reached behind him, grabbed the first shelf, and pulled himself along the track bolted into the floor. The oiled bearings moved soundlessly. As he swung by the final tier, he grabbed the coat he'd set there, pulled it on over his T-shirt, and grinned as he met Neely's friendly gaze. "Sounds like a real storm up there, huh?"

"It's shaping up to be that way," the man agreed lightly. He offered a hand, and though every part of Jonas's pride rebelled, he took the man's help. Getting out of the van was getting easier with time, but he wasn't made of steel. The van creaked as Jonas stepped off the bumper.

As his weight settled to the wet pavement, he glanced around. The gravel lot outside the lower street Mission offices was only dimly lit, and the lights affixed to the outside structure flickered as they always did. The electrical grid this far down didn't promise anything but a headache. The Mission had generators to handle the indoor power.

Pain rippled down his twisted legs. Climbed up through his spine. He must have made a face, because as Neely set his crutches down, angled perfectly for Jonas to slip his hands through the arm braces, his dark eyes flicked to his legs. "How are you feeling?"

Some of the agents just never stopped asking. "Every day's a win," Jonas said cheerfully. "So what's the director need me for?"

"Same old song and dance." Neely steadied him as Jonas tightened the straps. "We're good, but we're not you up there. Hey, maybe you'll finally accept that promotion to topside offices, huh?"

Jonas's grin hurt. "I like my van."

"You and that bucket." Neely slammed the doors closed, and Jonas tapped in a series of numbers on his comm.

The other missionary watched the van. Raised his eyebrows when nothing happened. "And?"

"I'm good," Jonas chuckled, "not flashy. She's safe."

"All right, then." Neely gestured toward the dark lane between the Mission building and the training facility beside it. "This way."

"Where's your car?"

"I parked on the other side of that alley," he replied, and Jonas's chest twisted.

A lie. Another lie. They compounded into a drum of fear. As Jonas's awkward footsteps clanked into the dark crevasse, as the padded ends of his crutches splashed through gathered puddles, he heard a subtle click behind him.

His heart pounded. Fear gnawed at his guts, but he firmed his grip on the crutch supports and set his jaw. No going back now.

The Mission didn't allow resignation.

He looked up, squinting against the clinging summer humidity and smiled as the city rose high above him. Layers upon layers of lights, of streets built on top of each other.

He didn't mind this city so much.

"Jonas?"

"I'm going," he sighed and pushed into the darkness. The alley swallowed them.

As the air thrummed with the constant flow of electricity, as lights flickered and the city thrust glittering fingers into the black sky, three gunshots echoed across the gravel alley.

The van stayed dark.

CHAPTER FOURTEEN

Splat.

Parker stirred. Warmth filled her, a sweet lassitude clinging to her mind as she surfaced slowly from the deepest sleep she'd had in a long time.

Simon's body tucked against her back. A hard arm folded over her ribs, securing her tightly against his chest. She sprawled back against him, her cheek pillowed on her folded arm, her legs tangled with his.

It'd been a long, long time since she'd woken up wrapped up in a man like this.

Smiling, she raised a hand to scratch at her itching shoulder.

Froze when her fingertips encountered something warm and wet.

Splat.

Parker sat up fast, every trace of sleep screaming out of her head. The daylight filtering around the pulled drapes lit the room to a muted glow, soft enough to allow for sleep but bright enough to pick out the dark stain smearing her fingertips.

Her stomach turned over.

Blood.

"Simon!"

He was already struggling to his elbows, not quite awake but moving, as if fine-tuned to his environment. To his name.

Her presence.

As bile welled in her throat, her shocked gaze lifted to his face. Blood dripped from his nose. Splattered to the comforter as he strained to push himself upright. "Son of a bitch," he growled.

It came out thick. As if caught in phlegm. Grasping the sheet, he yanked it to his nose.

Icy sweat broke out across her shoulders.

Unabashedly naked, Simon hunched at the edge of the bed, his powerful shoulders rounded, sheet gathered against his nose. "Sorry. Not the way I'd planned to wake you up."

Parker stared at his back. "It's because of that faulty DNA, isn't it?"

His head lowered. Crimson edged the material. Slowly, as she forced her stomach to settle, as she breathed in deeply and let it out in a slow, calming exhale, her limbs unfroze.

"I'm going to get you a towel," she said, summoning every ounce of brisk practicality she could. She slid off the bed, balanced herself with a hand on his shoulder.

His skin seared her palm. Too hot.

"God, Simon—"

His shoulder pulled away; he didn't look at her. "Just get me a towel," he muttered.

Hurt needled at her.

So did relief.

Parker hurried to the bathroom, paused only long enough to retrieve her jeans. She found her bra tangled with her shirt, balled them together and stepped into the fragile sanctuary of the bathroom.

With shaking hands, she ran water over a hand towel and carefully, determinedly wiped the blood off her shoulder. She didn't throw up.

Maybe she was getting a handle on this after all.

She dressed fast. Avoided looking at herself in the mirror, sure she'd see what she always did—a woman claiming to be the boss of soldiers, of men and woman who bled every day, shaking in her skin at the sight of it.

She was still standing. And right now, she was all Simon had.

Swiping a soft, lush blue towel from the rack affixed to the wall, Parker fled before she met her own eyes in the mirror.

Simon hadn't moved. Head bowed, the sheet draped over his lap, he held the edge to his nose and didn't even open his eyes as she pushed the towel into his hands. "Here."

He caught her hand. The hem of the sheet slipped to his lap. "Parker."

Blood coated his upper lip, patterned over his chin.

She winced. "Just—"

He didn't let her finish. His grip tightened, but to

her relief, he brought the towel back to his face. Held it there, his eyes searching hers over it. Fierce, intensity trapped in a yellow-green haze. "Mattie had a formula," he said, but too thickly. As if through a long tunnel. "She called it the Eve sequence."

Parker caught his shoulders as he swayed. Broke his grip without even trying. "Is that what you need?" His eyes closed. "Simon, what's the Eve sequence?"

"Maybe nothing," he muttered. "Maybe . . . it's too late. She made . . . us. Made us like this. *Degeneration*."

As his weight dragged at her, it was all she could do to guide his slow descent back to the mattress. He crumpled, his head missed the pillow, but at least he didn't slump forward onto the floor. Heart racing, she tucked two fingers at his neck.

His eyes, though closed, crinkled into a weary smile. "Not dead yet," he murmured from behind the cloth.

Where did this come from? A nosebleed? His fever?

How could this be genetic? What did it mean?

Damn it, why hadn't she paid more attention in her science studies?

"Simon," she said urgently. She knelt over him, pushed his hair back from his forehead. "You're sick, Simon, we have to get you to a doctor." And she needed to get home.

To hell with the odds.

"S'okay." He wouldn't open his eyes. "Just need rest. Got a headache."

Another headache?

Parker bit her bottom lip.

Maybe he'd sleep some more. His skin looked sallow, yellow-tinted under his darker coloring. Although sweaty, hot to the touch, he seemed to breathe all right—not counting the constant swallowing he had to maintain to keep the blood from drowning him.

The mere thought sent chills up her spine.

"You need that syringe, don't you?"

"Maybe."

"Okay." She couldn't stop herself from pulling the blankets up higher, tucked them around his broad chest.

"Rest."

He cracked open a bleary eye. "Don't do anything stupid."

There was the Simon she knew. "Count on it."

His eyebrows knotted. "Afraid of that."

But maybe he trusted her anyway, because his eye closed again, and he said nothing else.

Parker eased off the bed as quietly as she could and dragged shaking hands down her thighs. As if she could scrape away the memory of his blood.

Of his skin, hot against her palms. Smooth and ridged and—

She shuddered.

Degeneration, he'd said. Breakdown. Was every Salem Project subject suffering this? Every witch Lauderdale created?

The horror of it bottled in her chest, locked behind an iron cage of anger.

Simon couldn't go like that. While he slept, she'd get a bead on current events. Figure out how to get in touch with her agents.

Figure out which agents to trust.

Was he right? Were half her operatives turned already?

Were her team leads dead? Worse?

Parker hated not knowing. She was the Mission director. They were her responsibility. And with Simon's comm, she'd be able to contact someone, anyone. Jonas?

With his help, she could get back home. Slip any electronic surveillance, collect the syringe in her safe and get back here before Simon even woke.

She bent, picked up Simon's jeans as silently as she could, and padded out of the bedroom. Unclipping his comm, she draped his pants over the back of a chair and flipped it open with a flick of her thumb. The screen warmed up quickly.

And with it, a list. A familiar list.

She scrolled through it, first in curiosity. Then, the clean anger of righteous indignation flipped. Fury licked at her.

Name after name. The previous five she knew well enough to recognize on sight—victims to Operation Domino. Each checked off like a shopping list.

"What the hell is this?" she whispered, but she knew.

The list scrolled on.

J. Fisher.

One of hers. A missionary, assigned to Eckhart's team. Partnered with Agent Miles in the mid-lows. She'd never met him, but she knew her roster.

Found dead yesterday.

P. Adams.

Simon had already warned her about that one. But as she scrolled through the plain text list, fear seized her heart. Fear, and fury.

A. Williams.

D. Smith.

Missionaries, both of them. One topside, a new analyst from the orphanage training. Drew Smith had just finished training before Peterson was exposed. He was a fine man, a good agent. She'd handpicked him herself.

Her knuckles whitened.

Pain shot through her chest, a vise squeezing the breath from her lungs.

J. Stone.

Were her people nothing more than expendable pawns in Lauderdale's sick game?

A. Silo.

Her eyes burned. Her throat ached with it, but she gritted her teeth. Forced back the knot of anger before it exploded from her chest in a scream of rage.

That wouldn't do anything.

Except expose precisely what she'd turned her back on.

Her best tech, up to his neck in classified information, and Silo, one of her few friends in the Mission. She'd gone to the same orphanage with her. Now she appeared on a hit list. With her.

Because of her.

She flipped open the screen, dialed Jonas's frequency with shaking fingers.

The line thrummed, that toneless note that told her he wasn't picking up. She disconnected, tried once more.

Nothing.

Parker lowered the comm, eyes leveled sightlessly on the empty fireplace beside her. Her mind worked, burned through plan after plan until the only thing she *could* do became clear.

She'd known about her chances. Simon—to his credit at least a little—had made it clear. She'd accepted it. Accepted it only inasmuch as she intended to tear the roof down around Lauderdale's smug head.

But he hadn't told her about her people. Jonas, Silo, Williams—agents she trusted. Who trusted *her*. He'd hidden her away from the real battle, hoping . . . what? That she'd forget about the missionaries?

That she'd never find the list of people she knew—knew without a shadow of a doubt—were still hers. There was no mistaking it.

She'd always known he was a double agent, but he'd been sitting on a hit list of Parker's best and never so much as breathed a word.

Setting her jaw, Parker forced her shoulders to straighten. Locked her knees, spine rigid, and blew out a hard breath. She knew what she had to do.

She couldn't take the time to feel sick about it.

Grimly, Parker scraped her forearm across her face, then jumped as the comm pulsed in her hand.

Her grip tightened. Her heart rate spiked, and as adrenaline flooded her system, Parker didn't even look at the number. The comm clicked softly as she accepted the call.

"Wells, where are you?"

Black rage licked at the last fringes of her fraying control as Kayleigh Lauderdale's voice snapped through the unit.

"You haven't reported in." Her voice hardened. "You need to come in, Simon. I don't like the implications of this—"

"Hello, Dr. Lauderdale."

Silence filled the line. Tense, weighty. Then, quietly, "Director Adams. I understand there's a warrant for your arrest."

Parker chuckled. The sound grated, even through her own ears. "You'd know." Ice replaced grim humor as she added, "So your father has finally tipped his hand, hasn't he?"

"Director, you need to come in—"

Parker's fingers spasmed against the case. "Don't you start with me. You've been killing my people, you *bitch*."

Kayleigh's voice rose an octave. "It's not murder, they're subjects."

"*They're mine*." Parker raised the comm, lowering her voice to a venomous whisper. "You made a mistake, Doctor."

"I've made a lot." The raw honesty of the reply kicked Parker in the chest.

Her fingers tightened. "I have something you want."

The doctor gasped. "What? What did you do to Simon?"

The outright concern in her voice nearly sent Parker to her knees in hysterical laughter. She bit it back, clenching her teeth. "You mean that *subject* degenerating in the other room? Does he mean something to you, Kayleigh?"

The doctor swore, hard and low across the feed.

Parker looked up at the ceiling, blinking as guilt swamped her. Bloody, sharp. Made of jagged knives. "I'm told you're looking for a serum. Something that'll glue all these *subjects* back together."

More silence. But she knew Kayleigh was listening; she had the girl by the throat with this performance.

God, she wished it were only a performance.

Was Jonas dead already? Was she too late to help the others?

"If you ever want it, you'll make sure my people are alive," Parker said, and the edge leaked out of her. Left her feeling drained, her voice dull. "I'll come to you."

"How—"

"Jonas Stone," she said tightly. "Amy Silo. Anderson Williams, Drew Smith." One by one, she listed missionaries by memory. Men and women she grasped at random; whose names felt right on this list. "Alan Eckhart, Seth Miles, Elizabeth Foster, Peter Neely—" Fuck this. "*Every single one of my agents.* I want them freed, Doctor. Unharmed. If you don't, I'll destroy the serum."

"Wait! Those aren't—"

Wordlessly, Parker shut the comm.

The room spun.

Simon sighed from the doorway. "You can't leave well enough alone, can you?"

Parker's head jerked in his direction, but the damage was done. As Simon clung to the door frame, the world shifted out from under him, and he only knew it was too late.

Nothing he said would undo the pain he read underneath her twisted anger.

He let out a quiet, steadying breath. "I told you not to do anything stupid."

She blanched. Her features white, she dropped the comm as if it burned a brand into her palm. "I didn't think using your comm qualified." The excuse barely managed the volume of a whisper.

Simon braced himself, struggled to make sense of the room as it swayed in rotating spin cycle around him. The fact he was still naked didn't bother him.

Not half as much as it obviously bothered her.

Her gaze jerked up, cheeks red. Eyes wild. "What was the plan, Mr. Wells?"

He managed a smile, thin as it was. "Back to Mr. Wells, huh?"

"Don't you dare. Not now, not after *that*." Every word sliced through the air. Frozen, honed to a razored edge and flung at him with admirable precision.

He couldn't let her see how much he bled.

"Did you plan this with her? Did you tell the good doctor you were going to screw the Mission director to keep me out of the way?" she asked bitterly. "What's the big deal, you're dying, right?"

His heart wrenched.

Stupid, stupid move.

"It's not like that." Simon pushed off the door frame, forced himself upright and focused on her. The only thing in the room bright enough—*real* enough—to give him a beacon.

She couldn't know that.

"Then explain it to me," she began, and cut herself off with a savage, raw sound that didn't quite reach laughter. "Never mind. Don't lie. I saw the list, Mr. Wells. *You've* been killing my agents."

"Please." He strode across the living room,

managed to find the back of the chair. His hand closed over his jeans. He jerked the pants over one leg, struggled into them. "I've been killing *Salem* agents. I gave up everything to get *you* out safe. You heard her."

"Did you know I had the syringe?"

"No. But it's a sure bet Sector Three found out." Parker stared at him. "You've been reporting on me."

"I haven't." Patience fractured. So did the truth. But he couldn't tell her everything, not like this. He sucked in a breath as he pulled the jeans over his hips. The floor tilted. "Did you leave it at home, Parker? Is that why you won't tell me where it is?"

"It's *Direc*—"

Simon didn't let her finish. Leaving his jeans unbuttoned, forcing himself to move through the pain shattering his skull, he closed the distance between them.

Caught her hand as it flailed at him, seized her by the front of her blouse and forced her back. So fast, so savagely, that all she could do was stumble until her back slammed against the wall and the painting he'd already rattled crashed to the carpet. Wood splintered.

Simon panted, his heart hammering within the cage of his ribs. His fingers ached from the force of his clench around her wrist, pinned against the wall above her head, but he didn't care.

She wouldn't break. She'd promised him.

But he'd broken her, all right.

"It's not," he growled. "It's Parker. Parker fucking Adams, Church heretic, Mission traitor, dead woman walking."

Love of his goddamned meager life, for all the good that did her.

She jerked her hair from her face. Her cheeks blazed red, anger and something worse. Something hurtful and vicious.

Something betrayed.

Like he didn't see that coming.

"You can't—"

"Yes," he said, a violent growl over her, his fist clenched at her blouse collar. "I can."

Without giving her the chance to evade him, to answer him, he jerked her body off the wall and seized her lips in a kiss that would prove it.

He could. He could take from her this act of disobedience, could force her to confront the *real* reason she was so angry. It wasn't just the list. She knew as well as he did that he'd had plenty of time to kill her and hadn't. That the agents on that list were double agents, degenerating witches. It wasn't even the lie, although that didn't help.

What it was came on a groan so frustrated, so impatient and angry and torn, that it wrenched out of her chest. Even as her mouth opened under his, strained against his as if she'd climb into his mouth and wear his skin. Her free hand speared into his hair, fingers clenching as her tongue stroked against his in desperation; a need so intense he could practically taste it.

He'd gone and stolen something from her. Because he was an asshole and couldn't help but trade his useless, deteriorating heart for hers. And she hadn't even noticed yet.

God damn it.

His body responded even beyond the pain. He

pushed her back against the wall, but this time, as her back hit it, she dragged him with her, until he pinned her hips with his. Her chest flattened against his own, so right and so wrong and not nearly enough contact. Never enough.

Need and anger and regret all warred within him. He wrenched his mouth away, gasping for air. For sanity, for . . . God, for a chance.

No more chances.

Her eyes, dark and endless, opened. Shuttered. Her fingers loosened from his hair. "Let go of me," she ordered, so softly he almost could have missed the ice. Almost.

Even with her body straining against his, clothed against his seminakedness, soft and warm and everything he wanted, he knew he'd lost her.

No less than he deserved, anyway. He got his final fling.

But he still had to try. At least try to get her out of this mess, talk some sense into her.

"Listen to me," he said evenly. "And then you can do whatever you want."

Her jaw set, her lips, swollen from the brutal kiss she'd encouraged as much as suffered, gleaming damply. So beautiful.

Not his.

"I already told you how I was made," he said, but wearily. He couldn't help it. Last-ditch effort. "Mattie made damn sure that no matter what, we'd never live past a certain age, but she made a fail-safe. A fix."

Her eyes narrowed. "Why?"

"Because I think that she suspected even then that we'd become a problem. That her husband's in-

tentions would . . . change." His hand fisted against
the wall. "Juliet Carpenter was her attempt to re-
dress the wrong. It's one part DNA, one part . . ."
He shook his head, eyes squeezing shut against the
vicious clamp around his skull. "One part witchcraft. Juliet's power ties in to the fix."

Her eyes, vividly blue and somehow emptier
than he ever imagined, met his without reserve.
Without fear.

Without . . .

Well. He never had a right to expect anything
more than a few wild hours.

"I fail to see the relevance," she said, wrenching
at his grip.

"God damn it, Parker, I'm trying to explain!"
He glared at her, stared down at her too-white face
and felt like a fool. But he had to try.

She had to hear him. He had to make her understand. Had to.

"Juliet's name was Eve. If that syringe came from
Mattie, then it carries the Eve sequence. Don't you
see? You can't tell Kayleigh—" Her eyes flinched.
He verbally stumbled, caught himself and finished
grimly, "You can't tell her where it is. Tell *them*.
That sequence will give Lauderdale everything he
wants."

"He already has everything he wants," she spat.

Maybe. "But he doesn't have you."

He watched his words strike home—saw it in
the sudden way her nostrils flared, as if he'd scored
a hit. Drew blood.

So it wasn't fair. *Fuck* to fair.

He pushed on, doggedly. Desperately. "Mattie had the opportunity to give me the data. She

didn't then. Maybe she knew I wasn't ready to turn, not all the way. Maybe she knew the time wasn't right. I don't know. She killed herself instead." And it cost him to watch her do it. He couldn't do it again.

"How could the time be wrong?" The question ripped out of her; so much anger. So much pain. "How could it be *any more* right than before —" Her teeth clicked together so hard that he felt the aftershocks in her body.

Simon flinched. "If Lauderdale gets that code, there will be no stopping his army. Mattie wanted me to fix her mistakes, not add to them."

"All you want is that syringe for yourself," she threw back. "You'll say anything, Simon. Whatever your end goal is, you'll throw over anyone to do it. I'm not like you."

How could he make her understand? His fingers tightened on either side of her head. Spasmed with the force of it, of the wild storm of emotions unleashed under his skin. His heart.

"I know," she said quietly, her eyes bright. Too bright. Too many secrets too dark. "It's the only thing that can save your life."

"*Fuck my life.*" Her eyes widened at his near roar, and she wrenched her face to the side as if she'd escape him just by shaking his gaze. Simon wouldn't let her. Couldn't let her. Forcing her to face him, his fingers digging into her jaw, the side of her head, he met her furious gaze with his and growled, "It's not about my survival anymore."

"You're lying."

"Believe what you want, but I won't damn this city for your pride, Parker. Don't give them that serum."

Her lips curved, but there was nothing warm about it. "You already damned me. You damned the only people I *know* I can trust. Why stop there?"

The casual cruelty with which she flung the accusation carved a hole in his chest.

His grip loosened. As pain fractured his senses, he slumped, managed to brace his elbow against the wall beside her and didn't fight her as she slipped out from beneath him.

Leaning against the wall for balance, his forehead thudded against cool plaster. "It's too late, Parker. Don't do this."

She said nothing, but as he turned, grasping for support, he watched her collect her shoes. Her coat.

He closed his eyes. "Mattie killed herself so that I wouldn't have to."

Parker hesitated, hand on the doorknob.

"So that I wouldn't have to pull the trigger on my own mother, or lie about it to Laurence. He'd know. He owns us all, Parker. He made us, he monitored us, he fucking wrote the program."

Silence.

God, he hurt. All over. Inside, outside. Too much. "Now," he continued wearily, "he's made his move, half your team is dead or worse. I wasn't fast enough to keep up with the old man, and time's caught up with me. You can't fix this, Director." And for the first time, he couldn't bear to drawl the title.

The door opened beside him. Parker hesitated. Then, quietly, evenly, she replied, "I can't let them die."

"You can't save everyone," he retorted, pressing

his palms against the wall. "You can't even save me."

"Jesus, Simon. You wouldn't let me if I could."

Simon winced as the door shut, hard enough to send echoes drumming through his head. "You're wrong," he whispered roughly, knowing it didn't have a chance in hell of reaching her now.

The closest he'd ever get to confessing the chaos of emotions under his skin.

They didn't have time for this.

He didn't have time for this.

As he dug two fingers into his temple, his gaze fell on the comm she'd dropped to the floor.

That was it. He'd done his best.

Maybe he could tell that to Mattie in whatever kind of hell the devil reserved for people like them.

Slowly, every muscle aching with effort, Simon knelt to the carpet. He dragged the comm toward him, flipped it over and found the list. Skimming it fast, he cursed.

I can't let them die.

Stone, Silo, Williams, Smith—four people he knew weren't Salem Project agents. Four people likely to turn against the glut of witches in their midst.

Pawns. All of them, pawns to Parker's queen.

Devil take it all, what had Kayleigh done? He cleared the screen, input a number. It only thrummed once.

"Where the hell are you, Wells?"

"Why is Jonas Stone on the hit list?"

"I—What?" The word cracked. "He's not! He's not a Salem— Damn it, Simon, where are you?"

Fuck. *Fuck.* He pushed a rough hand through

his hair. Sucked in a breath and said grimly, "The director's in the wind."

"What?" Another crack. Another octave higher. "Wasn't she *just*— Look," she added sharply, cutting herself off. "You need to report back here. There's a lot happening. I— I need to talk to you."

"Yeah, I know." Simon studied the comm. "You get one question."

She sucked in a sharp breath. "This isn't a game, Simon!"

"Don't I know it?" He swayed. "Ask."

Kayleigh hesitated. Then, slowly, "Did you manipulate your records?"

He swallowed a laugh. "That isn't what you really want to know, is it, Kayleigh? Yeah," he added, humor fading just as fast. "Maybe one day, you'll find out why."

"Simon—"

"I did my part, kiddo. Now it's your turn."

"What the hell does that mean?"

He grimaced. "It means try to remember who your mother was." Because he'd done what he could. And it wasn't enough. Maybe Mattie's own flesh and blood could do better.

He didn't have it in him to try.

Kayleigh made a frustrated sound. "Simon, my dad has—"

He snapped the comm closed as the floor slid out from under him.

CHAPTER FIFTEEN

Amy Silo loved her job.

The Holy Order's library rivaled anywhere else she could think of. From the prettiest, richest penthouses to the wildest clubs in the lower streets, none of it compared.

A vast landscape of knowledge and learning, the library featured six floors of shelves filled with stacks upon stacks of books. She'd apprenticed here as a little girl, placed with the previous head librarian when the orphanage teachers realized how quickly she learned.

She'd spent her whole life in these walls. Knew them inside and out.

Silo lived in the top floor, a loftlike flat originally serving as an extra reading hall. Large windows overlooked the vista of the city, sprawled out in tiers beneath the highest tower.

The rest of the library tended toward thick, heavy red drapes and the dry, musty fragrance paper achieved once old enough. The lights were designed to be as natural as electrical lights could be, which kept the damaging daylight away from the pages and spines she and the staff maintained.

No book was less than fifty years old. And so many more were older.

Silo lifted a thick volume from the cart beside her. Its leather binding still gleamed, as unmarred as the day it came away from the press that created it. Raised letters under her fingertips glittered with faintly tarnished gold leaf, such a complete waste back in the day.

But so perfect, too.

Silo loved books. She loved the words inside them, the knowledge they imparted. The messages they carried, from the leanest pamphlet to the thickest encyclopedia.

She loved them for the same reason the Church didn't.

But she was happy here in the Holy Library.

She found the empty slot in the shelf for the book and slid it gently into place. She reached for another, smiled as the title caught her eye.

She'd read it fourteen times.

Silo liked books, loved the library, but that didn't mean she didn't pay attention. She knew a lot about the people who came here regularly. Director Adams was one. A good woman. A little overly focused on her job, but who wasn't in the Mission?

Though Silo was a missionary in the strictest sense of the word, she answered to all the leaders in the area. The bishop, Director Adams, Director

Lauderdale. Each had reason to send their people to her library.

All of them had reason to be watched. Carefully gauged. Reported if Silo sensed something wrong in the knowledge they sought.

To date, her own people requested more access to restricted areas than the Church.

But less than Director Lauderdale's scientists.

Change was in the wind.

Silo only hoped her library survived.

She shelved the worn book, somewhat more dog-eared than the others.

As she collected two more, she tilted her head. Her long, pale blond hair slid over her shoulder as she said, "It's still early. No one is here but me."

A footstep rasped behind her. A quiet, subtle click of metal. "Amy Silo?"

She shelved the two books side by side, a matched set. Tenderly, her fingers stroked along the neat row of dark spines. The dyes they'd favored in those days tended toward muted colors. Reds. Blues, greens, and browns. All darker hues. All gilded.

"Are you Agent Silo?"

She braced her hand on the shelf as she turned. "Yes," she whispered.

Silo loved the library. Loved the early mornings most, when the staff hadn't yet clocked in and she could work on whatever project fascinated her for the time. Shelving books, reading, researching when the Mission required something more.

She'd hoped to spend her life here.

She got her wish.

As the muzzle flare lit the interior of the fifth-floor archive, the report slammed into the thick drapes, the muffling weight of thousands of books. The Holy Library swallowed the sound of a body thudding to the carpet.

Blood and gobbets of gray matter splattered the colorful bindings. A wet, viscous spray that would have horrified the librarian whose skull it had once belonged to.

CHAPTER SIXTEEN

İt didn't make any sense.

Parker let herself in through her front door, the hair on the back of her neck prickling under the certainty that she was being watched. She had to be. There was no way Sector Three would leave her apartment unmanned.

Not unless Lauderdale assumed Simon would do his job.

Then it made perfect sense.

Parker swallowed the spike of anger, of tears. There was too much work to do, too many things to fix—people to rescue.

Please, let there be people to rescue.

The alternative was unthinkable.

Parker shut the door behind her, surveying the strangely neat living room. As far as she could tell, everything remained in its place. Which bothered her.

Wouldn't Lauderdale's people have tossed it? It's what *her* people would have done. No cushion unturned, nothing left to chance. Evidence mattered to Parker.

Maybe not so much to previous directors. Or to Lauderdale.

Sloppy?

Or a trap?

Parker leaned against her door, listening for a long moment. The rain had let up, leaving the roads wet enough to splash as cars drove by the complex. She could dimly hear the faint strains of movement—other tenants above and below preparing for their days.

Unaware that anything was wrong.

Beneath the subtle hum of the electrical grid and her own blood in her veins, everything was still.

No bell. No Mr. Sanderson to greet her.

Damn it. Had they let him out? Did they take him, did they do worse? Parker pushed away from the door, bit her tongue before she called for the animal that had been her friend for over a year.

The cat had been a designer castoff, that strange mix of white hair and blue eyes that all the genetically created litters seemed to throw once in a while. Parker didn't care. He was adorable; playful and lovable and a little bit grumpy.

And now he was gone. One more thing this whole mess had cost her.

Come on. Of all the things she could be worrying about, a cat should have been the least.

Parker glanced at the small table by her coatrack. Her coat still hung on the peg where she'd left it.

Every sense straining, she strode through her living room. "Mr. Sanderson?" she whispered.

Like it mattered.

"Kitty?"

No bell. No gravelly meow.

Parker wanted to cry.

Instead, firming her jaw against the ache building there, she turned and headed for her office. Her gun was gone, left behind in Simon's car, but her safe held a few extra things. Another gun, smaller but just as useful in a pinch.

The syringe.

But no extra identification.

As she input the code into the security panel, she barely kept from laughing. A little over a year ago, she'd considered developing a fail-safe—a plan in case things went badly. But she'd talked herself out of it.

Why not? She'd just made Mission director. What could possibly go awry there?

Such a fool.

"Not that it matters," she muttered.

And especially not now. Because as the door swung open, her gaze quickly cataloged the contents.

Gun. Jewelry. Documents. Cash.

No syringe.

"What the hell," she breathed. "What the *hell*." What kind of God did she piss off?

Quickly, she withdrew the small bag with her backup weapon inside. The zipper hissed free, and a nylon holster spilled out. The gun inside wasn't loaded. She fixed that, too, and slammed the safe closed.

She'd just run out of options.

Lauderdale had his sights on her missionaries. Her people. No matter how many of them had turned—if any of them had turned—she owed it to them to get them out. They deserved better than this.

That serum was her best chance. Now she'd have to scale back the odds.

Parker took a moment to lean against the wall, wincing as her body pulled in all the places she didn't want to think about now. The dull ache of her muscles only reminded her that she didn't *care* what Simon was doing.

She didn't care if he bled to death in that godforsaken safe house.

She didn't care if she lied to herself.

It was time to go. To her death, probably. But it was something.

Click.

She froze. Adrenaline pumped through her veins, heightening every sense to overwhelming acuity. She raised her gun, muzzle pointed at the ceiling by her shoulder, and held her breath.

Someone was here.

The ambience changed, in that so-subtle way of another presence nearby. Parker's eyebrows knitted as she strained to hear something, anything that would tell her who—or what.

Simon?

Something rasped in the living room, something clattered softly, as if the intruder had picked up an object and set it back down.

So her place was under surveillance after all.

Parker blew out a silent breath, seized her courage in both hands—right around the handle of her loaded gun—and stepped out into the hall. She pulled every footstep, tread lightly to the corner and flattened her shoulders against it.

Holding the gun to her chest, she squeezed her eyes shut, counted her pulse.

A voice, male, muttered something unintelligible.

Not Simon. She'd recognize his voice forever.

Say you're mine.

Never.

She rounded the corner, gun held at arm's length, grasp steady. "Don't move," she ordered.

Her voice cracked through the silence.

The man by her fireplace froze, a small frame in one gloved hand. His back to her, all she could pick out were his clothes—dark wash denim, a hip-length neoprene jacket—dark hair clipped short and styled fashionably back from his face, and gloved hands held up by his head. Lean, but not scrawny. Still, nothing like Simon's powerful athleticism.

Disappointment, painful and worthless, squeezed her chest.

She fought it down. "Who are you?"

"I'm going to put this down, okay?" The voice wasn't overly deep, not as clear as Jonas's tenor but youthful. Steady enough, even if it wasn't as cool as she would have expected from an operative.

A fresh recruit? Newly minted out of GeneCorp?

"Do it," she snapped, "and turn around. Slowly."

The frame clattered faintly against the mantel. Indication enough of his less-than-steady nerves. Score one for her.

She braced the gun, arms already starting to complain at the weight as the man turned. Sculpted features, smooth jaw. God, young kid. Maybe mid-twenties. Maybe less. He had a youthful charm about him, even as serious as his features were as he stared at her. Handsome, in a naturally charming way. He had the bad-boy look but none of the vibe.

His eyes were dark enough to nearly be black, and they met hers without fear.

Well, without too much fear.

Young enough to play at bold, old enough to know a bullet hurt. But not one of hers.

Her eyes narrowed. "I know you."

His grin, rueful as it was, revealed a dimple at the side of his mouth. "From the café. Yeah, let me explain."

Parker took two steps into the living room, but she didn't lower the gun. "Ten seconds. Talk fast."

"I'm not here to hurt you. My name is Danny—Daniel," he amended, fast enough that her eyebrow climbed. One part amusement, one part pity. He was taking her order at face value. "Everyone calls me Danny—"

"Streamline it, Danny." Parker gestured to the sofa with her gun. "Sit down."

"I'm not—" His mouth twisted, pride as far as she could tell. Following the line of her gun, he sidled over to the elegant piece of furniture. It wasn't the most comfortable thing in the world, but it was pretty and she liked it.

He sat gingerly. "Can I put my hands down?"

"Keep them where I can see them."

Slowly, he lowered his hands to his knees. His gaze slid to her gun, her face. Back to the door. Her gun, again.

"Are you expecting someone, Danny?" she asked pointedly.

"I'm not sure." Surprisingly candid. "I didn't expect you to come back here. I wonder if they would."

They. Her finger tightened on the trigger. "It's been a long twenty-four hours," she said evenly. "You need to get to the point. Who are you working for? Sector Three?"

"What?" He flinched. "No way! I'm not a witch hunter, either."

"Clearly."

"I'm here for something else. Someone else," he amended. He watched her for a moment, raising one hand to rub at his smooth jaw. "Look, I'm not here to fight with you or anything. I'm supposed to bring you to safety."

"Then why did you come after us in the café?" She watched her question arrow right between his eyes. He winced, tried to hide it, and only ended up scrubbing that gloved hand down his face.

"Yeah." The word crept out from behind his palm. When he dropped his hand, he looked tired, but nervy. Jumpy. "Okay, so, my name is Danny, like I said, and I'm acting on behalf of someone who isn't part of the Church."

"Who?"

"I can't—"

Parker crossed the room, close enough that he could stare down the barrel. "I've had a really, really rough couple of days. I'm tired, I miss my cat, and I'm pretty sure the next thing I do will get me killed. So you tell me how likely I am to shoot you down and get you off my back."

The blood drained from his disarmingly handsome features. "I know, I know, but I really can't say. She wants me to—I mean, you need to meet her yourself."

"Why?"

"I don't know!" He threw up his hands, fingers splayed. "Please, I'm just the messenger. You know you're not supposed to shoot the messenger, right?"

"What's her angle?" Parker demanded, ignoring the twinge in her chest that threatened to give in to sympathy. The kid was good. Just the right amount of charming.

Danny looked her in the eye. "Same as yours," he said. "We all just want to right some wrongs."

It smacked of truth.

But then, had she really been a great judge of character lately?

The gun wavered. Lowered slowly as she shook her head.

Of course she had. She'd pegged Simon the moment she'd met him, had read Mrs. Parrish's intentions within seconds. It wasn't her ability to gauge people that should be called into question.

It was her decisions after.

And now she had to make another one.

"I'm supposed to tell you something, but I'm going to reach into my pocket, okay?"

When she nodded her assent, he slid one hand into his inner jacket pocket. His eyes on hers, he eased the edge of something blue out.

Parker's eyes narrowed on the plastic case. It crinkled. "How did you get that?"

"Luck," he said, the word a sigh. "And one hell of a safe-cracking program."

Her jaw shifted. "I didn't write it," he said hurriedly. "For what it's worth, I'm really sorry to be violating your privacy like that."

He was too young for this. The real regret stamped on his features forced Parker to swallow her angry words. "But we ran out of options. I'm . . . It's an offering," he added sheepishly. "A show of good faith, okay?"

Her fingers closed over the case. When he let her take it, Parker lowered the gun to the floor.

Relief filled her. And with it, a wild curl of hope.

Danny visibly relaxed. "That's not our only offering," he said, slower now. Firmer. "You'll see when you come with—"

"No."

He flinched. "Aw, come on. Don't make my life difficult."

"I have to get to my agents."

"But they're—" His jacket beeped, three signals and nothing. Danny's eyes widened.

Parker raised the gun, but he didn't pay any attention as he clawed at the snaps of his jacket.

The comm he pulled out was smaller than the kind she usually saw. Not as sleek as the newest ones, but not standard, either.

"Oh, *balls*," he hissed. He stood, pushed away her gun with an impatient hand, and said fast, "We have to go. Like, now. Like, right fucking now!"

"Danny, calm down and tell me what's going on."

He ignored her platitude, grabbed her hand, and pulled her for the door. "If we're lucky, we can—"

They weren't lucky.

As Danny reached for the doorknob, the heavy

panel burst open. Slammed hard into the kid's face and sent him careening backward into her. She stumbled, tried to catch him as he collapsed in a tangle of his own limbs.

Two operatives darted through the door, guns drawn, masks firmly in place. Hers? She couldn't tell. They didn't register anything but professional training as one circled Danny and the other dropped a boot against his neck.

"Nobody move!"

Parker braced her arms, gun held tightly, but too late. As fear filled her, as adrenaline surged through her too-wired body and sent her stumbling backward, the other man in black body armor leaped at her.

She swung the gun like a golf club, reacting in pure anger, scared to death and tired of it. The metal caught the underside of the man's faceplate, cracked it up the center and sent him sprawling.

He didn't swear. Her missionaries would have sworn. They were only human, after all.

She spun wildly, made it two steps when thunder cracked behind her. It split through her eardrums, froze the blood in her veins.

But it didn't level her. Didn't even hurt.

The bullet wasn't aimed at her.

Danny.

Parker turned, her heart in her throat.

The man she'd hit grabbed at his mask, shaking his head as if she'd stunned him, but the other lowered his weapon from the ceiling. Plaster coated the carpet. Speckled white flakes across his black armor.

"Try that again," came the modulated voice

from within the other man's helmet, "and I'll put a bullet in the kid. Drop your gun."

Her gaze dropped to Danny, his face mottled beneath the pressure of the operative's boot. He clung to it, struggling to wheeze around it. "Go . . ."

"Drop it, Director."

What did she care? Danny was just some unknown agent. A soldier in this strange, no longer subtle war.

"Go!" he rasped.

Only Parker had never been like that. She couldn't start now.

She dropped the gun.

"Good," said the man. He raised his boot. Danny sucked in a gulp of air, red-faced, choking. "By the sanction of Holy Order of St. Dominic, you are hereby accused of being a witch."

Parker's mouth dropped open. "*What*?"

"No!" Danny struggled to sit up, but the operative casually backhanded him. He didn't change his gun to his other hand to do it. Danny's whole body rotated with the impact, slumping to the floor as blood gleamed on his lip.

The man with the broken faceplate seized her by the shoulder. "Payback's a bitch."

Her heart lurched into her throat. "No!" She twisted; his fingers tightened over her collarbone, bit cruelly. "Stop—"

She didn't stand a chance. The operative swung a fist wrapped around the butt of his gun, and her head rang like a bell, stuffed with fireworks and white-hot pain.

Her vision seared to red, white. And nothing.

If hell had a taste, it lived in Simon's mouth.

He didn't know how long he'd slumped on the floor, or what time it was now. He couldn't decide what part of his dreams were fever hallucinations, wishful thinking, or the torment of demons as he flashed from one hellish landscape to the next.

Degeneration at its finest.

Slowly, the skull-wracking pressure at his ears lessened. Sounds, real sounds, crept through pounding beats trapped in his head. The rhythmic rasp turned into the sound of his own breath, and a faint hum became the electric buzz of appliances, furnaces, more.

The world coalesced into focus.

His right hand vibrated steadily.

Simon raised his fist, squinted at the comm he'd clutched for who knew how long. Daylight streamed through the curtains, lit the blood-soaked carpet beneath him to vivid red and fading brown.

He was filthy. Saturated in his own blood. Tasting that metallic tang in his mouth and the salty remnants of the blood-laced mucus he hadn't managed to force down.

And the world still wouldn't leave him alone.

Every limb felt weighted with lead.

Groaning, he elbowed himself up, flipped the comm screen open. "What?"

"Simon? You're alive!" The voice fractured through the silence. Familiar . . . but strained.

Simon rubbed at his gummy teeth with the back of his hand. "Jonas?"

"Jesus, man, I've never been happier to hear your voice."

The raw relief in Jonas's weary tone forced Simon's attention to sharpen. To arrow on the screen. "What happened?"

"Before or after Neely tried to kill me?"

Jesus Christ. "Short version it, Jonas."

"There's been a coup. We're talking full-blown overthrow, man, secret police and all. Operatives I've never seen before have taken over the Mission."

Well, that wasn't a surprise. "Taken over how?"

"As far as I know, not a single bullet has been fired. Well, not up there, anyway." The analyst had a way of injecting verbal expression, and the grimace Simon heard hurt. "The one lodged in my leg probably doesn't count."

Why would they—Simon shook his head, hard enough to send the loose pieces of the puzzle clattering inside his thoughts. "Neely tried to kill you. Did he say why?"

"Nothing. Just, 'Come on up to see the director, Jonas!' and then *blam*. Lucky for me, someone was watching my back." A pause. "Your doing?"

"Jonas, I don't know what the fuck you're talking about." Simon managed not to growl it. He even somehow succeeded in a kind of calm.

But the shit had definitely hit the fan.

"Okay, okay. I'm in the feeds and I've been monitoring the broadband for hours." Keys clicked behind him.

And something new. A murmur, as if conversations happened around him.

Wherever the tech was, he wasn't in his van.

"It's bad, Simon," Jonas said seriously. "Mainstream media's all talking about a witch attack from earlier this morning. Not a word about the mess at the quad."

"Details," Simon demanded. "I need details."

"Right." More keystrokes, clicking through a brief silence. Simon squinted blearily. "The only thing I've been able to piece together is that a bunch of operatives in Mission armor showed up at the headquarters. General staff has been replaced—I dunno where they put 'em, but they aren't home. And, Simon? They got her."

"Her?" And then his brain kicked in. He straightened fast enough for his vision to swirl, but he clenched his teeth, forced himself to his knees. *Parker.* Where?"

"Chatter says they picked the director up at her place."

Fucking hell. She'd gone back. Why the hell would she go back?

Because that's where she stashed it.

"She was—get this—with an accomplice. Until about an hour ago, I assumed you were him."

"No." He growled the word. Who the hell had she picked up? What *him*?

Who was he going to have to murder?

He struggled to his feet, swayed. Damn, he felt like death warmed over. "Jonas, where are you?"

"With, uh . . ." He cleared his throat. "With a mutual friend, I think."

Simon slitted one eye in fierce concentration. Where was his shirt? Oh, right. The bedroom. The noise he made was noncommittal.

"Simon, uh . . . I have to say. You are one *bastard* of a conniver."

"Jonas, for the second time—"

"You've been stepping out on me."

"Oh." Simon padded into the bedroom, found his shirt where he'd discarded it. "That friend. Tell me something, Jonas."

"Yeah?"

"Is he really a friend?"

There was a pause. And then, very seriously, "You didn't know, did you? You risked it all on a gamble?"

Simon's smile lacked humor. And hope. "Yup."

"You manipulative son of a bitch." But it didn't sound like anger. Jonas sighed, the sound crackling through the frequency. "I don't know if friendship is the word, but there's at least a temporary kind of alliance. The ghost is damn pleased with the data-dump you handed over—through me, might I add. I'm patched up and alive when I should be smeared in an alley, and Neely's dead."

"Good enough."

"No, it isn't." There was an edge to that fine tenor Simon couldn't recall hearing before.

Then again, he couldn't recall much of anything at the moment. God, his head hurt.

He dug his thumb into one eye socket. It didn't help. "What?"

"How many people were you playing?" he demanded. "Who did you manipulate?"

"Everyone." A flat answer.

"Why?"

Simon was too tired to mince it. "Because Lauderdale's a psychopath, his daughter doesn't have the sense God gave a kitten, the bishop's a tool, your little witch team moves like goddamned molasses, and Parker's too fucking good to sacrifice on the bloody altar of Church politics." He took a deep breath. "And I'm fucking tired, Jonas, so what the *fuck* do you want?"

Silence. And then, in quieter tones, "I won't hold this against you on one provision."

Simon wasn't in any sort of condition to make promises. Jonas didn't wait for him to agree.

"Director Adams—I mean, Parker." Even her name sent a shaft of anger through Simon's gut. And something worse. Something he didn't deserve. "You're right, there. She's a good woman. Get her out of this."

"I plan to." And as the words left Simon's mouth, bypassing his brain entirely, he knew he meant it. Anger or no. "They'll take her in to the jails. You have access to your usual stuff from there?"

"Sort of," Jonas replied, but slowly. As if he wasn't sure. "At the very least, I can figure it out fast."

"Good." Simon collected his boots, dropped them by his pile of clothes. "Get me the whereabouts of every known missionary on the roster."

"Easy." Keys clattered, but as the pain faded from Simon's head, he realized it wasn't the same sound he'd gotten used to in the past two weeks. Different keyboard. Different tone.

He hoped to hell the man was in good hands.

"The orders went out about an hour ago. All missionaries are directed to muster topside."

"Fuck." Simon stabbed the button to transfer the call back to the smaller speaker, raising it to his ear. "This is not good. It's too soon."

"Too soon for what?"

"They've moved on the whole Mission. Okay,

Jonas, listen to me very carefully. We need to know who the hell is on our side and where they are. You need to make this happen."

"Done."

"Are you serious?"

"As a bullet," he replied, but his voice strained. "Parker had me working on it days ago. Simon . . . Man, I have to tell you. The only reason I'm trusting you now is 'cause you saved my life."

Simon frowned at the bedroom. His eyes settled on the rumpled bedcovers. The bloodstain he'd left on the sheet.

Saved Jonas's life? Not intentionally.

"You may have *risked* it, but I think I see what you're getting at."

"Fine." Simon spoke over him, and didn't realize until he'd started that he borrowed a note from Parker's frigid repertoire. "Get to those missionaries, get the word out."

"What should I say?"

"Your call, Jonas." Simon turned his back on the bed. And the memories made there. Too late for that.

He had one more shot at this. It had to start with a shower.

"Hey, wait. There is one more thing I can do."

Simon would take almost anything. "What?"

"If you can get her out, then I can get you safe."

Simon stepped into the bathroom, made a face at his reflection—he looked like shit with a serving side of raw meat. "How?"

"I know a few people." Cryptic as hell. "And I'm told we'll have a certain amount of, um, sanctuary. So I'll be in touch as soon as I can pinpoint them."

"Better find a different comm. It's only a matter of time before they lock you down from mine," Simon warned.

The tech's crystal laughter labored, but the smug edge to it made Simon shake his head. "It's me," he said lightly. "Already got it covered. You go get Parker."

At this point in the game, Simon didn't care about anything else.

CHAPTER SEVENTEEN

Parker's eyes opened slowly.

Lights. Stifling silence. The strange, clinging filaments of her subconscious faded to bleary awareness. Of pain. Of uncertainty.

Of restraints.

She raised her head, bit back a groan as her neck muscles cramped with the effort.

Damn, she hurt. The dull echo in her head slammed in time with her heart, centered right over her left temple. If this was the kind of headache Simon battled, her sympathy had just ratcheted up by about a thousand.

"Good. You're up."

She squinted through the light, testing each limb cautiously. "In a manner of speaking."

"Brilliant." Kayleigh Lauderdale stepped into Parker's field of vision, her hair pulled back into a high ponytail and her features set into grim lines. She'd forgone the suit this time, settling for gray slacks and a cap-sleeved blouse in butter yellow, but she carried her ever-present digital reader in one arm.

"Do you know the date?" She caught Parker's face in her free hand, held it straight. Searching her eyes. For what?

Brain trauma, probably. Parker managed a thin smile.

She knew where she was. Where they'd tied her up and dropped her.

The interrogation cells in the Mission weren't elegant things. Plain gray walls, plain gray floors. Typically one chair, and whatever else it took to get the job done.

Parker didn't pretend not to know what kind of confessions unfolded in rooms like this. And now it was her turn. She occupied the only chair, and a heavy table beside Kayleigh was the only other piece of furniture.

Parker blew strands of her hair out of her eyes, wincing with the effort. Her temple throbbed steadily. "I hear I'm accused of being a witch."

A flicker. The doctor's eyes narrowed. "Whatever it takes to get the quarry in, right?"

"Wrong." Parker jerked her face away from the woman's grip, her tone sharpening. "That's the difference between a good director and a bully with a mandate."

"And you're a good director?"

"No." Parker's smile edged. "I'm an accused heretic strapped to a chair in an interrogation room with the daughter of the man who just betrayed the Mission."

The digital reader dropped to the table, a clatter that echoed sharply through the small room. "Let me be clear," Kayleigh said, her voice tight. "You're obviously not a witch. Your blood lacks all the markers."

"Obviously," Parker replied coolly. "But the public wouldn't know that, right?"

"Exactly the point."

"Bully." Parker's mouth twisted as she met the woman's fog-blue eyes. They narrowed again. "This isn't the first time your people have screwed with lab results, is it?" The woman had the grace to look away. "I knew it."

"I knew you'd figure it out."

Small comfort. "I trusted you," Parker said quietly.

"No," Kayleigh retorted, raising her chin. "You never did."

And how. "So you tell me why my Mission is now in your father's hands."

The woman stared at her. "You have a lot of confidence for someone tied to a chair, Miss Adams." She pulled the reader closer to her, flipped it over, and keyed it on. "How long have you been working against the Church?"

Parker almost laughed. "Are you serious?"

"You've been stealing classified information," the doctor said, dragging a fingertip across the screen. Parker watched her, the set to her shoulders and rigid line of her back.

Kayleigh didn't want to be here.

Well, great. Neither did Parker. So what?

"Where is the Wayward Rose folder you stole?"

Parker raised a spiteful eyebrow. "What's wrong? Your pet not checking in with you?"

"He checked in," she snapped, clearly stung, "but he says the folder was stolen from him. Did you arrange that?"

"Arrange . . . ?" Parker couldn't help it. Her laugh broke on a sudden, painful surge of disbelief. Of . . . of pain so deep that it twisted all the way inside her heart.

He'd never said a word. Hadn't once indicated that he hadn't turned in that folder, hadn't even hinted that someone else had taken the data.

Who?

She had one guess. And if they were interrogating Danny now, Parker wouldn't be the one to turn him over.

"Did I *arrange* to have my home watched around the clock *just in case* Simon ever broke in to steal from me?" she queried, weary humor strained to the point of breaking. "Don't be ridiculous." Exhaustion filled her; resignation.

Regret.

She bent one hand back as far as she could, quietly testing the manacles locked around her wrists, but nothing so much as shifted.

Think, Parker.

"You aren't a missionary, Dr. Lauderdale." Parker strove for calm. Forced herself to breathe—through the fear, the anxiety riding her chest. The anger. "You're a scientist. Why are you here?"

The woman looked up, her pale brown eyebrows furrowed. "Do you even understand that this is your funeral? Do you get the importance of this?"

"Yes." Parker raised her chin. "I absolutely do. Sector Three has officially taken over the Mission, marrying the two in a monopoly that gives your father the run of the Church. Nobody has to answer for anything now. Not for crimes committed against innocent people on the streets—"

Kayleigh's jaw set.

"—or for crimes committed against innocent people in classified labs," Parker finished flatly.

"My father isn't like that."

"Salem Project."

Kayleigh's mouth tightened. "So you do know the details."

"Of course I know," Parker replied evenly. "How many of my agents are Salem witches in uniform? Are any of my people still mine?"

"What?" Kayleigh shook her head, bemused. "Of course they're yours, all but the few Salem subjects seeded in." She hesitated. "Were yours."

Parker stared at her. Studied the line of her mouth, the deep grooves at each corner and the furrow at her brow, and barely restrained a laugh. "You don't know. You have no idea what your father's been up to, do you?"

"It's not like that," Kayleigh replied sharply.

Such an echo of Simon's denial earlier, shades of his inflection. Parker wrenched her shoulders. Winced as the restraints pulled. "Then explain what he's doing."

"I don't have to explain anything to you. You're a prisoner."

"Oh, for God's sake, Kayleigh!" Parker's chair creaked as she leaned forward, but she couldn't go far. "Your father has been ordering innocent people—my agents—to be *murdered*. Don't you think that matters?"

Kayleigh stepped forward, her fists clenching. "No, he hasn't!"

"Then why was Jonas Stone's name on your list? Where is Amy Silo?"

Kayleigh's mouth compressed.

"The only people standing between you and the active witches in the city are on that list you sent to Simon. What do you think'll happen when we're all gone?"

"My father," the woman replied, drawing herself up indignantly, "is going to save this city. He's not *murdering* anyone."

"Hannah Long," Parker spit out, knowing the names wouldn't mean anything to the doctor and desperate to try anyway. "Jonathan Fisher."

There. A flicker of an eyelash. A twitch. Guilt.

But Kayleigh shook her head. "Those aren't innocent people, Parker. They're subjects. Property of Sector Three."

Parker's mouth fell open. And as rage slid like poison into her calm, shattered it completely, she strained at her bonds. "*Subjects,*" she said from between her teeth, lips peeled back. "He's killing people, but it's okay, because they're just *subjects.*" She spat the word. "You and Simon . . . Oh, God."

"I don't—"

"You were working with Simon the whole time?"

Kayleigh flinched, but her shoulders squared. "Simon owes us his life!"

"Simon owes Matilda Lauderdale his life," Parker shot back. She blinked hard as Kayleigh reeled back. As if Parker had slapped her. A button?

A chink in the girl's armor.

"Your father didn't make Simon. Matilda did," she pressed. "She's Simon's donor. I bet he didn't tell you that, did he?"

Red climbed into the doctor's cheeks. Her eyes crackled, filled with ice. "That's enough," she whispered. "Simon isn't— He's just another—"

"What? Test subject? Sure. One that carries your *mother's* genes."

White-faced, Kayleigh took a step closer, fists clenched. Parker didn't care.

This wasn't fair. It wasn't kind.

But she wasn't going to get anywhere with kind.

And hearing Simon's name come out of that pretty mouth only dragged Parker's sympathy further into the muddy depths of her anger.

"Simon's your half brother, regardless *how* he was born," she said, disgust twisting every word. "But it doesn't matter, does it? He's just a *subject*."

The door swung open, and one of the men in black armor stepped inside behind Kayleigh, sans helmet.

Parker's gaze flicked to him. Stubbled chin, square features, plain. Determined.

Cold.

No memory of his face. No visible tattoo.

"We're going to try this again," Kayleigh said, summoning a thin calm. She didn't bend, didn't crouch. Nothing to make the angle easier on Parker's neck as her eyes darted back to the doctor. "Why did you steal the Wayward Rose file?"

"Because your operation risked my agents' lives, and I wanted to know why." The truth might not set her free, but what did she have to hide?

Kayleigh's eyes widened, her arms folding over her chest. "Curiosity? You risked everything for simple *curiosity*?"

"No." Parker's stare shifted to the man. His pale skin was freckled, but there wasn't anything kind about the rigid line to his features as he watched her. "I risked everything because this kind of internal warfare destroys people. Someone was abusing his power."

"My father—"

The operative shifted.

Parker's glare jerked to Kayleigh again. Pinned with every scrap of anger and loathing and, hell, with fear she felt. "Your father is involved with witches, with the Coven of the Unbinding, and with human testing."

Kayleigh paled. But her jaw set. "You don't know that. He wouldn't ever deal with witches." When Parker only stared at her, incredulity warring with pity, the woman flinched. "I mean *actual* witches!"

"Dr. Lauderdale—"

Parker spoke over the dark-haired man with glacial emphasis. "Open your eyes, sweetheart. Your father is *butchering* people."

Crack! The pain of Kayleigh's slap was nothing compared to fierce satisfaction at breaking the woman. Parker's head snapped to the side, cheek burning, but her teeth bared in a hard, angry smile.

The man grabbed Kayleigh by the arm, pulled her physically aside. "Dr. Lauderdale, let me handle this."

"I can—"

"It's important," he insisted. "Go wait in the viewing room. Now."

Parker watched the conflict on the woman's face. For a moment, a flicker, that sympathy stirred as anger and uncertainty warred with pride.

But it wouldn't last.

For all Parker's bravado, she knew she had no proof. Nothing to force Kayleigh to see what Laurence Lauderdale had done.

Would do.

Kayleigh herself had access to all the proof she could ever need, but the bond between father and daughter was a strong one. She'd never look.

Parker closed her eyes.

"I can handle this," Kayleigh said quietly.

"No." The door opened, and Kayleigh huffed something indignant as footsteps scuffed across the floor. "View from there if you want, but this is Mission business now."

"What? You can't be ser—"

The door clicked shut. Locked.

Parker's smile faded, leaving behind a knot of fear, anger. Anxiety and resolve. She opened her eyes as the operative approached, his blue gaze empty.

"You're a good little tin soldier, aren't you?" she asked, but wearily. "So what part of all this do you come from? GeneCorp? Lauderdale's pet projects?" Her wrists ached, shoulders mirroring the strain.

Shortly, this would be the least of her problems.

The man reached for his belt, withdrew a foot-long tube. It didn't look like much, but she knew it for what it was.

The Mission used it for interrogations often.

Sweat bloomed across her shoulders.

"Make this easy on yourself," the man—the missionary?—said as he thumbed the switch. A faint hum filtered through the stifling room.

Every fine hair on Parker's arms lifted.

"Who else did you talk to about Sector Three?"

"So you can kill them?" she demanded, but it shook. "Please."

"What did Simon Wells tell you?"

Her teeth clicked together as the man crouched in front of her. "I don't tolerate anyone putting my people in danger," she said, forcing herself to sound as calm as she didn't feel. "Lauderdale will regret this."

"What information did you have Jonas Stone pull off the mainframe? Who did he send it to?"

That got her. She frowned. "What are you talking about?"

The man studied her, head tilted. "Jonas Stone was in touch with someone else at the time you first ordered him to find the data. We have logs. Related, you met with an informant recently at his behest. Who was it?"

Logs, he'd said. As in . . . "You tapped my comm?"

He didn't bother to answer. "He gave that data to someone else. Who?"

Phin Clarke. It had to be.

The electric prod hovered. Her skin crawled. "Where did you get that syringe?"

She clenched her eyes shut. "Go to hell."

Simon strode through the Mission lobby as if he owned it.

Three guns leveled on him.

One lifted. "Let him pass." It seemed telling that most of the Salem Project operatives Simon had met were men. He knew women were involved—hell, fully a third of the subjects were female—but Laurence Lauderdale didn't seem to share Simon's appreciation of the gender.

He nodded to the men guarding the front entry. "Where's the party?"

The man he knew only as Jones—like Simon and the rest of the lost souls the Church took in, the name had been given—jerked a thumb down the hall. "Interrogation rooms. We've rounded up most of the resisting missionaries, but there's a few still insisting we've got it wrong." He shouldered his gun, tilting his head. "You were supposed to bring that woman hours ago. Where the hell were you?"

Simon raised an eyebrow. "Trying to locate her sources," he returned evenly.

The man frowned. "Sources? More rebels?"

Rebels. As if they'd earned the right to call themselves some kind of standing army.

For Christ's sake.

Turning his back, Simon strode in the direction the operative indicated—although he didn't need the help. He knew where the interrogation cells were.

Putting Parker in one didn't promise a happy fucking ending.

He couldn't run. Every alarm in his body screamed at him to haul ass, kill every last bastard in the room and shoot a few more for emphasis, but he couldn't do that, either.

Everything depended on him.

Her life, anyway.

The rest was a lost cause.

His head hurt, but at least he was clean. More or less. He stepped into the elevator, hit the right button, and waited as the motor kicked in. The Mission elevators rode smoothly, and he was acutely aware of the security camera in the corner.

He schooled his features into something mildly impatient. Mostly indolent. The same mask that had gotten him through years of training in Sector Three.

Funny how Parker hadn't responded as well to that mask as she had to the man he was inside.

His heart thumped hard.

He couldn't be too late. They wouldn't kill her this fast, they'd want her information first. See what she knew, who else she'd told.

Maybe, after all this was over—if they survived the day—she could forgive him the pain he'd caused her.

And maybe her cat was a magical tooth fairy.

His fists clenched as the elevator slowed. The doors opened, a subtle whoosh of compressed air, and two heads lifted on either side of the hall.

Two guns followed.

More operatives. More faceplates.

And a hall full of cells.

"Where's the doc?" he asked, strolling out of the elevator as if he had every right to be there.

"Operation number," barked one.

Simon didn't bother moderating his sneer. Curling his fingers into his collar, he yanked the fabric far enough down to reveal the seal of St. Andrew imprinted in his skin. And beneath it, the bar code.

They'd both have similar.

Both guns lowered. "Some shit, huh?" the first man asked.

Simon couldn't tell if he knew them. The helmet modulated the voice too much, and neither said anything to suggest they knew him.

How many men had Lauderdale hoarded away?

Christ, how many facilities besides Simon's birthplace still functioned?

"Yup," Simon drawled. "Some shit. Where's Dr. Lauderdale? I've got a report for her."

"Two doors on the left," the second man said and tucked his gun behind him. "Don't go sticking your nose anywhere else."

Simon grinned. "No, thanks."

He made it three steps, squarely between the two, when a scream—muffled, female, and ragged—ripped through the hall.

Neither of the men so much as twitched.

Parker.

"That's three," said the first man. "Pay up, John."

"Son of a bitch."

Simon didn't think. Didn't even hitch a breath as he reached out beside him. The man digging in his pants utility pocket strangled on a curse as Simon wrenched his gun around, hauled the man backward with the strap and fired a semiautomatic burst in a wide arc.

It almost drowned out Parker's screaming.

The bullets slammed into the wall, tore plaster and paint into ribbons. Impacted the operative with rounds too big for armor to completely stop. He staggered back, blood flashing, smeared on the wall behind him.

Simon spun, wrenched the gun to his side. The second operative stumbled, struggling to disentangle himself from the strap, and met Simon's fist with his faceplate.

The tempered plastic cracked.

So did Simon's fist.

Swearing, teeth gritted as waves of pain radiated through his hand, Simon let the man drop to the ground. The gun collided with the man's side.

Within seconds, the semiautomatic was pointed at the operative, and he scooted farther away, crab-walking awkwardly.

The gunfire would have triggered an alarm somewhere, must have gotten attention. The interrogation rooms weren't soundproofed.

Prisoners listened to other prisoners scream. Sometimes, psychology did the rest.

The operative glared through his cracked faceplate, sights leveled on Simon. "Who are you?" he demanded, a strange amalgam of real voice and fuzzy computer filter.

Simon smiled. Even through his pain, humor licked at the black edges of his rage. "I'm a missionary."

The operative froze as the weapon's cartridge hit the floor at his booted feet.

Simon knelt, retrieved the dead guy's weapon.

"You can't—"

"Let me repeat myself," Simon cut in, and this time, there was nothing amused about it. He tucked the stock into his shoulder, stared at the man on the business end.

And felt nothing.

No sympathy. No shared past.

No mercy.

"I hunt people like you."

"Please—!" Bullets splattered through the linoleum. Through his armor.

Simon dropped the weapon as he stepped over the twitching body. Metal met sticky floor, but he didn't hear it. Didn't care.

Dead was dead.

And as Parker's screams filled the hall, his head—his worthless heart—he palmed the Colt from under his shirt and kicked open the door.

The observation room was dim, but the speakers feeding the events inside the deeper interrogation cell told him everything he needed to know.

Kayleigh's arms folded on the counter beneath the wide glass window. Her face was hidden, but her shoulders shook soundlessly as Parker's screams shifted to panting gasps for air.

"Who are your fellow conspirators?" a man demanded.

Parker sobbed for breath.

"This can all end." The man in the window bent, laid a hand on her shoulder. "All you have to do is tell me who you worked with. Who's your informant, Miss Adams? Who brought you the syringe?"

They had it already.

He should have been pissed. He should have felt something else, something more, but all he felt was elation. She was alive.

Her face tear-streaked, mottled red and white, Parker shook back her tangled hair. "Go to hell," she said between clenched teeth, with the exhaustion— the strain—of someone who'd said it already.

Many times.

The man sighed.

Kayleigh muffled a sob as Parker's scream crackled through the speakers once more, courtesy of the electrical prod applied to her side.

Simon sighted down his weapon's barrel. "End it, Kayleigh."

She shook her head.

"Kayleigh!"

When she stood, the chair flew backward. Clattered to the opposite bank of electronics so hard that it briefly drowned out the sobbing pleas in the window behind her. She clutched both hands to her chest, knuckles white. "I can't! I can't— This isn't what I was told."

Simon's jaw hardened, points of pain in his back teeth. "Look at me."

Fingers clenched, Kayleigh turned. Tears streaked down her cheeks, caught at her bloodless lips. Her eyes shimmered, impossibly fractured.

Hurting.

His grip on the gun firmed.

She wasn't hurting nearly as bad as Parker.

"Do you get it now?" he demanded. "Do you see the truth?"

Her gaze dropped.

"Why do you make it so hard on yourself?" came the reasonable tones of the interrogator.

"I don't understand what's happening," Kay-

leigh said, chin quivering. She looked at him. Back
at the window as the man circled Parker, slumped
forward in her chair. Kayleigh closed her eyes. "All
I ever wanted to do was find the Eve sequence. Fix
what my mother tried to."

Disgust rose like a venomous tide. "Instead, you
let yourself do your father's dirty work."

"It's not dirty w—"

Simon took a step forward, murder in every
screaming nerve.

Kayleigh paled, bone-white as she sank to the table's edge. "Please," she whispered. "He's my father."

"And blood is thicker than water, right?"

"Yes!" And then she jammed a hand against her
mouth, shaking her head. "N-no, I just—"

He shook his head, sickened by the truth he read
in her eyes. Just like her father's. "I'm not your
blood, Kayleigh. You come from *him*." He lowered the gun, unclipped his comm, and keyed in
a stroke. The list appeared. "Your inability to see
the truth isn't my problem. Right now, Parker is.
So you have a choice."

She met his eyes, flinched at what she saw there.

"Get out now, and start running. If you're good,
you'll make it to the mid-lows before everything
really goes to shit."

She looked down at her clenched hands. "I
can't."

"Then you stay here," he said quietly, every syllable a violent promise. He threw the comm to
the table in front of her. She flinched as it cracked
against her reader. "And you suffer the consequences with the rest of them."

CHAPTER EIGHTEEN

The current tore through her side, electrical teeth shredding, ripping, tearing. Parker screamed until she didn't have a voice left, words piling up in her head. Her throat.

Words of blame. Names, places.

Anything. God, *everything*. Just to make it stop.

She clenched her teeth around them.

When it finally ended, an eternity later, she sobbed wildly, panting for air, twisting against her restraints. Everything hurt, her skin itched, as if it wanted to sizzle off her bones.

Sucking down oxygen, Parker let her head hang. Her hair covered her face, a tangled curtain to hide her tears.

She could do this.

As her body shook uncontrollably, Parker knew she couldn't.

Danny. Her missionaries. Were they going through this?

Her interrogator shifted.

"Stop," she pleaded raggedly. "Stop . . . You have— You have what you want. Why?"

"One little vial of goo isn't enough," the interrogator said. He crouched, pulled aside her hair with a gentle hand. Kindness filled his eyes; so sincere. So sympathetic. "Just give me some names, and this will all be over."

Over, sure. Terminally over. And then this same torture would be inflicted on anyone she coughed up.

Names she desperately wanted to give.

A sob wrenched itself free. Fear clawed through her throat, seized her heart. As her gaze fell on that black prod, she shook her head. Over and over.

It was all she could do.

She screamed, hysterical even before the current touched her skin.

Thunder cracked; maybe it was her head. Her resolve. As her will crumbled, the current suddenly ceased. She sobbed, for breath and for the men and women she knew she couldn't save.

Couldn't even begin to know how.

"Please," she croaked. It broke. "Please . . . no more. I'll—" Her ears ringing, she raised her face.

Two men struggled in the small room. Simon.

Simon was here?

Her sob wrenched his head around. His eyes burned, wild and hopeless and filled with so much rage.

The interrogator lunged at him, tackled him hard into the wall. The prod came around—Parker screamed as it gouged into Simon's side.

He jerked, cords standing out in his neck as his body writhed and twitched. A strangled, hoarse scream locked in his throat.

She stared, every muscle shaking.

He'd come back. For her?

For the serum?

It didn't matter. He'd come back, and now that pain—all that agony and torture and horror—filled him.

She couldn't stand to watch it. Tearing at her restraints, the chair rocking, all of it—the fear and anger and, oh, God, the love—came out of her in a shriek. "*Simon!*"

The interrogator's head whipped around.

Simon wrenched to the side, fell toward the gun dropped from nerveless fingers. In seconds, the space of a breath, he whipped it around, teeth bared as he hissed out a painful breath through them.

"I'm here," he gritted out.

The gunshot ricocheted through the small room. Loud enough to slam through her eardrums, to shred the last ounce of resolve she had left.

Parker flinched, sobbing wildly. She yanked at her wrists, unable to force her body still—the restraints tore at her flesh. She couldn't stop. Couldn't sit still as the report faded into sudden, overwhelming silence.

But for her tears.

Warm, firm hands caught her cheeks, framed her face. "Parker. Parker, you're okay."

She opened her eyes. Met Simon's raw, desperately searching gaze.

Thank you, God.

Her smile hurt. "Fancy . . . meeting you here."

She sucked in a shuddering breath as her vision turned black at the edges. "Mr. Wells."

"Stay with me." He pushed back her hair with trembling fingers. "Damn it, Parker, don't you pass out on me."

She winced faintly. "Not," she mumbled, but knew she lied.

The void sucked at her consciousness—sweetly empty. Promising nothing but peace.

She wanted peace.

"Parker!"

Her restraints gave way, but she didn't have it in her to hold herself up. She slumped forward, couldn't even bring herself to brace for impact with the cold floor.

She fell into warmth instead. Simon's arms banded around her, one hand speared through her hair, tucking her head against his chest.

His heart hammered beneath her ear. An ethereal beat, rapid and solid and *real*.

"Don't do it," he ordered roughly, his arms tightening. He sank to the floor, held her as she fought to remain aware.

She had to tell him.

He didn't have to die.

"Stay with me," he whispered, gut-wrenching intensity. His voice shook. Were they still in the cell?

Of course they were.

Parker's fingers tightened in his shirt.

"I'm sorry. I'm so sorry, sweetheart," Simon rasped, every word low and painful as it filtered through his chest, thrummed under her ear. She shuddered. "I thought if I could get to Mattie first, if I could get that serum first, everything would be fine. Then she died, and everything . . . everything changed. I didn't count on *you.* I never counted on—"

His voice broke, his large hand tightening at the back of her head. Parker inhaled, took in his scent, the tang of blood and sweat.

The sterile fragrance of the Mission cell.

"If I could do it all over again," he whispered against her hair, "I'd tell you everything from day one. *Fuck* the consequences."

Her fingers opened over his chest. His heart. Bracing herself, she struggled to sit up. To raise her head from his shoulder and meet his eyes. They glistened, roiled in a sea of so many emotions that she couldn't pick out just one.

With trembling fingers, she cupped his jaw. "You're here."

"Always," he promised roughly, seizing her hand and drawing her fingers to his lips.

Something inside her chest turned over. Something stronger than she thought she could be.

She jerked her hand away. "Why the hell are you *here*? Simon, you're—"

The observation room door slammed open.

Simon moved so fast, the world tilted in a blurry spiral. One minute, he'd held her upright—the next she found herself tucked behind him, pressed to his broad back as two men spilled into the room.

They froze at the sight of Simon's gun pinned on them.

Parker's eyes widened. "Simon, no!" She lunged around him, grabbed Simon's arm to the side.

Bald head glistening with sweat, Alan Eckhart whistled a wavering, three-note tune—a questioning slide. He kept his hands up, a gun held in one and pointed to the ceiling. Unlike the operatives, he wasn't dressed in Mission armor. His worn jeans and T-shirt had seen better days. "You scared the hell out of me, ma'am." His eyes slid to Simon. Hardened. "Are you all right?"

He wasn't asking Simon.

Simon's arm twitched in Parker's grasp. She held on tightly. "I'm fine," she said, summoning every last ounce of calm she had left. She couldn't lose it, not in front of them.

She wiped her face on her sleeve.

"Those fuckers," the second man seethed. Seth Miles, lacking his fedora, his youthful face lined with anger. "Those motherfucking sons of—"

Parker's smile was faint, but she managed. "Okay, Mr. Miles. That'll do. What's the status?"

Eckhart didn't move, his gaze on Simon. "What's with him?"

"He's with—" *Me?* She caught herself. "With us." Slowly, she let go of Simon's arm, but she watched a muscle leap in his jaw.

"Are you sure?"

"She's sure," Simon growled. He hadn't moved, but he didn't step aside, either.

Miles looked at Eckhart. Then at her.

Parker swayed.

"Ma'am!"

"Touch her, and it'll be the last thing you do." Simon didn't bother raising his voice. Instead, he curled an arm possessively around her waist, angled himself to support her without breaking eye contact with the older missionary.

That three-note tune fractured on a sudden

snort. "All right," Eckhart said and stepped aside. "There's about twenty of us left."

"Us?" Parker repeated, her stomach knotting. "Did they kill the others?"

"The *fuckers*." Miles, anger evident in every syllable. Every breath.

Eckhart put a hand on his shoulder, but he met Parker's eyes. No fear, no reticence. "Some killed in the fight. Silo, Williams, and Smith were murdered ahead of time. We got out with Stone's help. The rest . . . um. Well, most don't work for *you*, ma'am."

"The fuckers," Parker breathed. Because anger, because grim humor, beat the pain of betrayal. She'd known. She'd suspected long enough to get used to the idea, but no amount of speculation softened the reality.

She'd worked hard for the Mission. All of them. And only twenty remained?

At least she'd been right about Eckhart and Miles.

Simon's grip tightened at her waist.

"Most of our agents are waiting in the cells," he said as Parker shook her head. It wouldn't clear, not completely.

Too much juice in those damned interrogation prods.

She clung to Simon's side, her fingers tight in his shirt as she struggled to focus on the missionaries.

Miles bent at the Sector Three man's side. Checked his pulse.

"Can we free them?" Simon demanded.

"Only if we get to the main computers," Parker said before Eckhart could. "We need a plan."

"We need to get you out," Simon countered.

She stiffened. He didn't let her go. "I'm not—"

"He's right." Eckhart wiped his arm across his forehead, his weary gaze calm as it met hers. Held. "Ma'am, we've got no love for Sector Three. If we can keep you out of their hands, anything else we do is gravy."

"I agree," Miles added, rising. His jaw, much less square than Simon's but edged, set. "Those bastards can't have our director."

Her eyes burned.

"You just get her out," Eckhart said over her, his gaze flicking to Simon. "Long as she gets safe, there's a chance the rest of the city'll hear about this."

She expected Simon to argue. To throw out a plan, demand obedience.

Instead, his hand tight at her waist, he looked at her.

His expression softened.

"Consider it done," he said quietly. Implacable as hell.

"Good." Eckhart glanced up, then jerked a thumb back through the viewing room door. "Because we have maybe two minutes before the distraction team makes a mess."

Parker disengaged from Simon's hold, forcing her knees to lock. The world dipped, but she braced one hand against Simon's arm. "What distraction team?"

"They locked up a handful of the analysts together," he explained.

"Foster came up with the idea," Miles added.

"They're down in the server room wiring things to overcharge."

Simple, but effective. Parker hesitated.

Despite Simon's glower, Eckhart reached over and touched her arm. His grizzled features softened. "They know the risks, ma'am. We all do. Let us help you out."

Parker stared at him.

Simon shifted. Stepped away, his gaze on the door.

As if he were giving the missionaries time. As a unit.

A team.

Miles folded his arms awkwardly over his chest, rocking back on his heels. "You helped us when we needed you most, ma'am," he said. More than a little sheepishly. "After Peterson."

"You kept us running smooth and you knew when to look the other way." Eckhart touched his forehead, a kind of salute. "None of us saw this coming. But we're damn well going to see it end."

"We're going to need you, ma'am."

Simon looked back over his shoulder. "The elevator's coming. Six people inside."

Parker studied the mid-low missionaries. She didn't have to try too hard to remember their files. Good men, fine agents.

Extraordinary people.

She nodded. Once. "All right. Both of you have Jonas's frequency, right?"

"Yes, ma'am."

"That's your link to the outside." She took a step, wobbled as her muscles cramped.

Miles caught her arm. "We gotcha."

Yes. They really did.

Let's move it."

Simon glowered at the small group, his gaze settling on the grip Miles had on Parker's arm. But he didn't say anything.

She needed the help. More, she needed to understand that her people—the good people—respected her.

Always had.

That much he'd never doubted.

Behind him, the elevator light blinked. He didn't know what was coming, only knew six shapes filled that shaft. Given the ruckus, he'd bet armed soldiers.

Miles led Parker out first. She followed, but her face lifted as she passed Simon. Grim, worried.

He touched her cheek gently. "I'm right behind you."

Eckhart studied him as Parker hurried down the hall, Miles protecting her flank. "Go," he ordered.

"I can—"

"Just fucking go, Wells," Eckhart ordered dryly.

Simon did. The agent followed.

All of them knew the layout of the cells. They moved as fast as Parker could, and when her legs gave out for the third time, Simon holstered his weapon and scooped her into his arms.

"I can walk," she snapped.

"No, you can't," Simon replied. The fury locked behind his thin veneer of calm trickled out through each word.

Parker stilled.

"Let me do this," he added, striving for something less violent and only partially succeeding.

"Time." Eckhart touched his shoulder; a warning tap. "In three . . . two . . ."

Simon braced himself.

On cue, the walls shook as something detonated somewhere in the quad. Plaster crumbled from the ceiling, floated like snow through the hall.

Whatever silent alarms he'd triggered earlier, they erupted into full-blown sirens. Alarms triggered throughout the complex. Warnings flared.

They ran like hell.

Parker clung to his shoulders, her face white, hair dusted with plaster. His muscles burned, but he followed Miles's lead to the far end of the hall.

Gunfire erupted behind them.

"One way out," Miles yelled. The stair exit was wired for alarms, but it didn't matter now. He kicked the safety bar, slammed the door open.

Voices echoed from above. Shouts and warnings.

"Move it!"

They made it down half a flight, Eckhart behind Simon and Miles in front, before the first bullets cracked through the echoing stairwell.

Parker twisted in his grasp. "Give me a gun!"

"*Shit*." Miles ducked, turning to return fire. Shadows filled the space between the landings. Muzzle flares lit up the gloom.

"Hurry." Eckhart pushed Simon, slammed his weight into Simon's back hard enough that Simon half dropped Parker. Her feet hit the stairs and she grabbed the railing, wrenching herself out of his hold.

"Damn it, I can walk!"

Bullets pinged off the metal stairs. Voices shouted orders, swore.

Simon looked up.

Blood glistened on the railing beside Eckhart's white-knuckled grip. His eyes met Simon's over Parker's head. Steady.

Resigned.

"I'll hold them off," he said through clenched teeth.

Simon unholstered his gun, fired off two more shots. He'd only have three more, at this rate. "Eckhart, move!"

"No." He sank to the stair, lips white with strain. As he turned, his T-shirt darkened. Red licked through the fabric, a gory stain at his back. "Get her safe, Wells. That's a fucking order."

"Alan?" Ducking low, Parker clung to the railing. "You're hit!"

Simon nodded. Once. "I will."

"You better." Eckhart's smile stretched over teeth suddenly bloody.

Fuck. He'd been hit somewhere vital then.

"Go!"

Simon bent, grabbed Parker as she tried to push past him.

Footsteps tromped over the stairs, clattered and thudded. For a brief moment, the gunfire ceased.

It didn't matter. Simon's senses told him exactly how many operatives filled the stairwell. Too many for them to handle.

Too many to assume they'd be taking prisoners.

"We can't leave him," she cried.

"Go," Simon snapped as Miles watched, transfixed with horror. With anger and grief.

He knew.

Hell, Parker knew.

There wasn't anything to do for Eckhart now.

Simon bent, threw Parker over his shoulder and followed Miles down the stairs. She grabbed Simon's shirt for balance, propping herself up.

As they sprinted down the stairs, gunshots riddled the landing behind them.

Parker twisted, too hard for Simon to hold. He cursed.

She hit the ground on her feet, wobbled, but caught herself against the railing. White-faced, blue eyes too brilliant, she set her jaw and faced forward. "Let's go."

Miles didn't bother to hide his tears. "Yes, ma'am," he said tightly.

They ran like hell itself burned at their heels.

As smoke filled the stairwell, Simon knew it did.

CHAPTER NINETEEN

The alarms wailed, adding to the cacophony as Miles pushed out into the underground lot. The air remained clear, but lights flashed on every pillar.

Parker resisted the urge to cover her ears. It wouldn't help.

"My car is down here!" she shouted.

Miles shook his head. "Impounded," he yelled back. He looked . . . Well, he didn't look much better than she felt. Drawn, hounded.

Behind her, Simon shut the door, jammed his now empty gun into the handle.

"How do we get out?" Miles asked.

"You don't know?" When Miles only shook his head helplessly, Parker caught his arm. Squeezed in whatever silent reassurance she could give.

"Parker, hot-wire something," Simon ordered. "Miles, get her out of here."

Her head snapped around. She whirled, eyes wide as she stared at Simon's implacable features.

He wasn't looking at her. His gaze pinned somewhere beyond them.

Toward the Magdalene Asylum, on the other end of the lot.

He wouldn't.

"Where are you going?" she asked.

"To even the odds. Miles," he snapped.

The missionary flinched.

"Stop it!" Unthinking, panic rising like a tide, overwhelming even the memory of pain, Parker grabbed the front of Simon's shirt. Jerked him closer, hard enough that seams popped. "Don't you dare. Don't you *dare* commit suicide on me, I won't let you."

He covered her hands with his, but his mouth tightened. "I'm not out to kill myself."

"You *liar*." Parker's fingers twisted into his shirt.

Behind her, Miles tucked his Colt into his belt. He walked a little distance away, peering at the cars parked closest. As if he could give them space.

As if their voices didn't echo between the sirens.

She ignored him. "If you're going after the syringe, I'm coming with you."

Simon's eyes banked. "No, you aren't."

"You can't stop me."

"Miles—!"

Parker slammed her fist into Simon's chest. Hard enough that he cursed. That her knuckles cracked. "Don't look at Miles," she ordered icily. "Look at me. It's my fault that serum has vanished, it's *my* fault Kayleigh Lauderdale has it. My responsibility, and I won't have you dying for it."

Rage lit like a fire in his eyes. Simon let go of her hands. Reached up, grabbed a fistful of her hair and gritted out, "The only end for me is death. Don't you get that? Either I die getting the fucking syringe or I die without it, but I'm not giving them the key to an unstoppable army."

Her scalp pulled, neck muscles tight, but Parker didn't care. She stepped closer, stepped into him, until her body pressed against his and he had no choice but to soften his grip or cause her real pain.

Tears filled her eyes. "That serum is worthless without you," she whispered.

"I am worthless without that serum." Slowly, his fingers opened. Gentled. His palm cradled the back of her head. "I'm going to die, Parker. One way or another."

"Then be man enough to look me in the eye when you do."

Simon stared at her.

Behind her, Miles cleared his throat. "I've got a car," he offered, embarrassment mingled with the strained tone of a man who knew shit rode hard behind them and didn't dare ruin a moment.

She knew that feeling.

Her whole world rested on this single second. Suddenly trembling inside, her heart hammering in her ears, she opened her mouth to try again. To ask him, beg him. "Simon—"

She didn't get the chance.

He dragged her closer, forced her to her tiptoes. Her eyes widened.

"Fucking Christ," he said, dragged hoarsely out of him by some force she couldn't see. Couldn't understand. "I love you." Lowering his head, he claimed her mouth, covered her lips with his. Caught her completely by surprise.

But not as much as his words did.

Not as much as the rough, almost desperate way he kissed her.

Reeling, Parker stumbled as Simon pulled away. "Okay. You win, sweetheart." He glanced at Miles, arm curving over her shoulders. "Let's get out of here."

The missionary pointed to a boxy blue sedan. "That way."

Where's my daughter?"

"She checked into Lab Seventeen ten minutes ago."

Laurence Lauderdale studied the ribbons of smoke wafting up from the Mission-side quad. One hand tugged at his earlobe, twisting the wrinkled, malleable flesh as a window shattered. Sirens wailed, Church staff scurried like ants below, and he blew out a hard breath. "What's the word down there?"

Behind him, Patrick Ross adjusted his thick glasses. "It's still too early to count losses, sir, but the systems array took heavy damage. Not every prisoner's been accounted for."

"What about Adams?"

"Still not clear."

Lauderdale grunted, turning away from the window to glower at his assistant. "Keep a close eye on that situation. I want Adams found, you hear me?"

"Yes, sir."

"Will this cause delays?"

Ross raised the digital reader, a gesture that echoed Kayleigh's studious habit, and scanned whatever it was people like him kept on those technical things. "Maybe," he finally said. "I'll know more as the shipments arrive."

Damn it. Lauderdale sank back into his chair, shifting his bony weight into the padding as it creaked. He reached over, twitched the computer keyboard closer, and stared blankly at the monitor as he cycled through the options.

Adams was a threat. A real one. She knew more about the events in the quad than anyone else outside of this room, and if she was half as clever as Lauderdale suspected, she'd be long gone in the chaos down below.

"Sir?"

He glanced up, narrowed his eyes at Ross. The kid was young, bright. Studious. Sharp as glass.

Twice as transparent.

But he had that spark, that verve Lauderdale needed to succeed.

He tapped the reader. "I'll get press releases out to every news feed. If Director Adams is out there, she won't get two feet without seeing her face on a wanted line."

A real go-getter. Laurence allowed himself a smile. "You're a good boy, Patrick. Get it done. And hold all my calls for the foreseeable future."

"Sir?"

"I've got meetings to schedule with Bishop Applegate." *We deeply regret Parker Adams's defection . . .*

"What about your daughter, sir?"

"She has plenty to keep her busy," Lauderdale

said, already picking out keys with halting care. "She can wait."

"Right away."

The door closed. A muted thrum rocked the walls as another set of windows blew out across the quad.

Rest assured, we're doing everything in our power to restore order.

Nestled in his pocket, a small comm vibrated. He pulled it out, opened it between arthritic fingers, and pressed it to his ear. He said nothing.

He didn't have to.

"Green across the board, sir. One more trip into the trench, and we'll be all set."

Media queries have been handled, and I will continue to ensure that no stone is left unturned in the search for the traitors.

Smile widening, Laurence Lauderdale closed the comm, disconnecting the line, and tucked it back into his jacket pocket.

I remain your humble servant . . .

"Just as I said, Mattie," he murmured, squinting at the screen. "Everything's just as I said."

I win.

Miles handed Simon a key. "There's three other safe houses I can check." His voice dragged through Parker's doze, forced her awake. "Not every missionary reported in by the time they moved on us."

Parker stirred, exhaustion clinging to her like a black fog. After twenty minutes of dodging and weaving through the topside streets, the sound of the rain on the car hood had lulled her into a kind of doze.

Now she blinked blearily as Simon turned around in the front seat, bracing a hand on the driver seat to look at her. "Wake up," he said. Gently, for all that he'd gone back to implacable again. "Time to get moving."

She straightened, rubbed her face. "Where are we?"

"One of the safe houses we've got set up," Miles replied.

"How safe is this one?" Simon hunched, studying the luxury complex through his window. Rain hammered at it, colored everything inside the car in eerie light-patterns of gray and blue.

Miles ran his hand over his short hair. Impatient. Uncertain. "It's as safe as we can get. This one was pulled off the Mission roster, but the cleanup techs haven't been in yet to strip it. We've got maybe a day or so before they come knocking, but it's the best we've got for now."

"Good." Simon opened the car door, slid out and bent, one hand on the hood. "Get somewhere safe. Get a new comm and contact Jonas."

The missionary's smile twisted. "Will do."

Simon shut the door, opened Parker's, and didn't let her even try to stand on her own. "Hey, I can walk," she protested.

He ignored her, sliding one arm under her legs and the other around her back.

Miles watched silently in the rearview mirror. His eyes reflected the same heaviness, the loss and anger and helplessness, dragging at her every breath.

Every thought, every replay. Even while she'd

dozed, she'd watched it unfold. Over and over, and always with the same outcome. She'd failed.

"Be careful, ma'am," Miles told her.

Simon pulled her bodily from the interior. Rain splattered against her head, her cheeks—refreshing after the blood and bullets and icy sweat that was all she seemed to be able to think about.

"I'll take care of her." Simon slammed the door on Miles's faint, rueful smile.

Parker frowned, too tired to struggle. "That was rude."

"He's a big boy," Simon muttered, and shifted her weight.

Maybe she should have insisted he put her down. He looked drawn and ragged, the gaunt hollows under his cheekbones more pronounced. His jaw set in razored lines.

Instead, unable to summon the strength, she wrapped her arms around his shoulders and let him carry her through the gated lobby.

Topside didn't believe in low-key motels or modest appointments. The place reeked of money.

As a rule, the Mission frequently changed safe house locations. After they pulled a place from active roster, a cleanup crew would step in—stripping the location of all extra Mission security and tech.

Most of the time, topside safe houses went unused. There just wasn't as much need in the higher streets for them.

As Simon located the suite—this one on the second floor—and unlocked the door, she nuzzled her cheek into his shoulder and took a deep breath.

She was out. She was free. But how many loyal agents remained behind?

How many people had been sacrificed?

Her fingers tightened in his shirt.

Simon shut the door behind them, locked it with one hand. It allowed her legs to swing down to the floor, but he didn't let her go. Instead, one arm curved around her back, he pitched backward. Thudded his weight against the door and dragged her closer.

As if she were a touchstone, he held her close; clung to her with both arms—a cage of flesh and bone. His cheek rested against the top of her head as he took a long, shuddering breath, echoing her own.

Tears filled Parker's eyes. Knotted in her throat. "Oh, God," she managed.

It broke.

"I know." Simon's arms tightened; crushed her against his chest. Held her as the tears worked out of her chest on a ragged sob. "I know," he whispered into her hair. "Crack, Parker. It's okay."

She didn't want to. She had so much riding on her shoulders. So many things to fix.

It didn't matter.

Parker wept, burying her face into his shoulder. She clung to his shirt, cried as if the world had ended and grief was all she had left. It filled her to overflowing, poured out of her in gasping, wild sobs, until she couldn't breathe anymore and his whispers couldn't penetrate her sorrow.

Tears for Alan Eckhart, for Silo and Williams and every slain missionary. Tears for the way things used to be—for the ideal of the Mission, for the people she'd tried to protect from the witches cultivated by the same organization she'd defended so strongly.

She sobbed for Danny, for the names on that list. For Jonas, who'd only done as she'd ordered and became a criminal.

For Simon, dying every day because she'd been *so stupid*.

And he held her. Simply held her, one hand rubbing her back, the other cradling the back of her head. Supported her when her knees gave out, sank with her to the floor and rocked her—whispering reassurances, soft and tender.

Parker cried until she had nothing left to give.

Empty, aching with the force of her own grief as it dulled to a blunt edge, she listened to the silence. To the beat of Simon's heart, slow and steady. His breath.

When he stirred, threading his fingers through her tangled, damp hair, she flinched. "I—" What could she say?

"You don't have to explain." Simon turned his head, pressed a kiss to the top of her head that she felt all the way to her bruised soul. It warmed. At least a little. "You're only human, Parker Adams."

At a time when she couldn't afford to be.

"I should have done something with that syringe," she said bitterly.

"You couldn't have known." His fingers traced her cheek. "You sure as hell couldn't give it to me."

"Why not?"

"Because I'd have handed it right over to Kayleigh," he replied, brutal honesty. "Anything for the cure."

Slowly, every muscle aching with the effort, she braced both hands against his chest and leveraged herself upright.

He didn't let her go to do it, forcing her close enough that she couldn't avoid his gaze. Searching. Exhausted, but so . . . so intent. So focused on her that she looked away.

She didn't know what she needed. What she wanted.

All she knew was that she wanted him to give it to her. Even after everything he'd done.

"Then," he admitted quietly, his hazel eyes shadowed. "Now, I'm not sure I wouldn't do the same."

"To be fixed?"

"No. Yes," he amended with a small shake of his head, "but only so that I could live with you."

I love you. He'd said it then.

Did he mean it? Did she believe him?

She studied his features, reached up a hand to cup his cheek. "Simon." He covered her hand with his, warm against his stubbled jaw. "When were you going to tell me about everything?"

"I wasn't."

Too much honesty in one go. "Not even about the ghost?"

He froze under her weight. "How did— ?"

"I didn't." She sighed. "But Danny came from somewhere, and there's only one other player who hasn't shown his hand yet. For what?" Her fists clenched against his shoulders. "That kid, Simon—"

"Don't. Don't go there. We all made the choice to play the game."

The floor buzzed.

Parker jumped, but he only shifted enough to reach under his stained thermal shirt and unclip the comm. His eyebrows pulled together, features knotting as he studied the frequency framed in the small screen.

"What are the odds?"

She shrugged, fatigued to the bone. "I don't think even Sector Three would try to locate you by comm," she said, weariness dragging her voice down to a murmur. "If they are, just get off the line in under sixty seconds." Or they'd trace him.

Right now, she was too tired to care.

The revelation, one more in a stream of them, just didn't matter anymore.

As the unit vibrated insistently, he flicked the case open. "Who is this?" He didn't bother to raise the unit to his ear.

The line crackled to life. "You must be Simon Wells."

Parker slumped, shaking her head as he raised an inquisitive eyebrow at her. She didn't recognize the voice. Throaty, somewhat dry, she thought it carried a feminine slant, but she couldn't be sure.

"Yeah," he replied. He straightened, gently maneuvered Parker off his lap. Shifted away from her.

She let him stand without comment, letting her head fall back against the door.

"You can call me May." A woman, then. The voice on the frequency turned sardonic as she added, "As I'm not dead yet, it's preferable to being called 'the ghost.'"

Parker's eyes popped open. "You have impeccable timing."

"So I'm told." May's tone was brisk. "Hello, Parker. You've caused quite the stir. I'm glad you're safe."

Simon glowered at the comm, fingers tense around the case as he held it in front of him. "What do you want?"

"Want?" The tone changed. Turned abrupt. "I want to be sure that you know what you're getting into while you still have time. Can I call you Simon?"

"I don't care what you call me," he said tersely. "I know exactly what I just did, and I want something in return."

What he just did? Parker covered her face with both hands. "You conspired with Jonas, didn't you?" Simon glanced at her. Nodded, once.

May hummed a note of agreement. "The information you sent me is invaluable, you know this. And I rather owe you one for that stunt with the Wayward Rose folder."

Simon's teeth flashed in a grimace. "That was you?"

"One of mine," she allowed. "So if I can help, I will."

"Simon," Parker whispered, a knot forming in her stomach. She struggled to her feet, elbow planted on the door for balance, but he didn't look at her.

Didn't do anything but tense his shoulders. As if braced for a fight.

The woman—the ghost—sighed. "Simon, you didn't tell her, did you?"

"I didn't have to." *Yes, he did.* Parker glared at the back of his head as he added, "She figured it out."

"Good," May said, amusement ripe on the line. "Parker, I understand you expended considerable resources to find me. That young man, Jonas, is unbelievably good."

"Not that good, apparently." But she couldn't summon the strength to meet May's forthright tone with anything but wrung-out emptiness. "Is he okay?"

"He's fine," May countered firmly. "He had me on the run as often as I had him."

Simon looked up at the ceiling, a muscle ticking in his cheek. "Could you—"

"No," Parker cut in. It hissed out of her, poked at the last embers of an anger she wasn't sure she had it in her to feed. "I want to hear this."

Silence filtered through the line, cut with the occasional crackle. Static. Then, it clicked. As if May tsk'd. "Very well. The short version, okay? I've been tracking the Church's interests for a *long* time. It's taken me years to find what Jonas cracked in days, but once he did, I was able to put the pieces together."

"How did you get to Simon?"

"Through Jonas," she replied. "Through his tech, anyway."

Simon's shoulders jerked. A semi-shrug. "If anyone could find the serum, it'd be Jonas or the ghost. I hedged my bets."

"You stuck your thumb on the scale," May retorted sharply. "I've been watching Jonas's incoming transmissions for a while. Simon struck me as a . . ." She hesitated. "A likely source of unrest."

Parker winced. "This *whole time* I refused to move against you for fear of what Sector Three would pull on the Mission, and you've been the traitor. Do you know how that makes me feel?"

Simon said nothing, his features sliding into stone-faced determination.

May's sigh crackled. "He's not the only leak, Parker, but I want to make something clear. You couldn't be expected to see this coming."

"Bull," Parker began, only to flinch as May's voice sharpened to a serrated edge.

"I've been doing this longer than you've been alive, my girl. I bank my life on secrecy, and rest assured, Laurence Lauderdale is the same." Her tone gentled. "Listen to Simon. You were kept in the dark on purpose. The fact you managed to wiggle out what little you did is a testament to your dedication."

And her stupidity. She turned her face away. From the comm and its disembodied voice, from Simon. Gathering herself, summoning what energy she could, Parker pushed off the door and paced carefully through the foyer.

"Give her time," May added behind her, but not for Parker's benefit. She swallowed a laugh. It only hurt her chest anyway.

"The Lauderdales have Matilda's last formula," Simon said behind her.

He followed her. But at a careful distance. She didn't need to look to feel his eyes on her— weighing, considering. Wary.

"That means they have Eve's code. Shit." The coarse word seemed out of place in May's dry voice. "And you?"

Simon hesitated.

Parker fell into the sofa, its shimmering violet upholstery cool against her skin, and dropped her arm over her eyes.

She knew what May asked.

What Simon didn't want to say.

"The same," he finally replied. "Where's Jonas?"

"Safe."

"How safe?"

"*Safe,* Simon, I promise you. He's being taken care of, and his wounds will heal a lot quicker than anything else he's gone through."

To Parker, listening to the exchange, it sounded very much like the two bargained over something. This for that, each a give and take of information and assurances.

How long had he been in bed with Sector Three, the Mission, *and* the ghost?

Was there even room for Parker?

"I assume you have a plan?"

May's chuckle rasped. "Of course, boy. Not that you'll like it."

"At this point, I'll take what I can get."

Parker lowered her arm. Sat up with a deep breath. The living room swam into focus— beautiful gray plush carpet, dove gray walls set off to perfection by accents of purple. Someone had decorated this apartment with flair and taste.

All it was missing was a white cat.

She was all cried out.

Simon leaned against the sofa behind her. As if reading her mind, somehow tuned in to her thoughts, he curled his fingers around the back of her neck, thumb digging into her corded muscles, soothing the ache there.

"The roads are all blocked," May was saying, her tone once more curt. "The sec-comps are on high alert and you'll never make it down through the checkpoints. You're trapped topside for now."

Simon's fingers stilled on Parker's neck. She couldn't see his face behind her, but his voice flattened. "Bullshit, we are."

"The media is plastered with your pictures," May informed dryly. "The Church has gone public with . . . Let's say a *version* of the truth, and it paints you both as the perpetrators of a coven conspiracy. You're the most dangerous thing to hit the wanted boards since—" She paused. "Ever, actually."

His fingers tightened. And deliberately let go.

Parker reached up, caught his hand in hers before he could draw away.

She didn't look at him still, not sure what she hoped to see.

"No one's going anywhere," May continued. "But that's good, because it gives us time."

"Time for what?" Parker demanded, turning her head to study the comm.

A beat. May sighed. "Time to rescue my grandson. Rest for a few hours. I'll contact you again soon. Simon, find a new comm."

"How will—"

"I'll find you," she said over Parker's question.

The line went dead.

Parker stared at it. At Simon's hand, slowly lowering. Her gaze slid over his bruised and abraded knuckles, over the wiry muscles of his forearm. His shoulder, his chest—broader at the shoulder, narrow at his waist.

Until her gaze met his. Locked.

So many questions.

"She reached out to me after Wayward Rose," he said. Quiet. Cautious. He didn't move, as if afraid to spook her.

She watched him, afraid to move, afraid to tip the balance. To send herself spiraling into someplace dark and angry and . . . and alone.

Her fingers clenched over her knees.

"I didn't know her name, or that she was even a she. Just a message, and a frequency." As he spoke, his voice roughened. Developed a low urgency; reflected the same resolution in his steady hazel eyes. "Worst-case scenario, I screwed the pooch. If that happened, I needed a way to bring it all down."

"She was your way? The hacker?"

A short, jerked nod. "I sent instructions to Jonas. I knew . . . he . . ."

"Had doubts?" It took effort to keep her voice even. To keep it from shaking.

"And files. Lots of files," Simon admitted. "I knew he stayed in touch with Silas Smith and Naomi West."

Her eyes narrowed. "Silas Smith is—" *Dead.* A shudder rippled up her spine. Spread outward, carrying anger with it. Disbelief. "Of course he's alive. No body, no evidence . . . Why didn't I see?"

"Because people made damn sure you didn't," he said hoarsely. But his eyes banked hard; filled with something brutal and raw. "You're a first-rate director, Parker. Nobody doubted that. You lead and people follow because you're steady and strong. But you're too fucking good for the politics."

Her laugh twisted.

Simon dropped the comm. It clattered to the floor, skidded under the couch as his foot clipped it. He rounded the end, sank to his knees in front of her, his fingers curling around her upper arms. Bit hard.

"I'm sorry," he said, bleeding intensity.

"It's not enough." She twisted. "It's not enough, Simon!"

"I know." He let her go with one hand, cupped her face. His features twisted, mirroring the anger, the shame and hurt and everything tangled up inside her own skin. "God, I know. I thought I could play you, that I could use you to end this nightmare. I never expected—" He let out a breath. A hard exhale.

Slowly, as Parker stared at him, her heart suddenly pounding a staccato rhythm, he framed her cheeks in both hands.

"I love you, Parker."

Her chest tightened.

"Somehow, you got into my head and under my skin." His fingers shook, but he didn't look away.

She couldn't. No adrenaline this time. No bullets, no madness to blame.

Trembling, she reached up. Traced his lower lip with the tip of her index finger.

His dark lashes closed, veiled the sudden spark in the depths of his eyes. A golden edge. "If I only had more time, I'd change everything for you. But time . . . time is a commodity I don't have."

"Why didn't you tell me?"

"You're too upright for this shit. If I said anything, if I trusted you, you would have gone toe to toe with Lauderdale."

"I could have made a difference."

"No." Fear, stark and so alien, filled his features. "He doesn't play by rules, Parker. I would have lost you before I ever had the chance to—"

Her heart broke. "Stay," she whispered. He

bowed his head, forehead resting against hers. "Stay long enough . . . I . . ."

"I'm a dead man. I've got nothing to give you. Just this bank of lies."

Slowly, she reached up, interlaced her fingers with his at her cheeks.

His eyes opened. So dark, raw with everything he wasn't saying. She didn't have to hear it.

She knew.

It wasn't okay. Nothing was okay. Her world had gone upside down—everything she thought she knew had turned into a lie.

But this? This, at least, was real. "Let me, Simon. Let me love what's left."

His fingers tightened at her cheeks. Groaning, he tilted her face up, slanted his mouth over hers in a kiss that lit the last remaining cells in her body to a warm glow.

CHAPTER TWENTY

Love. Against all logic. All *reason*.

She loved him.

What a fucking tragedy.

Simon drew back, giving her the space she needed to breathe. To think without him mucking it up—he knew already how easily she reacted to his nearness.

"Think about this," he ordered. He rose to his feet, exhaustion plucking at his muscles, at his head. His radar pinged subtly, but it always did.

Nothing important. Not yet.

He'd have to stay on it. Risk the degeneration he could feel biting at his heels with every breath.

Parker's lips curved into a faint smile. Tired, but real. She caught his hand as he turned away. "I don't have to."

"You're tired—"

"Not that tired."

God damn, the woman had a wicked edge. She stood, lifted his hand to her lips. Brushed his fingers with a gentle kiss.

It had the opposite effect of what she probably intended.

The sweet gesture ignited. Burned a path from knuckles to gut to dick.

Maybe he wasn't that tired, either.

Simon reached out, caught her by the waist. Before she could deny him, he had her over his shoulder, true caveman style, and strode for the bedroom.

It took him two tries to find the right door, Parker protesting every step.

"Last chance," he half growled, lust knocking through his every nerve. Firmly, his hand came down on the soft swell of her ass. Not enough to hurt; just a swat, a warning.

She bit back a cry that didn't sound entirely like indignation. "Simon!"

His palm caressed the spot, rough on her jeans. "Going once . . ."

She struggled to leverage herself upright, hands flattened at his back.

The bedroom was nice enough. Rich enough, anyway. Simon didn't spare more than a glance for the trappings. The bed was large and looked soft. That's all that mattered.

"Going twice," he added and dropped his squirming burden to the mattress.

She bounced, laughing, hair streaming copper and gold in the rain-muted daylight spilling through the windows. Her cheeks flushed. Hurriedly, she kicked off her shoes.

"Sold," Simon said huskily and caught her ankle

in one easy hand. She gasped as he dragged her
back across the mattress, hooked his fingers into
her waistband, and made short work of the front
snap on her jeans.

"Wait!" She pushed at his shoulders, her eyes
wide, bottomless blue. "Simon, no, I—"

"No waiting," he growled, peeling the denim
over her smooth hips. Down her legs. God, she
smelled like heaven.

Like the sweetest drug.

He wanted. He'd always want. Until the day he
died.

Fingers tight at her waist, he pulled her to the
edge of the bed. Knelt on the floor, a man worship-
ping his goddess, and buried his mouth between
her legs.

Parker moaned.

Music to his ears.

He knew what she liked. What really turned her
on. He wasn't sure either had the energy for it, but
he didn't care. It wasn't about the words. The per-
ception.

It really wasn't about her. Not this time. It wasn't
about playing her, seducing her.

Simon feasted at her wet flesh, dragged his
tongue along her swollen cleft and tasted the only
reality that mattered. She loved him. She wanted
him. The way she arched as he laved at her, the
way she panted his name, all of it reached deep
into his heart, his soul, and set something on fire.

He'd make this work.

No matter what, Simon would protect her, love
her, until he had no choice but to leave her.

His tongue speared between the folds of her body,

earning a shuddering grip in his hair as she grasped at something, anything. He smiled against her flesh, tilted her hips just so and licked again. And again. Dragging the softness of his tongue against her clit, thrusting it into her, over and over until her hips twisted and writhed and she wailed as she came.

It wasn't about her. It was about *them*.

"Please," she gasped. "Simon . . . I want you."

"Not too tired?"

She shook her head, hair tossing around her flushed face.

Simon rose, running his thumb across his damp mouth. She was so beautiful. Her fragrance would haunt him long into the grave.

This time, she didn't stay where he put her. She rolled to her knees, fumbled to help him with his jeans. He laughed softly, divested her of her blouse and bra as she struggled with his pants. Somehow, together, they shed the rest of their clothes. Stripped away the barriers between them.

Somehow, Simon found himself sinking balls-deep into the woman who loved him, teeth gritted, pulse pounding in his skull. This was real.

She was real.

It was enough. For now.

She arched under him, her legs curving around his waist, holding him to her. Her nails dug into his shoulders, half-moons of pain fracturing through his control.

He thrust hard, her body rising to meet his, welcoming his cock, clenching around it. She moaned with every surge, opened her eyes.

He drowned inside them.

Beautiful, courageous, sexy, wild woman.

His. All his.

"Tell me," he said hoarsely, hips tightening, grinding against hers.

"I love you," she cried.

"More." He growled the command even as he withdrew. Pulled away from her, until only the pulsing tip of him remained cradled in her wet flesh.

"Oh, God." She shuddered, hips rising, back arching. "I love you. I'm yours. Please, please."

As his testicles tightened, as every visceral instinct in him surged to raging life, warmth flooded his heart.

"Mine," he whispered, dropping his mouth to her shoulder. Kissed her soft, silken skin to her breast. His lips found her nipple just as he thrust once more inside her; rocked her, pushing her farther up the bed as she panted.

She came apart with a wild, shuddering cry, her head thrown back, shoulders twisting. Her nails scored lines down his shoulders, his biceps, and he bit back his own guttural shout as the pleasure-pain sent him over the edge.

The world tilted on its axis. As his body uncoiled, as hers clamped down on his shaft and her legs tightened around his hips, Simon let go.

For the time he had left, he'd love her.

It seemed to be enough.

It would never be enough.

As the sweat cooled on her skin, Parker listened to the steady drum of Simon's heart beneath her ear and floated bonelessly across the landscape of her own thoughts.

One of his callused, powerful hands still curled into her hair, his grip loose enough to keep the tension slack, but there. Decidedly there. A mark of possession, maybe, or reassurance.

Enough that as he breathed, his chest rising and falling steadily beneath her cheek, she shivered.

You need someone to take care of you.

He was right. Not in a way that turned her into a housewife or some kind of pet. It was different.

He was different.

He watched out for her. Took care of her the way she took care—

Her throat closed.

The way she *had* taken care of her missionaries.

He stirred, skimming the fingertips of his free hand down her spine. Again, she shivered.

She loved him.

"What's on your mind?"

Parker turned her head, shifting her weight so that his body cradled hers more readily, and looked up at his jaw. His eyes were closed, lashes a thick line against his angled cheeks.

It said something that he could tune into her so readily even without looking.

"You," she confessed, easily enough.

His firm lips pulled up at one corner. "I like that."

"You'd better." But any wisp of amusement ghosted by too fast to appreciate. "I'm not okay with this."

Now he looked at her, dark eyebrows knitting as his eyes—brown in the dim light—opened. He shifted, gathering her in one arm to pull her higher up on his chest, tighter against him.

Close enough that her leg curled over one of his

muscled thighs and she could look down on him. He let go of her hair, letting the mass tumble to his chest in a wash of red.

Now he shivered; gooseflesh rippled over his skin. His eyes darkened. Lust, need.

Appreciation.

She liked that, too.

But she braced one palm against his chest, just over his heart, and focused on what she needed to say. Even if his erection nudged at her thigh.

"You can't die, Simon."

Regret replaced apprehension. Raw and so clear that it stole her breath.

"Stop it," she added quickly, her voice strained. Her chest ached with it. With all the fear and love and emotional chaos. "I'm not ready to give up on you."

"You have to," he began.

She covered his mouth with one hand, a move identical to the one he so loved pulling on her.

His eyes flared.

Narrowed.

But a glint of laughter mollified her. Just a little.

"I'm not going to sit back and let this happen," she said quickly. A rush of air, a promise Parker hadn't even been sure she'd intended to make. "I won't go marching into the Mission to demand that vial back, but I'm not going to wait you out, either."

His jaw firmed beneath her hand.

"I don't know what I can do," she continued. Fast. She had to get it out. To make him understand. "But you can't ask me to sit by and passively wait for you to die. You— You can't do that. I won't do it. I l— I love you, and—"

Damn it. The tears caught her by surprise. They filled her eyes, spilled over as her throat swelled with everything she wasn't sure how to say.

Warnings, promises. Challenge.

His gaze softened. Slowly, he curled his fingers around her hand, pulled it gently from his mouth. "Stop, Parker." He pressed a kiss into her palm.

It nearly broke her.

"Don't cry, sweetheart. It's going to be okay."

Meaningless words, but only because he didn't know how true that was.

She would *make it* okay.

"You— You just watch and see," she whispered. He cupped her cheek, his thumb wiping away her tears.

Simon said nothing. Instead, slowly, inexorably, he tugged her down. Tilted her head just so, and tenderly brushed her lips with his.

It was the softest, sweetest kiss she'd ever in her life experienced. No rush. No pressure. Even as her heart surged into overdrive, as her belly shuddered and her breath caught, he nuzzled her lips apart. Drifted across them as if he had all the time in the world.

It was a dodge. A neat one.

But as she moaned, Parker thought she'd let this one slide.

He deserved a break. A time when he didn't have to think about the threat looming over him.

And she had plans to make.

CHAPTER TWENTY-ONE

Kayleigh's stomach burned steadily, a knot of pain she imagined as a blob of acid—eating away at her insides, burning a hole through her stomach lining. As a scientist, she knew better than to let her imagination carry her off.

But as Kayleigh Lauderdale, the woman, she wondered if she'd eventually have to cope with a hole right smack in the middle of her gut.

It had been a full day since the mess at the Mission. Twenty-four hours, and she'd been unable to reach her father.

He probably had his hands full. She'd paced and fidgeted and hid in Laboratory Seventeen—her own lab. Over half of it remained sealed in plastic protectors, dustcovers protecting the equipment from time and wear while Kayleigh focused on her father's needs.

Since stepping in for Nadia Parrish, she hadn't had time to work on her own projects. Only Eve.

It had . . . consumed her.

It consumed *him*.

She paced by her workstation, her gaze falling on the small plastic tube propped in front of her keyboard.

She should have begun work on it.

But then, she'd been waiting to talk to her dad, and Laurence Lauderdale wasn't picking up her calls.

No, wait, that was dramatic, wasn't it? Kayleigh could imagine what her father was going through right now—reports to the bishop, hearings about Parker Adams's betrayal.

That made the second director to betray the Church.

Kayleigh squinted, hands shaking as she jammed them into her lab coat pockets. Staring at the capped syringe, her mind flashed instead to that room.

That horrible, stifling room, with Parker's screams and—and—

The overhead lights flashed.

No, that wasn't right. They flared, developing a low-key corona, an aura that shuddered through her head.

She flinched, rubbed at her eyes as her eyeballs throbbed into a fully formed eye-strain headache. She knew all about these. Added to her ulcer and insomnia, and she was falling apart.

Was this what it took to be a leader of scientists?

Kayleigh stumbled to her chair, found it by feel, and collapsed into the ergonomically curved seat. She squeezed her eyes shut, willing the tension wrapped up behind her forehead to fade. To at least ease off.

Stomach, head.

Heart.

She felt sick all the way through.

Resting her fingers on the workstation, they settled instead over the plastic tube with its strange substance inside. Was this it? The end to her efforts?

She cracked open an eye. The glare from the lights wasn't so horrible that she couldn't work.

And since her dad was busy . . .

He is butchering innocent people.

It couldn't be true. She knew it wasn't true. Those people were test subjects, already doomed to die.

And more would without her help.

But what does he want to do with them?

The thought wormed its way into the throbbing space behind her eyes. Wriggled there, slimy and seditious.

What was it he'd always told her?

Make a better world, Kayleigh.

She lunged to her feet so fast, the blood drained from her brain. Left her lopsided and clinging to the table.

A little darkness. That's all she needed. Just enough to take the worst off the eye strain. Then she'd begin analyzing a sample from the syringe.

Bury herself in work. In her task. One step at a time.

One hand over her eyes, she crossed the silent lab, ripped the plastic covers off two of the analysis machines on her way to the lighting panel inset by the door. The tech, programmed to waken when the covers came off, hummed softly.

Let her father work all of this out. She was going to save lives.

She drew the light sliders down to dim. The coronas faded from each lamp, down to a faint haze. It would do.

"Hey, computer," she called.

"Query."

"Turn on all systems needed for in-depth analysis of viscous contents." It was easier than listing all of them. The computer knew what she meant.

"Engaging."

Nodding, Kayleigh strode for the workstation—and the bit of murky liquid that was going to make her father very happy.

"The following equipment has—"

As she reached for it, her ears plugged.

The mechanized voice droned around her, unintelligible.

Her vision narrowed. Tunneled. The syringe slid out of her fingers, hit the edge of the table, and clattered to the floor as Kayleigh collapsed.

The plastic tube rolled across the pristine linoleum.

It left a trail of burning gold. A fiery comet, burning all in its wake.

And then she saw nothing.

CHAPTER TWENTY-TWO

Thunder crashed overhead, the end-of-summer storm turning the sky into a playground of blue, purple, and murky black. The rain slammed to the streets in a curtain of gray, limiting visibility to a narrow corridor of blurry lights and acid-tinged mist. The hour hovered somewhere between midnight and one.

Simon leaned against a lamppost, collar turned up against the rain and feeling twice over the consistency of hammered shit. Hands buried in his pockets, he shivered against a cold that leached the warmth from his very bones—a cold too intense to come from the rain.

Time. It all came down to time.

In the alley behind him, Parker waited with an impatience he could all but feel boring into his back. She didn't like having to wait in hiding. Simon couldn't blame her; this whole thing had been her idea to begin with. But he wouldn't risk the chance of recognition.

Every feed from entertainment to news to police band had gone supernova with the story. Mission Director Parker Adams, traitor to the Holy Order. Armed and dangerous. Wanted at all costs.

Dead or alive.

Preferably dead.

She was too recognizable, and they lacked the freedom topside to find the things Simon knew how to requisition in the lower streets. Her assets had been frozen almost immediately, and whatever allies she might have made as director were either too scared or unwilling to help her now.

He didn't have the money or the contacts up here to keep her safe.

But damn it, he had to try.

The comm, clenched in one fist, hummed, a short, staccato fluctuation Simon wasn't sure he didn't imagine. He waited. Another thrum against his palm cut off only halfway through its standard duration.

Simon flinched as his head spiked a complaint; a bolt of pain through the back of his skull. Why most of the pain started there, he didn't know. It didn't matter. Whatever the reason, dead would soon enough be dead.

When his comm vibrated again fifteen seconds later, he pulled the device from his pocket and flipped the lid. "Talk to me."

"Oh, man." Jonas's voice cut through the rain, his tension. Even through the pain, but it wasn't kind. Usually so pleasant, tonight it lanced through his senses and scorched everything behind it.

Simon squinted, wiping away the stinging rain from his eyes with his free hand. "That sounds bad."

"Let's just say that you are seriously going to love these guys," Jonas replied lightly. "Like, fall down and worship."

"I'll take that bet." He glanced down the empty street, then into the alley behind him. He couldn't see Parker from where he leaned, but that meant no one else could, either. The shopping district had long since emptied for the night. "Talk to me."

"Okay, between May and me, we've managed to cross enough wires to focus attention away from the sec-line for about three minutes."

"Not long," Simon said, frowning. "Are you sure we'll get through?"

"It's all you've got. They'll change guards at two-fifteen, and if everything goes right with our calculations, there shouldn't be a wait. It's the quiet shift."

It would have to do. "Who's our contact?"

"You'll be meeting them in about half an hour. Where do you want to meet?"

"You aren't arranging that for me?"

"What, and ruin your mysterious man in the rain routine?" Laughter filled the tech's voice. "I've got you tracked, and your ride's on the way. Stay there if you want, or meet somewhere less, uh, empty for distraction purposes, but decide now."

Easy. "We'll wait." Simon stepped out of the hazy light, fading into the alley as he transferred the comm to his other ear. "I've got Parker with me."

A shadow detached from the depths of the alley. In the broken light afforded by the violent display overhead, he saw her scrape both hands through her sodden hair, pulling it away from her face.

She looked exhausted. Smudges under her luminous blue eyes told a tale of strain and anxiety that he didn't have to be psychic to know was for him. He'd scared her earlier. That fucking nosebleed, which was starting to taste less and less like blood and more like he'd licked a copper wire.

It couldn't be a good sign.

"Thanks, Jonas."

"That's why I'm king of the wave." But Jonas hesitated, and even through the fog in his head, Simon recognized it.

"What?" he demanded. Parker tucked herself against his side. One slim arm wrapped around his lower back, under his jacket.

Like she could support his weight if he pitched over. One corner of his mouth hiked up, his heart torn between raw pain and something so much warmer. Love and loss. Fear and pride. He tugged her closer with one hand, pulled her fully into the shelter of his body; tucked her between the wet alley wall and him.

Jonas sighed. "How are you doing, man?"

"Can't complain." It was all he'd say with Parker right in front of him. Her free hand curled into the front of his jacket.

"He's lying," she offered.

Ears like a cat.

Simon glowered at her as Jonas's laughter spilled out from the frequency. "We'll be here when your contact arrives," Simon said sharply and snapped the case closed. Shoving the comm back into his pocket, he opened his mouth, but she beat him to it.

"I don't know why you hide it," she said, leaning back against the alley. Her eyes closed, red-tipped lashes spiked with rain fanning her cheeks. "He's seen the list of degenerated subjects, he knows."

Simon braced one hand against the wall by her side. It let him lean without crushing her with his weight, took the edge off the aches in his body. The exhaustion that was more than just fatigue. "Because I still have things to do. And bitching about it won't help. Parker—" Her wet hands, chilled by the rain, tunneled under his jacket. His shirt. He hissed out a breath as they found his skin, splayed wide over his stomach. "Dirty."

"Could be," she replied, a glint of blue laughing at him from under her lashes. Those fingers crept higher. Along his sides. Dug short fingernails into his skin, and even pain wasn't enough to dull the sudden pulse of need tightening low in his gut. "How much time do we have?"

Oh, Jesus. To think anyone ever thought her cold. Simon crowded her into the wall, bracing his weight on his forearms, and took her rain-wet mouth in a kiss that soothed him in ways he'd never be able to explain.

She didn't hold back. Her lips opened for him, sweet and warm despite the acid-tinged rain he tasted on her.

As her fingers tightened against his chest, as his cock made abundantly clear exactly how little time they had, Simon nipped at her lower lip. "Behave."

"Or what?"

Another nip. Hard enough to elicit a gasp, her

eyes flaring with heat and pleasure caught on this side of pain. "Christ," he murmured, soothing the hurt away with a flick of his tongue. "There isn't nearly enough time in the world to explore you."

This time, the pain that flickered in her bottomless gaze had nothing to do with the physical.

Clumsy. Simon gathered her in his arms, turned so his back flattened against the wall, and wrapped her in his coat. Wordlessly—what could she say?— Parker tunneled into his warmth. She was soaked to the skin, but he didn't care.

"I'm sorry," he said, nuzzling into her wet hair. His arms tightened around her. "More than you'll ever know."

"Quit it." Her fingers bunched in the back of his shirt. "You keep talking like it's a done deal. It's not. I swear to God, I'm going to get that syringe back—"

"Parker."

"—if I have to hunt Kayleigh down—"

"*Parker.*"

"—to hell myself—"

"Fuck." Simon caught her chin, tipped her face up and smothered the fierce stream of words with another kiss; another melding of lips and breath and heat that had her swallowing her diatribe on a ragged moan.

Not all heat. He heard her fear, tasted her frustration as he swept his tongue inside to rasp against hers. He poured everything he had into that kiss, everything he didn't know how to say. Love and need and fear for the future—*her* future, without him. Her body melted, boneless against his.

Lights cut through the alley.

Simon didn't think, didn't have to. Reacting

purely on instinct, he spun, tucking Parker behind him, one arm holding her in place against the alley wall as he reached for the Colt under the jacket.

A silhouette loomed into the alley mouth, backlit by the rain-hazed streetlamp. "Please don't shoot me," came a masculine voice easy on the ears, but unfamiliar.

"Hands up," Simon growled, shaking his head hard as vertigo slipped in under his senses. Shit.

"Okay. I'm unarmed." Hands splayed on either side of the silhouette. "Jonas sent me."

Parker stiffened behind him. "Mr. Clarke?"

"Phin's fine," came the calm reply, although the man didn't move.

Simon lowered his gun. "Phin Clarke. I should have known."

"I'm not alone." The shape of a hand beckoned. "We need to get going."

Parker gently pushed at Simon's back. "It's okay, Simon."

As far as her safety was concerned, *nothing* was okay.

But his director didn't take her cues from anyone. She sidled out from behind Simon, hooked an arm in his, and said flatly, "He's rocky on his feet."

"Parker, damn it."

Phin stepped fully into view, a lean man with dark brown curls plastered to his head and—

Simon squinted. "The hell are you wearing?"

The man's very white teeth flashed in a smile as he took Simon's other arm. Because it beat falling on his face, Simon let him. "The same kind of thing you'll be wearing in about ten minutes."

Carefully and fashionably shredded jeans, something that looked like a cross between a man-corset and a dress-shirt, a synth-leather jacket. Club-wear. The kind of getup a topsider wore when he hit the party streets. "Hell, no."

Parker smothered a laugh.

Phin only shrugged. "Come on, let's go meet the cavalry."

Parker slid into the back of a plain silver car—not too fancy, expensive but lacking in all the gilded edges of the topside elite—and stared at a neon pink blur as it filled her vision. Dangling from a set of callused fingers just on the edge of—

She hesitated to call them straps.

"Is this a dress or a freakishly bright bondage scenario?" she asked dryly, tugging the material out of her face. She scooted along the seat to make room for Simon beside her and raised her eyebrows as the large man wearing chauffeur black met her eyes through the rearview mirror.

"It damn well better be the former," Simon growled, plucking the material from her grasp. He opened it, gave the one-piece a cursory glance, then turned narrowed eyes to the man Parker had never met. She didn't have to.

She'd been all over that docket.

"Silas Smith," she offered evenly. "Most people think you're dead."

"That's the idea."

Phin Clarke slid into the passenger seat, his dark brown eyes crinkled with amusement as he shut the door. "Do you two know each other?"

"No." The man had a voice like a truck engine, deep and powerful. It fit. By all accounts, Silas Smith was a missionary who'd forged a path for himself after a mission gone wrong, long before Parker's time. His features were ruggedly square, carved of granite, and set in implacable lines.

The eyes in the mirror were gray-green. Cool, assessing. Every inch a missionary, no matter where he drew the line now.

But they hardened to jade ice as his gaze settled on Simon.

The silence between them held volumes—unspoken words, emotions, something. A give-and-take Parker wasn't keyed in to the right frequency to understand. Finally, Simon nodded. Once. "I owe you."

"You're damn right."

Parker's mouth curved up. Wry humor. "Nice to meet you, Mr. Smith."

He grunted a non-answer.

"I suspected you were alive. And Naomi? She was your partner, wasn't she?"

"Manner of speaking." Not a forthcoming sort, then.

"Okay." Phin pulled a bag from the floor at his feet, passed it over his shoulder. "There's towels back there, and clothes for you, Simon. Change up."

"Into this?" Parker snatched the slinky pink material from Simon's grasp, flushing under his suddenly all-too-wickedly amused scrutiny. "What're we going to do, make security blind?"

"Oh, they'll be blind, all right," Phin said, but his smile evened into a straight, no-nonsense line as he met Simon's narrowed gaze. "You, too, Simon." He turned back around, deliberately shielding his view with a hand as the car pulled out into the street.

"I'm not wearing a dress," Simon declared.

Parker grimaced. "This barely qualifies." But she unzipped her jacket, aware that Silas raised a large hand and tilted the rearview mirror to the roof.

How chivalrous.

Simon wasn't remotely the same. He watched her as she shimmied out of her coat, helped her when her sleeves caught on her wet skin. His eyebrow quirked as she unbuttoned her blouse.

The look she shot him didn't help anything. He only grinned, a wicked slant, and traced a line from her collarbone to her navel as she struggled out of her shirt.

Ripples of nerves, of awareness, shimmied out from that imaginary line. Curled deep inside her body.

"I don't suppose," she said to break the awkward silence, "there's a brush and makeup in there?" Her voice betrayed nothing of the butterflies Simon's touch lodged in her belly.

His grin deepened.

"Jessie said she put everything you'll need in the bag," Phin replied without turning around. "Including a wig. If you need a hand, I'm—"

"Don't even think about it, pretty boy." Simon's voice held nothing back. The leashed menace in the order earned a snort from Silas—that surprised her—and a fierce frown from Parker as she flipped her hair off her shoulder. It slapped him in the chest.

"Thank you, I'm good," she told the man. "I've been to too many meetings to not know how to freshen makeup in a car. By Jessie, you must mean Jessie Leigh."

Simon caught a handful of her hair, tugged in warning, but tucked it neatly behind her back with gentle fingers.

"Yes, she's on our side."

"What part of *our side* do you mean?" Parker asked mildly, planting her feet and raising her hips to peel the wet denim down her legs.

Simon growled something almost under his breath as he dug through the bag.

"It means that she's no fan of the Salem situation."

"Because she's a Salem witch," Parker said, tucking her sodden clothes at her feet. "Like Juliet." The cool air in the car settled over her damp skin, coaxing gooseflesh over her limbs. She shuddered.

Simon pulled out a bundle of clothing, his angular features settled into a hard scowl, but he nodded. "Different batch than me, but stamped all the same."

"Forgive my candor," she said as she pooled the slinky pink material through her fingers, "but she's not dead because of Matilda Lauderdale, right?"

A beat, and she saw Silas and Phin exchange a glance.

She didn't need confirmation at that point. She'd suspected as much. Pulling the dress over her head took effort, and she rapped her knuckles on the ceiling twice before she managed to pull it over her wet hair and face. "I guess you know about the syringe."

"We know," Phin said.

Regret kicked her in the spine, hard enough to hunch her shoulders as she straightened the halter dress. It clung to her like a second skin, an electric bright sheath that barely capped at mid-thigh. "I was . . . I couldn't keep it—"

Simon closed the distance between them, tucked her so firmly against his side that he might as well have planted a flag in her and named her his. The bare skin of his chest warmed her cold flesh, seared a line down her side. It helped. A little.

His teeth flashed as he snarled, "Too many games. Too much politics. Parker got caught in the middle and Lauderdale has the serum."

"It's all right." Phin almost turned, caught himself. "We'll figure something out. We always do."

"Thought it'd happen, anyway," Silas added grimly. "Let's focus on getting you through the sec-lines."

Right. One thing at a time. "Hand me the makeup bag."

"And a brush," Simon told her, putting both in her hands. He dropped a kiss on her temple, sweet and exquisitely tender, before bending in the cramped quarters to pull his boots off. The streetlights and district signs they passed gilded his muscled shoulders in ripples of color.

Parker took a deep breath and bent her attention on applying makeup without a mirror. As she did, she listened to the rustle of Simon's clothing, his muttered swearing as he struggled to change in the small space of the backseat.

She wanted to laugh, but given her precarious position with an eyeliner pencil, she asked instead, "What's going on up here? The feeds aren't helpful." And she was used to a constant stream of information. It bothered her to be so blind.

To her surprise, Silas's dark rumble answered her. "As far as the media is aware, the bishop is now in control of the Mission. Sector Three is still playing close to the vest, but it's a sure bet that the real power lies with them."

Parker shouldn't be so surprised. The man was a trained missionary, after all. No matter what he fought for now. She nodded—caught herself as the eyeliner pencil came dangerously close to her eyeball and said aloud, "Director Lauderdale has always been the keystone to Sector Three. He'll have half a dozen strategies in place to secure Bishop Applegate's loyalties."

"Which is why we've got to move fast," Phin interjected, "before this has a chance to gel."

"Any solid plans?" Simon asked. An elbow narrowly missed Parker's hip as he struggled with his wet jeans.

"First, we get you out of the line of fire."

"And then?" Parker pressed.

"Then we try to get as much data as we possibly can using Jonas and his new buddies." Silas glanced over his shoulder as he eased into a lane of light traffic, his gaze briefly touching on Parker as she hunched over the pencil she struggled to apply. His eyes flared, a glint of something warm and reluctantly approving, before he looked quickly back to the windshield. "Fuck me." It wasn't an invite.

Parker bit back a smile as Phin chuckled. "I'll take that as a good sign. You done, Miss Adams?"

"Not yet. Do we know what Lauderdale's plans are?"

"No," Phin admitted. "But Jonas is keeping watch. It's strange that Sector Three hasn't made any sort of public move."

"Not that strange," she said slowly. "They're used to secrecy. Problem is, they're good at it, too."

"We're almost there," Silas interjected. "Hurry up."

It took a lot of concentration, a few starts and stops and a close call with the mascara brush, but she did it. As she brushed out her hair, pulled it up into a tight knot, and yanked the blond wig she'd found in the case over it all, she declared, "Good as it gets."

Silas's gaze remained on the road, but she saw Phin's head tilt. "Can I look?"

She ran both hands through the chin-length strands of fake hair. "Go for it."

Beside her, Simon struggled into his synth-leather coat, elbows narrowly missing the window and her head. As Phin turned in his seat, his grin split into a fully fledged smile. "Damn, you two."

Simon muttered a curse. "Shove it, Clarke."

Parker leaned away to study Simon's new look. Black synth-leather pants hugged his lean hips, outlined the muscles of his legs. The tank top he wore was just this side of *don't give a damn,* and the way his hair spiked back from his face looked as if he'd spent hours getting it just messy enough to tempt a girl to run her fingers through it. The crowning glory, the long synth-leather coat, made him look like a gunslinger out on the prowl. Or an extremely bored topsider.

He looked dangerous. Delicious. So completely outside the scope of his usual worn denim and flannel that part of her wanted to laugh.

The other part of her—the part barely covered by a strip of pink—wanted something else entirely. Her grip tightened on the tube of lipstick in her hand.

Simon glowered. "The pants are too short."

"Tuck them into your boots," Phin instructed and turned his critical eye on her. "Great job on the makeup. Too light for a real night out, but it'll do. Lose the bra."

"What?" Her gaze jerked to him. "No way."

"Lose it, Miss Adams." His smile turned wry. "No slummer would ruin the sightlines of a dress like that with a bra. Are you wearing a thong?"

"Am I going to have to get out of the car?" she snapped.

"Maybe."

"Damn it." Gritting her teeth, she worked her bra off as Phin once more turned away.

Another grunt from Silas, but this time, she swore she heard laughter.

CHAPTER TWENTY-THREE

The current splashed and frothed beneath the flat-bottom boat, dragging it along the rock wall. The god-awful shriek it made had Parker huddled against Simon's side, her hands over her ears.

Simon bit back a smile and only held her tightly.

"Sorry!" At the back of the boat, Phin plunged a long oar into the water, wrenching back against the water's grasp. "Almost there."

Getting through the sec-lines had been a piece of cake. Prepared for the worst, Simon had kept one hand on his gun as the car idled at the sec-line checkpoint. They'd timed it perfectly. As the guard peered inside—his flashlight had spent an inordinate amount of time on Parker's breasts—Parker had flashed a smile with enough wattage to fry a lesser man, and Jonas's promised distraction had gone off.

Whatever it had been, the man's comm crackled with orders from the security station, and he'd waved them through hurriedly.

Simon hadn't expected it to go *that* easy. He hadn't expected the drive to go as smoothly as it had, the shift into a battered orange pickup truck, the route into the ruined carcass of Old Seattle buried under the metropolis, and he sure as hell didn't think about the Old Sea-Trench as *somewhere safe*.

But then, this is where Matilda protected her people.

This was where she'd died.

Parker's hair gleamed in the summer sun, a fiery red and copper braid flung over Simon's arm as she clung to his arm. Molten flame, as cool and silky as it was vibrant. He loved her hair. Thank God the wig was gone. "Where are we?" she demanded. Exhaustion bruised the skin under her eyes, but she didn't complain.

She wouldn't. Still the same Parker.

"Near as I can tell," he said, looking up, "we're about half a mile out of the city. Maybe more." He knew exactly where they were—but he hadn't known about the water entry. The only way he'd found Matilda's sanctuary had been directly through the ruins.

And even then, he suspected she'd led him there.

"Will Silas be okay?" she asked Phin, shifting on the boat bench. The dress rode up on her hips, but she'd pulled her jeans on underneath once they were safe enough to get away with it.

"He knows the way in," Phin assured her. "There's two that we know of."

"In to where?"

"You'll see," Phin chuckled. "Hang on."

She shuddered. "I never want to go through Old Seattle ever again."

It amused Simon. After so long in the lower New Seattle streets, he forgot that Parker had never really been off the beaten path. She was a topsider, through and through.

The ruins buried beneath the paved streets of the towering city remained among the most dangerous places Simon had ever been. Liberally littered with pitfalls, rotting structures ready to collapse and worse, he'd only stared at Phin when the man suggested they go there.

"Trust me," he'd said with a grin.

Not on his life.

But Parker had taken the choice out of his hands, and here they were. Nestled in a boat in the middle of the Old Sea-Trench, watching craggy cliff walls slide by.

The sun had come out an hour ago, a rare day. Although its muted warmth helped take the edge off, anxiety still draped over his shoulders.

It'd been a mere thirty-six hours since the Mission had gone dark, and too quiet.

"Here we go," Phin warned. "Brace yourselves!"

Simon gripped one edge of the boat, his knee nudging hers. She held onto him with both arms, but she stared out at the formless canyon. Fascinated?

Or cataloging every turn. He had more than a suspicion about how her brain worked.

Phin navigated the boat along the fast-moving current, his mouth pursed in concentration.

Simon frowned. "All I see is—"

"Hey." Parker pointed, her eyes widening. "There's a fissure."

"What?" He looked out over her head, but all he saw was more rock. More faceless cliff and stone and craggy edges.

The boat scraped along the cliff side, metal screaming over stone. As Simon braced himself, held Parker as they rocked, he glanced back at their guide. "Are you—"

And then it stopped.

Suddenly, without warning, the boat slipped through a cavity Simon hadn't seen, pitched forward, and sent him sliding backward off the small bolted seat.

Parker's laughter ended on a squawk of surprise as his arm tightened around her ribs, pulled her with him to the boat floor.

Her elbow nailed him in the chest. He grunted, but for the first time in what seemed like too long, warmth—genuine laughter—filled him.

"Whoops." Phin bent, propping the oar on the boat floor, and offered Parker a hand. "Sorry about that." His brown eyes twinkled. "Welcome to the sanctuary."

From Simon's position on his back, all he saw was blue sky muted by a faint trace of clouds. But it was warm—a lot warmer than it had been only seconds ago in the trench.

And it smelled like sulfur. That warm, spicy mix he'd only ever smelled here.

Parker managed to get to her knees with Phin's steadying hand. When her face lit up, her beautiful eyes shining like the sun, Simon's heart filled with it. "Simon. Look!"

Gripping the edge of the boat, he pulled himself upright.

The crescent-shaped canyon carved into the trench had stolen his breath the first time he'd ever set foot into it. On one side of the point, Matilda had built a green house—small, cozy enough for one but clearly stretched for more. Tents had been erected on the shore, and a wooden pier jutted into the greenest, stillest water he'd ever seen.

"Oh," Parker breathed. She grabbed his arm. "It's so warm."

"Volcanic hot springs," Phin told her.

Simon knew.

The boat glided across the bottle-green water. As they approached the pier, the door in the green house with its mismatched windows opened.

Parker went still beside him.

Naomi West stepped out onto the porch—the same porch where Matilda had taken her poison. Where she'd shot him.

And died.

Simon's hands clenched at his sides.

"This will be fun," Parker murmured. Her tone slid into the even, cool notes he'd learned meant she was reapplying her armor.

He didn't blame her.

Naomi was a wild card.

The boat nudged the pier. Quickly, Phin stepped onto the creaking wood, offered a hand. "Ladies first."

She glanced at Simon.

He nodded.

When she took Phin's hand, Simon met the man's forthright scrutiny. Though his lips twitched, Phin said nothing as he helped Parker to the dock.

Simon climbed out on his own.

He'd never met Naomi. Not directly. Reports had suggested she was a knockout, and as Simon and Parker crossed the shore and approached the porch, he couldn't help but affirm the description.

Her black hair was a spiky, magenta-streaked black mass, short enough at her chin to bring attention to bone structure even Simon recognized as exquisite. Her mixed-Japanese features lent her an exotic beauty the rest of her fulfilled—long legs, trim figure. Lethal as hell, by all accounts. It was no wonder Parker had chosen her to deal with the Clarke problem. She'd fit right in with the beautiful people.

Well, assuming she'd lost the array of facial piercings at the time. A silver hoop nestled into the center of her lip glinted as she braced her folded arms against the porch rail. More rings decorated one eyebrow, a stud and hoop glimmered in her nose, and he'd bet there'd be more under her shredded jeans and loose sweatshirt.

Her eyes, a mix of blue and violet, weren't kind. "Well, well. Little Miss Parker goes on walkabout."

Simon's lips twitched.

"Miss West." Parker halted several feet from the porch.

Phin strode past them, his mouth set into a crooked slant. "Quit it," he said lightly as he jumped the porch steps. A boundless font of energy, Simon thought. Phin's jeans were worn and stained, and his flannel shirt—much like the ones Simon favored—didn't mark him as anything special, but the way he moved did.

Confidence, assurance. Like Parker, something

about him suggested *topsider,* but here he was. As far from topside as a man could get.

And he seemed to be doing all right.

At least, if the way he snagged Naomi's arm, spun her around, and pulled her into his arms was any indication. "Phin, hey!"

"Hey, yourself." Phin held her tightly. "I'm glad to see you again, sweetheart."

"It's been three hours," she protested. The compressed edge to her mouth softened. Just a little.

"It's been too long," Phin countered, nuzzling her color-streaked hair. "Be nice to our guests."

Unable to help himself, Simon reached out. Laced his fingers with Parker's.

Her palm was damp.

Nervous? A chink in the armor, after all.

"Relax," he whispered.

She shook her head.

"Trust me," he added dryly. "Of the two of us, you have the least to worry about."

"I know," she murmured.

The calm acceptance, the flicker in her eyes, gave him pause. She knew? Knew what?

Another figure stepped out from the lush foliage to the right of the pretty green house with its roof of purple flowers, and Simon's shoulder squared.

Showtime.

The woman who approached from the hidden cove on the other side of the crescent point had short black hair, a rounder figure, and a face Parker recognized immediately.

She stiffened.

Simon's grip tightened around hers in silent warning.

Juliet Carpenter transferred a small basket to her hip, her green eyes shuttered as she approached the porch. She didn't smile.

But she didn't run, either.

Simon met her accusing gaze. "Hello, Eve."

The basket Juliet carried hit the black-sand ground just as Naomi vaulted over the porch railing, a curse on her lips.

Beside Parker, Simon braced himself. Secrets and unspoken accusations filled the too-tense air.

No. None of this. No more.

Parker stepped in front of Simon, arms outstretched to the side, squaring her shoulders as Naomi closed the distance in a smooth, leashed surge of fatal intent. "Stop it!"

Phin jumped down the porch steps. "Naomi, don't."

"That's not her name," the ex-missionary snarled.

She filled Parker's space, a bullet ready to tear through anything in her way.

Enough was enough.

As Simon grabbed her shoulder, Parker stepped into Naomi's approach—grabbed her by the sweatshirt, one arm curved around the woman's waist.

She might not fight, but Parker knew how to get in the way.

And angry missionaries didn't scare her.

"That's *enough*," she yelled.

Her voice pierced through the canyon, echoed back eerily.

Naomi stopped. With one hand twisted in Simon's collar, she'd managed to brace her forearm against Parker's throat—one flex of lean muscle away from crushing her larynx, or worse.

Slowly, her eyebrows climbed, fine black arches pierced with rings on one side. "Holy shit," she drawled. "Look who's suddenly got a spine."

"I always *have*," Parker said evenly despite Naomi's arm at her neck. "You never bothered to look."

"Let them go, sweetheart." Phin's arm tightened around Juliet's shoulders. She hadn't moved. White-faced, she stared at Simon behind Parker.

Pretty girl. A witch named Eve.

Matilda's chosen.

Simon wasn't a complete blank slate. Parker didn't need anything else to fit the pieces into this particular puzzle. Slowly, she loosened her hold on Naomi's waist.

The woman drew back, but her eyes glittered dangerously as they flicked to Simon. "One wrong word—"

"We're all on the same side here," Phin said tersely. He squeezed Juliet's shoulders. "No one's going to hurt anyone. Juliet's safe, Nai, I promise."

Simon's hands settled over Parker's shoulders in like reassurance. She stumbled as they pulled her back, well out of Naomi's reach, fingers tense. "The hell are you thinking?" he demanded.

She shook her head, shrugged off Simon's grip. "Juliet. I'm Parker Adams. This is—"

"I know who you are." As greetings went, it wasn't promising. The girl patted Phin's hand on her shoulder but pulled it off with a lift to her slightly square chin. "He was there in that facility."

Simon stepped into Parker's peripheral. "I'm sorry."

Juliet's eyes widened.

"Look," he added, pitching his voice to carry. It firmed. "My name is Simon. I wasn't born with it." He reached up, dragged down the collar of his thermal shirt. The tattoos inked on his tanned skin stood out in stark relief. One seal of St. Andrew.

One bar code.

Parker watched Juliet's face. Every sign seemed to point to her as the key to this reunion. The cue the others would react to.

Someone they all wanted to protect. A good girl. A girl with the secret to Simon's survival.

Juliet's eyes flicked to the stamp. She swallowed hard.

"Like you," he continued, tone gentling as he let his collar go, "Matilda made me."

"Why?"

Parker stepped aside as the question slipped from the witch's lips.

This wasn't her conversation.

But as she backed away, folding her arms over her chest, she watched Simon just as closely.

His jaw was set, features ridged with strain. Tension. Only part of it was the effort he was making to remain steady. She knew the signs by now. But did they?

"I don't know," he admitted. "It's one of the many things I don't know. Who I am or what she wanted from me."

Juliet's arms folded beneath her breasts, twined into the pale blue T-shirt she wore. Too big for her. Maybe Phin's. "Go on."

Naomi shook her head. "What's it matter?" she demanded.

"Christ, Naomi," Phin murmured and folded

his hand over her mouth. He dragged her against his chest, her back to his front, and grunted as her elbow collided with his side.

A pang hit Parker's heart.

"I don't have anything left to go on with." Simon spread his hands. "All I know is that Matilda made me from her own genes. She wanted me to do something, but before I could ask, she—"

His eyes flicked to the porch.

"She died." Eyes flashing, Naomi tore Phin's hand from her mouth. "You shitfucker son of a—"

Parker tensed, ready to throw herself at the woman—risk the ass-kicking she knew the ex-missionary could level on her. But Phin grabbed the woman by both arms, more daring than she would have given the topside playboy.

"Stop it," he ordered. "Naomi, let him finish!"

"I'll kill him," she snarled. "He practically just admitted to killing her!"

"No." Simon stepped back, hands raised. But he didn't square up. Didn't meet Naomi's challenge with anything but raw honesty. "I came here, it's true. But by the time I arrived, she was already—" Pain flickered in his expression. "She chose to drink poison. I'm not lying."

"We couldn't fucking tell if you were," Naomi shot back.

Juliet flinched.

"He's got the scar from where she shot him," Phin said, and somehow, when he spoke, even Parker felt soothed. The man had a way about him. He spoke, and she wanted to listen. A real charmer.

"It just proves he was here," Naomi spat. Her eyes flashed. "Why are we trusting him?"

"Why *are* we trusting him?" Juliet echoed, but quietly.

Parker couldn't let this degenerate into something worse. "Please," she said.

All eyes turned to her. Sudden and direct.

Simon's banked, pain to anger. Anger to the cold, shuttered edge she was starting to associate with some misguided attempt to *fix things*.

What could she do? Please what?

She didn't know, but she had to give it her best shot. And she knew how to crack Naomi's edge. The woman had been the best missionary Parker had ever seen.

But she'd softened.

Slowly, Parker sank to her knees. The black sand shifted underneath her.

Simon rocked back on his heels, expression pained. Shocked. "Parker, no—"

"Matilda Lauderdale knew her husband still controlled the witches from his lab," she said over him.

Juliet watched her, worrying at her full upper lip.

Simon took a step toward Parker; she threw up a hand. "No," she said flatly. "Stop. I'm not doing this again." Let Naomi see the ex-director on her knees. Let her see how far Parker would go.

What it would cost her.

Pride didn't mean that much when the city—and Simon—was at stake.

"Laurence Lauderdale is the man behind all this," she continued, her gaze on Naomi now. Challenging. The woman's too-full mouth twisted as her tongue slid out to lick the jewelry in her lip. "He's been creating witches by the dozens, maybe even the hundreds."

"We know," Juliet said tightly.

"I know you do," Parker replied, gaze shifting to her. "But what you don't know is how bad it really is. The Mission is now run by his witches. His daughter—a respected geneticist in her own right—is trying to crack the code that will fix the thing that's breaking his army. And if she's half as smart as her parents, she'll have it done within weeks. Maybe sooner."

As one, every eye turned to Simon.

His fists clenched by his sides. "It's true," he said quietly. "I'm dying. So are all the subjects. They call it degeneration. I'm thirty years old and my generation has lasted the longest, but we're still—"

"Broken." Juliet shook her head. "We know."

"But you aren't dying now," Parker said, her eyes on the woman who'd started it all. Juliet Carpenter. *Eve.* "I need . . . Please, can you help us?"

"You had the fucking syringe," Naomi pointed out, but even her volume lowered. Tense, her posture rigid, but her fists remained at her sides.

"It wasn't her fault," Simon growled, not for the first time.

"Of course not."

"Of *course not,*" Phin replied, more firmly. Sincere where Naomi bled sarcasm.

"Shitfuck." With that snapped judgment, Naomi shook off his hand and stalked away from the group. Within moments, she vanished back around the house.

Phin tucked his hands into his pockets, smile crooked. "That, for Naomi, is polite."

"I'm well aware," Parker murmured, but without heat.

Juliet knelt, gathered her basket and the odd purple tubers that had spilled from inside. "So the Church has the last of the serum," she said quietly.

"It's my fault," Simon said before Parker could.

She glared at him. "No, it's—"

"It doesn't matter whose fault it is." The witch with the pale green eyes looked up, her expression sad. "Simon, I'm sorry. I can't help you. Jessie and I used the other two syringes Matilda left us. Whatever she needed from me, it's locked up in my chemical makeup, not my power. All I can do is—"

"I know," he repeated, his arm tightening at Parker's waist. "You boost others' powers."

Juliet glanced at Phin. "Then why are they here?"

"You didn't say we were coming?" Parker narrowed her eyes at Phin.

Running a hand through his curly hair, Phin shrugged. "Jonas got in touch. Jessie planned the rest. I just figured if there was a way . . ."

"I came to say I'm sorry."

Parker's heart swelled as Simon's words settled over the small group. Quiet. Earnest.

Honest.

"Before everything, all I wanted was the Eve sequence. I intended to steal it, cure myself, and get the hell out of this city no matter what it took. When Matilda died, I—" He took a deep breath, let it out on a whoosh of unspoken frustration. Anger. "I didn't care about any of you, any of this, until Parker, and I failed her. I failed all of you." He looked down at Parker, his jaw shifting.

"You didn't fail me, Simon. You're the reason

I'm not in an interrogation cell right now. Maybe worse."

She cupped his cheek. "There's time."

"No, there isn't."

A new voice fractured the tenuous peace. "There might be."

CHAPTER TWENTY-FOUR

The foliage rustled, large, tropical fronds swaying as another man strode out of whatever lay hidden behind it.

Parker's eyes widened. Blond hair, incredibly blue eyes. His features were unmistakable. It couldn't be. "Caleb Leigh? We thought you were—"

"Dead?" He turned his head.

Parker swallowed a gasp.

Scars climbed up his neck, tendrils of ropy flesh carving wefts over his jaw. His cheek. It slanted his mouth into a permanent smirk. He wore long sleeves, but his left hand gleamed in the daylight, shiny skin and corrugated edges.

Wordlessly, Juliet reached out.

Caleb took her hand. "That was the point," he said. His eyes, uncomfortably sharp, settled on Simon. "You son of a bitch."

But there wasn't any heat to it.

Simon nodded. "You of all people know what it means to do what we do."

"I know where your head was," Caleb confirmed, but rigidly. As if he didn't like even admitting that. "Doesn't excuse it. For either of us."

Juliet frowned. "Caleb doesn't have to act alone anymore."

"Neither do you," Caleb said to Simon, finishing her thought with ease. His gaze landed on Parker. Slid over her, from her braided red hair to the skimpy pink dress, her scuffed coat and stained jeans.

His permanently slanted mouth twitched. "I expected you to be more imposing."

"Caleb," Juliet protested.

"I get that a lot," Parker replied evenly. "I have a file filled with the names of people you murdered in my office topside."

"It's true." Brutal candor. "I'm not excusing anything."

She blinked.

Phin shifted his weight, an awkward gesture.

Simon watched it quietly. Watched them all as he stood solid and still against Parker's side.

"Let's go sit down," Phin suggested. "There's tea and food. We can talk there."

"Okay." Parker spoke before Simon could refuse, aware of the sheer will he expended to stay upright. Show no weakness.

They didn't have that luxury anymore.

"You know what I do," Caleb said to him.

Simon nodded. "Most of the new Coven of the

Unbinding witches are Salem Project operatives. You and your sister's . . . abilities are known to Sector Three."

"Then you know I mean it when I say there's still a chance." Caleb plucked the basket from Juliet's hands, caught her hand as she tried to grab it back and brought it to his mouth for a kiss too tender for Parker not to look away. A gold ring on Juliet's finger flashed.

Juliet's features darkened. Uncertainty. Mistrust. "Another vision?"

Worry, most of all. Parker knew the feeling.

"It's okay, Jules," Caleb murmured.

What Parker didn't know, didn't know how to really name, was a strange feeling of . . . solidarity unfolding within her. Of sympathy, shared knowledge.

Caleb's gaze seemed to take everyone in, studied them all, catalog them. File them away.

They settled on Parker again, briefly.

Understanding flashed there.

Simon's hand flattened on her back. So possessively that Phin tried and failed to hide a grin.

"I saw a vision," Caleb confirmed. "I saw two paths." He tucked the basket under his arm. "At the end of each, I saw death standing with a scale."

"A scale," Phin repeated. "What?"

"The future is a mess of riddles," Juliet said wearily. "Signs that aren't what they seem. Or maybe are."

"He's seeing the future?" Parker demanded.

"Saw it," Caleb corrected. "Ask him." His chin

thrust at Simon in a kind of acknowledgement. "He knows how it works."

Simon looked away.

The blond witch's smile quirked at the scarred edge of his mouth. "In this vision, one path led to a slaughterhouse. Hundreds dead, hanging from hooks. Infants lay strewn upon the floor, forgotten. Everything's dark. And cold." Caleb recounted this quietly. Grimly. Phin scowled. "The other path leads to total destruction. Thousands of corpses, *hundreds* of thousands, piled high. Men, women, children all scattered over the broken ground."

"Oh, God," Parker whispered.

Juliet flinched, cheeks paling. "I hate this."

As if he couldn't get enough, as if he both offered comfort and demanded a touchstone, Caleb laced his hand with hers. His scarred hand.

Parker's throat closed as Juliet didn't pull away.

Love. Real love, the kind that would last forever. She was surrounded by it.

Was this what it could have been?

No, she wouldn't think like that. She'd made a promise. Wordlessly, she rested her head against Simon's shoulder.

Caleb shook his head. "I'm not done. At the top of the corpse pile stands a man I've seen before, but this time, I see his face." His eyes pinned on Simon. "It looks like yours."

Parker stiffened. "There's no—"

"It's allegory," Caleb said over her.

"It's crap," she shot back.

Simon said nothing.

The witch smiled faintly. "The point is that

those are the things I see. But it's not a total wash. Last night, the vision became clear enough to recount, but as I watched it, I realized something."

"What's that?" Simon asked, but cautiously. Resignedly.

"It's *not* you. Not really." His eyebrows raised. "It's the same man I saw in the vision that led me to Juliet, the man in the shadows holding the chains that bound her. It's your father."

Shocked silence filled the group. Filled Simon beside her.

Then, with a low, strained "*Fuck,*" he turned away. Strode past Caleb and Juliet, his fist clenched.

Parker took two steps after him, hesitated when Caleb put that scarred hand on her shoulder. "Give him a minute."

She looked up at his face, the twisted edges of his burn-marred flesh, but all she saw was compassion. And a dangerous kind of determination.

Beside him, Juliet touched her arm. "There's been a lot of secrets, decades of the stuff. We're still sorting it all out."

"We need a plan." Parker closed her eyes briefly, drew on the Mission training—her own strength—to lock her knees. Keep from tearing after Simon, holding him. Reassuring him.

The urge nearly took her breath away.

When her lashes lifted, she found Caleb smiling at her. "You're a tough lady, Parker Adams."

"You have no idea," Phin said behind her. It was almost a complaint.

Parker stepped away, smoothed the pink dress without hope of getting it to lay right over her jeans. "What does your vision have to do with any of this?" she asked, calm now. Steady. She was good at useless information.

"I'm not sure," Caleb replied.

"It sounds," Juliet mused, "like there's going to be sacrifices on both ends."

"It's war." Parker glanced at the emerald green water, still as glass. Her mind churned, filtering through what she knew. *Focus.* This would help. Anything would help. Help her, help Simon.

Help New Seattle.

She frowned. "Miss Carpenter."

"Juliet," the witch corrected with a small, cautious smile. "It's okay."

"Juliet," she repeated. "Thank you. You used the serum?"

A nod.

Parker glanced at Caleb. "And you saw Lauderdale standing on the pile of corpses in your vision." Was it strange that she wasn't discounting images from a witch's imagination?

No. At this point, she'd use anything she had.

Caleb nodded. "But he wasn't anywhere on the first path."

Phin hummed a thoughtful sound. "Because he's dead?"

"I don't know."

Parker nodded slowly. They had one shot at this. And maybe, just maybe, it'd come through. "What if I could get you the one person who could unlock everything?"

The other woman frowned. "Who?"

"Kayleigh Lauderdale. Laurence's daughter." Parker's gaze touched on all three of the coconspirators she never would have imagined herself standing beside, unless it were at an execution. The world was a funny place. Varying degrees of uncertainty looked back at her. "If we can get her, we can force her to extract the sequence from you, Juliet. Or even Jessie. We can cure Simon *and* give ourselves leverage against Laurence."

She recognized the glint in Caleb's startlingly blue eyes, but she also noticed that he glanced first at Juliet.

All right. She could respect that.

But it was Phin who surprised her. "We're not going to hurt her." It wasn't a question.

Missionary, once. But never that kind. Parker shook her head. "Not if we don't have to."

"Jules?"

The witch leaned against Caleb's shoulder, her hand clenching over the front of his T-shirt. Her gaze locked on Parker. "What about the vision?"

"We have two choices," Parker said slowly, glancing beyond her. To the foliage Simon vanished into. "One, the director lives. Two, he dies. If I have to choose between New Seattle's citizens" *Simon*— "and being *good*, I'll pull the trigger myself."

A ghost of a smile touched Caleb's mouth. A faint nod.

"Let's talk about it with the others," Phin offered and touched her bare shoulder gently. "You should go check on him."

She didn't need to be told twice.

Simon's fist collided with the cliff wall. Pain shredded through his knuckles, his elbow, but he didn't care.

He was going to kill something. But he wasn't anywhere *near* the man he wanted to take apart with his bare fucking hands.

And Matilda was already dead.

She'd *known*.

"Simon!"

Parker's voice. Urgent.

Concerned.

He spun, just in time to catch her as she launched herself into his arms. A flurry of intent and red hair and—Christ, every inch the woman he loved.

His head throbbed, warning that he was pushing it, but it didn't matter.

His hands sank into Parker's hair, cupped her head to hold her for his kiss. Angry and raw, but it softened as she eagerly raised her mouth to his. Gentled as her lips opened for him, cooled his fury. Channeled it.

Carried it with him.

She clung to his shoulders as he drew back. "It's okay," she said urgently. "It's okay, Simon. This doesn't change you."

"I should have known!"

She winced as his fingers tightened in her hair. But she didn't pull away. As the strange mist curled over the emerald green bay, the only bit of privacy he'd been able to find after Caleb's announcement, he stood in the center of Matilda's secret sanctuary and felt so alone.

And yet, with Parker's body pressed to his, so very not.

His head ached as he closed his eyes.

"Kayleigh isn't just my half sister. *Laurence* is my father." He laughed. It broke. "Why would she mix the genes in a vial if my parentage is the same as her daughter's?"

"Are you sure Kayleigh's natural-born?"

"I don't know!" He jerked his hands away, too raw to risk hurting her in his anger. His confusion. "I'm a test-tube creation, Parker. I wouldn't be degenerating if I wasn't."

"Maybe you are. Maybe you aren't." She caught his face in her hands, stared up at him with so much in her eyes. Love, reassurance. Concern.

Fear.

"All I know," she said, every inch the authoritative director that had haunted him, "is that I love you. No matter where you come from." Her wide mouth quirked. "And I also know that you got played badly by the people you were trying to play."

It shouldn't have made him laugh. But it did. As humor welled up beneath the anger and pain, Simon's hands mapped down her back. Molded her to him, shaped her body against his. Perfect in every way.

"You said Matilda had a plan." Parker's fingers traced his jaw. "What if she didn't really? What if all she wanted was for you to be free?"

"You can't know that."

"You're right. But the way it sounds, she concentrated on two of you. One to help break the genetic fail-safe, and one—you—she made from her own body. Test tube or not, Simon, she wanted you."

"She wanted someone to fix her mistakes."

Parker's smile undid him. Slow, so sweet. "That's the beauty of being human, Simon. You get to choose your own path."

"Why bother?" He broke away, didn't get far before she caught his hand and hauled back with all her weight. He stiffened, barely managed to keep from stumbling.

"Caleb's vision isn't absolute," Parker told him sharply. She laced her fingers with his, wrapped her other hand around his wrist and held on as if afraid he'd vanish if she didn't.

The way his head knocked, he might. Out with a bang.

"And the way I'm reading it, it's saying that Lauderdale is going to end up on a mountain of bodies if we don't do something." She tilted her head. "May wants our help, the people here can help us, so we're going to help them. We have plans, Simon."

"I can't keep fighting, Parker."

And there it was. The truth, on a ragged growl.

She raised her chin. "Then don't. I'll fight for you."

She would, wouldn't she? She really would throw herself into the fray—join these outcast witches and their overwhelming goal to take down Sector Three.

She really would risk it all. Risk time with him. "Why?"

"Because I love you." Her eyes shimmered, unshed tears bright enough to send a knife through his chest.

He hated to make her cry.

He never would have thought that. Tears didn't bother him.

Her tears, though. *Ah, hell.*

Simon pulled her to him, step by step; tugged her into his embrace and nuzzled his lips into her hair with a long, shuddering breath. "Then stay with me here," he said, appalled to find the words coming from his own lips.

He didn't want to die alone.

"No."

His heart stalled.

Parker braced one hand over it, raising her face to his. Her cheeks gleamed, damp with her tears. "I refuse to sit by and watch you go. Kayleigh has that damned serum. Maybe she's got it cracked now. Maybe not. But your cure is up there, and I will get it."

"I don't know what I have left," he insisted roughly. "I could break *any* time."

"Don't worry." The words, curt but laced with resignation, followed Naomi West out of the foliage. Her smile sharpened. "*We* can be trusted. And like it or not, we're on your side."

It was so similar to what he'd told Parker only days ago, word for word a *fuck you* of support, that he almost laughed.

Parker looked up at him. A world of hope, of pleading in her beautiful eyes.

"I can't make up for Matilda," he said.

"Matilda had a mysterious stranger routine that drove me up the fucking wall," Naomi cut in, flicking that away. "I hate that she's dead. But she knew exactly what she wanted and how to get it. I don't know what she had planned, I don't care. If you want to ask her, go talk to her grave." She jerked a thumb back behind her, somewhere in the foliage. "What I know is that shit has hit the fan topside, and until Lauderdale is wrecked, we're as good as dead."

Simon closed his eyes as the pressure in the back of his skull drummed, painfully loud.

Last time he'd come, there had been only two bodies on his radar. Matilda, her life fading, and Jessie Leigh.

Now he read seven. Nine, including him and Parker.

Not quite an army.

"Silas is back, and Jonas contacted us," Naomi said, her tone gentling as much as he suspected it could. A real hard-ass. "He's got a list of potential friendlies and a plan that may get us killed, but if it works, we'll nock a victory on our belts that Lauderdale won't forget. And he says he's on the trail of something else."

"What?" Parker asked.

"He won't say until he knows it's worth investigating," she said, "but knowing him? He'll find it."

"What about the serum?"

"According to the comm chatter he's monitoring, that syringe doesn't exist," Naomi replied. "Which means someone has it, somewhere. He's going to find it. Him or his weird ghost friend."

"Good," Parker said quietly, her tone low. Intense. "I'm in."

Simon looked at her. Studied her face, set in determined lines. Bloody obstinate woman. "Fine," he said. "But when I die—"

"Pessimist," Naomi snorted, and turned away. "Come back to the house to talk about these plans of yours. And Jessie wants to meet you. Again," she added, with a subtle emphasis that wasn't lost on Simon.

He'd met her. He'd kidnapped her.

All because he'd needed that fucking serum.

Naomi's footsteps receded back toward the main clearing.

Parker's eyes shone. Too bright. "You aren't going to die."

"I wish—"

She raised up on tiptoe, pressed her mouth to his in a kiss that threw him utterly off balance.

When she stepped back again, her cheeks were flushed. "Not," she repeated.

His mouth slowly eased into a smile. "We'll see," he allowed.

"God damn it, Simon, what do I have to do?"

He hooked a finger into the knot on her halter top. "Convince me."

Her breath caught as the material gave. "We have to go back," she protested, even while her fingers tunneled under his shirt. Seeking his chest, and the suddenly frenetic beating of his heart.

He sucked in a breath as her palms found his skin. She electrified with a touch. Through pain, through anger and fear. She stripped it all away.

He couldn't get enough. Didn't want to stop, to let her go for even an instant.

Forever was an awfully long time. But maybe . . . As her dress came apart in his hands, as she pressed her body to his in willing abandon, Simon groaned.

Maybe he'd try. Maybe he'd force himself to make it, force his body to obey his will and survive the coming storm to see the sun shine on her copper hair one more time. See it reflected in her eyes.

Maybe, God willing and a shitload of luck, he'd succeed. Just for her.

Just for *them*.

*G*ive in to your Impulses!

These unforgettable stories only take a second to buy and give you hours of reading pleasure!

Go to *www.AvonImpulse.com* and see what we have to offer.

Available wherever e-books are sold.

AVONIMPULSE

IMP 0811